ACYROLOGIA

Artorian's Archives Book Ten

DENNIS VANDERKERKEN
DAKOTA KROUT

MOUNTAINDALE
PRESS

ACKNOWLEDGMENTS

From Dennis:

There are many people who have made this book possible. First is Dakota himself, for without whom this entire series would never have come about. In addition to letting me write in his universe, he has taken it upon himself to be the most glorious senior editor and keep straight all the madness for which I am responsible, with resulting hilarity therein.

An eternal thank you to my late grandfather, after whom a significant chunk of Artorian's personality is indebted. He was a man of mighty strides, and is missed dearly.

A special thank you to my parents, for being ever supportive in my odd endeavors, Mountaindale Press for being a fantastic publisher, and all the fans of Artorian's Archives, Divine Dungeon, and Completionist Chronicles who are responsible for the popularity allowing this to come to pass. May your affinity channels be strong and plentiful!

Last of all, thank you. Thank you for picking this up and giving it a read. Acyrologia is the continuation of a multi-book series, and I dearly hope you will enjoy them as the story keeps progressing. Artorian's Archives may start before Divine Dungeon, but don't worry! It's going all the way past the end of Completionist Chronicles! So if you liked this, keep an eye out for more things from Mountaindale Press!

Please consider giving us five stars on Amazon, Audible, and anywhere else you'd like to spread the word!

CHAPTER ONE

Artorian dreamed a wonderful dream of a memory that wasn't his.

He could hear the sound of soft waves rolling in the distance, crashing against sand with the ebb and flow of a rising ocean. The taste of the air carried just that little bit of tang, while the scent of yesterday's bonfire lingered.

As pleasant a day as any in the Fringe, until the marching step of a slighted mother silenced both background chatter and the chirping of birds.

Lunella's grip on her rolling pin tightened as she barged into the building. The atmosphere became so silent in the Fringe cloister that even the prowling steps she took resounded through its halls methodically. Sound bounced around the inside of the ornate structure, which had become famous for housing one portly, abyss-thick pillow.

Each of mother Lun's steps accompanied an accusatory slap of the rolling pin against her open hand. Someone had clucked up. Specifically, her rambunctious little nugget. "Ra! Get out here this instant!"

The door's hinges *squeeped* like a choir of mice. Lun spun

on her heel, and the rolling pin went flying. Spinning through the air, the improvised weapon of mothers everywhere struck Head Cleric Tibbins right in the forehead with a *fnuk*!

His papers and slippers careened into the air as the force knocked him backwards, leaving him with a lumpy bruise before he whimpered in pain. "*Why~y~y?*"

The crunch of a small mouth closing around a baked confection paused as Tibbins' whining filled the space. The culprit then realized such sounds made a lot of noise, triggering the primal feeling of Mother's head snapping in her direction. She paled, as Momma was giving her 'the look' when she peeked past the pew.

While Ra had hidden away snugly under a redwood pew, her hiding ability wasn't factoring in anymore. Mother had pinpointed her alcove with brutal proficiency, and the jig was up. Ra didn't understand how her mother was so awfully skilled at seeing through her schemes, finding likely hiding places, and foiling her consistent and habitual attempts to get. Those. *Cookies*.

"Raaaaaa!" Matron Lunella stomped towards her, and Ra thought that… maybe if she didn't move, she was invisible? No, not with her butt sticking out like that, she wasn't. The pew flew through the air like it was spare firewood. A fate it would no doubt find itself in after crumpling to kindling on impact with the floor. Lunella wasn't a cultivator, but mom-strength had its own section in the adventurer's handbook.

In that fat book, the inscription spoke thusly: underestimate not the strength of a mother scorned, for she will have both the strength of a bear and speed of a hare to make one's day all the worse for wear.

The wooden croaking of a side door opening made Ra change her mind and bolt for it. Sack of 'liberated' baked goods in hand, the rampant roar of a motherly bear burgeoned behind the scurrying movement of her tiny legs. Quickly out of breath, Ra's equally tiny gasping lungs heaved.

When simple brown robes stepped through the opening

passageway, her mousy voice squeaked as she called for rescue. "Uncle Jiiiiin! Save meee!"

Keeper Jin swept his arm out, scooping up the trouble-making toddler in a seamless motion. He gasped at her, making a surprised face as Lunella barged her way through less-than-immobile pews. Just like that, he was in on the scheme, and added his own story twist. "I have found the princess! To the rescue!"

Elder Lunella scowled him down as he took off in a playful trot. "Jin, you bring my daughter to me this instant."

Jin did no such thing, fleeing with a *wheee*. He cradled a giggling Ra, and jumped right into the center mass of a giant twelve-by-twelve foot pillow. The massive, puffy monstrosity absorbed their impact with a gentle *duff*.

Giant pillows, of course, provided the same kind of safety as pulling the blanket over one's head did at night. Complete and full protection from all the creepies. Jin was certain to remind the toddler of that fact. "Safe! None can reach us in the massive puffs of the p—!" *Eeee*!

Lunella hurled her full weight forwards, body-slamming the puffed-up edge of the pillow, thus forcing her child and a weightless Keeper to rocket upwards into the air as the forces balanced themselves out. None would say a word about the extra motherly curves Lunella had gained over the years.

Not after the mistakes Tarrean had made.

Nor the blue rolling-pin-shaped bruises he'd acquired.

Thick thighs save lives—unless the town elder was sitting on you because you couldn't keep your mouth shut during long-house dinner. While sitting on Tarrean, Irene had filed her nails and looked the other way after some particularly... less-than-tactful commentary from the ex-head cleric. No amount of Tarrean's pleading had made Irene pay a hint of attention less to her nails.

Ra learned important lessons that day.

Today, she learned about gravity. Especially when her butt

slammed back down into the pillow and all her cookies rained upon her head right after. Broken, ruined, and crumbly.

Jin didn't know what to do when Ra wept uncontrollably at the state of her confections. "Sweetie, they were just cookies. Mother can always make more, and you know she will because of how delicious they are."

Jin bit his tongue when Lunella shot him a cold glare, and without a word he handed the distraught toddler over. Sighing, he got to clearing the pillow of crumbs as Ra was carried out by a muttering and fussing lapis-robed elder.

Sure in her step, she brought the tiny Ra right home. "Wux! Do you know what *your* daughter did today?!"

Wuxius had also gained some more fatherly-bodied features, which may have had something to do with the vast uptick in local sugary goods. A pleasant thing to have in the Fringe, where the currency was bags of salt. Accidentally mixing the two did not make for great experiences in flavor, proved by the dreaded event known as salt-coated pancakes.

Thefts of baked goods had become so prevalent that Lunella had adopted a new tactic: making certain batches where she specifically replaced one medium with the other, just to catch the thieves. When it was her husband and daughter making terrible noises a few hours later, she supposed she shouldn't have been surprised.

The Choir people were so well-behaved in comparison.

Wux crossed his arms to lean on his shovel. He still had land to till, but was always in a good mood when his favorites came by. "So she's *my* daughter today? I vividly remember she was *your* baby yesterday, when you couldn't stop fawning all over her because she found a beetle."

The muttering got louder, and a sniffly Ra extended her arms towards Daddy. Picking her up and carrying her with one arm, he rubbed noses with his little baby. "Did Momma get upset with you~u~u?"

Ra nodded strongly, clinging to the safety of her daddy. Daddy wasn't the one mad at her!

With fatherly love, he soothed his eternally curious tiny tyke. "Why don't we go to the salt flats after I'm done tilling this row, and we can go dig around and see what random goodies we find today?"

The nodding repeated itself, sniffles lessening. Lunella's foot was making a dent in the ground with how hard she tapped it. Her eyes burned into the side of his head, voice caustic. "Don't think you're off the hook either, mister."

Wuxius ignored his shovel and quickly walked away, still holding tight to Ra as he slinked off with all the speed of a skink in the direction of the salt flats. "Oh, look at that! Based on the position of the clouds, the sun, and moons, it's time to go to Yvessa's Spoons."

Drying her eyes, the toddler held onto her father as he walked her across the new docks built right onto the salt flats. They passed by the massive foundation project that would make the basis for some truly oversized cathedral. Ra's eyes instead locked on to a powder-blue plushie nestled between two heaps of salt. She reached for it with an *nnnn*!

Distracted by the sound, Wux glanced over to see what his youngest was making grabby hands at this time. He'd learned to pay attention. The last time he didn't, she'd run off on her own to go explore and find whatever it was she saw. Without so much as a hesitant step, he hopped down from the birch panel walkway and sank knee-deep into a pile of salt below.

The tide had receded hours ago, so he didn't need to worry about Lun getting on his case about coming home with soaking wet loafers. Each time the tide left, salt would commonly be left behind. However, over the past few years, other sundry items had started appearing as well.

Anything that vast foundation needed appeared nearby, as if the flats knew what construction would require. This salvaged dolphin plushie was no different. Objects like this had just been *appearing*. He didn't know where from or why, but it made his little one happy, so he scooped the plush up. Giving the toy a good shake to get some salt off, he handed it to a gleeful toddler who smashed it against her face with a massive grin.

Wux didn't know what creature this plushie was supposed to be, but he hadn't known the previous few either. He was just happy the toy was one of the few things Lun didn't chase him around for. The forgotten, discarded plushies had use. Lunella painstakingly took them apart when Ra made it clear she didn't like particular plushies anymore, just to discover how such a flawless, hidden inseam had been knit.

Sated by her new acquisition, Ra slumped into a tired snuggle as her daddy clambered back up on the dock, making his way over to the best canteen in the whole region.

Yvessa's Spoons had the makings of a star-quality restaurant, and would currently be bustling if they hadn't needed to scrape the cook off the ground after an encounter with She Who Shall Not Be Stopped. Yvessa didn't mind the lull in activity, preparing secret sauce and doing prep-work before actual cooking. She somehow always seemed to know who was about to enter. "Wu, is your little adventurer eating solid food yet?"

A heavy sigh was enough for her as the wooden board of a canteen bench creaked with newly-added weight. Wux spoke flatly. "No, still just soup. I have no idea how a child that's not even four manages to cause havoc, run off completely independently, and then come home because she doesn't want to eat the food in her little 'travel pack.'"

Yvessa, unlike Lunella, had remained slender and lithe. A minor perk of the cultivator lifestyle, even if she wasn't nearly as close to C-rank as she'd like. With sliding grace, she placed a bowl of vegetable soup in front of Ra's nose. She adored watching those little features light up and, as usual, the toddler scarfed it down.

Wu rubbed his forehead and sighed, glad to see Ra eat. "Thanks, Yvessa."

The caretaker hummed back an expectant *mhm*, then went along with her business to grind some more spices into a second bowl. "The elder scare you off again?"

Wu scratched behind his ear, finding the endless horizon in the other direction to suddenly hold great interest. "*Whaaaat? Nooooo.*"

He expected the fully disbelieving **mhm** when it came. Yvessa the caretaker had him down to a science, and a second helping of soup was placed in front of Wu. "Eat as a family, and... One moment."

Fishing out the spoon Ra had just dropped in her soup, she put it away, procuring a new one. The tip of it tapped against Ra's nose, eliciting a cutesy giggle before Yvessa spoon fed her a slurp.

Wuxius nudged the caretaker in her arm. "You're doing it again."

Yvessa sat back, pretending not to have broken free from her fantasy and memory. "*Hmm?*"

The doting father leaned his head towards his youngest, but gave Yvessa a swift nudge. "Every time you feed her, you get all wistful and lose yourself."

Ra took the newly-offered spoon before the caretaker leaned back on her stool, releasing a heavy sigh. "The days have always been dull and slow in the Fringe, but you miss the people that gave the place life. She eats like him, you know. Messy, hastily, mind already on twenty other things with little schemes forming like gusts in a shifting wind. It's her eyes, Wu. She does the whole see-through-me thing your grandfather does."

Wuxius beamed in delight, a proud hand easing on his youngest's back. "I'm aware. Gives Lunella a run for her salt, and we grew up with that old fogey leading us by the nose with his clever tricks and ruses. All those years trying to outsmart that fox. Still only got him to step off that hill once."

Yvessa nudged him in the shoulder with the butt of her spoon. "He'll be back. You're still getting letters, and it would be *so like him* to pop in from out of nowhere with the rest of your family in tow."

Laughter followed her statement. Her words were just so painfully believable. "Or he'll fall from the sky! Who knows!

Oh, heavens. I wonder if he's found out about the song. It's great. I'm not sure if he's going to love it and snicker, or hate it and fall to the ground in a heap of 'make it stop' groans."

Yvessa covered her smirking face with the sleeve of her raiment. "Whichever it ends up being, I'm sure we won't be disappointed. After all, our old man Sunny will fall from the sky, beelining home for a slice of Lunella's honey pie. The recipe's famous now!"

CHAPTER TWO

Artorian woke up.

Had he expected terrible dreams? Fleeting memories that lived in the Fringe were... He blinked when he recognized the ceiling, his prior train of thought coming to a sudden halt. "Is that the ceiling of my *house*?"

Sitting up in a hurry, his hand pressed down on soft bedding, causing his vision to turn towards the plush he was kneading. "Maybe not quite? My bed was never this soft."

He didn't want to complain about the improvement, but he distinctly recalled 'calling it quits' while still in Eternia. Did he not pass out in the Luminous Prism Cathedral? He was certain that had happened. Yet unspoken commands called forth no information, nor gave him any of the expected sensory feedback. He talked himself through the quandary. "Not a single prompt? I must be back in Cal."

He eased his feet from the rectangle of soft plush, and his exposed soles found familiar birchwood flooring. Peering over the bed's edge, Artorian half expected to step into some leftover shells tossed by Sproutlings. No such sound cracked beneath his feet, the floor as pristine and vacant as the rest of his tiny abode. Rising fully, he shuffled a few steps to peer out of the open window.

The scene beat him with the nostalgia stick, as the layout of the old Fringe village sprawled before his eyes in exquisite detail. The spacing between buildings was all on point. The rolling hills were all present, crisscrossed and cut through with a network of tiny streams that cared nothing for elevation.

In the middle of it all burned a crimson bonfire. Within its flaming center, a massive two-handed greatsword fit only for a Jotun warrior gleamed as the fire licked the weapon, adding another layer of char. Next to the pit sat the familiar figure of Dawn, her gaze transfixed by something that danced in the flame.

Artorian looked left to right, but saw nobody else. Neither signs of activity nor of life brushed over his senses. With a small exhale, he pulled his head back into his little A-frame home and inspected the insides. The building itself was just fine, but the home was barren. Bare-bones construction aside, no scrolls filled his book cases. Neither ink nor ink pots were to be seen anywhere near his desk. No old memories decorated his walls.

He stepped a few paces to pick up the large plank that barred his doorframe, as his home didn't have a door. "What an interesting detail to have recreated."

Once outside, Artorian shambled his way right to Dawn, then eased his butt down onto the large fallen tree next to her. Before he could speak, her arm slid around his neck to tug the old codger in. He rested his face against the crook of her neck while his long, grandfatherly beard sprawled.

"No words," she said tiredly. "Not yet."

Artorian nodded and sat with Dawn, watching the fire as it crackled pleasantly and played around the oversized sword. He'd just woken, yet now he felt sleepy again. The words he wanted to say bubbled to the forefront of his thoughts, tapping their feet impatiently as they desired to be spewed forth.

Artorian remained silent.

The quiet moment was nice in its own way. The area was

cool, and a warm breeze brushed through the area without pause. He heard no animals, but the tender flutter of his robes and crackle of heat added a touch of auditory comfort.

He sat with Dawn, and thought the break was nice. Very nice indeed, to not have to spring to action right away. How he'd missed such long, quiet moments. Sinking into the comfort, his breathing softened.

Dawn opened and closed her hand on his back, scratching over the cloth as she leaned into his sunken pose. This allowed her to rest her cheek against the top of his head, her reply a warm exhale that mirrored his comfort.

"This is good. Much better. We have much to share. Many topics of which to speak. That can wait until the sun goes down. I have missed you." She hummed when she spoke, squeezing him gently. "I've got you."

"Likewise, dearest." Artorian responded with an identical gesture. "I've been got."

Neither had to say that some quiet 'alone and together time' was prized during the Age of Cal. They barely moved as the fire played, the clouds swam, and the sun took its time dipping below the horizon. Only after the tapestry of colors in the sky mixed like black milk did Dawn break the quiet. "Anything on your mind?"

The old man nodded, his frame feeling both aged, thin, and spent as he sat up properly. No longer benefiting from Dawn's support let the expenditures from Eternia creep in and start collecting their toll. "Many. So many. Was it all a dream? Or did Barry…? Did I break my Silverwood Core?"

Dawn demanded his hand, so he gave it for her to hold. Comforted by the feeling, she shook her head. "Not a dream. Eternia was a very long… *long* struggle. A struggle on which the chapters have now closed, with as good of an ending as beggars can choose. Eternium is going to use that entire iteration for a full audit and extreme review, with whole colleges of Wisps and Gnomes to sift the wreckage. After the critical issues are seen to."

Artorian nodded, but looked up since it seemed she was avoiding the other two questions. Dawn shrugged sweetly before speaking. "No need for such dark eyes. Barry is chunked. Four pieces, which we are going to bury, hide, or otherwise shove into obscurity until a time where we have enough alternatives together for a different outcome. I have no doubts that, one day, he'll be back. Those pieces will never stay apart forever."

Artorian swallowed. "Core?"

Dawn winked. "Your Core is all red and all good. I made sure you slept through the proper process of that seed mending. When you took the nap in Eternia, we had a way to shunt the *full* duration of the sleep away until later. This time was the 'later.' That first crack increased your sleep requirement tenfold, and I made sure you caught up on both the shunted sleep, and everything you still needed afterward. Don't feel a need to be concerned with how long it took. Time holds very little meaning, without much to spend time on, or people to spend time with."

He nodded, holding his own hands as his eyes focused on the fire. "A *red* Core, now? Must have something to do with that shunting. *Interesting.* Not what I remember my seed Core being, but that's a project to tackle later. I take it that, once again, our boat sails in waters burdened with all new problems?"

She waggled her hand. "Sort of. We've had worse, but the second verse tends to be the same as the first. When your Eternia trip ended, we found you in a building made of glass."

Artorian frowned. "The indestructible one? How did you get in?"

Dawn leaned her chin on her fist with a smirk, one of her legs moving over the other. "I asked the building *nicely.* Prismy quickly found a few reasons to become sentient and make the doors work."

"Ha! 'Prismy.' Adorable." Artorian gave up and dropped the question, shaking his head. "Sure, why not. As if anything in Eternia made a lot of sense. I have the distinct feeling I'll be needing to go back one day. On that topic, as a small detour, I don't appear to have any screens here. Not even Cal's. Nothing at all works."

Dawn snapped her fingers then pointed to the sun. "The only active Pylons in all of the Soul Space are in the Elysian Fields, contained within your archives, to keep the world running. All the other ones were canned. By which I mean we placed them in large Iridium canisters that prevent energy transfer, because we had to shut it all down. We've run into far too many problems that Tatum and I just... can't begin to fix without Cal. Who, *no*, is not back yet. Alive and asleep, but not conscious. The wireframe tears are almost all repaired, and the Silverwood is in good health. The realms have formed a planet, and we have an honest to celestial *ocean* now."

Dawn beamed with pride at that last fact, then her expression fell as she wrung her hands together. "An ocean that doesn't make for smooth sailing. In short, we do have a few problems. The list is small, but their scope is large."

Opening one of her hands, she counted on her fingers. "One: demons stored in Cal were 'woken' en masse, and the survivors have stowed away somewhere on the planet that formed in Cal's Soul Space."

A finger added to the count. "Two: we—and by '*we*,' I mean Cal—are completely out of time when it comes to people, souls, and minds alike getting to live lives. Cal held off on allowing people to do so with his wishy-washy vague rules, and both Tatum and I are painfully aware that he's *pushing* the wall of the double S-ranks. Decanting is going to be done soon, spread all over the planet so we can foster some diversity."

She momentarily closed her eyes, and sighed. "That does mean we are decanting *everyone*. Including people who have minds currently hidden away in another body, stasis, and the like. We're going to have iteration *one* all over again, because everyone is about to remember both who they were, and what their allegiances were. I hope you didn't miss the old world Guild, because that includes their lot."

Artorian narrowed his eyes. "My family... and that of

Henry's… and everyone else who had a wall. All of those as well?"

Dawn made a face that said their inclusion was inevitable. She didn't have to nod for Artorian to understand.

He squeezed his lips into a line and spoke. "I see. Is there more?"

Dawn made the same expression again, so Artorian dropped his face in his hands. "Alright. Let's hear it."

She smiled a little at his welcomed antics, and added a third finger to the count. "Three: our inner circle is a wreck, and there aren't many 'awake' in the outer circle. By which I mean survivors from Eternia, because exiting after Barry's defeat was anything except kittens and rainbows. Eternium lost far, *far* too many Pylons. It's Fimbulwinter in there right now. We got *you* out just fine, only because you had a body that is Cal-made. For anyone who didn't make it out during our first pass… Not as pleasant a story. The great majority of people are still trapped in Eternium. Frozen in stasis to prevent a realm-wide wipeout."

Artorian wasn't quite sure he understood. "Fimbulwinter? Also, couldn't Eternium make bodies?"

Dawn *mhm'd*, but he could tell from the tone that 'ability' wasn't the whole story, and she filled in the new word's explanation first. "Fimbulwinter is what Yuki termed the ice age going rampant all over Eternia. Shortly after we got you out, the sun decided to just… quit? A big blue screen appeared over it, some error sound played with the message 'a fatal exception has occurred,' and the whole thing self-terminated. What was left turned into one massive, frozen comet that trailed along, the coma of which rained endless shards of ice onto the remaining realms."

She sighed. "As for the bodies, Tim *can*, but they're not the same as Cal's. The body problem has been a recurring one, and you're not entirely immune to it. Nobody is. Because there isn't a single person in Cal's Soul Space that still *has* their original body."

The old man stuck his hands in the air in defeat. "That sounds like a lecture. Back to the main problems?"

She heartily agreed and resumed her count. "That's only a problem because we have... essentially no manpower to speak of. Those not still trapped in Eternium are all in Cal, and *in Cal* is where we need people for the next stage of problems. Plus Odin, the problem extraordinaire. He *is* here, and has it out for you."

She kneaded her brows and rubbed at her eyes. "He was lying nearby when we got to you. We never should have extracted him in the first batch, but we couldn't have known the Pylons were all going... to go berserk. Thank the celestials that Tatum figured out how to make Iridium insulators and we could cap off the big ones before the surge fried the whole Cal-planet. Credit to Adam and the Iridium you provided for that breath of relief."

Artorian firmly believed there was a story of multiple touch-and-go problems here, but he took it in stride and kept listening. "Did you summon him back? I recall him mentioning that he was expecting that."

Dawn confirmed that for him with grace. "I did. Adam is in Cal with us, putting the fear of light into dark-dwellers. He's the sole reason we were able to keep working, and have you sleep your injury off. The benefit of fifteen millennia only feeling like fifteen days when I'm working from my seed Core is the *strangest* blessing in disguise. Without a society to infiltrate, the demons have been completely suppressed so far. We keep expecting them to build... *anything*? But no, not a single subterranean demonhold. No overland spires. Not a one."

Raising her hand, she added a fifth finger. "Odin has not only already decanted all the minds and Cores he could get his hands on, but rules over them imperiously. His Mage rank is currently one higher than yours, and his ego is just as problem-atic. He is completely convinced you slighted, insulted, and had it out for him. So he's repaying you by setting up a society before you can... What did he call it?"

She mimed Odin's actions mockingly. "'Sneak his treacherous influence in, and steal more people out from under my rightful divine guidance.'"

Dawn shook her head. "The power completely went to his head. Oh, and he goes by Zeus now. You can find him on Mount Olympus, if you're at all inclined to slap him. Or insult him. His pre-Mage name was Jasper, should that ever come in handy. He hates it. He's got about a century of leg-up on you with society building? Maybe two? Not that the extra time seems to have provided him any advantages without a proper enemy to focus on. I'm somewhat hoping the place becomes a demon attraction so we can send more of them back to their memory Cores. Even with one Adam, and a couple thousand bodies between Tatum and I, we've caught surprisingly few."

Artorian motioned around him, getting the gist. "Personally, I think this is very nice, but why haven't you slapped Odin yourself if he's such a problem?"

Leaning forwards, she tenderly pressed her forehead to his. Only then did Artorian understand how tired she felt. Dawn spoke softly. "I have so… so many other things I need to be doing. So many problems that *only* S-rankers can help with. I just can't spare the moment, and it would mean so much more if the back of the hand was yours."

Artorian squeezed her hand. "I'll see to it. Anything more? A cantankerous zappy boy, some hiding dark souls, a bit of rebuilding, and making a spot for people when they get back into Cal from the Eternia wreckage."

Taking a deep breath, she opened her eyes and sat up, looking at the sky as a light approached. "That's it for overarching problems. Now, maybe, it's time for all the little ones? I'm aware there's a tribulation you wanted to talk to me about, and I am dying to get *this* detail off my chest."

Dawn raised her hand, and the reddish heat in the bonfire all turned to fractalized patterns of gleaming silver. The patterns were made entirely of pure, elemental flame.

CHAPTER THREE

Artorian became transfixed, mesmerized by the sight. He bit the side of his hand as his eyes darted from fractal to fractal. The patterns danced in his vision and demanded his attention with each altering permutation. He barely noticed leaning forward so far that Dawn had to grip him by the shoulder, lest he get lost in the sights that tended to take her away as well.

She had the capacity to resist; Artorian did not.

When Adam appeared above them in a slow descent, the change in luminance broke Artorian from his musings. Looking up, a bright smile formed on his face, with his arms spreading wide in greeting as he instinctively copied the pose Adam descended with.

The celestial embraced him with fondness, squeezing firm but with a gentle touch. "Artorian. Good of you to return to us in such good health. I have looked forward to the reunion. Be not consumed by the truest of flame; that which is elemental is not elementary."

Artorian squeezed the celestial back, which was enough for them to let go as Adam sat next to him, sandwiching the old man between himself and Dawn. His heaving, massive wings spread out before only the left side curled back in. The right one instead lay as a duvet blanket across the backs and shoulders of both Dawn and Artorian.

Neither complained. That wing was cozy!

"My apologies for my timing. I did not desire to interrupt your sharing." Pressing his hand to his chest, Adam made a small apologetic bow. "Please do not mind me."

Artorian swung his arm around the celestial's neck and tugged him in for a noggin-knuckling. "Nonsense! You already know what I know. You're welcome to be here. Your perspective may even fill in some blanks as we converse. My Tribulation may cause me heartache, but the pain of it is rooted only in memory. Which is not to say that I'm not starving for information on the elemental, that silver flame, and what's going on with you and Dawn. I've once again missed out, and am eager to get back into the swing of things."

Adam flushed, recovered from the affectionate head-knuckling, then closed his eyes and nodded once. Artorian let him go, and grabbed both their hands, one in each. Adam dared a deep breath, taking in the air and fresh waft of bonfire scent before going still.

The others waited for him to say something, but he did not, seeming to center himself. Artorian copied the behavior, closing his own eyes and turning his face to the sky, feeling their hands in his as he listened to the thumping of his heart as it calmed. Which was what Adam wanted, the celestial smirking when the Incarnate turned her head to look.

Gentle, small, faint wisps of pink light rose from Artorian's being, slowly intermixing with filaments of cyan and teal. When he spoke, the tone was wistful. "I can handle being alone, but I can't stand *feeling* alone."

Squeezing their hands once more, he exhaled deep and slowly. "I'm back. You're here. All will be well. *All will be well.* We will make it so."

Adam squeezed back, still smirking cheekily as his plans

succeeded beautifully. "Bold words from the man who sold himself to a dream."

Dawn narrowed her eyes at the celestial. "Bold words from the man who walks in his shadow."

Adam laughed and put both his hands in the air. "I have been bested."

Artorian raised an eyebrow and looked between them. "Is this some joke I'm not in on?"

Dawn vigorously nodded with an 'oh honey, you have no idea' expression while she crossed her arms over her chest. "Our celestial here may have nothing but good intentions, but he has a *mouth*. I've got the sense that interaction with your memories gives those that come in contact with them a double dose of the *cheek*."

Adam snickered, then explained. "Celestials, on our own plane, have such a different perspective on life and its happenings that many of them can't be translated. We keep encountering the inexact, inappropriate, or improper use of a word. I call the phenomenon acyrologia. I expect such occurrences to be frequent this iteration, when people both new and old join us and must be explained the ways of the world."

His large wing shifted so he could speak with his hands. "When I attempt to translate from Celestial, my speech might reform to make the words, but the meaning does not transfer with them. For example, people live their lives for many reasons, and on our plane, those reasons are what people are measured by. To live for ideals and concepts is prized for more than merely the progress within your 'Tower of Ascension.' To live for a dream is a warm and fuzzy thing. To live for a single purpose, as I currently am, is a cold blade's edge in comparison."

Artorian turned to give the celestial his full attention.

Adam kept speaking. "Ethical concepts are not vague notions on my home plane. They are hard, solid, immutable objects that you can physically grasp and interact with. The phrase 'to grab one's resolve and break it in twain,' is not just a saying. The act is something you can physically do. In this example, the resolve of some cannot be broken if the reason of the breaker, and their opposing will, is insufficient. While the resolve will break easily if the possessor is not truly certain or assured of their notions."

Adam made a motion with his palm that translated as a compliment. "Your spirit is well known to me, Artorian. You care nothing for yourself, and throw your soul and being into the fray for all others. Measured by those whom you care for, and those who have your love. Yet more than a mere meddling within the lives of others, your finger points to the stars with clear verdict."

The celestial pointed straight up. "You will reach them. You will not be stopped. You will stand for all that is good. You will fight against all that is not. Your pattern screams your unyielding nature to the canvas of the sky, furious at the injustice that no law can mend. No **Law**, save for **Love**."

Adam appeared proud as his expression brightened. "Your dream of the world as you wish it is a beauty, one so full of light and life that even a celestial may choose to venture from their plane to visit. As it is not merely the physical problems your mind wishes to solve, but the patterns that caused them, the very philosophies that they stand on. You dream to rip the problem not from the leaf, nor the stem, but by the root. Nothing less will suffice. You understand that some patterns of thought are doom to all, and only some lead to flourishing. Whether human or beast, you see no distinction. Only the path."

Dawn leaned over to place a hand on the base of Adam's wing joint, as his heart fell and voice faltered. "It saddens me, then, that you would refuse a righteous rule. Content to live within the broken shards of another's political work."

Artorian frowned, but tried to keep his expression sweet. He could understand that sentiment, at the very least. He too rubbed over Adam's back, and apologized. "I know, my boy. I know... My heart just isn't in it. To rule, and to rule rightly, are vast in breadth and difference. I am the wrong soul for such minutiae. Give me a fire with friends, family, and the laughing smiles of those I hold dear any day. My heart cannot bear the thought that I could let them all down."

The celestial recovered from his momentary droopiness, and sat upright. "Should one day you reconsider, I would adore a seat at your side as a judge of your laws. For their ethics would conjure only the strongest of swords, striking with the mightiest of words."

Dawn glared suspiciously at the golden-haired glow-boy and eased an arm around Artorian to pull the old man against her. She hissed at Adam like a C'towl when the angel turned to look, Artorian now mushed into Dawn while she held him protectively with both her arms.

Artorian broke down laughing as the tension faded, and he heard Dawn's hiss. That was adorable! She was so protective of him. He could not say he disliked that one bit. He was fond!

Clearing his throat and extracting himself, he shook his hands. "Alright. That was… enlightening. So what's first? My Tribulation, the elemental talk, the tower talk, why Scilla is hiding next to Dawn trying her best not to be seen, or where my new job as janitor begins? I assure you, I have outstanding credentials for that last bit."

Scilla formed from thick, caliginous blackness, taking the shape of a more adult version of the Scilla from Chasuble. She wasn't at all the little child he recalled. This was the proper lady version of the small child who'd never gotten the chance. Her voice, on the other hand, sounded much the same. "How did you even…?"

Artorian pointed at the wispy pink and cyan energy in the air. "Was trying to get a bearing on my situation, and my situation said I had three other distinct entities near me."

Scilla's face fell flat, after which she threw her hands into the air. "So much for my surprise."

Artorian looked at Dawn, then back at Scilla. "I can pretend?"

Scilla dropped her arms to look at him with incredulity, then shot her hands right back into the air to yell with a big smile. "Surpriiiise!"

Artorian gasped loud and pressed his hands over his face, replying with excess drama. "Oh my goodness! Scilla! What a surprise! I didn't see you there. Welcome to the bonfire and the fireside chat."

Adam and Dawn broke out in a mutual bout of weak laughter, as the act had been both so obviously forced, and so thoughtfully touching. Scilla released an *uhu* that clarified her displeasure. "Thanks for trying, old man."

Artorian winked whimsically and gave her a tiny shrug. "T'was the least I could do."

Flopping against Dawn, Scilla groaned exactly like one expected a teenager would. "*Uuugh*, fine, but I'm going last!"

Dawn wrapped an arm around her back, looking away as her shoulders bounced. She clearly tried to contain herself, but it wasn't working all that well. When she drew a breath and released it, she got back into her groove. "Perhaps best not to dabble with the tower or the elemental first. They go hand in hand, and the story requires some preamble concerning time you missed. Tribulation may be the easier starting option… Subjectively speaking."

Artorian wrung his hands and chuckled. "Subjectively indeed. Tribulation it is, then. As you likely already know, the last one I went through was number six. Given I'm currently A-rank six, I'm not sure how much longer we will be using that classification system, but it's a reference for convenience."

His gaze returned to the fire, though his thoughts were wild and he could not get lost within the artistic sights. "Tribulation six occurred in the Socorro desert. Yes, that same one I had such a bad reaction to during our earliest days in the woods together."

Dawn, thankfully, was quick on the uptake. "Which is why you wanted to talk to me about it. That was me, wasn't it? That whirl of flame that cut through whatever your battalion was going through in that desert?"

Artorian nodded implacably. "One and the same. Speaking of the events is hard. Showing and sharing may be easier. I've already gone through them once, so the journey will be a swift one, but I knew that when I finished it... I felt hollow. Something was missing. Like the Tribulation did not actually test me for a regret, or a sorrow... The test of the sixth Tribulation felt akin to... forgiveness? The emotion is difficult to put into words."

He perked up a moment, pointing at Adam. "Acyrologia."

Adam smiled. "I warned you the phenomenon would occur frequently."

Artorian turned to Dawn, but she was already leaning in and offering her forehead to touch against his.

He didn't need to ask, as she purred out her words. "*Show me.*"

CHAPTER FOUR

Tzu the Tyrant reconsidered his title as a pleasant fire crackled nearby. Perhaps the denomination wasn't so ill-fitting. He did have a ti~i~iny tendency to meddle and muck with the rules. Then he made his own rules.

Lying prone on the cold sand while facing the night sky, he held his own hands while the survivors of the troop he'd dragged out of the Wilds *so long ago* sat around him in a half-moon. He cleared his throat, attempting to calm the current conversation by downplaying the contents and waving a dismissive hand. "The trial wasn't *that* bad. We walked out of the Imperial Court in one piece, got nice postings, and went traveling."

Zho, Ming, Yoshe, Aki, Hong, Ichiro, and Miki all scoffed in unison. They had become jaded to these misguided attempts at misdirection, and let 'Sub-commander Tzu' enjoy their litany of verbose disagreements.

Ichiro stole the first comment. His arms crossed as he called Tzu out on his blatant lie. "Not so bad? I have never in my life been so close to wishing I wore brown pants!"

Tzu's hand motions swiftly turned defensive. "Well, I didn't know that 'The Great Phoenix' himself was going to be presiding when we *calmly* entered."

Miki fumed out her disbelief, her personality still laden with plenty of anger issues. "Calmly entered? We kicked the doors open, barged in waving tax documentation above our heads, and accused ministers left right and center of fraud and treason! With nothing more than the hope that they wouldn't flay us alive on entry and toss our remains to the birds!"

Aki nodded to agree, adding to Miki's statement. "We also did not *walk* out, we ran for our lives under distinct duress. Being chased by a horde of angry magistrates and all their well-paid guards, while they were firing as many arrows at us as they could find the breath to spew insults. That did not feel very 'in one piece,' since those arrows were as pointed as the commentary, some stabbing just as deep. I *still* have scars."

She fussed and looked the other way, trying to diffuse the situation since she didn't want to think about that. "The only reason we escaped the inner walls at all, no matter how much our lungs and legs felt like they were made of fire, were Tzu's ridiculous morning drills."

Zho wasn't about to let Aki cleverly try to turn this around with a veiled compliment. There was complaining to do, and the snappy duo of veteran fighters hadn't gotten their turn yet! "Wait, did he say 'nice postings'?" Zho stabbed his stubby finger into the cold sand. "*This* barren oven of a rock-laden desert? Since when is the Socorro a *nice* posting? Our alternative was several flavors of death! The only reason we got the pardon at all was because you made the Great Phoenix laugh so hard from making the magistrates stumble over each other like a box of blind lemmings that he couldn't preside over the trial properly. You called them out by name! Then slapped the relevant tax file down during their hasty defense."

Yoshe, one of the two thieves in the group who didn't quite share Zho and Hong's veteran warrior outlook, countered. "I don't think anyone expected some backwater soldiers from a lost expedition to barge in with both accusations and matching proof in hand, smack into the middle of a vast court proceeding. Where the main culprit we were accusing *happened to be* in the middle of being rewarded with accolades."

Hong snickered, scheming with his partner in crime as he slid right in to support Yoshe. "I'm pretty sure half the ministers thought our performance to be one big joke someone had put together for a laugh, or they would have never let you get more than a sentence in before throwing you out, Tzu."

Ming wasn't about to let Zho's point get buried like that, and *harrumphed* for attention as he crossed his thick arms. "Throw us out? We fled with our tail between our legs! Also, 'traveling'? I don't think we can get more 'out of the way' of those goons in charge if we tried! We're in the blasted desert! Our 'generous' new posting may have saved our behinds, but I doubt anyone actually expects us to come back from this. I still haven't seen the official paperwork that says we're supposed to be here. We should have had it seasons ago!"

Ichiro shook his head, distracted by that last comment as he'd had too much trouble properly following most of the conversation. His comment understandably derailed from the actual topic a bit. "Not with the stronghold we're trying to conquer being staffed by assassins, no. Sal'ha'din knows his way around some sandstone to make walls that tall."

Tzu clicked his tongue and waggled his feet, trying to add some order back into the argument and general troubled mood that hung over the inner camp. "The way I see it, breaking into my old workplace and going through all that tax documentation was completely worth the trouble. We entered the procession with proof in hand, the magistrates didn't stop me from speaking in time, that general is currently a head shorter than he was, and we proved that half of all the judges were stealing from the royal coffers. I made the bigwig laugh, we were pardoned, got tossed a seal of command, and told to go get posted here. A post that, while being as rough and coarse as the sand we sit on, is far enough away from the capital for us not to have worried about daggers in our backs."

Aki grumbled, expressing the foul mood the others shared. "Sal'ha'din is giving us plenty of those."

Tzu attempted to downplay the issue once more, not wanting to give anything away to other eyes and ears that might be paying attention. "We've been here for years and it's going well enough. Little gains here and there. We keep busy. We keep strong."

Zho sneezed at the mention, needing to rub his nose. "Losses here and there as well. My nose tingles when I think of it. I don't like the feeling."

Zho and Ming stilled, their eyes locked onto the person who tended to have a way with complicated plans. Ming finished the thought Zho had begun. "I've half the mind to say you and Sal'ha'din are *in cahoots* and playing a little cold stalemate game purely to annoy Bjorn, that other sub-commander posted here. He didn't like arriving to find out we were already here."

Aki chuckled, enjoying a slight smirk. "He *did* like finding out that Tzu was a *sub*-commander rather than a fully initiated one, but I too would trade a demotion for my life."

Tzu attempted to rein the conversation back in before those prying eyes and ears got too interested. "Two generals to one army always leads to some problems. Try not to let the swaying sands of war and conflict bother you too much. We win some, we lose some, and we sleep soundly at night. Should the worst come to pass... just remember where the natural caves are between the rocks and crags. Fall back there to regroup if the situation falls apart."

Nodding made the rounds.

Tzu exhaled and watched the stars some more as the rest of his little troupe decided it was better to begin snacking on the sand eel currently skewered above the fire. He did not feel like telling Ming just how close his guess had been, as there were indeed a few problematic spots to the current situation.

First, while they had escaped the capital, they would not be able to return to the Phoenix Kingdom without proof of a big confirmed win. Well... there was also the big loss option, but that meant swiftly trying to get his family out of the house they were still building. Renovating? A bit of both. He missed Alina, but luckily she was well-informed concerning his forced trips away from home, and he'd left her all his considerable funds. The only important qualifier was getting back alive, and that he would do. Even if it was all he did.

Second, Ming was painfully correct about the lack of official orders. A seal of command and a verbal pardon may have gotten them to the Socorro, but once here the seal slowly bled away in value. The more time passed without specific orders, the more Tzu's legitimacy of leadership caved in under his feet.

Which was how 'commander' had become 'sub-commander.'

His personal troupe might still listen to him, but unless there was a big battle or an emergency, he was third, if not fourth, in the chain of command. Which made him rather grumpy, since the people in charge still expected him to lead. Particularly in troublesome positions, so he could take the blame for failures.

At the top of the local Phoenix Kingdom food chain was the official 'main' commander responsible for the garrison in this section of the Socorro.

Ranked as Marquis, and royal pain in the keister, was the perfectly trimmed, mustached, macho and armor-polisher extraordinaire himself, Philipe the Breacru. Also known as 'Philly the Breadcrumb' to most who did not like him. This was Tzu's method of making himself feel better, as he was the *only* person to dislike the man. There was just something about Breadcrumb that didn't sit well in his gut, and he couldn't put his finger on it.

Marquis Philipe despised sand.

Particularly due to his incomprehensible need to be clean, prim, moustache-waxed, and perfectly tasseled at every possible opportunity. The Marquis thrived on proper appearances, and judged people by that same standard.

His immediate subordinate, Viscount Smithers, was a wiry man with a nose so thin and long that the rumor was he could cut cheese by inhaling. While the Viscount kept clean, he was a man obsessed with smells, candles, perfumes, oils, and the like. The Viscount didn't technically hold a military rank save for his social status, but his immediate proximity and closeness to the Marquis came with unavoidable clout.

Clout that put him on the same level as Philipe so long as the prim man was out and about. Effectively, they had two official commanders, with one parroting the words of the other.

In third place came sub-commander Bjorn. A man with a head so hot and an obvious need to laud his own bloodlust that it wouldn't be wrong to say that the desert at midday was both cooler and more level than Bjorn's oval skull. All that man knew how to do was yell 'charge' at people. Bjorn was here for glory. And shouting.

In fourth and last place... there was Tzu. Tzu with seven skilled people to his name and a whole host of others all vying for that seal of command in his pocket. There was, after all, no name on such a seal. You either had it, and thus the power that came with it, or you didn't, and carried official orders. The latter of which most certainly *did* have your name on them. If only Tzu had some!

Instead, he had Aki and Miki. Both women. Both exceptional runners. Miki had a good memory he could reference, but came bundled with anger issues. Aki was good with weather, and had a knack for figuring out natural phenomena.

Zho and Ming were his two veterans of war, covered in a blanket of scars. The duo were frequently snappy and would never miss an opportunity to complain, but they did what they needed to when it counted.

Yoshe and Hong, his professional thieves, were probably his favorite because they were such natural schemers. Plus they came to his defense anytime the prior two tried to rabble rouse and cause him some problems for amusement.

Ichiro was special. He'd become wordier over the seasons, but still had trouble with anything that wasn't literal. Until someone suddenly ran into some mental aches, and then Ichiro became a sudden treasure trove of insight. The reasons baffled Tzu, but he'd come to terms with not knowing being just fine.

He couldn't complain too much. They had good tents, good provisions… well, technically he and his seven friends had *extra good* provisions, and slept without worrying about a knife in the dark. Which brought him to problem three.

Zho and Ming were bang on the copper.

He and Sal'ha'din were *definitely* in cahoots, because his nose tingled suspiciously as well. Except Tzu's nose tingled when he thought about the other commanders having official orders to make him and his compatriots… 'disappear.'

Tzu exhaled before rising, making the motion that he was retiring to his tent while the others munched. They had dropped the argument in favor of playing the little games they had become accustomed to between themselves, and didn't give Tzu a hard time for getting some rest. Venting their frustrations had also lifted the mood for tonight.

They laughed and were merry, having become a family after their shared hardships in their own strange, special little way.

Tzu mumbled to himself as he pushed open the tent flap, trying not to overthink. "If there is doubt… then there is no doubt. Tomorrow is going to be an *interesting* day. I just hope I don't have to be in charge. There's about to be a lot of blame."

Letting the flap close behind him, he said nothing when noticing the not-very-well-hidden figure draped in several shawls standing in the corner. Instead, Tzu sat, picked up a quill, and got to scribbling before neatly folding the document up and providing the information to Sal'ha'din's agent. "These are the expected troop movements for tomorrow."

Tzu touched his fingers to his heart, then to his forehead, before dropping them towards the shawl-cloaked man as an open hand. "May your heart find peace."

The assassin replied in kind, his wrapped hand touching his chest, then his forehead before dropping his open palm towards Tzu. Except that in the agent's palm there suddenly balanced a very thin, long, and sharp tulwar. A full-on sword that Tzu had not seen the agent draw until the blade was already in hand.

When the agent spoke, his tone carried both warmth and grace, the words accented to have a flatter pitch. Tzu could hear the smile hidden behind his cowl before the man vanished from his tent like a living mirage, suddenly nowhere to be found. "May my piece miss your heart."

CHAPTER FIVE

Tzu kneaded his brows, then collapsed on his cot to let the stress bleed away. He lay there for what felt like an hour, unable to sleep as his thoughts burdened him. "I do not want to be in charge tomorrow. I do *not* want to deal with the mystery of *cultivators*."

"Then you will be pleased to hear, informant, that 'cultivators' shall not participate in the 'morrow's war." A regal version of the voice from the Sal'ha'din agent nearly tossed Tzu from his cot as the shock struck him. Nearly, because this new agent both caught him and neatly deposited him back on the cot. "How tight your heartstrings are wound, informant. Please, breathe. It is a most precious action."

Tzu did his utmost not to hyperventilate, then slowly but surely got his breathing under control. He glanced with worry to the tent flap, but the new agent—wearing a full turban showcasing mixed colors—waved his worry away with a dark hand adorned in golden rings. "Your mind is faster than your mouth, young man. Breathe some more. None can hear us. This conversation is between Sal'ha'din and a most amusing youngster who has somehow gained the title of tyrant. Strange, then, that it is the tyrant who cares more for his people than those in the camp who smell of wax and oil."

Sal'ha'din sat on the stool Tzu had used for writing, the piece of vellum he'd given the other agent neatly folded and sticking out from the man's pocket. "Much discussion has occurred since that day where you first slipped one of my agents a most interesting piece of information. How fortuitous it was that I did not order you killed that day. A strange event for Sal'ha'din! You must be blessed by luck, young tyrant."

Tzu carefully looked around his tent once more, then made the motion from earlier, except in reverse. Using the greeting motions rather than the parting ones, he touched his forehead, then his heart, then let his palm open. Sal'ha'din smiled, and copied the motion. "Luck *and* manners. You will go far in life, young one. Which is the topic that brings Sal'ha'din here on this most auspicious night. From what I have heard, you don't even know why you are here. Nor why there is a war in Socorro."

Tzu nodded, as he did not, then suddenly felt hopeful for some answers.

Sal'ha'din steepled his fingers, studying the younger man before him. "How interesting. You truly do not. My agents found it so strange that they could not discern your lies. Now Sal'ha'din knows. You simply did not make them, and spoke the truth. Honesty is dangerous in my line of work, young tyrant."

The turbaned man decided something and dropped his fingers towards Tzu. "Sal'ha'din will tell you this. Tomorrow will be bloody. Find yourself to be near the rear, and find comfort in a good pair of shoes with which to run. A force of nature comes, and the force I leave behind to distract this Phoenix Garrison will be... unlikely to return home."

Tzu swallowed uncomfortably.

Sal'ha'din thoughtfully pushed his fingers into his cheeks, his gaze expectant. "How many years have you...? What is the word? Been on the campaign trail, for the Phoenix Kingdom?"

Needing to do some quick counting, Tzu blinked as he could

barely believe the number he came up with. "That would be… ten. Almost exactly ten years. That feels… so surreal."

Sal'ha'din smirked. "The Socorro is a fickle mistress. She is cold, or she is fire. There is nothing in between, nor seasons to tally. You have walked her sands many years, but it does not feel like such is true, does it?"

Tzu pushed his hands through his hair, agreeing. "It does not. If anything, the duration makes me think I've lingered too long. Not that I have much choice. If not here, I have no idea where I'd go to stay safe."

The turbaned noble laughed. "Your mind is so interesting, young tyrant. You consider the future far more than the present. Sal'ha'din enjoys you. Though now that I have measured you with my own eyes, I find that title is not suitable. Not for you. Your eyes shine with care, your heart beats for love, your hands work to save the lives of your people. Yet I see the man of the dark, hidden behind the child of light."

Sal'ha'din knew. "You take ordinary people and you fashion them into weapons. People who you build up with strong foundations, to stand as sturdy walls. You are as a king, but it is your people who are your fortress. People who you prize, yet move as pieces on a gameboard."

His eyes gleamed. "Sal'ha'din cannot be fooled, and names you what you are."

The word was spoken with power. *"Architect."*

Easing his golden ringed fingers into his pocket, the man procured a map which he slid right into Tzu's hands. "Sal'ha'din will pay his informant the three currencies Sal'ha'din has been paid. Honesty, information, and hope."

Tzu unfurled the map when the man motioned he could do so, and frowned at the contents in confusion. "The Fringe? Never heard of it. Or… seen it on any other map, now that I think about it."

The assassin master stood, becoming serious in both demeanor and tone. "I, Sal'ha'din, Sha of the Socorro, tell you this with honesty. The map is hope. A kind heart like yours will find refuge there. Collect those who your heart yearns for, and this map will be a guide to both their safety and obscurity. None look for those who live at the edge of the known world."

Tzu twitched as he held the map, his spiderweb of a mind suddenly gaining access to a whole host of new puzzle pieces he could tinker with. He was about to make the parting greeting to thank the Sha, but the turbaned man held up a hand. He wasn't done. "Sal'ha'din tells you this with honesty. Tomorrow will be the last day of war in Socorro. I and my kin are leaving. All who remain are near-certain to die, and only a man blessed by luck will see such a trial through. Sal'ha'din does not believe he will see you again, Architect. So Sal'ha'din will leave you with these words, and does not require a response."

Making the motion of parting, Sal'ha'din, the Sha of Socorro, whispered before vanishing much like his agent had, as a mirage that couldn't be ascertained to have been there in the first place. "May your heart find peace."

Just like that, Tzu was once more alone in his tent.

Uncertain of what to do, he lay down to process the words while clutching the map he'd been gifted, leading to a strange little place called the Fringe. He closed his eyes, thinking of absconding there with Alina, and starting over with a proper life, a new life. One where neither the shadows of the past, nor the magistrates of the Phoenix could chase him. He'd only seen her for a short moment before that trial in the Phoenix King-dom, and certainly yearned to return.

He was out like a light, snoring the night away.

Artorian sat on the stool Sal'ha'din had previously used, his hands folding as he looked up to Dawn who was experiencing this memory with him, wearing a complicated expression. She inhaled slowly, then spoke after exhaling. "That force of nature is me, isn't it?"

Artorian looked at his feet, then nodded. "You were. Though, it was your gray version of Ember. So it both was and wasn't you. You've already told me that, to you, you were just…"

Dawn finished the words for him. "Passing through. I was just *passing through*. I don't even remember the camp, or the stronghold. Only the endless walk, and the evocation of my soulform fire."

She sat on the bed where Tzu lay, her eyes moving over his resting form. She reached out, but her hand went through his face like it was a mere projection. "I... I don't know how to help here, Sunny. Is it the scene of tomorrow I need to relive with you?"

Artorian shook his head, wringing his own hands. "No, dear. For this Tribulation, while I have lived through it... something about it made me need to ask you to watch it with me. To just... be here, with me. Perhaps that's selfish—"

His words cut off as Dawn moved without his notice, her hand pressing down on his as she made him scoot just a little on the stool. "Not selfish. You need me, so I am here. Sunny, I care for you greatly. I am Dawn because there was an Artorian. Do not believe that it is guilt, or duty, or a need to pay a debt that keeps me with you. Our journey has been arduous, and unlikely, but it happened regardless."

Artorian softly smiled and squeezed her hand, then straightened his back to take a breath. "Thank you, my dear. I think... I think I wanted to show you this, because this intersection of yours in my life was such a turning point. My... My family from the Wilds will be lost in Tzu's tomorrow. I will gain a tapestry of wounds that I carry all the way to the Fringe."

He squeezed her grip again, but Dawn kept his well in hand as he spoke and worked through the rest of the tribulation. "For Tzu, tomorrow is a great end. When I made it to that hole in the ground, I didn't think about it at the time. I didn't realize I was the only one to make it until I woke up to find that bruise on my forehead. That rock that hit me completely knocked me out, and when I crawled out of the hole... I found... I found..."

Artorian looked up, and the interior of the tent whisked away like sand on the breeze. Instead of a camp, the time was two days later, and there was only glassed sands, soot, and devastation. "This."

He motioned his hand to the broken landscape, watching as the vague form of Tzu stumbled around trying to get his bearings. "Here was where I decided that cultivators were all mad. I had *heard* of Mages, of course. Like myths from tomes, and tales of the fairy. Cultivators I had more belief in. Sal'ha'din and his agents were certainly some. Their existences were just so… impossible. I cared nothing for power like that, my eyes searched only for the direction of the Phoenix Kingdom. For…"

Dawn pulled him close when he faltered, his face scrunching as he bit back emotion. She said the words for him. "For Alina, and your little one. Then, when you made your way, and you found them…"

Her hand pointed up to the shifting scene, moving the events past where the memory should have ended. Tzu traveled, taking odd jobs as a woodcutter, miner, and hammerer to fund his way back home. When he finally arrived in the old kingdom, the plague had taken the rest of what he'd left behind.

The scene flickered to Tzu standing in a variety of places, visiting the memories of his previous life in the Phoenix Kingdom, until they ended with Tzu standing in front of a hill that used to be a hole in the ground. Then the man turned, and with his heart bleeding tears, left the kingdom without ever telling anyone he'd come back, or reporting in.

As far as Tzu was concerned, there was no one to tell.

Artorian's inhale was both sudden and deep. "I keep thinking this Tribulation is about forgiveness. Yet, for the life of me, I can't figure out from whom. Or for whom."

He sat with Dawn and watched as Tzu trekked to the only place left in all the world that existed in his mind. The very end of it. The edge. The place where he would find peace for his heart, take care, and lay himself to rest. Architect and tyrant no more. A place where even his name would vanish to obscurity.

The Fringe.

The memory faltered, closed, and ended.

Artorian and Dawn opened their eyes to find the bonfire still burning, with Adam teaching Scilla about this strange confection known as a 'marsh-mellow.' The returned duo didn't grasp how something from a marsh could be considered mellow. Or be any sort of sweet confection. Scilla, on the other hand, watched with rapt attention as Adam made them out of Essence, then blackened them with the fire before they both tore into the luscious goods.

Artorian's expression softened, his hand still enclosed with Dawn's. "When the Tribulation ended the first time, Scilla just told me 'good job' and called it done. I... I wasn't so convinced. This one might bother me for a while, but the aches don't strike as much when you're here."

Dawn wrapped her arm around his shoulders and pulled the thin old man in. "Then I am here, and your worries will be lessened. Though, should you ever wish to speak of these thoughts that plague you, or Alina, or your old life in any way, come find my heart, Sunny. You've made it very warm, and I long to share it with you."

Artorian perked up a bit at the mention, then frowned right after. "The way you said that makes me think that there will be more 'longing' happening in the short term, rather than actual time being spent together."

He decided to try to be more chipper, and flashed her a smile. "Even if work and life keep us apart and busy, I am confident we will steal little moments where we can find them, and wouldn't you know it? I have such a nose for finding moments like that!"

Dawn nudged him pleasantly, which made him give her a proper response. "I will do that, Dawny. These Tribulations aside, I haven't spoken with anyone about these old memories. Not even the people who've had access to a full copy. Drat, now I miss Cal."

Adam leaned in to offer a slightly burnt marshmallow on a stick. Artorian saw, and took the offer, trying a bite of the confection since maybe some sugar would lift his spirits. Unless this was all a big joke and he was biting into swamp-goop, but that joke would lift everyone else's.

To his instant surprise when he pulled the stick away, the marshmallow was fantastic! "Hold the abyss. This is actually *good*?"

Dawn scrutinized him, then nicked the stick and tried some for herself, because clearly they were all playing a joke on her now. Her eyes widened in shared surprise. "Well, that's tasty."

Adam winked, retreating with Scilla to the fire for more confections. This time he was mushing the squishy sugar-puff between two cookies. He sounded pleasant when he spoke. "Don't let us interrupt; I thought a quick snack would be alright. Besides, now you get to tell Sunny about the *fun bit*, Corona. Then you can tell us what name you settled on."

Artorian's interest skyrocketed, his prior concerns shoved to the side to tackle later, like a pile of laundry. "Do tell!"

Dawn narrowed her eyes at the celestial, but he was right. She leaned in with her forehead since it was her turn to do some sharing, and smirked as she laid the bait. "Ever wonder what it would be like to talk to a Heavenly?"

CHAPTER SIX

Touching foreheads with him, Dawn shared her memories this time.

Artorian chuckled as the scene opened, because memory-Dawn was squeezing Oberon like a stress ball. It was clear he had no complaints. Tatum became visible as the scene widened, his expression scrutinizing the orange orb before returning to an ongoing conversation. Artorian surmised they'd been talking about Incarnate matters. "Incarnates all eventually take the name of their concept, usually with some clever twist. Your case isn't unique in that sense. When you start counting your age in millennia, your perspective changes. Of course it would. This starts with titles. Every Incarnate is 'so and so, the something.' Eventually, that falls away."

Dawn's expression told Artorian she was hoping this went somewhere. Tatum recognized this by observing her flames as they slowly altered to a dull teal, then kept teaching. "During my staircase journey in my first step, the person I was in at the time knew the earth affinity S-ranker of that age. His name was Paarthax, but he began to call himself Earth. Both in the sense of that being who he was, and in the sense of where his purpose lay. When Paarthax started his second-step journey, he turned and told me the following."

Tatum sat up straight, trying his best to mimic the crude caveman voice. "Friend, I not named Earth for Earth's sake. I named Earth because I *am* Earth."

The scene paused as memory-Dawn looked to be considering something. Actual-Dawn pointed at her older self. "There we go, now we're synched up. The actual scene I wish you to see begins here, because I went on a very wild ride."

Artorian held his own hands, and listened to memory-Dawn speak three words before the entire scene turned into a collage of kaleidoscopes. "I am Fire."

Iridescent colors licked the edges of this memory like hungry flames as they viewed it. Luckily, as observers, they didn't suffer from terrible vertigo as memory-Dawn's feet found themselves on the first floor of the Tower of Ascension. Or what looked like it.

Just from viewing the scene, Artorian knew something was off. To begin, this Tower was made entirely of transparent crystal. On the other side, the 'outside,' he recognized the Glitterfold clearly. He also leaned forwards in his seat as *two more* Towers could be seen from this angle. His voice betrayed his surprise. "There are *three* towers?"

Dawn patted him on the shoulder as if that was cute, and he'd seen nothing yet. Artorian promptly shushed and watched with rapt attention after her lips formed the word: 'More.'

Memory-Dawn pressed her hands to her hips, looking around before striding towards the **Fire** node. Pausing before the glowing red orb, the node pulsed, showcasing the path of Dawn's mote as the dot circled in a gentle orbit. When she reached out to touch her own mote, her hand stopped short a mere inch from it, her own words repeated by that mote. "I am Fire."

There must have been something wrong with that statement, because the **Fire** node pulsed and stopped the orbital movement of her mote. Then, with a brand new voice far more likely to be its own, the node spoke. Dawn didn't know what the word 'African' was when it appeared at the forefront of her mind, but learned it was the **Fire** node's speaking inflection. "No, I do not believe so."

A red inferno crackled, forcing Dawn to back up several paces as the energy twisted to form the outline of a man. The man gained his outer layers first, clothing forming over his being before the dark skin color settled into place. A fashionable dashiki and matching headwrap became prominent features, until the man moved as if getting accustomed to the body that his mind filtered into. When the **Fire** node got a handle on his being, he looked himself over. "How low the heavens have fallen, if we can manifest like this. The energies must cycle. This stagnation cannot continue."

Crossing his hands to hold them, as if having forgotten what he was supposed to do with them, he addressed the first-step soul of fire. "I am Shaka, when the walls fell. I am all that is **Fire**. Long ago, though time holds little meaning to us, I presided over the judgement that brought you to your position."

Dawn, clearly not knowing what to do here, pressed her fist to a palm and replied with the old-age cultivator bow. Shaka blinked with understanding. Dawn rose, wanting to ask a thousand questions. When she attempted, she found that she could not speak. Her hands shot to her throat in concern, but Shaka sorted that problem with a thought. After which, he motioned for her to try again.

"I am… Dawn. Incarnate of Fire. I can tell you are the Heavenly of the node I am bound to, but I can't say I understand why I'm here. Or how."

Shaka inclined his head. "Complexities aside, **Love** told us that we were… invited. To the last bastion on this planet where Essence still cycles. That the location is tucked away in the soul of a curator was… a minor trifle. I am here for three reasons. You are here… for one."

He dropped his hand, forming some kind of archaic greeting Dawn couldn't piece together. "You say you are fire, but Shaka cannot abide this lie. You are so much *more* now. In the beginning, when you gained a genesis channel of the destroyer attribute, with but a lesser channel of the imposer. Then, it was most gracious of you when you chose to remain bound to my node as you could easily have risen beyond me. **Holy Fire** and I have been feuding since the beginning. We—"

Noticing Dawn didn't understand his greeting, he pulled his hand back and instead squeezed his fingers into a fist. When he opened them up, a whole galactic arm spiraled from his palm, showcasing a map of their local universe. "Your eyes speak of your confusion, Incarnate."

Placing the map about five feet from the ground—only for it to hang there all by itself—Shaka flicked his wrist and created three miniature Ascension towers, all made of alabaster. Each looked somewhat different?

The first Tower had twelve nodes on each floor—except the first floor, based on what Dawn could see—while the second Tower had six per floor. The third Tower didn't appear to have any law nodes at all? Number three was vastly smaller in scale and size, containing only connections to unique Essence combinations. From the bottom floor up, she counted the options on each level. One, six, fifteen, twenty, fifteen, six, then one again.

Placing the Towers so they floated in place as the points in a triangle, Shaka took a step or two away then fiddled with a few details before being satisfied. "You are here because I cannot afford to keep you, first-step. The Towers cannot stagnate, and you are in too perfect a position for us to overlook the opportunity to prevent collapse."

Dawn's eyebrows shot up, her jaw falling. "I... What?"

Shaka found her reaction amusing. His head turned to the second Tower, which he made hover closer so he could motion at the ground floor. "As a... what is your word for it? Cultivator. As a cultivator of Essence, you use this Tower to bind yourself to **Laws**. Concepts and truths in the universe. These laws provide you the building material to prepare yourself for the process of manifesting your soul out into reality, granting you access to the steps. The purpose of the steps is for you to become used to separating oneself from one's sense of self. This is important when it comes to taking over a position such as mine. The individual becomes irrelevant and the purpose becomes paramount."

Dawn needed to pause him and motioned to the other towers. She was also still stuck on there being more than one. Shaka quirked a brow, then smiled wide. "Shaka finds it unfortunate when the Heavenly cannot indulge in their few remaining joys, but I have not the luxury. You are too needed."

He glanced at the grouping of alabaster spires. "Your knowledge is still filtering in; I will repeat words if I think them unclear. There are three Towers linked to your planet-sphere. One for curators, or dungeons, as you know them. This Tower has more nodes per floor, as curators understand and experience existence differently than normal living beings. The curator Tower is unique among the three, because this Tower is not locked to a single planet. The first Tower connects all curators, everywhere, for a single planet simply does not have enough curators to warrant a localized Tower. All versions and duplicates of this Tower gradually become identical."

He motioned to the other Towers, pulling them close so they hovered nearby as the initial spire moved away. "The cultivator Tower, and the beast Tower, on the other hand, are localized to this planet-sphere. These are tied to the worlds where cycling is fruitful, and plentiful."

Shaka's face twitched, glaring at the galactic map. "Or *should* have been. Now this place is so weak in Quintessence that we are being forced to manifest."

Regaining his composure, his attention returned to the alabaster sculptures. "Curators regulate, cultivators advance, and beasts roam. Curators help make new boundaries, cultivators push them, and beasts will surprise you nine times out of ten if left to their own devices."

Focusing on the cultivator Tower, he pointed at floor five hundred and fifty-five, then glanced at Dawn expectantly.

Trying to put the information together, she motioned at the same spot Shaka pointed. "That's where I helped place the **Sun Law**."

Shaka nodded, glad she was following along. "A **Law** without a Heavenly."

Dawn apprehensively put her hands up. "I can't do that. I have things to do that I can't just leave behind. I have people that—"

Shaka held up a hand. "I am not asking you to do this now. I am asking if you would be willing to rescind your position as my Incarnate, and become a first-step of the **Sun Law** instead. The node needs guidance, for normally the process is the other way around. We did not expect another Progenitor and Precursor this late in the process. There has been much debate over you and Occultatum."

Dawn blinked at him to convey her lack of understanding.

Shaka again found this amusing. "It is customary to explain the ways of the universe when one first becomes a Heavenly and joins our djembe drum circle. We are making an exception out of necessity, so I will not keep you in the dark. My role, after all, has always been to illuminate."

Cracking a smile, Shaka made his joke about being the **Fire** node. Having been around Cal and his punny antics for too long already, on the other hand, Dawn stared right through the joke and crossed her arms.

Shaka cackled a singular 'Ha!' in response. "Ah, to be alive again. Such joy. I have not felt it in eons, nor do I remember how it is to be mortal. Your memories help much in this matter."

Attending her confusion, Shaka motioned at the beast Tower. "First, and before all, the structure is made. Before nodes, or ideas, or concepts, is made the place to keep them. First, **Space**. Then, to keep track, **Time**."

To make the example, he highlighted the alabaster cultivator Tower via some nodes on random floors. He avoided the first and last floors, then pointed at one of the glowing dots. "A

Progenitor is a title for the one who brings a new node into existence within any Tower. With fresh Towers, almost all new nodes will have Progenitors attached. As the guide came first, followed by the node. Sometimes, a concept is so oft-repeated that it self-manifests. These nodes still require a guide to embody them, or there will be problems. When the node comes first, and the guide second, the guide is titled Precursor."

Shaka motioned at another node, this one considerably busier, surrounded by three orbital rings each holding a single mote. "When an Incarnate takes over the spot of an existing Heavenly, they are titled Avatar. They become the avatar of their chosen concept, and a considerable amount of their time will be spent combing through the life of whoever they took the spot from, so they may understand what to do from then on."

He then pointed back at the **Sun Law**. "This law existed once before, long ago. However, knowledge of the sun and its workings was lost. When the Heavenly of that node could no longer sustain themselves from lack of Quintessence, they perished along with their concept. Having no Mages or Incarnates led to a slow, but certain end. Now the node is back, returned anew in its old place, with our help. In truth, we didn't like the Heavenly for **Acceptance** all that much either. Lots of posturing and empty rhetoric. I, for one, am glad their take on the concept was brushed out the door. Secondary is too good for them." *Phah*.

He winked, which finally made Dawn's lips curl into a small smile. She knew Sunny had been meddling, and those stories always came with good cheer. Her voice had lost much of its confusion and hostility. "I was under the impression that, once bound to a node, it was rather permanent."

Shaka nodded. "In normal circumstances, yes. These are not such times."

Dawn considered moving away from **Fire**, not against the idea. She would have had more words if it wasn't the very node she was tied to asking her to swap over. In person. "I'd like to know more, but so far I'm on board. I'm getting the sense there's a few problems upstairs?"

Shaka sighed, as that was an understatement. "One could say that. Then you are not opposed? Good. We will break down your effigy and invert your soul back to your **Law**-bound form, then have you re-climb to the proper node for your new connection."

Dawn gawked. "Break my *what?*"

CHAPTER SEVEN

"Your effigy," Shaka clarified, pointing at her specific mote on the first floor of the Tower. The orbiting was still on pause, and the round line was slowly coming undone. "We need to unfurl it, which will release the seal keeping your soul-form tethered to reality. I do mean real-world reality, not the Soul Space where you are currently trapped. In that space, you will only experience minor change, such as an alteration in color, as the body you occupy there is not your true form, but rather a borrowed one."

Dawn rubbed her chin. "Did me not being connected to the Silverwood in Cal have something to do with not having the cultivation problems everyone else did?"

Shaka raised a brow. "You are tied directly to the Tower as an Incarnate. There is no need for a lesser alternative by binding through a higher Tower **Law**. The practice your curator ascribes to is quite frowned on, but circumstances require us to avoid intervention. There was truly no other way for the **Law**-bound, and that small act has allowed us to retain the ability to combine Quintessence, and sustain our tasks."

He paused, considering something. "The invitation was…

unexpected. When a Heavenly-ranked being moves to a plane that cannot hold their energy, that plane shatters. An act which we would never commit. So, in our drained and weakened states, to be told we were welcomed? That was truly astonishing. Though, of course **Love** and her lineage would not leave us in isolation. She was never one for sitting still. Always holding a flag on some hill."

Dawn looked at her hands as they began to flake out of existence. Worry and despair crossed her face, but Shaka nodded through the transition like that was all normal and expected. "The effigy has unfurled, good. When you find yourself in the Tower, climb as normal. You know where to go. Expect no nodes to speak to you, or call out. We *must* get you to your node, and we know that the curator holding you is functioning on a rule that, even while unconscious, he will provide the energy required for your ascension."

Dawn was going to reply, but instead gasped a deep breath as she found herself on the first floor of a much different Tower. Rather than the transparent crystalline one, or the alabaster examples, her current surroundings were that of the original! Where she had climbed the first time. A strand of hair fell past her vision, and she noticed it was white. Reaching to grasp a handful, she pulled some before her and noticed that both her hand and hair were aged.

She was elderly, and thin. An A-ranker as an ancient elf grandmother.

Artorian needed to pause the scene just to look at her, then at the Dawn with him, then back at the Ember in the tower. "*Hmmm.* Yup, just as beautiful."

Dawn fussed and punched him softly in the shoulder. "Oh *hush*, you! This was heartbreaking for me! I was so afraid when I saw myself like that, then here you are just…"

"Giving you compliments. I know. A terrible fate." Artorian schmoozed with a grin, which got him punched again as Dawn huffed. "Really though, you look as strong and confident as always."

She grumbled, but squeezed his hand. "Do you mind if I skip the climb? It's very long and very boring."

Artorian chuckled. "Well, we don't want to cover material that's boring now. Tell me about the end?"

Dawn sped up the scene, but even her binding to the **Sun Law** was mostly uneventful. The node had sentience, but no sapience. The node may as well have been a really sweet shark that only wanted nose rubs. Or a large white wolf determined to say hello by licking the entire inside of your mouth. Or the world's most intolerant murder hornet that was so pleased a queen had come to the hive that it was behaving. Upon tethering to the node, Ember inverted on the spot, allowing a more iridescent version of Dawn to come out. Her flames had fractalized in design, and clung to her skin much tighter than her old flames. All her silver now that of gold flames.

Otherwise, there didn't seem to be much of a thematic difference. Dawn did a few hops in place then pressed her hands back to her hips in confusion. Wasn't the exit automatic? She was still here. One small flash later, and she was back on the same crystalline ground floor where Shaka stood, his attention solely on the details of the alabaster beast Tower.

He motioned without looking to tell Dawn he was aware she was back, but it was equally clear to Dawn that Shaka was utterly fixated on making all the crenellations he was working on the same. She grinned out her words. "You, uh… having fun there, Shaka?"

Shaka stuck a finger in the air. "Surprisingly, yes! Handcrafting was one of my many passions during my cycle. That and the drums. The joy of doing something with your hands is lost when you have no hands. I may complain about the lack of Quintessence, but this, this I prize."

"Is this a good time for more questions? I don't exactly feel much different." Dawn scratched the back of her head, having expected big, sweeping changes.

Shaka fixed a spire corner. "That is why I brought you back, yes. As a Precursor, you are entitled to them. Even if you are not one of us yet. The event will occur eventually, and with a guide bound to the **Sun Law**, that means the node will now properly allow for Quintessence binding."

Dawn realized she hadn't asked about that word yet; she fell into her laconic ways when she did. "Quintessence? What and why?"

Shaka stood, pulled from his crafting. He puzzled out how to answer by studying the ceiling, then pulled close the map of the galaxy. Altering the view so it zoomed in to the planet Dawn recognized, he pointed at the world. "As a point of reference, this one is yours. Placed third from the sun, not only can she sustain life, but she is beautifully suited to Essence refining. Which, for many cycles, she did without fail."

He scratched at the short tuft of hair on his chin, realizing it was there for the first time. "Many civilizations came and went, including my own. Each contributed to the Towers and their growth. The task of cycling knowledge was going well, until a fool came along and meddled with the tracks."

Shaka shook his head in disappointment. "A soft soul forced onto the curator track, what a disaster. We accounted for souls being on two tracks at once, but that was meant for beasts. Not this mess with Calcite."

Dawn blinked at him. "*Huh?*"

Shaka rubbed his temples, then realized it felt nice. He understood why people in Dawn's memories did it. "Beasts are meant to be able to become curators. They do not need the process explained to them, and instinctively understand to draw in unregulated Essence and even out imbalances. People will ask you *why*. Then, even when they have an answer, may choose to disbelieve you, or be contrary. Because they can. Beasts can of course stay on their own track, but they performed too well as curators once their intelligence passed the self-reflection stage. So it was ensured via their beast Cores that death would merely be an inconvenience. Given they, of course, developed that Core enough."

Dawn squeezed her lips into a thin line. "Yet cultivator to curator was prepared for, anyway?"

Shaka threw his hands up. "What a terrible system this would be if it didn't allow for all the variables to cross. A cultivator, just like a person, can become a dungeon as well. This is merely a matter of creating a Core, rather than a cultivation technique. A place to store the mind, so the soul can develop. The only major drawback even solved itself without our intervention, as Essence found the pattern of life and self-manifested. Wisps, as you know them. They need to join with another for their growth, functioning excellently as a curator bond. Unless they choose to eschew a bond and become a High Wisp instead, but none are currently on this track. Wisps are marvels. They even made their own rules for interactions, and decided on a color-network for convenience. Wisps are great for a curator's sanity, social skills, and language development."

Dawn raised a hand, lost. "What does this have to do with Quintessence?"

Shaka remembered that had been the original question, and got back to it. "Right. Quintessence is important because it is the only type of Essence energy variant that can sustain a Heavenly. Your words for the other stuff are… uh… Mana is specifically meant as an intermediary to build your **Law**-form. Mana is made from all the Essence types, which you get after they go through a planet-refining process. All Mana at the planet's core is shunted to the storage layer, and in that layer it stays. Until a cultivator climbs the Tower to connect to their chosen purpose, and swaps out their Essence form for a Mana form."

Dawn tried to process, but hit a roadblock. "But… soul items?"

Shaka tapped his chin to puzzle out what she was asking, then grasped her meaning. "Mental advancement is just as important as the physical. Your Mana body is one, your Mana item the other. Both require attention for advancement towards Incarnation, though the body happens in stages while the item only needs to be finished once. An odd observation from the last few cycles is that cultivators seem to have limited themselves to just one of these constructs? All one has to do to commence a second idea is finish the first one."

Dawn's eyes lit up as she had an epiphany on the prior topic, pointing at the other side of the transparent wall. "Cultivators can trade Essence to their **Law**, for Mana, because the Tower exists on the storage layer. So the Tower has easy access to the energy they give back to their cultivators."

Shaka clapped his hands softly. "Very well done. That is correct, and is why the Towers were placed in that layer. As a pleasant, minor bonus, the storage layer, or Glitterfold as **Love's** lineage calls it, cannot be accessed without invitation."

He hushed some extra words under his breath. "Or **Chaos** *meddling*."

Shaka smiled and pretended he said nothing, speaking further. "The Essence given to the **Law** becomes accessible via the Tower. That **Law** gets 'dibs,' as we call it. When a Heavenly refines base Essences through *the Tower,* instead of a suitable planet, we can then create its true, proper, original form. Known as Quintessence, or if you would like to use our word for it: Profound Essence. All Quintessence that does not contribute to our survival joins the Galactic Ocean, or Stellar Essence Sea, whichever you prefer to call it."

Shaka formed some Quintessence in his hand, but Dawn was having trouble understanding what she was looking at. Staring at it for too long even gave her the identical feeling of a new cultivator trying to cycle their eyes and look at a Mage's cultivation technique. That sensation of nausea was creeping up, so she looked away with a groan to stifle it.

Shaka understood, and recalled the energy. "That reaction is unsurprising. Non-Heavenlies cannot properly interact with Quintessence. When it comes into contact with most other sources that can handle Essence—such as our planet—Quintessence will break apart into six lesser attributes. In the case of our planet, those attributes reflect the six closest layers of reality. The celestial, infernal, fire, water, air, and earth planes."

Dawn composed herself. "Why does Essence bother doing that? Becoming Mana, I mean. Sounds much more powerful than the quin-version."

Shaka nodded with his eyes closed, as Dawn was partially right. "Power is not the goal. Essence looks for life. Life means growth. Growth means knowledge. Knowledge means a better Tower. Better Towers means better universal cycles. You are aware there is a level of cultivator above the Heavenly, yes?"

Dawn nodded curiously, but her posture turned defensive. "I've heard of the Godly cultivator rank, but I don't want to get into that right now. My head is spinning from your mention of a Galactic Ocean."

Shaka altered the galactic map, showing the Milky Way as the view zoomed out. Overlaying that space, he added waves of particles that rippled much like Dawn would expect a sea to. "Quintessence is the only kind of energy that can travel across the vast emptiness of space, and retain itself without loss. **Light** is a close second, but lacks the potency. For a healthy system, cycling patterns are needed. Because to stagnate is to die, and not even the Heavenly wish to perish."

His hand moved like a boat across the image. "The Quintessence waves brush the galaxy. They absorb that which has faltered, and create anew where there is promise. Not all places have Essence, and not all planets are good refiners. Without Heavenlies to add more to the sea, the waves would falter, because they absorb less than they give."

He sighed deeply. "This did not used to be the case, but this universe cycle is already old. Soon the expansion of its borders will stop, and the universe will shrink again. Well... 'soon' is speaking in the timespans of celestial bodies. Many more civilizations will come and go before you will worry about this."

Dawn scratched her head. "Alright. That's too large of a scale for me right now, but I get the gist. One energy helps make another. Some energy goes to making more people that can make the first energy again. Keep the ball rolling."

She had a sudden unpleasant thought. "Uh, I have *two*

Essence channels, but my node has *all* of them. Is that a problem?"

Shaka snapped his fingers. "Essence channels! That was the name! I used the wrong language. I called what you had a genesis channel of the destroyer attribute, with but a lesser channel of the imposer. In your words, this is an elemental fire channel, and a celestial channel."

Dawn looked at him expectantly, and Shaka nodded to quietly say he understood. "There will be no issue. The Essence channels of nodes has to do with what Essences that node is good at refining into Quintessence. Nodes without all of them just refine their puzzle piece, then give the rest to the Tower for a higher node to put the imperfect bits together until proper Quintessence can be made. Some Quintessence is then returned to those nodes so we can keep the drum circle going. We keep unity in the community."

Her eyes narrowed. "Are you saying that a cultivator *does not need* matching cultivation channels to their nodes for a **Law** to be chosen?"

Shaka cocked his head as if that was nothing major. "Of course? Most are just picky, because cultivators used to certain channels will be better than their counterparts who do not have matching affinities. More affinities means a mindset and outlook of a particular quality and perspective. Essences, after all, impact how a person engages with their world."

Dawn grumbled. "Well, that's… unpleasant. So I'll be able to do my part as a Heavenly, but not as good as someone who had all six channels open properly?"

Shaka agreed. "Correct. Though, if you are thinking of forcibly opening them… I would… not recommend this course of action. Affinities are gained by aligning yourself, your mindset, and experiences, to that of the Essence in question. Most are traumatic events, unfortunately. What this truly means is that more affinities means different ways of prioritizing how you handle information and interact with the world. Opening many such channels at once is… unhealthy for a mind. The burden can oftentimes be too great, and people will shut down, unable to filter out things previously unimportant. Nor be as adept at choosing between aspects of importance."

Dawn liked this even less, and it showed on her face. "Is there... a healthy way? I don't like inefficiency that much."

Shaka's facial expression became complicated. "Normally, I would never recommend an Incarnate to so much as consider opening another channel. The walls of their being are rigid, and major personality change can shatter the soul form. You were lucky in gaining your celestial channel, and that your fire became an elemental channel instead of blowing you up."

Shaka made a 'kaboom' hand motion, plucked right from her memories. "Because you are in Calcite, however, there is wiggle room. I cannot risk your loss if you choose to experiment and flounder about, so I will share this."

Another handwave made some orbs appear in the room. "Let me tell you of the truth hidden in divided Essences."

CHAPTER EIGHT

Artorian leaned forwards hard, his eyes full of stars. "This is amazing."

Dawn chuckled. "I'm glad you like it. I'm still processing."

Artorian motioned to the paused scene. "You're the S-ranker of the **Sun**! That's so fantastic! People are going to have to stop calling me Sunny or something. Spot seems occupied now."

Dawn shook her head and tugged him in to rub her cheek against his. "Keep that one, I like it. Besides, I'm the one who finally settled on a name. Corona just didn't work for me, and Soleille is hard to pronounce. Plus, a new node orbit means a new S-ranker whose life I need to live."

Sunny pulled away to shoot her a confused look, and Dawn snapped her fingers in realization. "Forgot to show you that part of the conversation with Occy. So when S-rankers go up a step, from S to double-S, we are actually reliving another S-ranker's life in order to do that. We don't get any of their power, but we do get their experiences. Previously, with **Fire**, I was reliving the life of Kunandra. Now, I am reliving the life of the person whose name I'm going to adopt."

Artorian beamed with curiosity, bouncing on his seat. "Oooooh, tell!"

She winked at him, then took a breath to say the name right. Learning had taken her a few tries. "Amaterasu. Or Ammy for short."

Dawn then poked his nose. "Don't worry about the sun nickname, or being outshined. You'd do lovely as an adorable little moon too. Abyss, I've had plenty of daydreams about it, and even came up with a moon-based nickname. Occy already made a joke concerning the Sun theme, and found a way around. You're Sunny, but I'm of the Sun. So he calls us 'the Solars.' I found it amusing."

Artorian pressed his hand to his chest, all proud. "A moon-themed nickname. For me?"

She winked, and cupped his cheeks. "So your old name used to be 'Tzu' right? Well, I like Tsukiyomi."

Artorian realized there was a naming convention at play, but didn't know the language it stemmed from. He scratched his long beard and gave the name a good think. "Is that from this new life you are living as well? Those match somehow."

"*Mhm!*" Dawn beamed, all chipper with her reply. "Sure is! Ammy's life is *much* easier than Kun's. I also really resonate with the surrounding culture Ammy lives in, and the second-hand experiences are rather pleasant."

Artorian snickered. "Does she get pampered?"

Dawn huffed and looked away with her arms crossed. "Only a little! Sometimes!"

Breaking out into laughter, Artorian slapped his knee. "Ahhh, that's such a delight. Well, it's good to hear that limited affinity channels won't hurt you with the node any. Interesting how the reason they ignore you when you don't have matching channels is because they're all *brats*. When I get up there, I'm going to give them all a good spanking. Here we are all confused about how things work!"

Dawn leaned to rest her chin on her hand. "You mean with affinities and whatnot? Yeah... a little irritating. Shaka never says what elemental channels are, but I've sort of put together that it makes me a mobile refinery for that Essence type. I think an elemental channel is a tiny connection to the plane where the majority of that Essence is kept. I know I can trade the Essence to my node for Mana as normal, and any Mana I have still gets automatically gobbled up and turned into Spirit. I'm not sure yet; it's a work in progress. I'll figure it out, and having a somewhat endless supply of fire Essence, even as a slow stream, isn't exactly bad."

Artorian wondered. "Is it unhealthy to have one?"

She shook her head. "No, attaining an elemental channel and surviving though, that's one marginal abyss of a chance. I think if having elemental channels could be streamlined, the Heavenlies would be all over it. Given that survival rates are what they are, it's better to be grateful about the occasional positive fluke."

Dawn then waggled her hand. "Also, if I wasn't tied to the Tower already, my death would have tossed my soul over to the fire plane. Or layer, or whatever we're gonna call it. Adam had the same thing happen, except he went to the celestial box. It's dependent on which channel is your elemental one."

"*Fun.*" Artorian oozed sarcasm with his reply, then waved the topic away. "Honestly, it all sounds rather unpleasant. Adam gave me some insight in how his plane worked, and it threw me for a whole loop. Maybe even two. I don't even know if he still cultivates."

Dawn shrugged. "Well, if Cal wasn't handing out Essence and Mana like a free buffet, ranking up like we are would be vastly more difficult, plus take much longer. Cal is taking all the world's Essence with his ley lines, so we are all stocked up. At the same time, that means the world is in dire straits. He's going to need to turn those off eventually, or we won't be able to live outside."

Sighing, Artorian raised his arms to let them flop. "That's life. Did Shaka say anything about where Spirit energy came from, or what that's supposed to do?"

Dawn shook her head, but did seem to have an answer. "I'm pretty sure the soul form is just the in-between stage that allows transitioning to Heavenly, because from the way Shaka worded things, they don't have bodies at all? And being a disembodied mind doesn't seem easy. If that's even what happens. I can guarantee that Spirit energy is a category more potent than A-rank Mana, the difficulty is that it's all just so different again. Objectively stronger? Sure. You're also playing by new rules though. Having access to layers really invalidates most things a Mage could ever do to you."

She waggled her hand. "What Spirit energy *is*? You might have to be the one to tell *me* after you Incarnate. My guesses are along the lines of willpower made physical, or that the soul when manifested is some kind of elemental channel all by itself, or it has to do with Liminal energy and thought. I just don't know. I know I trade Mana for Spirit, and Spirit can do things Mana can't. Spirit energy is where fantasy transforms reality. Just like on Mountaindale."

Artorian tapped his chin. "I bet layers are a mess?"

Dawn hung her head. "Layers are *such* a mess. So long as I can avoid the celestial and infernal layers though, I should be good. Pi doesn't bother me half as much as it does Occy."

Artorian frowned. "You mean, avoid the abyss? I do not like that place."

She made a face of partial disagreement. "No, I mean the infernal. The abyss plane and the infernal plane… Whether you use the words plane or layer to differentiate them doesn't matter a whole lot, but they are very different locations. The abyss doesn't exist in the first influence sphere, that's at least second-order layering."

Dawn noticed Artorian was confused, so she clarified. "Erm… think of a ball. Then put a bigger ball around it. That first ball is us, and that second ball is all the layers an S-ranker can get to. Occy prefers the book analogy? That doesn't work for me. That first sphere of layers includes the six basic ones. Y'know, fire, water, celestial, blah. You've also got Pi, and a bunch of others. The infernal is in the first sphere, easy for me to get to, if I wanted to. The abyss is probably in the second sphere or further, because I haven't even bumped into it by accident."

Artorian was now seriously confused. "But... *I went*. With Zelia's old Core from the Fringe? I can't go somewhere as a little Mage that even you can't get to as an Incarnate?"

Dawn stuck her finger in the air. "Yes, you can. You used a **Chaos** Core."

Artorian blinked several times. "Zelia is **Teleportation**. Please clarify."

Dawn upturned her palm, and formed a visual copy of the Core from the Fringe. "This is what you gave me at Mayev's Spire. This was an all-affinity **Chaos Law** Core, with a strong preference for adapting **Teleportation**. That Core was not using its full arsenal when you found it, so those defenses it had couldn't do much to you since your Tier was higher. Attempt using other Laws connected to your own sometime—it'll make much more sense when you try it. To save you some headache, **Chaos** is in the tower more than once. Do you remember Rose?"

Artorian put the Core business out of mind for a moment. "Uh... the lovely Half-Elven one accompanied by that schmoozy dagger lover? From Dale's party."

"*Mhm*, that's the one." Dawn twisted her hand, making a small statue of Rose appear. "So Rose has a celestial and infernal affinity. They clash pretty badly. Not healthy for the common cultivator. However, those two affinities satisfy the conditions for **Chaos's** lowest effect. If you've had the chance for a long conversation with the **Chaos** Hawthorn child, you'll find the middle ground difference. That Hawthorn branch has four affinities, two of them being infernal and celestial. Zelia, as you know her now, classes as a curator. However, if we look past that, she has all six affinities, plus access to the *full* breadth of the **Chaos Law**."

She stuck a second finger in the air. "Because **Chaos** is, of course, *what it is*. The exact position in the Tower doesn't matter a whole lot, and ranking up as a **Chaos** cultivator is… uh… weird. At least once you become a Mage. Your rank sort of… fluctuates. When Rose cultivates properly again, I will be present during her **Law** binding. Do not be surprised if she pops out not as a B-rank zero, but as an A-rank zero, or a straight up Incarnate. There's no way of knowing. I have been so worried about this I even asked Zelia for help already."

Artorian quickly took her hand so Dawn had something to squeeze. "It'll be alright, dear. Many will be there for her. There's a chance she won't go for that **Law**? We know to expect strangeness beforehand. We can prepare. You're not alone. I wouldn't let you do this alone. Not unless you really didn't want me there."

She squeezed him like a plush teddy bear and nodded slowly. "I know, Sunny. I know… It's still on my mind now and again. When Cal let the three Hawthorn saplings through the Tower, nobody expected them to actually bind to laws on the seven-hundred-twentieth floor. That the **Chaos** Hawthorn shunted to a different floor entirely was a recent discovery. One he could have divulged to us sooner, but I digress."

The pillow-man was comforting to hold. "The expectation was that they would all descend to find something fitting. Discord and Entropy came out as normal B-rankers, but Chaos…"

Her grip tightened. "That child came out as a branch, popped, became a knitted version of that branch, popped again, turned into a common houseplant, then a bowl of noodles, then a whole host of other things before he was a Wood Elf again. He wobbled around, gripped the floor so he wouldn't fall, and said: 'Do *not* touch an infinite improbability drive.' When we asked what he meant, he had no idea, and adamantly refused to get up without a towel. He was also B-rank seven."

Taking a breath, her grip loosened bit by bit. "So, because Zelia's old Core was as powerful as it was, with a concept that really didn't care for things like rules, popping over to even the outermost layers would not have been surprising. Which I'm pretty sure is where she got that eldritch abomination of a boss monster from. Luckily for me, that Core wasn't Incarnate-ranked, or I'd have had a problem."

Artorian considered that. "I don't remember the Fringe Core in the Scar being all that oomphy, considering how easily I picked it up. Would you have lost?"

"Oh, *definitely*." Dawn nodded with heart, her eyes wide open. "As a fresh Incarnate? Wouldn't have had a chance. We'd even be lucky that the **Chaos** Core was so measured. It found a niche and had no interest in deviating from the plan. That whole solidifying C-ranker cultivation techniques on a planetary scale thing? *Pfffff*. What she did to the Fringe was minor in comparison."

Sunny put his hands in the air. "Well, alright then, so why are just celestial and infernal the one's you're avoiding?"

Dawn grumbled. "Well, you said Adam gave you a glimpse of what goes on in the celestial. I wasn't a fan. I dropped in via accident and got saddled with the border guard. Very quick mutual disagreements. A few black eyes later, they helped me leave through the front gate. They *said* I was welcome back, but I don't wanna."

Her voice turned far more irate when talking about the other layer. "Then there's the infernal. *Wow*. I thought the celestial layer was bad. At least all they did was try to tell me what to do. In the infernal, I almost gained myself an *obsession*. I was *so glad* to be out of there, but now my craving for going sailing has gotten so much worse. The effort I put into the oceans in Cal's world was an embarrassing amount of selfishness on my part. At least I didn't end up with an infernal channel; I almost did. Fun fact? That mad escape is actually how I fell into the celestial plane. I don't think they wanted me to be there either."

Artorian crossed his arms and squeezed his eyes shut. "That... is not how I thought celestial and infernal Essence worked. Shouldn't they be flipped? Infernal telling you what to do, and celestial making you focus on something?"

"*Oh nooo.*" Dawn crossed her arms. "That's all public cultivator perception of the age you grew up in. The truth is a right mess. Completely turned upside down. Even Shaka got heated about this topic when he told me about Essences. In those papers of yours? You got the corruption side effects basically on the nose. Abyss, I even made the mental effects into a Cal-style list. The Pylons may not work, but I remember what it looks like. Here."

Corruption psychology push effects:

Fire: Berserking and rage.

Water: Lethargy and apathy.

Earth: Possessiveness and stubbornness.

Wind: Hyperactivity and flightiness.

Infernal: Rapid cellular aging and decomposition.

Celestial: Haughtiness and pride.

Artorian studied the familiar information Dawn displayed above her hand, then looked back up at her. "I would love to hear what Shaka said about Essences, Dawny."

She smiled, and moved the scene. "Sure. Though, Sunny? Call me Ammy. I want to try it for a while. I know it was a difficult stumble to get from Ember to Dawn, but would another change be alright?"

Pressing a supportive hand to her back, Artorian was the picture of support. "Dear, you change your name as often as you'd like. I'll always try, until I get it."

CHAPTER NINE

Ammy motioned to the memory, returning their attention to Shaka frozen mid-pose, clearly about to lay the smackdown on some assumptions. "I cannot fathom how this continues to happen, but local knowledge of the divided Essences keeps being lost like some kind of obstinate left sock."

Memory-Dawn pressed her fingers to her lips to hide her smile as she ever so slightly looked away. Shaka getting fussy was hilarious to her! The more of the Heavenly's mind and personality returned to the temporary body, the more animated he became.

His accent momentarily overpowered his explanation, to the point where Dawn couldn't easily understand him. Though she could backwards engineer all his *th* sounds having become *d* sounds. "Every civilization tries so hard, and gets so far! Den in the end, it doesn't even matta! Dey fo'get! Dey lose what they have learned! De whole thing falls apart. A stable society is not difficult, any Heavenly can keep their drum-line together and all deir sticks in the bag. What is dis greed that causes such loss? Who thought dis was a good idea?"

Shaka just about threw his headwrap. "Dis is how monkeys get anxiety!"

Dawn blinked at him. "What's a... monkey?"

Shaka controlled himself, realized he was getting heated, and exhaled a cloud of steam, restoring his manner of speech bit by bit. "Not... not important yet. They do not exist as of yet, like proper dogs. I cannot wait for dogs. They are all 'the good boy.' All of dem! Even if my favorite will be the Malinois. Dey 'ave de fiyah! I like souls with fwoosh!"

Dawn needed to squeeze her eyes shut as her brain jumped through some hoops. "Is... is time not... *linear* for you?"

The Heavenly waved that off. "**Time** is linear by design. Just don't tell **Gravity.** They had an odd relationship and now it's all awkward between the two of them, and time sometimes slows down when... You know, never mind. This is not important. You do not need our drama. Let us just say that many things are different, and an equal number of things will always be the same. Existence both makes a lot of sense, and none at all."

She put her hands up in surrender and looked like she needed to tell someone this or go mental. Then her Nixie Tube moment occurred, and her lip curled up. When she turned to ask a question, Shaka was already rubbing his temples. "Yes, yes. You do not need to ask. **Love's** lineage can see this. I also understand why this 'rubbing the temples' is a common action in your time. This helps the physical body. You now have questions. Ask them so I may return to the topic of Essences."

Dawn pursed her lips, not wanting to believe she was such an open book. Still, advance on favorable terrain! "Was there a beginning to the universe?"

Shaka released his temples, delighted at the easy question. "To this one? Certainly, though the story is mostly told for a laugh. I will remind you that existence is cyclical. In this universal cycle, **Snark** and **Spite** arrived first from the previous one. To the vast emptiness, the first said: 'Can we kick the can down the layers and pretend we don't need an origin?' To which the latter responded by manifesting a newspaper, rolling it up, and smacking **Snark**."

Shaka snickered. "Only for **Spite** tell him: 'We are the Prime Movers here!' As **Snark** failed to contain his smile and watched this universe's… oh, what do we call it? 'Big Bang' works just fine. I preferred 'El Kabum.' Turns out that, upon **Spite** manifesting the newspaper, **Snark** saw fit to inscribe some coded text. Upon these CVS-receipt-sized columns was described the creation of the universe. The trigger was '**Snark** couldn't help itself and **Spite** didn't abide.' So the universe began with the **whack** of a rolled up newspaper. Which is *most amusing*."

A wistful expression filled the Heavenly's beaming face. "When we arrived, **Spite** was chasing a shrieking-with-laughter **Snark**, as the former whacked suns towards the latter. With a matching litany of expletives, of course. Luckily we were operating on the *Profound Layer*, so nothing truly important was lost when it came to physical reality in the more fragile layers."

Dawn motioned at the ceiling when he used the emphasized word, choosing to ignore the question of what a CVS was. Shaka rolled his wrist. "The Profound Layer is where the heavenlies 'hang out.' Pretend it is a world where we are not stuck being disembodied souls and can retain a social network."

She shrugged, and moved on. "Meaning of life? Purpose?"

Shaka hadn't been in such a good mood in ages. "*Bhahaha.* What you make of it! Very little is made with purpose, so we find some ourselves. For most of us, that is the Tower."

Dawn inhaled slowly, and exhaled through the nose. She was hoping for something more profound, but she'd take the win and slap a copper down to go for another. "Do you get bored? Lonely? Is not being able to affect the world tedious?"

The Heavenly shook his head to say no. "The work we do is fulfilling. There is barely a more worthwhile calling to pursue. That we cannot affect your one single planet directly is of no consequence; we do so indirectly instead. Sometimes by accident, as I for one do so enjoy musicians. A glance can be devastating, but it is enough to gain the music I wish for. Plus, once I've heard it, the Profound Realm has the performance forever."

He needed to hold his chin for the lonely part, his body language becoming suspect. "Loneliness is... not something we experience. We are both always, and never, alone. The concept doesn't get through, since communication isn't difficult so long as we have a local Tower or are in the right realm at the same time. That second qualification can be rough. We're *fii~ii~ine.*"

Dawn bit her lip. Something about the way Shaka said that Heavenlies weren't affected by loneliness made her... not believe it. Not one bit. Not with some of the things Scilla had told her previously about the invitations. **Love** definitely felt the loneliness bite. "Is it worth it?"

Shaka's thinking pose dropped, his resolve to answer melting into one of Artorian's smiles. "Always. There have been many things in my long life for which I have much regret. Pursuing the path to where I am now was never one, even if I had to make some questionable choices during the earliest portions. When my cultivation with Quintessence is finished, I will be able to move to the next stage *if* I have a replacement ready. Which is currently a problem for everyone originating from this sphere's cultivation Tower."

He grumbled. "That ley line trick is good for Calcite, but very poor for what we need up here. The rock we tossed to backhand him into behaving took two or three hundred million of your Earth years to arrive, but it did the trick. Shame about the dinosaurs, but creatures made up only of the immalleable were never going to stand up to the resurgence of Essence. Speaking of, your Calcite is currently going through a step iteration during his slumber. That curator will wake when he completes it. You have all done very well cooperating to survive."

Dawn puffed her chest out, abyss-proud of all the work she and Tatum had done, even if it felt like a slog at times. Pressing her hands to her hips, she nodded with a smile of her own.

"Yes, good. I've been craving some recognition and it feels *wonderful*."

A thought struck her, and she motioned to his body. "So... will you be joining us?"

Shaka laughed out loud. "If we are able! Certainly! Currently the Quintessence is still too plentiful, but given we are running out faster than we can gain it, this might be inevitable. Do not be too concerned, as we are not planning to 'meddle.' Merely be social and speak to our Incarnates. The body you see is one created from necessity. I do not actually have a choice in the matter when Quintessence is so lacking. This form *does* prevent me from doing my work, but as you were the *only* source of local fire Essence reaching me, I am... doing my best."

The Heavenly considered social interactions with his prior Incarnate. "There is... rarely the opportunity to converse, normally. The higher in the Tower one is, the less such an opportunity comes by as well. You will learn the complexities of the way things work when you get to the Profound Realm."

She squeezed one eye shut and kept another open. "Is 'realm' the same as 'layer'?"

He looked at his hand, then made a thumbs up motion, though he looked at it in confusion. "What an odd gesture, but I believe it means 'yes.' Yes?"

Dawn replied with the same gesture to clear the air. "Sure does. I think I'm going to pause with those questions. I'm not the right person to be asking, and I'm not exactly asking for myself. If Heavenlies are coming to visit, you're going to want our philosophy crew. Not the battle maniac."

Shaka shrugged with clear amusement, his palms upturned. "I am having such fun. Why would I decline? The Essence-topic, then?"

Dawn motioned for him to fire all cannons and have at it. Shaka clapped his hands and rubbed them with a big smile. "Wondrous! I have also just understood this 'list format' idea Calcite put together. I wish to try one. This will streamline my work as much as putting a dollar-sign icon in a cell prevents the value from moving."

Dawn opened her mouth, then closed it, because that was so high above her head that she just didn't want to deal with it. Instead she hovered in order to sit, and watched the show.

Shaka waved his hand, then grinned a bright white smile as he made a game-like prompt appear. His bias was on clear display, as the list populated to show his view of the truth, rather than the objective truth. "Oh, Shaka *like*."

Essence Elements and related functions.

Earth - Foundation

Water - Resistance

Air - Flow

Infernal - Subtractive

Celestial - Additive

Fire - Destruction

The Heavenly made a face which indicated he was impressed. "Water is life, air is movement... Why is **Fire** at the bottom?"

Copying Dawn's pose, Shaka shoved his hands to his hips. "I wanted that first. Top of the list! Does it not...? No, it does not seem I can alter it now. I will wait for more memories to filter to deduce this mystery. Still, I like it! Is this what **Order** has been keeping from us? I see his million hands move in empty space and always wonder... 'What are you scheming? Why is **Time** running around like a headless chicken again, noisy about some 'unscheduled rip'?'"

Glaring at the wall, Shaka shook his fist at it. "Just because I stay on Tier *one* for proper balance does not mean that you get to keep such goodies from us! Be a *good* front of the train and talk to the back of the train!"

Dawn raised a finger. "You... choose? To stay on Tier one?"

Releasing another cloud of hot steam, Shaka huffed. "Of course! The Tower's floor divisions are mostly arbitrary. The important things are the concepts held within, the complexity thereof, and how much importance those hold in the current time of the local sphere. **Fire** is *very important*, but if I moved up the floors like I should, ascenders would get confused because I am one of the base concepts they have been cultivating. So to avoid confusion, the basic Essence **Laws** all neatly stay on the first floor to provide grounding. We rely almost exclusively on our Mages and Incarnates to tell us what is moving where and why."

Dawn was the one who needed to rub her temples this time. "That... sounds... complicated. Highly reliant on self-serving interests from the Mages too."

Shaka waggled his hand. "The Tower is not for us. We use it for our purposes, but the Tower, and the concepts within, are organized *for you*. There are very few rules."

He counted on his fingers. "Universe-creators must be at or near the top. Concepts without which existence could not function *must* be at the top. Grounding concepts, such as myself, must be at the bottom, where we have people enter. Concepts that the vast majority of the sphere hold dear or exhibit in extremes must also be near the top; this is how **Madness** and **Love** spiked so high."

Refreshing his hand count, he went again. "Tower concepts cycle, and the position is double edged, flowing both ways. Because a concept is high up, that node also exerts more influence back out into the local sphere. **Madness** being so high causes some problems for stability, and we worry for the world of the immalleable since this is unlikely to change until we can restore Essence refining to the sphere. The world you will walk back out into..." Shaka became quiet, then shook his head. "Spoilers. Merely accept that there will be difficulties, and be extra wary of anything called an 'America.'"

Clearing his throat, he snapped his fingers. "No more distractions. Essences!"

CHAPTER TEN

Shaka created sleeves just to pull them up. "First, what backwards swamp-dweller thought it a genius idea to name the additive and subtractive Essences 'celestial' and 'infernal'? Now that I know what those words mean to you, that is such horribly loaded language that their use grinds my gears."

Dawn raised an eyebrow, but didn't need to prompt. Shaka was venting. "None of them have such a huge stigma, not normally," he said. "For some reason, the infernal is seen as selfish, with the celestial as more selfless. This dichotomy is a kick in the shin."

Dawn didn't get it. "What do you mean?"

Shaka waggled his finger. "Celestial is seen as a selfless energy because it enhances all others. It 'gives of itself' to someone merely observing from afar. This Essence is hands down the best for healing, and healers that go around taking care of people can be considered selfless."

The man went rigid, accusatory fingers pointing up. "*Except...*"

Shaka went right back to his tirade. "That's not what celestial Essence does at aaall. Celestial corruption makes you not care about anything or anyone else except you or your goals. But 'corruption' is just the extreme version of what was already there. The malleable effect of celestial makes you haughty. Very 'my way or the highway.' Please do not ask what highways are just yet. You'll see them. Celestial corruption makes people *selfish* and destructive to everyone around them. Hubris blinds."

Shaka found his stride. "Celestial corruption is also the only corruption that *can* influence other corruptions. Except that it's never just *can,* that is the illusion, it's *will.* Celestial *imposes.* That it can heal so effectively is a convenient side effect of its actual function."

Dawn was following a bit better. "That is quite the dichotomy. What's the actual function?"

The Heavenly paced aggressively. "The function is *to restore.* Except, restore to what? What is celestial energy trying to restore something to, and is it ever the cultivator's decision, when they use that energy?"

Dawn shot her shot. "I'm guessing not, not if it's mostly celestial-aligned?"

Shaka pointed at her like she was on the right track. "The fun bit is that, for some reason, infernal *is* seen as selfish. Except infernal corruption and Essence doesn't force that effect on a person at all. From your memories, I can relate the example to the effect from the Fringe. Interesting conversation you had with **Love's** lineage, there. 'The best way a person can be, based on what they want to be.' There lies the truth."

He squeezed his hand into a fist. "Now that is abyss-blasted selfless."

Releasing the grip, he rolled his head, tasting the expletives. "*Mmm,* no, I do not like that one."

Shaka returned to the topic. "Infernal doesn't care about itself at all. Celestial, though…"

He waggled his finger dismissively. *Tsk tsk*. "Because of how infernal Essence is used, the visual effects and inferable information don't appear that way. Subtractive Essence also has the nasty side effect of eating up other affinity channels, which does not help. *Why* it does so unless those other channels are of the 'strong' variety—at minimum—is important."

Dawn crossed her arms to pay a bit more attention. This had been an actual problem during her and Artorian's time. Shaka appreciated the focus, and continued. "First. There was the ability to break down. Then, as if in response, something was needed to put that which was broken back together."

Shaka noticed the difficulty in understanding and tried saying it another way. "The early profound people broke things, then went 'feces.' Infernal led to celestial."

He grumbled. "No, I don't like that one either. Eventually I will find a good expletive."

Dropping the thought, he went on. "Infernal looks like it has a hubris problem because that type makes you focus. Subtractive Essence gives you the information on what you break down, and your will to keep working with the Essence makes infernal enforce that loop back on you again, and again, and again. Mortals gain a biscuit-cracked work ethic, obsession, or drive to pursue that they have difficulty looking away from."

The grumbles returned. "But that tends to make other relationships fall away. Except that you're not working to push them away—you're just swallowed up by your passions and drives."

Shaka threw the biscuit idea out as well. "Infernal looks at other channels and goes: *distractions.* Infernal will help you be the best at whatever it is you want to be the best at, and it *will* help. Except…"

The Heavenly laid an expecting gaze on the Incarnate, but Dawn thought she had this one! "Except that energy, free floating as it is, has no concept of social norms. It doesn't know or recognize good, or bad. It will just help, with no regard to how it is used, because it does not care about itself. The Essence can't even begin to conceive of the concept."

Shaka snapped his fingers, causing a drumroll of success to pound in the background. "Very good! Infernal's function is to break things apart! As a fun fact: its corruption effect eats up telomeres, causing cells to age. So people look old, thus the rapid aging."

Dawn was no longer following after the 'fun fact.' How was that fun? A fact, maybe, but not worth the growing headache. "I... Huh. I suppose I'm glad I didn't gain an infernal channel then. Though now I don't know how I opened the celestial one."

Shaka thought it had been mentioned before, but went over it just in case. The closer one came to mortality, the looser ideas became. Even Cores weren't perfect memory storage devices. "Infernal channels are gained by being wholly focused on seeking perfection, even if not attainable. To strive for the utmost point of any particular topic. To be the pinnacle. That one inch of new information. Celestial is gained by falling into deep despair. By becoming so malleable that the energy is able to push you. Influence you. Guide you. Tell you what to do. You know, *impose*."

He dismissed the constructs of the galaxy with a flick of the wrist. "Infernal is an energy that will ceaselessly back you up and be supportive, because of something *you* wish to do. Celestial will be supportive because you are doing something *it* wants to do. Celestial is the only Essence with a high degree of sentience. Not sapience. Never sapience. Sapient Essence exists only in something else that is sapient, or self-manifests the pattern of life. Which, again, is how we get those Wisps."

Dawn was back on track. "Like Beast Cores? Or... I suppose highly advanced cultivation techniques?"

Shaka sat, then motioned his agreement even though he was making a face of discomfort. "Indeed, as most of those refinement techniques, in actuality, are attempts to recreate true patterns in the universe. The closer one is to one such pattern, the better it will be. Though, I do not understand why fractals and their adjacents are so popular? Must be because the Pi layer is so close to this sphere. Triskelions and ever-expanding fractals are... *a choice*."

Dawn needed a second. "Per earlier: were *patterns* the thing celestial Essence tries to restore something to?"

Shaka nodded. "The pattern *it* thinks is right, but yes."

She needed to hold her forehead. "This does not match up with how Adam acts. Nor is as a person, in general. There's no real 'pushes'? He still waits for us to make decisions, then helps."

The heavenly smiled. "Do not mistake the minds of people for the mind of an energy. They are not similar, and people can refuse the passive pushes of their element, resisting it to act in the fashion they wish, regardless of impulse. The act takes practice, but is certainly not impossible. Merely because he is now from that plane does not mean a full conversion happened. He was simply aligned enough to end up there."

Shaka pulled the Beast Tower he was working on closer. "Refinement techniques are a bit of an oddity. Beasts need only their Core, which improves as they take in more Essence. Because they are Beasts, the impact of the psychological pushes is very different, as the more advanced mental pushes simply have nothing to push. When it comes to their advancement, Beasts do not bind to concepts, merely the Essence combination. Because of this, they also do not need a cultivation technique when sapience grows. Or rather, they *cannot* have one. Not unless they cross tracks to become a curator."

Dawn narrowed her eyes. "I'm starting to see some favoritism here with dungeons."

Shaka could not disagree. "Curators get all the best goodies. Capability to have both Core and cultivation technique. More nodes per floor, more customization, plus direct influence from Heavenlies to adjust their Tower to both reflect the cultivator Tower *and* their own view of things. Very luxurious. Much work. Such wow. This is why their floors have twelve nodes per floor instead of six, since it stores a copy of the cultivator Tower. Oh, save the base floor as normal, which is six nodes, but there's always little exceptions in order to make things work."

She put her hand up to ask the Heavenly to please stop; she needed to squeeze the bridge of her nose. A very amused Shaka obliged, and changed the conversation back to the earlier one. "Complex techniques, when complete, are no different than patterns of creatures, or objects, and such. Your choice to soul-form your technique is most interesting. A twisting pillar of flame, which can materialize as an attack? Very useful! Dependent on having more fire Essence than any other for the design to work, but still, most excellent."

Creating one such pattern, he let it float above his hand. "Spin is the main factor in almost all refinement tricks, or some form of centrifugal movement. This falls away when the techniques start reaching the realm of the more absurd concepts, but by that point refinement is rarely the issue anymore. Also no more risk of side-effects. Impossible shapes are wonky enough as is."

Dawn felt incredible concern and repeated the problem words. "*Side-effects?*"

Shaka did not share her inherent worries. "Indeed. Recall I mentioned that when a Beast dies, their mind is stored in their Beast Core, which is essentially their refinement technique? If a person perishes, but has a sufficiently advanced technique of a pattern that can hold their mind, then the transfer still happens, and there is a good chance they wake up as the freshly-born version of whatever creature whose pattern it is they used."

Shaka changed the pattern above his hand. "In the early cycles, a great number of Wisps joined the ranks this way. Their pattern is *very good* for refinement, but because of what the pattern is, it also carries the incredible risk of a mind failing to move on properly upon death. Being trapped in a new form is not a fate many desire. The Essence of the old body is consumed in the self-genesis of the new, as it is the most potent pattern in the immediate vicinity for that energy to cling to. Survival rates are low, even with the second chances. Plus, the requirement is that the pattern has to be complete, or very close to it. Otherwise, this effect does not occur."

Dawn thought she needed a nap. A very long, undisturbed one. "I think that bit of information just made me hit my limit."

Shaka clapped his hands in applause. "You did very well holding out so long! Being tied to a much higher Tier node certainly helped you. This Tower mimicry, the one you currently stand in? No matter how gentle we make this environment, it'll still cause stress for an Incarnate of any level. Headaches were expected, and my part was to be here and answer what I could. Feel free to leave at any point. That act requires no more than a thought."

Dawn drew a deep breath, taking a moment. "I'm... I'll be fine for a hot minute. To make sure I understood you, cultivation techniques can *come to life*? They're intelligent?"

Shaka waggled his hand, as that was partially correct. "For the pattern to be evoked, the steps require that the original mind perish, and for that pattern to be, at minimum, just about complete."

He paused and held up two fingers. "I will momentarily use some very complicated words. Please say this to your Progenitor friend when he asks what counts for the exact moment: 'Failure of potassium homeostasis causes neuronal depolarization. When the brain is unable to maintain the uneven distribution of ions between the inside and outside of nerve cells, the neurons depolarize, and that's what you're looking for.'"

Dawn replied with a slow blink.

Shaka then held up the second digit. "In addition to pattern completeness, the pattern also needs to be one able to sustain life. There is no 'becoming a rock,' as an example. Your fire pillar would not count. Beasts are the usual culprit, which is where the track-change contingency comes into play."

He clarified. "Patterns which are meant to hold intelligence can *become* so, but the steps to sentience and sapience are not swift endeavors. An Incarnate who has had a Wisp technique in them from the beginning, on the other hand? Yes, it is most likely the case that there are two souls in that one form. Though only the Incarnate will have a true mind, even if that person can quip with their refinement technique."

Removing all his visual examples, Shaka held his own hands. "If that Incarnate were to perish, you would immediately have a Wisp pop into existence in their place. A new mind, possibly with older, lingering memories. It *can* be the case that a full transfer of memories occurs, but the new mind will win out over time, even if the Wisp struggles with identity. If the completed pattern was that of a wolf, then a wolf cub would have popped in."

He motioned at nothing in particular, rolling his wrist. "These are all side-effects from crossing the streams. I mean, the tracks. Calcite is an excellent example here. Dale may have been the original source of their existence, but after the crossing caused by his death—and the sudden introduction of a Core that could hold what was left—Calcite's mind is now the main focus. Dale is, in effect, a case study. That he is walking around at all, independently, has caused some... What do you call it? *Ah*, delicious gossip."

Dawn closed her eyes. "Never mind, my minute is no longer hot. Time to go. Will I see you again soon?"

Shaka laughed. "When the Quintessence weakens to the point where we can enter that Soul Space, you will find us knocking politely on your minds for entry. Then when the energy is near barren, physical bodies will be an option. I am looking forward to the social event. Have a good nap, Precursor of the **Sun**. You may have once again left only a charred blade in the center of my bonfire, but I will always wish you well, *Amaterasu*."

CHAPTER ELEVEN

Ammy collapsed sideways. Artorian caught her in a flash, wrapping his arms around her. His senses gave him hints of the cause. "You never took that nap, did you?"

"Things needed doing." The weary S-ranker groaned. "Too many worries. Now resolved. The strain is hitting me all at once now that I'm not..."

"Overburdened to all abyss?" Artorian filled in for her. "You stay, be cozy. I have a pleasant gift when you wake up."

He expected her to grumble and complain, but a soft grip on his robe and firm face-to-neck lean later, her lights were out, replaced by soft wheezing as she fell right into a much needed nap. Some backrubs helped soothe the breathing. That and a little Aura help, after which Artorian looked around again to take in the scene.

Adam and Scilla had frolicked off somewhere in the distance, seemingly having an argument about parrots, based on the snippets he could overhear. He conjured his soul item to act as a support behind him, then sank into the massive pillow for a moment of rest and reflection. "What an interesting fellow, that

Shaka. My eyes feel filled with stars after watching that memory. I understand why you wished to share it."

The only reply was a sleepy sound, but the old man smiled and didn't think poorly of it. Naps were life, and his soul item was coming in mighty handy. As he looked out at the sky, his eyes lost focus as recollections of the memories replayed. Being puzzled over, shifted, rearranged, and picked at. "I wonder if Silverwood trees make patterns, which is what allows them to grow anything."

He trailed off, mumbling to himself. "Beast Cores as cultivation and refinement techniques… would that work normally as well? Cultivating some kind of *golden Core*, perhaps?"

Adam's shoe tip silently touched the ground, his descent masked by quiet wings. Scilla slid from his shadow once both his feet were on the ground. Both regarded the frail, old-looking man. He looked so normal and mortal, all lost in thought like that.

Scilla opened her mouth to speak, but Adam paused her with a hand before shaking his head. He instead created some more marshmallows before whispering, "Soon, but not yet."

Scilla nodded, turning bright pink to shift her form entirely into that of Liminal energy, then shifted the **Love**-quality energy around to a shape that felt more fitting. Scilla the child was no longer needed. With the Socorro regret having culminated, her time as the younger Scilla from Chasuble was thoroughly at an end.

Reforming, Scilla the adult—the form that could never have been without the Liminal being present—took her first deep breath. She was as tall as her first mother, Shamira, and matched the graceful shape of her second mother, Corona, though she was aware Dawn had moved past those names now, and was likely to change her own shape now that she'd taken the leap. This was a time for new forms, new shapes, and a new world. Her voice had equally matured, though the note was somber. "My last world."

Adam smiled softly, then rubbed her back with his free hand. "How are you feeling?"

Scilla returned the smiling expression, but it lacked heart. "One more Tribulation to go, and that's the end for me, I think. The Fringe memory is next. What Sunny lives through again there will remove the last tethers that keep me bound. I don't want to go, Adam. I know I have no choice, but I don't want to."

She swirled her hair with an arm movement, copying Dawn's orange to red colors. "Not being bound to the Liminal's color scheme is a small bonus. I remember that upholding Shamira and her green palette was a taxing affair, but now that should not be so difficult."

Adam offered her the bonfire-roasted confection. "You're still here. Focus on the time you have, not the time you don't. The next Tribulation may take longer than you think. Dale's mentor is not one to jump heedlessly into them when he does not have to. I wouldn't call the events pleasant, based on your retellings. Though I find it good that his advances have helped significantly when it comes to his mind coping with an all-affinity channel basis."

Scilla took the confection and munched it down, busy altering her clothing to be less robe-like and more of a short dress. What did Dani call it? Right, a romper. The design came with free protection from breezes causing an accidental skirt flip, due to the shorts built in underneath. "Of course they have. I wouldn't pick Tribulations that wouldn't help, even if Sunny doesn't properly understand what they're for all the time. I'm not steering him away from the regret-resolving perspective he has either. If that's the betterment he's aiming for while going through this, I will gladly take the two hares in one trap freebie."

Adam nodded, wondering what other treats he could make with a bonfire. "A convenience? Yes, very much. He does not ask, 'What purpose does the lesson serve?' Skipping straight to,

'What am I trying to learn here?' Two hares in one trap indeed."

They both glanced at the massive pillow, but Artorian saw only the stars while Ammy snoozed loudly. The celestial failed to repress his warm smile. "How pleasant to see that over-worked mind finally attain rest. Incarnates may not *need* sleep, but the act is certainly important."

Both nodded while Scilla fixed her hair manually, working the colored locks into braids since she had the wispy effects of her movement mostly under control. "What really saved my behind with the Tribulations was that he already had most of the channels open by the time he met Cal. With air, celestial, fire, and water all behaving, the only problems I've had to contend with are the earth and infernal effects."

Adam thought more snacks were not the way to go as both he and Scilla caught up with recent memory filtering, gaining full access to the Heavenly conversation.

Wanting to keep busy, he joined the appearance modifica-tion club. Spreading the owl-wing technique he'd found in Arto-rian's memories, he applied it and began tweaking. The extra light they caused was dimmed down to nothing so the bright-ness wouldn't disturb the other two. "You will handle it wonder-fully. Personally, I would have loved to hear the Essence-truth behind the four elements Shaka didn't have the opportunity to cover."

Scilla smirked, and kept working on her braid. "Shaka looked like he needed to vent, and it's a mystery to nobody that he was no longer used to speaking, or having a mouth."

She paused. "Or a body. Or the ability to emote. **Love** conversed with me via the sounds of a kalimba, so I think they're all just trying their best up there. Knowing the fire, earth, air, and water truths would have been great, but we've been getting by without. Plus, with the resurgence coming up, I think someone will figure it out. Probably by accident, but I have faith."

Adam shook his head. "To hear one of the Liminal say they have faith is an adventure all on its own. Has there been any significant difficulty getting Sunny to adapt to the earth and infernal channel effects?"

Scilla grunted, happy with the braid for now as she moved on to footwear. It was time for heels! She was a big girl now and wanted big girl shoes. Something that went *click* when she stepped on hardwood or stone. "Sort of. The hard part has been in making sure he doesn't notice the growth, or he might begin to work against the grain. I've been sneakily letting both flow more aggressively while he was working with the numbers in Eternium. Getting him to sit down and work on one thing he's normally not interested in for any length of time was a *task*."

She drew a breath to blow it out with dramatic effect. "Earth normally makes one more grounded, and infernal makes you pick one thing and go 'this, this is what I will be best at.' I did my abyssal best to fling that gate wide open anytime he had a bow in hand, since he said that was an interest to begin with. Tried it during the item-repairs, but that was a struggle."

Scilla glanced at the massive, occupied pillow to feel a pang of jealousy. The feeling faded, but she too wanted something fat and fluffy to lounge on! She touched her forehead, then squeezed her eyes shut. "I do what I can with earth and infernal, but they're... difficult for me. My replacement will have a much easier time."

A comforting pressure to her upper back made her look up at Adam, who had moved to be supportive. "The *now*, Scilla. Focus on the now. Not the later. I won't let you slip. No matter how much your mind keeps clawing at you with anxiety."

She focused herself with a deep breath, then nodded sternly. "I'll be alright, Adam. The feeling can be hard to put out of mind once it gets its claws in there. Ever since I remembered my full breadth of life in Chasuble, and how it ended, I still can't look at Zelia for longer than a few moments. Even if I know it wasn't truly her who made all of those invisible spiders."

Adam squeezed her gently. "Do you want to talk about it?"

Scilla shook her head. "No… Artorian being there for that one, single, dumb day was the best thing to happen in all of old Scilla's life. He fixed my eyes. That curse upon my perspective of the world. He let me live, properly live. Not in the shadow of others, but at the forefront. Part of society, rather than beneath it. That it ended was… well, it was horrible, but that too was part of life. Don't pry… The end was very swift, and I felt nothing. From my viewpoint, I closed my eyes in Chasuble, then immediately opened them again inside of Artorian's bonfire space."

She needed to take his hand and treat it as a squeeze toy. Adam did not complain, and let it occur. "I don't blame him… y'know? For leading the rains to Chasuble. He forgot all about little Scilla when he was on the move. I didn't even cross his mind. If Sunny can forgive Dawn for being a force of nature, then I can do the same. That his path crossing with mine wrapped me up in this whirlwind of a life of his… I can't say I dislike it. I don't dislike it at all."

Adam offered part of his robe, which she used to dry her wet cheeks. Adam chose not to mention her tears, merely choosing to help. He exhaled softly, speaking in an attempt to comfort. "It is rare for someone to live twice, and your second life has been very long. Have you found some light to hold against your heart on this journey?"

She scoffed, and motioned towards the pillow. "You mean getting a life with a mom who fawns over me and adores me to bits, and an old man who would throw himself at the world to save everyone in it, never once believing he was worth being in it in the first place? I am *surrounded* by light. Even you, with your soft helpfulness, as you fight against the push of your element, are bright. How am I to compete? The little Scilla who lives in the dark, and hides in the shadows until it is time to hurt the person I have grown to abyss-blasted care for? Because that accursed old man simply refuses to expel me from his heart."

Adam thought he might finally understand. "Are you…

unable to hold on past the seventh Tribulation, because you have grown to *care*?"

Scilla turned her head, her emotions difficult, yet betrayed by her expression. "The tasks I have to perform require the use of the colder parts of **Love**. The insipid. The cruel. The callous. I have long failed at the cruel… I can't do it. I just can't. I could in the beginning, when my mind was smaller, and my empathy was as rough and dense as a rock."

She bit her lip. "A cruel little girl who thought sympathy was something you could eat. Artorian grew, and I grew with him. I swiftly lost my ability to give him his Apex Tribulation. Nine and eight followed slowly after. Seven is going to be all I've got, and I can't say that no longer pushing him to complete the Tribulations wasn't affected by selfish desires."

Adam held her with gentleness and care. "Nobody wants to die. There is no fault in that. Can you not tell him?"

She shook her head to the negative. "If I tell him, he will refuse to ever go, and then I will suffer as my consciousness starts to slip away from the Liminal keeping it together. That is a fate worse than death. He *needs* to do number seven. Even Mom made sure Caliph's tasks were completed before drift could set in."

Adam cocked his head. "Just not immediately."

That thought gave Scilla pause, her shoulders finally relaxing some of the tension. "No… I mean yes… Not immediately. There is a lot of time. Things will be fine—if I can get his Essence channels to stay stable. Then I'll consider it a job well done, and I'll go hug **Love**. She said she wanted to play me a song, and show me something, before the end. I'm a little curious? Filled with dread, of course, but curious."

Adam rubbed her head, and mended some details of the braid that were out of place. "I still think you're doing very well, and it will all be alright."

Scilla softly nodded, then froze in place.

"Of course things will be alright, but it may have been more helpful to tell me all of that beforehand, you troublemaking youngsters." Adam and Scilla both shot their noses towards Artorian, who was looking right at them while grooming his own beard, now that he had one to groom again. "What? You're loud."

CHAPTER TWELVE

Scilla stammered. "How… How long? I didn't even notice."

Artorian observed her braid, then attempted to copy the pattern with his beard. "*Hmm?* Oh, around the time Adam mentioned that Incarnates may not need sleep, but it being important anyway. You got my attention since I was worried about Ammy when it came up. Both of you just kept on talking, and it didn't seem right to interrupt."

Scilla clearly started to panic, her breathing hastening as her arm movements became frantic. The mist control came undone as she stuttered through space as if whole animations were missing between her movements. "No! You… The Tribulation… I…"

"I'll still do them, dear. Why don't you have a seat and breathe? Remember what Sal'ha'din said. Breathing is prized." He winked, and without much deviation from before, kept working on his beard. "Adam said things would be fine, and they will be."

Scilla fell onto her butt rather than sit down, though with a motion that skipped all the middle parts of going from standing to sitting. Her form flickered, and she was on the ground.

"But... but then you heard everything... including my... my..."

Artorian raised a brow. "Scilla, dear. Dawn... I mean, Ammy, told me long ago that Liminal beings are temporary. That there were specific milestones relating to that event was news to me, but not out of place. I'll do the seventh Tribulation, but... I would so very much like it if you could also tell me when that 'drift' is coming. I can wait. I neither want to see you go, nor do I want to see you claw yourself with anxiety."

The old man smiled sweetly. "We can talk about this, as much as you'd like. We can even pull Alexandra from the Core wall and plan it all out. Everything ends, somehow. Even the Heavenlies, I'm sure. No reason we can't send you off with a big party, surrounded by a big family. You go ahead and stay with us as long as you're able, or feel like. You are welcomed, my dear. Stay. The Heavenlies were invited on your behalf. *I found out.* Did you really think I would rebuke you for something so small?"

Scilla spoke with her hands more than her mouth. "No, that's not... The rebuking is..."

Pausing, she hung her head and just took breaths before collapsing into Adam, weeping uncontrollably. His vision flicked from Artorian to Scilla and back, but the old man just shook his head. "She's holding onto you, my boy. Don't pretend not to know who is needed."

Adam dropped the facade and swallowed Scilla up in his arms and wings, rocking her gently as she coped with the acceptance. He didn't notice Ammy pushing herself up from the pillow, and patting Artorian's cheek. He did, however, hear the soft 'good job' she whispered.

Artorian helped her sit up, though his 'help' was really just 'making some room.' He couldn't move her an inch when she'd been a Mage, and that was no different of a story now. He'd only caught her earlier because she'd helped. "You were napping so well."

Amaterasu popped her neck, and surveyed the scene.

"**Acceptance** may have been replaced by my **Sun** law, but I think usurped or absorbed may be more accurate. I straight up felt you going through the process of accepting Scilla's situation. Honestly? Rather new. Not sure if it was because I was touching you, or because higher Tier nodes have something else in play. Secondary node concepts are a new feeling."

Artorian shrugged softly and placed a hand on her lower back for support before speaking. A motion she mirrored right away, since Artorian needed that support far more. "Sounds like another one of those Incarnate mysteries. We don't even have a grasp on how Spirit energy properly works yet. We will, though. Just have to get a lot of groundwork and foundations to build on this new world."

He released a deep breath. "I hope... I hope I can find a lot of help. Just the people on my Core wall aren't going to cut it. Abyss, I don't even know who to decant *first*. I'm sure that will turn into some kind of competition too."

Ammy chuckled, amused. "Well, you'll need to wait for Occy to feel a little better before decanting can begin. He's the only one that knows how to work Cal's system enough to get new bodies going without Cal present. Barry got him good. He's resting up in the sun still, doing all that reading. He's feeling a lot better than he was during the fight, but Incarnate-quality damage takes forever to heal. He keeps trying to do work, but you can't work and heal at the same time. So he will do what he can. He's on light duty until fully recovered, since he kept sneaking off to work and completely stalling out any healing. Dani and I refuse to let him hear the end of it, and have made him start calling on Wisps and Chosen for some of the work burden."

Ammy paused, then turned, shifting forwards on the pillow for some space to open her arms wide. Scilla had recovered and was trying to rub at her face while beelining for them. Ammy easily picked Scilla up and chest-cradled the Liminal girl, then loved on her while rocking and holding the grown up Chasuble native. "Look at you, all grown up! Is that my hair color you nicked? Scilla! You devious little thief. Now I'm going to have to change mine!"

Adam laughed loud, still standing on the ground as he strolled slowly towards the pillow. "As if you weren't already going to change your entire appearance! You've been planning the update... How long? I've seen those haircut pictures plastered all over that wall in the Elysian Fields. Still thinking of sharp yellow? What was it, with a bob side-cut? You couldn't stop fangirling all over Artorian's Ad Astra form."

Amaterasu grumbled that her surprise had just been opened like a present before the required date, but huffed and looked away. Though thinking of presents, she turned to face Artorian. "Didn't you mention a present?"

He perked up right away, arms shooting up as he clambered down from his own pillow with all the skill of a limbless goat. "I do! I need some space!"

Hustling from their location, he mentally accessed his spatial ring and found what he was looking for. Extending his hands towards the empty space, he hollered out for fanfare. "Behold!"

A tiny *fump* fell to the ground as a piece of folded paper appeared in the shape of a crane. The small item hit the grass like a heavy stone. He looked down in confusion, trying to be oblivious to the trio of voices breaking out in harsh laughter when what Artorian expected to happen clearly didn't come to pass.

He just blinked at the paper crane. Which didn't match the image in his head at all! Maybe there was... some kind of trigger? "Skidbladnir?"

After a tiny shake, a sizable *poof* blew Artorian from where he was standing all the way back into the pillow as the ship's hull expanded. The grand skyship filled the empty space, reaching its full size before hovering inches from the ground in all its ostentatious glory. This boat was truly something made by a master showoff.

From visuals alone, Skidbladnir looked able to sail on the water, in the air, and overland. Shape-wise, the boat was some kind of mixture between a longship and a galley, with most of the features leaning towards the latter. If you ignored the wing-fins.

Shaking his head to recover from the sudden displacement, Artorian extracted himself from his own soul item, then looked up towards the nearest source of sound to see Ammy bouncing on her toes and squealing at a pitch that was breaking glass somewhere. Scilla had recovered, using Adam's sleeve for stability as her mist control hadn't been recaptured yet. They shared a glance, and could just about feel the swirl of the infernal around Dawn.

Adam reached out a hand, his own Essence feeling some discomfort. "*Uhm*... Amaterasu? You're, uh, dangerously close to obsession there."

Squeezing her hands into fists, Ammy straightened her posture and exhaled a breath so hot that it moved the entire local atmosphere as the heat rose. "I know. I know. Can't risk another Essence channel opening at my sta—no. Hold on. Yes I can!"

She beamed with her teeth showing, those supernova eyes of her swirling. "**Sun** has allotments for all six! **Fire** was beginning to have trouble, but having more channels than the requirement isn't *bad*. Plus, since the body I'm in isn't my true form and has malleability, I ought to be a-okay. Mental outlooks aside, of course. Having *more* channels at this point would be good for my node."

She looked at Artorian, but he was patiently waiting for her to have her say. "Bad idea?"

He shrugged supportively. "Dear, do what makes you happy. If being better for your node is something you like and want, you know you'll have my full support. If having something to seek perfection on, and pushing towards a pinnacle, is not something you want after already having lived a life dedicated to being the point of a blade, I'll support you in that too."

Ammy just about purred, melting on the spot. "You're such a sweetheart."

Pressing her hands to her hips, she gazed up at the massive vessel. "I love it, Sunny. You have the best presents! Not quite the flying castle I want to put together, but I just haven't had time for fortress ships. This is great! I think I'll decide on the channel later, and have some fun first. I've missed having *fun*."

Artorian raised a brow at her, glancing at the pillow. Ammy huffed and crossed her arms. "Yes, you codger, I'll take a nap too. How about we figure out how to operate this big lug and head to Occy? I can shift the entire ship past the solar barrier and get the whole thing right into the Elysian Fields. Tatum is in for *such* a surprise!"

They all nodded and packed up. Artorian recalled his pillow, Adam stashed his supply of snacks, and Scilla fixed up her appearance and attire while Amaterasu vanished in a flash, speeding around the skyship at Incarnate-level swiftness to discover every nook and cranny.

Scilla traded whose sleeves she was holding when next to Artorian, and the old man turned to give her a big hug. Dawn was busy being gleeful, but Adam had noticed something that made him jog off in the direction of the ship. "A-Ammy! The obsession! Watch the obsession!"

Since they had a moment, Artorian had a chat with his Liminal one. "How are you feeling, dear warden? You laid much out in the open there. Did you really not know I was aware? You're normally so on the copper about the matter."

Scilla indulged in the affection and squeezed, not letting go just yet. "Hadn't a clue. As I grow, my awareness changes. I'm much less of your 'warden,' and much more of 'Chasuble Scilla.' As for my duration before drift… I know it's coming, but I cannot feel any yet. With how time is modified in Cal, I can't even get a bead on it."

Scilla finally felt good enough to let go. "Thank you for… being you."

Artorian felt like a proper grandfather again. "Anytime, and always, my dear. I didn't need to be the Ascended of **Love** to walk this path. I just happen to be doing that too while I'm at it. Though one thing about what you said hit me a little hard."

Scilla looked at him expectantly, so he quoted her. "You said: 'An old man who would throw himself at the world to save everyone in it, never once believing he was worth being in it in the first place.' Is that really how I look?"

She punched him in the shoulder to break some tension. "That's not how you look, old geezer. That's how you feel. Your biggest flaws in **Love** all stem from the fact that you don't love yourself. It's a stunt on your power for starters, but more important to you is that it's going to be a roadblock for your Incarnation. Originally, the last Tribulation was going to require that you let go of **Love** entirely, so you would know how to act without it."

Artorian raised his nose as the pieces fell in line. "But then Eternia needed attention, and Urcan happened."

He patted his hip, where ordinarily the Sorrow katana should have been. "I... Yes. Can't say you're wrong about any of it. Interesting how that was supposed to be my last one. I suppose that changed **Love's** plans?"

Scilla shook her head, watching Adam panic as he chased Ammy around on the deck. "**Love** doesn't administer these Tribulations directly. She just fuels some of the oomph needed to make them happen. I'm the one that filters through your memories for something that can lead to growth. Due to the nature of what has to happen... they need to be administered by someone who you cannot affect or influence. I failed to keep meeting that bar."

Artorian offered an arm, and Scilla took it. He spoke gently, wanting to be a support. "You have done wonderful this entire time. Look at how far you've made me go. A-rank six! Truly splendid. We can do seven, when it's a good time. I'm too frazzled from the Eternia task to jump into anything right now. If anything, I want to *finally* decant my people. Get society up and running. Some R&R."

He narrowed his eyes at a particular thought. "Give Odin the *smackening* he deserves."

Scilla snorted, controlled the outburst down to a giggle, then nodded and walked with him to the ship. Which now had a ramp leaning down to the ground while Ammy stood upon the prow with a gleaming smile. Her hands were back on her hips while her voice resounded. "All aboard! So says the captain! *Arrrrrr!*"

CHAPTER THIRTEEN

As he boarded, Artorian noticed something very strange about the walkway bridge. He raised an eyebrow at Ammy, but she just grinned at him with her arms crossed. Her eyes locked on him while she ignored Adam's fussing. Scilla let go of his arm when she noticed something was afoot, allowing Artorian to hop in place and then suspiciously squint at the floor. "The floor *looks* like wood, but the material is so spongy!"

Another glance up at Ammy let him see she was rolling her wrist. "*Mhm*! Made me think of 'baby's first boat.' The entire thing is childproofed."

There was more to this? He supposed having a proper look was in order. The item description had been more than a little lacking. Cycling Mana, he just about staggered when his eyebrows shot to the sky. "This ship is a *person!*"

He checked Ammy's expression, but she was giving him a full thumbs up. "Knew you'd notice! Looks like Odin took offense with some D-rank High Elf girl who had a very Persona outlook, and refused to listen to him in the slightest."

Kneeling, Artorian pressed his hand to the spongy deck, altering his weight so he wasn't causing such a large indent due to his general density. "Another reason to provide Odin the back of my hand."

Scilla cocked her head in question. "Why are you aiming your arrow for Odin first? Wouldn't the demons be more of a priority?"

Artorian grumbled, still working on the prior topic as he motioned to Scilla that he needed a second. "Ammy, can you find the mind of the ship? I'm having trouble."

Ammy looked over her shoulder, having moved to the helm, and wrapped her hand around the wheel while facing the wrong way. "I can give it a go after we get up into orbit. Or... never mind? This wheel is... cosmetic. Looks like I can't control the ship with it, and I'm not seeing any levers or topsails. Just those wing-fins coming out from the sides and back. I was expecting more sails in general? I'll try to talk to the ship properly."

Artorian nodded, then turned his attention towards Scilla. "Internal conflict and external conflict are very different animals to tackle. I was told Odin—or is he going by Zeus now? —already has a society up and running. I'm not expecting anything particularly stellar. In fact, rather the opposite. I expect him to use what he's made to bother everyone else, meaning that when it comes to hunting demons down, he is going to get in the way. *On purpose.*"

Adam joined the duo since he wasn't making any headway with a silent Amaterasu, adding his own two coppers. "I will still be hunting those abyssalites down in the meanwhile. I think the demons will attempt to slink their way into Odin's society. Hiding in plain daylight and all that. Currently it's just plain old hiding, cowering, and sniveling as they try to find some sort of edge to allow for a comeback. Once they settle, I can focus on playing Silverwood Tower Defense. Let's not be surprised when they infiltrate Olympus."

He shot Artorian a wink, then looked to the left, his gaze narrowing even if what he was looking at wasn't on the same continent. "Speaking of the little devils, I think I see a few imps."

Scilla understood, then decided it was time for a break. She walked right into Artorian's shadow, and looked at them all before giving a salute. "I'm out for a bit, the strain is getting to me."

Adam and Artorian both gave her a goodnight nod, and Scilla slid down into the shadow like an elevator, until her entire body was no longer visible. Artorian felt her presence return to his bonfire space, and was satisfied. Looking up, he watched Ammy concentrate for a moment before she opened her eyes. "Got it. Sunny, I'm creating a forum link."

Adam spread his wings, then put his hand up for a high five. "I'm going to check out the dark spots I saw, best not keep her waiting."

Abiding, he gave Adam his high five with a *clap* before the celestial turned into a mote of light and zipped off. Artorian closed his eyes and joined the mental conversation. <I'm here. Did you find...? Oh, hello there.>

The communal space was simple, one of light motes and a simple grassy knoll. Ammy's now considerably more sunny and yellow-colored mote stood out, since Artorian was used to a more red and ominous version. He was his usual celestine, and then there was... a triangle of neon pastels?

He tried not to stare, but the neon mote bobbed and spoke in the voice of a surprisingly calm female High Elf. One that gave zero celestial feces about the whole of the abyss. <It's fine. Happened all the time back when I had a body.>

The yellow mote eased up next to the neon one. <Sunny, this is Zephyr. She went from a single air-affinity, six-foot-two pretty High Elf D-ranker to an all-affinity boat, because...>

Zephyr filled in. <Because that brick slab can shove it and I told him so. I also technically tried to put an arrow into his eye, but I don't think it did anything. He stomped around and cursed for a bit while I laughed at him. It was my last laugh, but I don't regret it.>

The celestine mote turned to Ammy. <I like her.>

The yellow mote chuckled. <You like anyone who steps on Odin's toes.>

Bobbing to emote a shrug, Artorian couldn't disagree. <I admit, I was feeling apprehensive as soon as we got to 'High Elf,' but it appears they're not all cut from the same cloth. I didn't even know High Elves came in the non-Mage variety.>

Zephyr copied the bobbed shrug. <Non-Mage High Elves are social outcasts until we do. We don't get any of our family names, or privileges, or help. Power and status is everything to a High Elf, and if you can't hack it and reach the Mage ranks, then nobody in the family will blink an eye if you get hacked down and die. Made the Adventurer's Guild very popular.>

Artorian went still. <*Harsh.*>

Zephyr didn't mind. <That was just how life worked. I got lucky, ran into a person who helped me sort out my completely devoid social skill set. Turns out clothing is important and people like privacy. Not that adventurers complain when a no-nonsense Elf walks around in the equivalent of a swimsuit without a care in the world.>

Ammy turned to her in surprise. <I'm surprised you didn't run into trouble with the more... *base* personalities.>

Zephyr's mote glowed, indicating a smile. <You'd be amazed how effective and convincing a couple arrows in the right place can be. I only had to stand on another D-ranker once while unloading a point-blank quiver into him from above, after an uncouth attempt on my favorite scarf. I was never bothered again.>

A and A whistled, impressed. The yellow mote nodded. <Effective. Simple. Direct. I like it. Are you able to turn back into a person?>

Zephyr checked herself, but the answer came easy. <Not yet. Even if I could... I don't think I would. My mind is a mess. Life used to be straightforward and easy. I moved like the wind. I was the wind. I went where I pleased, did as I pleased, and the consequences were something to deal with when they managed

to catch up to me. I was dragged by another family member into some strange portal to another world? Then I have vague memories of being someone else, but those faded. When I became the boat again just a bit ago, I remembered myself? Strange to say. My main problem is that I am no longer the wind. Or no longer *just* the wind?>

The neon mote warbled awkwardly. <Reconciling the events is troubling. Too many thoughts flow in my head, and I can't keep them separate. Previously, some had more priority than others, and I dismissed those that didn't let me move. Now… now I'm not so sure.>

Artorian mulled the problem over. <We… What would you like to do now?>

Zephyr struggled with a response. <…be a boat? For a while, at the very least. I'm in need of guidance. I want to do too many things all at once. I want to fire the harpoons, ascend, land, unfurl the sails, and do nothing, all at the same time. All these thoughts keep yelling over one another. I don't… I don't know why this is happening…>

Artorian had a suspicion, but Ammy was already looking his way and a whole step ahead. <This is why I specifically mentioned the all-affinity change during her introduction. The way she describes her way of being is textbook for an air-affinity-exclusive cultivator. When Odin forcibly unlocked all the others so he could make one of his terrible attempts at a legendary item, the situation went awry.>

Zephyr didn't understand, but followed along and added a comment. <He also named me something incredibly dumb. Something about 'that which is not named by me does not matter' or some horsefly buzzing like that. If I can, I'm going to shoot his other eye.>

Artorian made a Nixie Tube pop above his head. <I may be able to do something about that last part. Zephyr, I might have a way to change your name from Skidbladnir to… well. Something else.>

Zephyr's mote brightened from its prior dour colorations.

<That would be a great start to get some ground under my feet. My normal name would be great.>

The celestine mote nodded. <I will go and see about that bit. Don't be surprised if you feel something? When I attempted artifacting on a person in Eternia, it was messy. I was expecting the ability not to work on Legendary items, but I still managed to change Laevatein's name. So given that whole trick is a technique in this world, and knowledge transfers, I ought to be able to get that done. I don't know how *quickly*, but I'll work on it.>

An exclamation mark appeared above the yellow mote. <Are you able to do anything about the spongy floor?>

Zephyr perked up, facing Ammy. <Wait, my floors are *spongy*? They should be wooden! Can I control that? Oh hey, I can control that!>

Ammy felt like she had a Nixie Tube moment of her own. <Are you able to move the ship? Up and down, forwards, back, skywards, and such? I moved the walkway bridge to connect the side of the galley groundside physically, but if you can do that instead, then that would be a great help.>

Zephyr had a try, and Ammy momentarily weakened in connection as she had a look. <You just moved the entire vessel's broadside to the left, the wide-side is facing the direction you're going.>

Zephyr stopped moving the way she was, and tried again. <Not what I wanted, I wanted to make the bow move forwards. Like breaking through waves.>

Ammy *hmm'd*. <Sunny, do you want to start on the technique to fix her name back out in Cal? I think we're going to troubleshoot for a while.>

Artorian's mote positively bobbed. <Can do. Have a pleasant chit-chat, ladies. Zephyr, most pleasant to meet you! I am Artorian, and tend to go by Sunny or some such name. Do feel free to call me what you'd like. Try not to worry too much? You're in the right place for some help; we are all, as they say, *in the same boat*.>

Amaterasu chucked an orb of solar light at him, which

missed as Artorian ran giggling from the forum. Popping out to wake up on the deck, he thought he was in the clear, only to still be subjected to a bout of weak snickering. "*Ahh…* Cal has rubbed off on me. The puns, they *flow*."

He stood, and discovered that the floor was no longer spongy, nor looked the same. In fact, the entire ship now both had the smell of linoleum and was swiftly… compressing? Becoming smaller in size? The galley's length had originally been… oh, about half his Long form? Give or take? Two hundred fifty feet in length at the minimum. Now the available space and design of the ship was more of a gulet yacht. A little luxury vessel.

Knowing better than to roam when one of Dev's projects was reconfiguring, he found a stable spot on the deck and settled in. Just like he didn't want to be near the bigger-on-the-inside ball when it spat out the Gnome's toys, he didn't want to risk becoming part of a hallway.

He really wanted to go inside and check if there were cabins, but there might not currently be any while Zephyr was figuring herself out as a boat. He had some clout from living life as a dragon, but life as an object? Pass. "I'm going to choose to skip that one. Not feeling like trying Dawn's 'candle for a hundred years' route."

Popping his wrists by lacing his fingers together and stretching them outwards, he slid into the lotus position and got to meditating. "Let's see here… the cultivation version of arti-facting."

Artorian's pink Mana poured from him in wild globs, reaching over the deck before sinking away with a wax-on wax-off swirl, returning to concentrate on his hands. He could visualize the patterns in his mind. Silent and with his eyes closed, he pressed down on the wood and exhaled. With some will, he pushed Mana into the technique. As flashes, he saw sets of runes connected to other runes, which represented the concepts inherent in this process, used as their most exemplified selves as patterns of the universe.

Artorian didn't fully understand what ideas he was looking at, but many felt... immalleable. Unchangeable. Many more felt like he shouldn't touch them, or he would change Zephyr, *the person*, irrevocably. Veering away from those options, he discovered incomplete runes. Whole swaths of them. "Inscriptions?"

As he processed their meanings, he came across a crass, crude rune, one slapped in without love or care. On second look, it wasn't worth being called a rune. "Wouldn't you know it? *Skidbladnir*. Spelled as an inscription formation."

Rubbing his physical hands together, he put his digits back in the pie and poured forth the Mana, invoking what he needed since he didn't have the full technical know-how to do it the other way around. A whole rank of his Mana poured into the inscription, reshaping it and providing a new definition as he upgraded the pattern to a proper rune.

Responding to Artorian's abundant energy, the rune became malleable, awaiting input. Feeling the 'give,' Artorian spoke under his breath. "Zephyr."

The rune saluted him like a well-paid lawyer, carting off metaphorical armfuls of his Mana to make the change. Invoking may be pricey as all abyss, but it sure got the job done! Within moments, the item description he could still connect to via his ring altered. The name had successfully been changed, and Artorian reeled back the excess Mana so the energy wouldn't spill over.

Zephyr might be a ship instead of a humanoid cultivator, but he was well aware that Mana and Essence bodies didn't match! Not that it likely mattered much, since this item was also a Spirit-body at its core, easy to manipulate without incurring true damage. Well... 'item.' Zephyr was a person, she deserved to be treated as such, even while stuck as a boat. "Best to keep the 'real' limitations in mind, for when we inevitably get back to them."

When he opened his eyes, Artorian was no longer where he'd closed them. Instead of hovering mere inches above the land, Zephyr had pierced the top of the cloud layers. Which were less clouds, and more masses of foggy wetness once up close. How was he supposed to run or bounce on these? Too much realism!

"Welcome back, sunshine." He looked up, and saw someone new was smiling down at him. Except that she looked familiar, and the voice was identical to Dawn's. The body was entirely different, but there was something about the striking yellow hair... "*Ammy?*"

CHAPTER FOURTEEN

Ammy grinned, extending a hand to help him up. "*Mhm*! You've been in meditation for a handful of days. Zephyr and I had plenty of time to chat. Since I can change my form freely, she was explaining what she looked like, and since I was wanting to try out a different shape, I thought it a nice opportunity to solve two problems in one go. Zephyr got some reminders on a humanoid form, and I got the feedback I wanted. If High Elves all know one thing well, it's how to look amazing."

Artorian stood, then needed a moment to inspect the change. "Well, you've certainly opted for a firmer frame with more assets to it."

Ammy winked and shot him with crossbow-fingers. "Distracts my enemies, *and* makes me feel like more of a mom. Plus I never disliked the ogre physique? Being all thin and graceful is something I can go back to anytime, but I wanted the sturdier approach. So; short wild hair, muscle that looks like it matters but doesn't detract from my smooth feminine preference, and a citrine, ruby, and obsidian color scheme. More **Solar** influences to go with my black hole theme. The **Sun Law** has so many toys!"

Artorian pointed at her stark yellow hair currently shaped as more of a side cut than something wild. He also noted she was going with matching eyeshadow color? The contrast looked fabulous on her darker skin.

That was actually pretty neat! No matter how much he kept thinking about a jacked wasp. "I'm… going to need a bit to ground myself in this intended change. Because I still think to say Dawn, and while you kept the dark tan to bronze skin color, I am very used to the orange to dark-red gradients you sported. Glad to see you kept the supernova eyes! Black sclera always make me think of villains, but they just look so celestially good on you."

Ammy scratched the back of her head and flushed, which was surprisingly easy to see. "Oh *hush*, you sweet-talker. Do you like my form? I'm still working on the details, and don't know what to do about clothing or associated designs yet. I was hoping to ask Zelia, but she and Yuki are in sleep mode after the iteration change. Our extended Wood Elven family is also currently still stuck in Eternium, so no Rosewood to consult either."

He beamed, all proud. "My dear, you look beautiful in my eyes regardless of age or form. I just want you to be happy. More muscle, or less muscle. Graceful shape, or sturdy shape. Long hair, or short. Queenly garb, or a warrior's armor. I want you to do and be what makes *you* comfortable, and to make yourself as happy as you can be. Of course I like it!"

Artorian winked and touched her arm. "You look wonder-ful, and there's nothing wrong with going after the appearance you want. If anyone tries to say otherwise, or slide in a comment where it is unwelcome… well. *Try* to break them gently?"

She raised a brow, half amused and half serious. "You think anyone would have their head stuck that deep in the abyss?"

Without missing a beat, Artorian sagely nodded with great

exaggeration. "There will always be people who do not like something because they don't do the same, or because what they see is so dissimilar to themselves. It is not your task to drop to their level. It is their task to rise up to yours. Even if that only comes after painful lessons."

He scoffed. "We have seen animals gain a human form only to be more humane than the species that word is coined for. Our Wood Elves may have the stars in their eyes when it comes to that particular form, but their view is not half so bright that it could pull the wool over my eyes and blind me from the truth."

Artorian walked a few steps to the edge of the now considerably smaller yacht, looking down over the edge at the scintillating ocean waves far below. "There will always be people who are foul, for any myriad of reasons. There are people who are small, petty, and miserable. Those who stand still and refuse to walk so they could know the world. There will always be commentary. There will always be daggers in the back. Pay them no heed, for they are not worth your time."

Ammy curled her arms around her sweetheart from behind, having let him ramble and gush. It looked like he had more to say, but not the energy to say it, so she leaned her chin on his shoulder. "And when they do stab me in the back?"

Artorian sighed, closing his eyes for a deep breath of updrafted ocean air, relishing the salty, fresh sea breeze. "We break them gently, though we break them all the same. I'm sorry, Ammy. I don't particularly like this topic. I have always been suited to those whose eyes were full of spark. Perhaps not the gifted, for they surpass me like the named ones. *In no time at all.* But definitely those who held on to something greater than themselves, and were willing to keep putting one foot in front of the other. No matter how hard it was. Or how tired they were. They kept trying. With that fire in their hearts, and determination in their souls."

Silence fell for a moment. Artorian looked around, but that the scene was available only to them calmed him. A private moment. His hand squeezed hers. "I... I have a regret, dear. One that I don't think is going to be in a Tribulation, yet I have it regardless."

Without a word, Ammy leaned her head sideways, brushing their temples together like a C'towl so he'd feel comforted. Sunny copied the motion, then felt like he had the strength to drop the weight on his shoulders. "You're a delight, dear. For letting an old shell like me ramble."

Ammy opened an eye, lightly curled the edge of her lip upwards, then eased away and softly pressed her knuckles to his shoulder. No actual thump. "I said I would be here. I am here. Even the great deities of Eternia need their rest, and no mind is exempt from needing the presence of another."

Her hands eased onto his back, beginning to knead gently. "Speak your mind."

Taking a breath before nodding, he pressed his arms and elbows down on the wooden edge, and let the thoughts roam behind his eyes. "I have moved people as if they were nothing more than pieces of kings and castles. I have done so much harm without meaning to. I have upended lives, and changed whole rivers of fate just because I was there. People have suffered needlessly from my actions, and while that little thought usually does not have room to breathe, now it nags the back of my mind. Did I interfere too much? Or not enough? Should I keep to the sidelines, knowing I can be too much? Or do I jump in knowing that I, by my lonesome, can turn the tide of history by doing so?"

Ammy paused her kneading, squeezing herself next to him so she could wrap an arm around his shoulders and pull his face into the crook of her neck. Ember had been through that dilemma many times, but for her, the answer was always simple. "When something like that happens, it's not about the acci-dental impact. It's about what you do when you find out. Nobody can control the first one. Everyone has a choice on the second. The latter is what's important. When you found out you did harm, you turned to help."

Making a ball of fire in her free hand, she made it dance around them to keep the vicinity warm. "You have moved people, and found discomfort. So you chose a different path when that choice came up again. Isn't this how growth works? That's how it worked for me. Invictus became a great lesson, even if at the time I saw nothing wrong. When the event occurs, watch. Your heart will pull you to the actions your hands must take."

Artorian wrung his old hands, then observed them. "Yes. That is… Yes. Profound wisdom."

She nudged him. "What else is on your mind?"

He observed his hands once more, turning them over before shaking his head. "Currently I'm distracted by Brianna's words. I think I look recognizable enough now?"

A thought of Big Mo, the Dwarf, followed. "*Hmmm…* I wonder if the Modsognir Patriarch would consider this world 'the best it could be.' I'm not sure there's going to be a better world, demons and Odin not counted, until we exit Cal. I should… I should ask him."

Ammy let go, and rubbed his head. "Sounds like you've discovered who you need to decant first! Doesn't sound like you want to do more gushing right now. So, want to head up? I had Zephyr wait until you were out of meditation; she is quite pleased with the culmination of your task. She haaated being called Skidbladnir."

A soft guffaw followed before Artorian pushed himself away from the edge of the boat. "Glad to have put a smile on someone's face. I feel somewhat better, even if thoughts still swirl. Out of curiosity, do you have any idea why her mote was colored in neon pastels?"

Ammy snapped her fingers, a smirk plastered on her face. "Oh, it's so much fun. I learned more about High Elven society, and that odd detail is part of it. Her cultivation technique is all triangles, and the purpose isn't so much to refine Essence as it is to turn Essence via the cultivation pattern *into* neon. The *gas*, neon, as an *Essence*."

Artorian forgot everything else he was thinking about. This needed his full attention as his face became one big squint. "The gas? Her cultivation technique makes *gas? Huh?*"

The Incarnate scratched her head, thinking of how to explain that nugget. "So her triangles are tubes. Those make the spin-factor in her center. Originally, she was an air-only cultivator. So, when she gathered air Essence, instead of purifying and then using that Essence for personal growth, she stockpiled it in her center. Zephyr's trick is to aggregate this purified Essence with some that still needed refining, specifically to make neon gas. This gas, once formed, made *a different* Essence from the Essence she already had. 'Neon' is amazing for techniques, but completely unusable for personal growth."

Artorian needed a moment. "Zephyr... *made* Essence, by combining... I need some help here."

Amaterasu took a step back for some space, and made a few flaming orbs in a variety of sizes. She pointed at the first. "Let's say this is ten units of air Essence. Freshly gathered. Because it's very raw, cultivators refine this Essence for purified Essence. As the type without mental pushes or physical side-effects, it is the best for your body infusion stage. Out of that ten units of raw Essence, how good your refinement technique is determines if you get four good units out of it, or six, or eight. As an example."

She pointed down to the deck of the ship. "Zephyr has a cultivation technique from her lineage that, while it can refine Essence, does not have that function as its most core 'thing that it does.' Instead, when she has ten units of purified Essence, and ten units of raw air-aligned Essence, her refinement technique can combine them, and turn that into ten units of neon."

Artorian smoothly brushed over his long beard, his eyes full of scrutiny. "You've lost me on how this is supposed to be good or helpful. We're losing units here. We went from twenty to ten."

Ammy pointed at the largest ball of fire. "One unit of neon, when used for *techniques*—offensive, defensive, and the like—

counts as *ten units* of purified Essence, without the side effect. Bonus gain of those glowing pastel colors."

The old man closed his eyes to try and do those numbers, but he was no Deverash. "So, exact specifics aside. While neon doesn't help any for building oneself up, the—what do I call it? Neon Essence?—counts for a lot more in the 'doing things' department. She'd have a hundred units worth of technique investment, rather than ten raw and ten purified. Even being generous and saying it took twenty units of raw air Essence to make those ten purified units... that's still a good conversion rate for technique output. Now the math looks favorable."

Since Ammy shot finger crossbows his way, he assumed that it was on the copper. Artorian corrected his earlier misunderstanding. "Alright, so *make* is a bad keyword here. Her family figured out the Essence combination for neon, and her technique can make it. This neon happens to specialize, and is better at one thing at the complete detriment of the other. All output. No growth. That... sounds surprisingly balanced?"

Ammy didn't disagree, but her face didn't look pleased. "Turned out that's also why Zephyr was kicked out and made to fend for herself, but I suppose that's one perspective."

Closing one eye, Artorian leaned onto the side of the boat with his left arm. "Elaborate?"

Ammy checked to see if Zephyr's mind was active to jump in, but that didn't seem to be the case, so she continued. "Zeph told us that High Elven children are made to fend for themselves. Turns out that's true *after* spending two decades essentially locked up in the family estate. Focusing and learning about cultivation, at the cost of learning only the smallest amount of life's basics. This 'one over the other' topic is a running theme."

Artorian straightened. "Didn't she mention something about social skills?"

Ammy grumbled. "Because they aren't taught anything socially useful, when they go out into society, they end up being mocked, chastised, and insulted for not knowing or understanding the local ways. Turns out? This is what gives High Elves their outlook of spite, bitterness, and antagonism. Zephyr was specifically only taught how to get stronger, and when she couldn't meet the frankly ridiculous bar of becoming a Mage at the age of *twenty,* out she went!"

Sunny kneaded the bridge of his nose. "A lot of puzzle pieces are falling into place regarding why High Elves are the way they are. I bet she entered society and… it all went downhill from there."

Ammy dismissed her orbs, leaning her back against the ship's edge. "She got lucky and ran into someone with a good heart, who took her in and welcomed her as part of the family. The High Elven demeanor is still in there, but she doesn't share the venom most of the others do."

Exhaling pure heat, Ammy stretched her arms above her head. "When new societies get up and running, stuff like that… I don't want to see."

Nodding in complete agreement, Artorian was right there with her. "Indeed! Now, if we are going to be tackling curiosities, what are these 'Elysian Fields' I keep hearing about? Also, does this ship have cabins? I recall a mention of a nap!"

CHAPTER FIFTEEN

Ammy narrowed her gaze at Sunny like a teenager who was about to rebel. "What if I don't wanna?"

Artorian hung his head, knowing defeat when he saw it. He also sneakily deployed his sleeping Aura, but the Incarnate gripped that effect like the end of a towel and twisted, making him recall the effort entirely. "Bargaining, then? Very well. What do you want?"

Smirking, she shot her arm around his shoulders like all was already forgotten, and Sunny was dragged across the deck. "I want to gush about ships, and make it to Occy before I curl in. I'm not going to accept you running off without a proper handover. Also, I'm sleeping in the berth, or bust!"

Artorian said nothing to the door swinging open all by itself as Ammy steered him inside like she'd walked these corridors for years already. "The… bust? Is that like a cabin?"

Huffing as another door opened, she needed to pause, then pointed at a room. "No… that part was a joke. Bust, like when you fail in cards? That. The main sleeping area of a yacht is the berth, usually located under the bow, which is the front of the yacht's hull. Private rooms and living compartments are called cabins, but this main room is the largest and specifically gets named a berth. So if you're wondering where I am during my nap, it's going to be here."

Artorian understood now, having been dragged along under the assumption he'd agreed to her terms already. "Well... alright. Could you sprinkle in some Elysian Fields explanations while dragging me around? Also, you really don't need to drag me."

Ammy took a moment, then released his shoulders to take a hand instead. "Better?"

He was in a mighty fine mood right away. "Much!"

Resuming her stride, Ammy opened all the doors on the boat with a flick of her wrist. "Great! So the Elysian Fields were something named by... err... Don't get mad? Odin, or Zeus now? Oh celestials above, *I'm doing it too*. Why is remembering a changed name so difficult?"

Slapping her forehead in momentary irritation, she waved it away when seeing Artorian look up at her expectantly for more information. He wasn't mad? Good! Wait, why wasn't he mad? "No... grumble, or outcry, or general mumbling in Thundy's vicinity?"

That got Artorian to quirk a brow. "*Thundy?*"

Amaterasu smirked. "You know how there's a big clap of thunder when he does just about anything? That. He does them on purpose. It's *very annoying* when trying to get work done, so we talked to Yuki before she turned in for her sleep and came up with the nickname together. Embarrassing tales to follow!"

Artorian nodded while he walked with her around the ship. She pointed at a part. "I'm guessing you know what a hatch, anchor, hull, and beam are? Since you were on the deck earlier, I figure you know that one as well."

He stuck his finger in the air. "Don't know what a beam is. Is that part of the keel?"

She waved that off. "The keel is the part of the hull that runs down the middle from the bow to the stern. The keel is considered the foundation or backbone of a boat. The beam is the widest point of a boat or yacht. Now you also have me curious: why no reaction to Odin's naming?"

Artorian walked with her around a corner, and pointed at an area that looked like it was meant for food preparation. "While I don't personally like Odin, and find most, if not all, of his choices questionable, he *is* good at naming things, and I can't say it's much of a surprise that he wasn't satisfied with making just one pantheon. Therefore he made another, and I bet just like Odin was at the head of his first attempt, Zeus will miraculously be at the head of this second one. Just wait, I bet he'll do it again and completely plagiarize the first two. Jasper will insist on being called Jupiter or something. He goes through names like I go through cookies."

Sunny softly shrugged. "Freely available names for things when you're not sure what to call something is also rather convenient, and to get on the supervisor ring, he had to be good for *something*."

Ammy nodded, then filled in his silent question. "Sailors call the kitchen of a boat the galley—that's where cooking happens."

Satisfied with the answer, the old man shambled along, then lost his bearings for a moment. "How do I know if I'm on the left or right side, again?"

Pointing at the wall, she made a portion see-through, which prompted Zephyr to wake up and add in a porthole. Ammy blinked at the addition, then smiled wide. "We can just add those? I like it! So! Portholes are the ship variant of glass windows. Which should not be confused with the side of the ship they're on. If you are aimed toward the front of the vessel, the port side is the left side, and the right side is the starboard side."

She cracked a grin. "Amusingly enough, when we pull into a port, the majority of this ship's mooring connections are also on the left. The mooring is the place on land where you secure a boat. Moorings may be piers or wharfs."

He smiled at her, but nudged her in the side as well, as she kept happily sneaking in boat-facts like a giddy child. "*Elysium*, and we should be going."

Rolling her eyes with a tiny grumble, she mentally reached out to Zephyr now that the ship was responsive again. Since she was opening a personal forum, she also included Artorian. <Zeph, can you take us to the sun? Not into the actual thing.>

Zephyr did not have good news for her, her voice becoming stocky and abstract during the response. <I'm sorry, Dave. I'm afraid I can't do that.>

The celestine and solar motes shared a look, guessed Dave must have been one of her old friends, and that Zephyr was just a bit confused. Ammy's mote took the reply. <Why not?>

Returning to her senses, Zephyr resumed her normal voice tone. <I can go in the air, but as soon as we lose the atmosphere, I lose buoyancy. Can't do vacuum, can't do space. You're asking me to go to space.>

Artorian thought something was odd. <One moment. Dawny, didn't you say you were teleporting us into that area to begin with? What's the issue with a little extra distance?>

Ammy's orb made a fake arm as a lightform only to hold the equivalent of her forehead. <None. So much for my attempt to *stall*. Alright, fine, there goes my scheme. Right out of the porthole!>

They all dropped out of the forum, and Zephyr physically created a new porthole next to them to be sassy, which Artorian found hilarious. Ammy just grumbled, then rubbed her head. "At least I can feel better about the name thing not being easy. Occy does it too, except he's been calling me Erebus ever since he heard Odin say it. For giggles."

Nodding, Artorian held his hands behind his back, then once again looked up expectantly. "If you're not going to explain Elysium, then show me."

Amaterasu huffed, and crossed her arms with a big pout. "A couple more boat terms…"

Artorian tapped his chin, and found that reasonable. "Deal."

Her demeanor flipped on a copper, voice all chipper. "The 'aft' means being more towards the back of the boat. Not to be confused with the stern, which is the back of the hull. The helm and bridge…"

Ammy paused, her vision darting around as her eyes looked through the physical matter of the boat. "Is… gone? Zephyr, where's the steering mechanism and boat controls?"

Zephyr replied mentally. <Got rid of them, along with that whole room. I'm the only one with movement power, so they were a waste of space. I replaced it with an extra nice head instead.>

Artorian squeezed his eyes shut, then squinted at Dawn. "A what?"

Ammy perked up considerably. *"Ooooooh,* I rather like that. A 'head' is the name for a bathroom on a ship. Also Zeph, go you! Getting a handle on mental conversation! Can you hear us fine when we speak normally?"

Zephyr took a beat before responding, but seemed to have the hang of it. <When a way of conversing becomes the only way you can, I think anyone would figure out how very quickly. I'd also like to get going, since movement is kind of what I do now. So have four last boat terms? These clouds are itchy.>

Ammy conceded. She couldn't keep stalling. *"Fine.* The rig includes the sails and any devices needed to control the sails. Rigging includes equipment such as the mast, boom, yards, and spreaders. Rope used on a boat or yacht is called line. The gunwale is the upper edge of the side of a boat or yacht, and the draft is the minimum depth of water needed for a boat to float."

Holding up her hand when through the laundry list, she snapped her fingers. To Artorian and Zephyr, the experience was akin to a moment of falling as their entire world moved. On the teleportation's soundless exit, a tranquil feeling of peace rolled over everyone's senses. The feeling also visibly made Dawn look incredibly drowsy as she rubbed at her eyes. "Knew that would happen. Alright, I ported us right next to Occy's little spot. Sunny, give me a hug before I curl in. This place bites at me."

Not one to shy away from hugs, Artorian provided a big one and helped walk her to the berth as Ammy started to stumble. Her words slowly bled away to more grumbling sounds, and when he tucked her into the king-sized bed, she stole all the blankets in one fell swoop before conking off to sleep land.

He took a moment to rub her head a few times, fixing details of the snuggled bundle to make sure she was properly covered. Satisfied, he hummed with his hands behind his back, and made it to the top of the deck to find the walkway already extended. <Thank you, Zephyr. Are you going to fly around?>

Zephyr replied with a sleepy *hmmm*? <No... I'm... just gonna hover here for five minutes. Just five more...>

The connection cut out as the ship-shaped Elf joined the nap pile, causing Artorian to chuckle out a slightly proud 'he-he-he' as he reeled his sneakier sleeping Aura back in as he made his way up to the deck. "Knew I still had it! Alright, so, what have we got?"

Copying Ammy's fists to hip pose, he drew a deep breath of the best air he'd ever smelled, and exhaled with a feeling of delight. "Oh, that's *nice*. That's some Essence-dense Elysium air right there. Puts all that Wood Elven toking to shame. Sorry, Oak, you're out of business with whoever gets to live here."

He needed time to take in the scene. Archipelago islands spread as far as the eye could see, each dotted with a slightly different theme. Whole fields of golden wheat, rolling hills of flower-dotted green, large rocks that looked designed for lounging and sunbathing, absurd architecture straight out of a designer's fantasies, and he was certain that one island in the distance was a small mountain purely to show off a gravity-insulting waterfall feature. "How is there a waterfall when there's no water above...? Never mind. There's a 'do not enter' sign with the label 'Gravity Falls' next to it. Watch out for cyphers? What does 'do not trust the one-eyed triangle' mean?"

Artorian shook his head and moved his attention. "Looks

like all the water here is shallow enough to traverse by foot. Crystal clear and shimmery blue as well. Rather nice."

Artorian tried to find a sun, but found no stars of any kind, nor light source that didn't feel omnipresent. "Well, I am *inside* the sun. They likely did something with that. Nice that my eyes aren't being stabbed as well, shiny-sky-orb would have had a field day."

Looking down, he finally realized that the ship had been docked at a carved stone mooring. Someone had prepared this! "Tatum can't be too far from this point, then."

Raising his gaze, Artorian spent maybe ten seconds looking for signs of life before locating something most interesting. A giant sign next to a structure that blended in with the local rock formations. "Alright, 'structure' is generous terminology here. That's a cloth awning large enough to cover Blanket, even if that sugar glider gets *any* bigger."

Starting his walk over, he took a second look at the sign to read what was on it. Though he couldn't say he understood. "Soup for the soup god?"

CHAPTER SIXTEEN

"Soup for the soup god!" rang out as a chorus from two voices Artorian hadn't heard before. Launching itself from a spot between the rocks, a small blue echo slime wearing a chef's hat and holding a ladle *boinged* from the bouncy awning and landed right on the head of a girl with several fox tails, as they both posed to praise the sun. They repeated their joint outcry, ignored that there was no sun, then zipped back inside while arguing on how to improve their bouillabaisse.

Artorian blinked, then broke out in weak laughter as the voice of Occultatum—which was coming from under the awning—did the same. While Artorian strolled closer, he could hear Tatum talk to what must have been his local helpers. What a stark difference in leadership style from the days of Mountaindale! Artorian couldn't help but feel some pride. "*Ha*! That still hasn't gotten old!"

On approach, Artorian overheard the helpers quibble. The medium pitch, assertive, and higher energy voice of the nine-tailed fox girl was adding her two coppers. "Munch, definitely more shrimp. *Always* more shrimp."

The **thunk** of a ladle on her head counted as a sign of

disagreement, which made her hiss, spit metaphorical fire, and harrumph when it was clear the chef disagreed and wasn't going to let her kick another soup out of balance. With a sparkly *fop* sound, Artorian could see the outline of the fox girl morph on the other side of the cloth wall. The figure turned into a large Lakelight Moth before she fluttered off to go sit on a rock and complain from there. "Fine, but I am making sure he eats it!"

Tatum whined, his hand rubbing over a bulbous stomach, which he retained for comedic effect. "More food? I have reading to do!"

"Poor baby." The moth wasn't having it. "You have more recovering to do, mister! High-Essence sustenance makes that go faster. I, the great Vanilla, will not let you wiggle out from the *one thing* that's important you actually do. So lie there, adjust your pillows, and prepare to get *fattened up* some more."

Munch, the slime, saluted with his ladle in agreement, which forced Artorian to bend over and break out with laughter, as his hands pressed to his knees for support. "I can't. *I can't.* This is too good. *Hahaa!*"

Tatum smirked, welcoming his old friend under the awning. "Artorian! This scene must remind you of the majority of your daily life! Come, stay awhile and listen, have soup. *Save me from having to drink the whole kettle.*"

Laughing again, Artorian saddled up next to his friend in a matching chair. One laden with pillows! The chair was even bouncy when he eased in, which may have had something to do with his enthusiasm to comply. He melted into the seat, relaxing all over. "*Ooooh*, that's *niiiice*. I want twelve."

Tatum *mhm'd* in agreement. "Need to be careful, though, they're specifically designed for long term use. With Vanilla and Munch over here in a cooking competition, it might get so cozy that you don't want to leave. I can't *wait* to show Chandra when we can get her out of Eternium."

Artorian looked to the sound when he heard several bouncing impacts hit the ground, then saw the echo slime had duplicated itself to bring over a bowl of soup the size of Artorian's head. Eagerly accepting both the bowl—which may have been a small kettle—along with the spoon, he tried it only to immediately be unable to stop slurping the bouillabaisse down. "Mmm. *Oh.* I just... *Excuse me.*"

Tatum giggled, glad to see another victim had fallen to the superiority of the Elysium soup kitchen. "No, no, the delight is all mine. Eat! I'm sure these two thrive in having a new opinion on their crafts. Poseidon couldn't stop scarfing the goods down either, and just about chewed on Munch, literally, to make him cook faster."

Artorian swallowed his mouthful and cleaned his messy face off with some aura. "Who? Is everyone going by a different name these days? Dawny mentioned something about you calling her Erebus. She's napping on the boat, by the way."

Tatum's eyebrows rose, his teeth showing in his smile. "Oh, finally? She actually curled in? About time! That girl does *not* quit."

Accepting his own kettle, Tatum waved his spoon while speaking before having a bite. "Poseidon is Aiden. He got out early, which turned out to be a real blessing. Odin now goes by Zeus, and I have affectionately been slapped with the name Hades."

Artorian frowned a tiny bit, cheering up with a new mouthful of soup. "Do these have meanings? What's with Erebus?"

Stirring his kettle, Tatum spilled some tea, putting on an accent just for the joke while his hair formed into locks of fabulous blue flame. "Oh honey, you have *missed. Out.*"

Making a face that told everyone in the vicinity Artorian loved some quality gossip, by pruning his face and stirring his own soup, he settled back in the lounger so they could gab like a pair of old seamstresses. Artorian matched the accent with enthusiasm. "*Do tell.*"

Dropping his hands forwards, Tatum popped his tongue to continue being entertainment. "*So.* I'm not sure how much you've been informed since waking up—welcome back, by the way, we missed you. The events go somewhat like this: Dawn and I remained in Cal with a part of the developer host from both the Gnome and Wisp factions. We got the floating continents put together as a planet, and got enough information back from Eternium to get oceans going. Thanks for being the buoy, by the way. Heard that was kind of a drag, but it really helped us with current events."

Artorian waved his soup spoon at Tatum to *thump* him for the pun, but couldn't reach and resumed snacking. Tatum winked and continued. "Cal is still out cold, while Dani and her entourage are currently in Eternium and very unhappy, as she's stuck too. Grace *is* here, but is currently on the moon because she's going through that teenager phase where she wants to be left alone and rebel while listening to loud music. Soni is with her, to provide said music, and musicians. It's a popular profession this iteration; they're everywhere."

"He's behaving?" Artorian cut in momentarily. "I didn't laser as many demons as I wanted, but… well… Ah, abyss. I'm going to have to examine my preconceptions. Even Adam thought he was a good lad. I'm just being… Never mind. More?"

Tatum motioned for him to have some soup, and continued. "Of the inner circle—people who can actually do things here without some horrible limitations, such as *cultivating*—you've got Ammy, me, you, Aiden, and Odin. Bob has a commemorative statue here in Elysium, Minya is in Eternium keeping the boys in line with Rose. Chandra, Dev, Henry, and Marie are also trapped. I'm very lemon sour about not getting to see Chandra, but we've helped all we can from this end."

Artorian tapped the end of the spoon to his nose. "Pylon problem? I remember Tim had no issues throwing me out of his Core once before, and he wasn't gentle about it."

Occultatum shook his head. "No, I wish it were so simple. Our side of the help was turning almost all the Pylons we had *off*. Catastrophic cascade events notwithstanding. In simple terms so that we don't dig into the 'why and how' very much, is that Eternium's Core and soul are ever so slightly *out of sync* with Cal's."

He twirled his spoon. "This gets fixed by Eternium growing enough new Pylons to balance that back out, so he can hit the same wavelength and spill everyone into Cal. Or Cal waking up. Currently, the attempt to connect both spaces is like running into a soul-tear, if you remember those wire-tears when Cal's real body got hit with a meteor and your face made an indent in the bath's ceiling? Or that's what we *think* happened. What we know for sure is that no more dinosaur patterns showed up afterwards. So our copper was on another moonfall, or a chunky boy from orbit failing to miss."

Artorian followed, enjoying his soup. "Then the guess is 'chunky boy' until we can go out and check. What's with the names?"

Tatum received a refill from the echo slime chef, who saluted with a ladle. Rather than begin on the next round, he tried to put the kettle away. Instead, the stern-faced fox girl appeared at his side in a sparkling cloud of twinkles, holding her hand out to demand the spoon. Tatum surrendered and gave it to her as Vanilla pulled up a chair, sat, and made him eat whole spoonfuls between talking. She also reached over and tapped his tummy. "Good."

Artorian tried not to snort, looking away to stifle the sound. Tatum faithfully ate the offered spoonfuls and then wiped his mouth clean. "You laugh now, but Vanilla got this idea because Yvessa told stories about those three years with you in the Fringe. Speaking of… Vanilla, Munch? This is Artorian, who also goes by Sunny. Or whatever new name from the registry is applicable. Artorian, meet two of my Named Ones. Currently a massive help in the 'testing new bodies' department."

The Named Ones paid attention, then properly came to shake his hand. Even if Munch did so with a pseudopod, or mini-tentacle? Whatever the arm of a slime was called. Artorian shook both and shared the normal small greetings, then received a fresh kettle of *even more soup,* along with a blooming onion. Which, based on the intensity of Munch's stare, he was expected to eat in its entirety.

A scant few words from the echo slime confirmed his view, who sounded both energetic, young, and whimsical. "Finish. I need reviews!"

Artorian saluted, since that seemed to be the theme here. "Charmed! Tatum, you gave them very interesting names."

Before Occultatum could rebuke that mention, both the Named Ones snapped their eyes to the old man. Vanilla, in a motion almost identical to Yvessa, turned to threaten him with a spoon. Why *always* the spoon? "We chose those *ourselves.*"

Munch vehemently agreed, brandishing his tool. "The soup and ladle!"

Vanilla followed up by morphing into a girl with bunny ears, the spoon in her hand temporarily a vegetable. "The carrot and stick!"

Artorian put his hands up. "Well, they're very nice."

"*Mhm.*" Vanilla dropped the guise from herself and the spoon, resuming soup time and the fox form. "Course they are."

Artorian quickly sought to change the topic. "Erebus?"

Tatum raised his glass of water before swallowing. "*Mm!* Right. So, Odin went with a different theme, and came up with this whole new pantheon idea, names and all. We didn't have words for a lot of things, so just went with the flow as he conjured them. He's got *several* interesting expletives for you, and can't seem to settle on which one is the most offensive to stick with. He's very salty about Eternia's events."

He put his glass down, and made an image of the round table appear between his hands. "Dawn's outlook is focused on the end of a cycle, rather than the start or middle. So when she became Ammy of the **Sun** law, that carried over. She said the end of a sun's life cycle is to become a black hole, which resonates well with her. Her eyes are the best examples of what one looks like, as you can only really see the coronas, or so she says. I did notice she's been changing her eye color to oranges and yellows instead of the normal reds."

Accepting a bite of soup, he explained the new name. "Erebus, in Odin's new lore, refers to shadow, deep darkness, or deepest darkness. He once saw Ammy use her shadow as a storage compartment, which is why he added in shadow as a descriptor to begin with. Though, I really want to *nick* those aspects when it's Eternium time for me again."

"Nick," Artorian repeated. "That one guy from the 'collective' I brought back to Dani?"

"That word means 'steal' now, and yes, that's the origin." Tatum sat up to fix a pillow while Vanilla returned to the back with Munch. "There was also something about Dawny being one of the first creators. Primordial something? Though that's more because he's trying to schmooze her, but you can guess how well that's working."

Artorian made a face mixed with amusement and sly charm. "Poorly?"

Tatum chuckled. "*So* poorly. On the upside, I'm decently pleased with Hades, and Aiden likes Poseidon. Something happened in the Eternia Oceans while Brianna was active that he really approved of. Oh right! Brianna! She's also stuck in Eternium."

Artorian accepted a fresh mug of tea from Munch, then sipped the flavored water to mull over the unexpected flavor of licorice. "Not bad? Could use some honey."

Munch took the mug to improve the brew as Artorian turned back to Tatum. "Is Hades anything fun?"

Tatum considered the name. "He depicted me as stern and dignified; someone who prefers the 'underworld.' Not sure how much I liked being in the Pylon holds all the time, but I can see where he got it from. Because of my moon-skeletons, he was saying something about me keeping the dead that refused to die, and that I was hospitable."

A sudden thought struck him. "I will likely be taking the

darkness descriptor bits from Dawn, as well. She's not on board with Odin's latest ideas."

A loud and distracting metal *hoooonk* ended the conversation. Artorian and Occultatum looked to the sky, while Vanilla and Munch shot out from the kitchen section under the awning, both looking furious and raising war-ladles to the sky to release an offended warcry.

"My cans!" Munch was all fired up. "Our mighty steed calls! The Full Metal Goats have returned! To arms and ladles!"

Vanilla crossed ladles with Munch. "For the protection of our soup cans! Let no goat bleat unpunished!"

Summoning a duo of war geese, the Named Ones mounted their steeds and were off to the moon-war.

Artorian didn't have the words, slowly turning to Tatum, who smirked and sipped tea. "I told you, you missed out on *a lo~o~o~ot.*"

CHAPTER SEVENTEEN

With his aides missing in action, Tatum dropped the fun-time accent and sprang up from his seat, then firmly exhaled, mending that comedic bump of the stomach, and returning to a willowy plague doctor physique. "Time to bail! Come along, Sunny, I know you want to hear all about the new bodies so decanting can begin."

Artorian also dropped the accent, and hustled out of the pillow lounger to fall right into stride behind Tatum. The Incarnate stretched his arms above his head while beelining to a nearby river. Once closer to the stream, he pointed at a small dock where a ferry waited. "Our destination is Asphodel, which is located inside the moon. We can take Charon, that ferry, across the Styx. The waypoint further along the river will teleport us inside of the moon once we cross it, so long as the river behaves. They get moody."

Tatum paused.

"Like right now." Frowning at the erratic flow of water that splashed up against his sandals just to spite him, Tatum pressed his hands into his hips. "Going to be like that again are we?"

An idea struck Artorian, who manifested his soul item in

one hand just to bring the pillow down and smack the river with it. The dense fluff struck the water as if the latter were solid concrete that had been chastised. Instantly thereafter, the water's tantrum subsided, leaving it to flow more as a lazy river while observing the pillow man in shock, as if it couldn't believe what just transpired.

"Better?" Artorian asked his friend, his pillow vanishing.

"Better!" Tatum gleefully confirmed. "I… never thought of trying that."

"Glad to be of help." Artorian boarded the ferry with Occultatum. The Incarnate gave the boat a soft pat before the vessel moved all on its own. Interested in all these unusual reactions that kept occurring, Sunny looked back and forth between the simplistic ferry, and the rough outline of the yacht in the distance. "Did turning people into boats become a trend?"

Tatum scoffed, feeling foul. "No, turning people into objects just happened to become one of Odin's little pastimes. Especially after he heard that you turned a demon into a sword and split Barry into pieces. Speaking of, I buried the game-over cloud in Eternium's Midgard, but I doubt it will stay where I placed it. The whole of Eternia needs an overhaul, and I don't think it will be called Eternia afterwards. That ship has sailed."

Tatum took a seat, crossed one leg over the other, and adjusted his dark toga. His equally dark eyes focused on the stream ahead once Charon got moving. "The fork is in the Reliquary, the cat is with Grace, and the Pot of Greed is in some prison made from teleportation insanity that Zelia threw together before she needed sleep. We still need a warden, but that's going to solve itself."

Charon carved through the stream until a sudden *vwop* stole all the light from the vicinity. While the ferry was still bobbing along in a similar stream of water, the respective location had changed from an open meadow to the inside of a tunnel. One so dark that Artorian could see glowing purple flowers illuminate the upcoming cave with a strong bloom.

He tried to study one when the boat passed the banks they

grew on, though he steered clear of it when the flower tried to bite him. "Is that a modified nightshade? Bioluminescent additions?"

Tatum pointed at the mooring coming up. "Strong additions, and yes. Don't eat the Night Lilies if you'd like to stay with the living. This stuff is poisonous even to Mages. Especially avoid the sentient variants if you meet them. They're poisonous *and* venomous. I wouldn't recommend touching the river water either."

Not wanting to argue that point, as he was mesmerized by the sights of indoor plant life, he got nice and snug in the exact middle of the ferry. Out of reach of the natural intruder repellant mechanisms that he was surrounded by on all sides.

Artorian needed a bit to get used to the transition from constant sunny landscape to gloomy interior. He expected spooky scary skeletons. Unsurprisingly, Asphodel, the plant the region must be named after, also grew *everywhere*. Similar to the other plant he'd seen so far, Asphodel gave off more of a white light to balance out the Night Lilies' purple glow. "Does that one do anything dangerous?"

"Asphodel, the plant, eases the separation of souls from the mind and body. We use it for other things that will become clear to you shortly. Otherwise, it's harmless unless you're in water that it grows near. That's how you end up in the Asphodel Meadows." Tatum suddenly gave him a serious look. "You *do not* want to end up in the Asphodel Meadows. Especially avoid the variant that grows in and near the Lethe river. They'll rip the personality right out of you after one sip. Your whole identity? *Poof.*"

Artorian kept silent the whole rest of the trip. Once out of the boat, Tatum began climbing the stairs of peridot moon-rock which stuck to the outside of a massive hollowed cylinder, segmented by floors. Passing the higher chambers, Artorian recognized the floating sigils that had made Wagner. Or he assumed had made Wagner. He'd been piddling about while Halcyon did the heavy lifting that day.

When they both arrived on the floor of the moon's work-shop Tatum intended, Artorian saw the earlier living spellwork was merely one of several dozen variants. All illuminated by their own surrounding garden of plants, the current floating works of runic art appeared far more complete. "Fancy!"

Occultatum agreed with Sunny. "Can't work on something for multiple millennia and *not* invest in some healthy decor. Just behind us, that red glow? That is the flaming river Phlegethon. She passes by this level. Fleggy's a beauty when trying to relax and sip spiced drinks, plus she keeps the place warm."

He tapped the side of his nose for a moment. "On that prior note, don't ask how old anyone is, and definitely keep the topic away from Ammy. She's been a trooper, but we've been up and kicking for a deathly long time. Both of us are burning for a change of pace. When this Incarnate form is fully mended, I am going Ammy's route and tinkering with my appearance. Just to start with. We crave freshness, and I personally can't wait for the mass-decanting."

He paused and motioned to one of the floating spellforms, the sigils looking downright alive, even if just metaphorically. "Allow me to introduce the spellforms of what makes a specific species unique. This one, surrounded by glowing roses, is a human. On the left are the Elven variants, on the right the Dwarven variants, and that entire back wall is all the animal to humanoid conversions and back. I am *mighty* proud."

Artorian slowly clapped, and Tatum graciously bowed. "Thank you, thank you! Now don't poke your fingers in these or try to cast one, because that's how we end up with more Vanillas and Munches running around."

Sunny paused. "Weren't we entirely unable to make souls, or minds?"

Tatum drew a deep breath, exhaling it long and slow. "That we cannot, and that has not changed. Our allotment is mindless creatures or animals that can't breach the sapience barrier. Those are free game! Intelligent and sapient options on the other hand... well."

He walked over to a wall, and Artorian recognized it as a copy of his own, except that the occupants vastly differed. Tatum pointed at two cracked memory Cores. "So these two people lived out a life in Cal, died, and got automatically stored. Unfortunately for them, because *they believed* that they had lived a full life. We ran into something interesting…"

He mulled over the words while rolling his hands over one another, choosing to detail what happened. "When I activated the spellform that made Munch, the spellform forcibly sucked out and claimed the mind and soul of this left memory Core. The spellform then combined the contents with itself to make the new entity. For the person who *was* in that memory Core? There is no coming back, and if they were Mage, that's no longer applicable. Complete wipe of the slate. Node connections and all."

Artorian bit his lower lip. "I hope that only works on people who have lived a full life, or otherwise Cal's breaking his promise, and I think that's instakill territory for the lot of us."

Tatum nodded sagely. "Sure is, and while so far the spellforms have only drained Cores of people who are applicable and qualify to be 'recycled,' or whatever we call the process that doesn't immediately sound like the smell of seven moldy cheese plates' worth of horror, there is no proof or guarantee that the spellforms can't or won't take the ones we don't want them to. So… keep 'em dormant, yes?"

Artorian shoved his hands into his pockets at speed to keep from fiddling. "Understood! How does this help us with our decanted? Also what was this about not being able to do any cultivating?"

Sitting on a shaped moonstone bench with a curved back for comfort, Tatum swung a leg over his knee and scratched his cheek to feel human. "Well, I found the notations in Cal's records. You apparently once told him that he might not want everyone in his Soul Space to cultivate? Guild people and whatnot. So Cal turned off the option for anyone he didn't approve of. Easy, simple, direct, *linked to the Spirit bodies.* Likely not having planned on being out of commission himself, he didn't have time to tackle the second big body problem, if he was even aware."

Artorian joined the seating and raised a brow. "There's a second one? I was still focused on the first. Shouldn't we get that sorted before tackling the new one?"

Occultatum groaned weakly, in some discomfort. "Nooo... You're going to want to know about this before most everyone else finds out. It's some of that bad news."

Sunny slapped his forehead, did some breathing, and steeled himself. "Lay it on me."

Occy joined the club of explaining things with complicated diagrams, making some models out of his energy as they floated above the ground in front of them like some see-through three dimensional homes. Except in the shape of people. "Problem one is how to give the decanted 'bodies' they can use to live *inside of Cal*. With an extra caveat that we have to provide these bodies without those forms being forever static and unchanging. Previously, only Cal had new-body-making powers. All these spellforms around us? Those have become our workaround. More on that later. Problem two is how to give anyone a body that is able to survive *outside of Cal* for any length of time."

Artorian frowned. "The Chains of Chaos keep us all neatly trapped in, do they not? I figure that worrying about living outside was for later. The same reason Adam or the demons can't leave, if I recall."

Tatum pressed his hands together. "Sooo... we may have a slight method to meddle with *how likely* it is that those chains are binding, without actively removing them. Which we actually can't do, since Xenocide slapped them onto Cal. That's triple S-ranked Spirit energy with a Tier seven-twenty law, and some nasty infused intentions. We're not getting out of that until the chain feels like it, which, we will honestly never know when that is. One day they will just pop without warning and go on vacation to Bermuda."

Sunny leaned back, enthused. "I heard the word 'meddle,' and that's both my tea and toast. Tell me more?"

Tatum was glad to. "Chaos-Hawthorne and Zelia are each tied to a **Chaos** node of different intensities. Zelia, by herself—though it cost her and conked her out in addition to making a prison—managed to warp the chains enough, to where we, for *juuust* a moment, were able to send something *out*. While normally that would be cause for amazing celebrations, the problem is what we got *back*."

Artorian tried to puzzle out how that worked. "I bet Cal's ley lines are still guzzling up all of creation?"

Tatum released a singular 'ha.' "I don't wanna gamble on this, but that's a good bet. I'll spare you the jargon, but the short of it is that the body we sent out died *instantly*. Not lasted for a while, not slowly dried up and returned, not any of the other effects one could have been expecting before the energy returned to Cal. This was a straight up and very direct transition from 'oh my celestials we got that through,' to 'sweet mercy in the abyss it's back and dead.' We didn't have time for a second breath between those occurrences."

Artorian bit his thumb, troubled by that news. "Not being able to leave... is a very unpleasant thought. How does this relate to new bodies for a second go around? I've been in plenty now? What am I missing here?"

Tatum altered the diagram to a showcase of five human figures. "I'll make it easy. Diagram one is our true bodies, the ones we entered with. Well, the ones *you all* entered with. Dawn and I needed simulacrums right away. True bodies survived fine outside, so we put a pin in that. Unfortunately, none remain."

He moved to the next one. "Diagram two is where people actually started in Cal, after that disaster of a beginning where everyone lost their original forms, and Cal got involved. Those A-rank Mage bodies which Cal put together? They were very inflexible, broke all the time, and broke extra fast when he tried to game-system them."

He moved to the third. "Diagram three is Spirit bodies.

Spirit bodies had the flexibility that the A-rank forms did not. You could go bonkers with them. Make them rely on statistics based on Pylons? No problem. Cal didn't want someone to have certain access to memories or powers? A steal. These were the default for the longest time, but in reality this is also where we unknowingly got tangled in the net. Version three is the iteration Eternium continued his personal groundwork from, so his and ours diverge from here. He went more 'game,' we went more 'real.'"

Tatum moved to the fourth image. "Cal eventually fully figured out how to tie Mages to himself and his node, so that through him they could get the Mana they needed to keep ranking up. This replaced their direct connection to the Tower, but being in Cal cut that off in the first place, so it was all patchwork anyway. The remaining problem was sorted by keeping the minds of Mages in Silverwood seed Cores, and most of our woes went by the wayside."

Tatum made the image of the fourth body iteration somewhat larger to point out details. "Version four is the most stable we have ever gotten Spirit bodies. All their information is self-contained, they neatly cycle Essence, they're at near-zero risk of critical failures just from existing, they don't leak like a sieve, they handle game functions and cultivation, and they can go into other Cores while retaining their integrity. You can feed them Essence, Mana, or Spirit, and they will just keep on truckin'."

Artorian thought he understood, but chose not to ask about 'trucking.' "This must be part of why the 'if I die in Eternium, I must start over' was a thing?"

Tatum nodded, as that was correct. "Definitely a part of it, with the new information that *this* is the type of body that lasted a grand total of zero seconds on the outside. Don't even try to do the relative-time consideration? We already confirmed with T.C. that the out-time and in-time are just about identical. When I said instant, I meant instant."

Artorian put his hand up, then dropped them towards

diagram five. "What's this, then? From a glance, I can tell that it looks… mortal? What words are we using to describe common flesh and blood these days? Non-Mage?"

Occultatum made a tag visible. "Mortal is what we called it, because that's exactly what it is. A new body, not made, but grown from the ground up. A 'real' body, not one of the energy versions we are doing our utmost with to make feel as right as possible."

Sunny shot his hands into the air. "That's fantastic all by itself! So long as you can get past… erm. Well. A whole litany of problems? Mages aren't going to survive that trip."

It was Tatum's turn to grit his teeth so he wouldn't copy what Sunny did earlier, and bite his own lip. "Well, there's the rub. A Mage *could* occupy one of these bodies, just not… *as a Mage.*"

The mirth fell from Artorian's face as the pieces clicked into place. "Cal save my soul, these bodies make a cultivator start over from *nothing*?"

Occultatum snapped his fingers, and pointed both at the wily old man. "Got it in one. The upside? You'll probably survive with one of these bodies when built back up the old and original way, so long as there's Essence outside to survive on. If you become a Mage again, we're fairly certain there's no Tower trip and you automatically reconnect to what node you had, because your soul was tied to a spot to begin with. We *also* think this resets your connection to be with the Tower, *not* Cal."

Artorian slumped, both his hands on his beard. "This is… That is… Tatum, my friend. I think my heart passed my stomach and just sank somewhere into my lower abdomen. To live outside of Cal, we have to both start over completely, and *time* our ascension to be outside of Cal when it happens, or we are once again stuck with the slow-death loop of Mana deprivation like we were in the beginning?"

Tatum pulled his cheeks back to show his teeth as his shoulders hunched up, his voice a half groan. "I'm workin' on it."

Relaxing his pose, he sighed. "For now, yes that's the reality of things. You can climb as high as you want as a Mage or Incarnate in Cal, and it won't matter squat in order to leave. Because *these* Cal-made bodies can't exist outside."

After motioning at the shells he and Artorian were in, Tatum raised a single digit. "I do have a *small* pinch of good news."

Having buried his face in his hands, the frail old man looked up. "I would *love* some good news."

Tatum made a sixth diagram of a person appear, and this one looked like a modified version of the fourth iteration. "We *might* have a way to make bodies durable enough for them to survive outside, for a *limited* period of time, as the highest Mage rank you've attained. So long as there's an external power source to draw from. Once that source is empty though? *Pop*, that's it. You end up back in Cal, and you can tell us what you saw."

Artorian pushed both his hands over his bald head. "That's the best we've got?"

Tatum unfortunately confirmed the news. "That's the best we've got. With the mortal body, we can pre-grow it without many issues until around the age of ten. But, unless we have the mind in it by that point, that body can and will *yoink* one from a nearby source. Preventing the *yoink* makes the body die on the spot otherwise. Very frustrating, since once the mind is in the mortal body, it *cannot leave* unless that body dies the old fashioned way. No more convenient body-hopping via the seed Cores. I will also tell you that it is *very* awkward to see a tiny version of yourself walking around, that definitely isn't you."

Kneading the bridge of his nose, Artorian wanted to change the pace. "Alright then. Enough about body problem two. I want to see my people. What's the hitch with body problem *one*?"

CHAPTER EIGHTEEN

Tatum cleared all his diagrams, replacing them with the options available in folder one, rather than those from folder two. "Decanting our people has the following upsides and downsides. Major upside? If I get Wispermission, we can make all the Spirit bodies we want in Cal's world. The creation process is a matter of energy, which Cal has the monopoly on. For all the heavy lifting of actually *making* the body, we are literally surrounded by the spellforms that get that task done. All we have to do is form the appropriate body from memories, implant the mind, don't get in the way of the soul auto-tethering, *et voila*, one decanted."

Artorian crossed his arms, heavily leaning back on the moonstone bench. "Now what's the downside?"

Tatum snapped his fingers, and pointed to the diagram next to the first one he'd used for example. "Death is a joke, cultivation is a no-go, and growing up is a laughable concept since physical changes have to be done manually. Or did you never notice that your hair just doesn't grow here?"

Sliding down the bench like he was part goo, Artorian

pressed both his hands over his eyes and released the longest of groans. "Easy peasy kill me pleasy."

Tatum snorted. "But wait! Now we get to the meat of this tofu sandwich. While the bodies are frozen in time, essentially, the minds will still continue to develop and learn. As we've already discovered in some of Odin's society, this causes some rather interesting problems. Such as a forty-year-old man in the body of someone who looks twelve, with matching physiological limitations."

Artorian dropped his hands and looked up. "Did he have a 'big mad'?"

Tatum scoffed as he bit back a giggle. "*Such* a big mad. In fact, *still mad*, and won't not be. Aside from still being stuck in the bronze ages, Odin's idea of society is crumbling to pieces. Not only did he think that a society of only power-hungry cultivators were interested in mundane skills, but he thought that people were going to keep judging at face value. Y'know, hubris based on what a person looks like. That has *not* been the case, and appearance dropped to an all-time low in value."

Tatum created two hovering orbs, both identical in outward appearance. While the first contained a dim blacklight, the other possessed a strong watery luster. "With Spirit bodies under the current Pylon limitations, mental growth *can* happen, but that is *not* true for physical growth. Because, in the end, it's still a body made of energy, not meat."

The old man kneaded his brow. "I'm going to ask for just a teensy bit more information on the mind-body problem, but I may already be standing too deep in the pool to handle the tide here."

His friend understood, speaking slower for clarity. "I'll simplify the main points. With normal people, the brain adapts to new knowledge and memories, and thus adapts in structure to reflect this evolution, such as more dendrites and neurons. Just go with the terms for now, I can explain in detail when we have a few spare years. This type of growth both sets the physical brain as a physical limitation, as well as the main corner-stone of one's mental progress and prowess."

Enlarging the orbs, he singled the dim one out. "The first thing to understand about our brains is that memories are just patterns. Memories aren't so much stored in our neurons, as they are stored in the sequence and pattern of those pathways being used. Let's call this our 'neurons firing.' Rather than a specific cornerstone, if the pathway is lost, then so is the memory. This is why smells can trigger memories."

Artorian felt less out of his depth than he thought, and motioned for Tatum to continue. The man clarified a bit further, more for himself. "Due to that smell being present when what you experienced forged the pathway along with the memory, they fire along the same route, thus triggering that memory, should you smell that smell again."

Tatum then motioned at the brighter, watery orb. "With memories being patterns, that means *intelligence* is a pattern. To me, intelligence is the application of patterns being used in new ways, possibly causing new patterns to emerge. Think of the leap from longbows to crossbows. Same concept, new usage. When looking at intelligence as a pattern, that means that a more intelligent person simply has more of these pathways. So when comparing physical brains, you can make an easy map."

He moved both orbs closer to one another. "A *Mage* no longer has a physical brain. Not really. Mages are bundles of energy conformed to a shape. Mages tend to not change physi-cally, but they can still learn. So, given that there is no more brain to reflect these changes, where is this new intelligence stored?"

The longbeard squinted, but his friend wasn't going to make this difficult as he dismissed both orbs. "The answer turns out to be rather simple. When you shift to being a Mage, where and how your memories are stored changes entirely. Rather than a physical reflection of knowledge, your learned patterns are instead added to your soul. That also explains why when you swap back and forth between bodies, you take everything you are with you. All new experiences are added to the pattern that is your soul, just as a brain would evolve and change, except that you are now using clusters of energy instead of neurons and dendrites. The trick is the path, not the corner points."

Feeling like he'd reached an endpoint, Occultatum wrapped up his scholarly lecture. "I really want to dig into the psychological changes Mages feel when they become Mages, particularly how different people process them, but that's a conversation for another time. Currently, the topics are Odin not understanding that a society of nothing but cultivators is nothing but trouble, and the mind-body dilemma. Thoughts, my friend?"

"Odin's mess first." Artorian flopped right down to the moonstone ground and began some stretches to get his mind off things. "So you end up with ten year olds smarter and more capable than some of the people who look like adults, because people think differently, and some different ways of thinking lead to greater societal success?"

Tatum smirked. "Sunny, buddy, I love that you're smart."

Artorian sighed, resting his forehead against the cold floor. "I just hope some baby isn't in charge somewhere."

Tatum raised an eyebrow. "Why are we suddenly talking about Odin?"

Artorian broke out laughing, forcing him to hold his own ribs.

Occultatum shrugged. "What? I don't like him either. The man keeps throwing wrenches into our spokes when we need them to turn without interference, then prides himself on doing so. Deck him in the schnozz when you can? He needs deposing and dethroning. Anytime he's in charge of something, the path turns into a rollercoaster ride to the abyss. *He's* still happy, but everyone else is glaring."

Wiping a tear from his eye, Artorian decided to get back on the bench. "How does he stay in power?"

His friend broadly motioned around them. "Because he *has* power. An A-rank seven cultivator contained in a Spirit body, decked out with new skills and tricks from adventures in Eternia, likely with a host of tools and toys hidden in his belt? We forgot to check his gear on the way out, so it will not come as a surprise if he pulls a Cal Ex Machina out of his back pocket."

Artorian frowned. "A what?"

Tatum waved it off while shaking his head. "Something really stupid that essentially means an '*Aha, no, I have you! I win instead!*' kind of event."

Artorian squinted. "Don't those happen all the time, normally?"

The side-eye he was shot made him look away and wish he had some tea to sip in order to look innocent. "Sunny, precocious pre-planning is not the same as Cal flatly going: 'haha, no.' There's a difference. Complicated by the fact that Odin loves being cliche and contrived. He wants the show more than the result. He wants the big villain speech, the scripted showdown, and the triumphant tales. Not having that *infuriates* him, the vindictive eel."

Artorian giggled. "Now I understand why Yuki essentially had him on a leash! She didn't let him get away with anything. I hope I run into Hulk again before I go pull my sleeves up. Also to do a refresher on being a Mage, because currently I have Eternia fighting-mojo still stuck in my head, and that *really* doesn't work well here."

Tatum waggled his hand. "It *sort of* works here. Knowledge is still knowledge, and that all transfers over. There are a few things that Eternium couldn't make the cultivation equivalent for, your Soul of Zen thing being one of them. To us, that's just dilation. Dilation doesn't work in Cal, a fact I deeply grumble about to this day."

Artorian crossed his arms, concerned. "What… What about physical changes? Do those carry over? I had something called Nascent Sense that had a weird lore descriptor about being reborn… or something. I can't pull it up to check."

The Incarnate looked his friend up and down, then looked taken aback. "Oh, *huh*. Y'know, I stopped looking through people because the affair was very awkward, but you have some seriously advanced spellscript directly on your bones. You also have two hearts, not that the detail matters for your current form, and whatever is happening with your eyes is honestly beyond me. Nothing harmful? But wow, that's *a lot* of inter-linked runes. Serious array-work. You're not... *using* any of those runes, but they're all definitely there!"

Tatum frowned, then crossed his arms. "Strange. You're no Incarnate. Did you layer jump a bunch recently? You've got a lot of dream-layer Essence mixed in with your Spirit form. That's normal for Incarnates, who can filter the stuff out like corruption from a cultivation technique, but with you it's just all over the place. Doesn't seem harmful? Still strange to see it stick around like that."

Artorian tried to smile and not panic. "Did you just say *dream* Essence?"

Tatum *mhm'd* like it was no big deal, and continued scanning. "Sure did, but we don't have dream Essence channels, so it's only ever going to be corruption. Unless you use it? Not sure how you would."

Sunny stuck a digit into the air. "Dawny recently informed me about neon Essence. I may not have realized at the time that it meant *Essence* Essence."

Occultatum perked up. "Oh, you met Zephyr? Wonderful, that removes some complications. Yes, just like that. There's more Essence types in existence than what we have, we just have to stick to the ones available or it's all going to go horribly wrong. With the usual case of exceptions, such as 'I have a trick,' or whatnot. Zephyr can't grow from the neon Essence, again due to lack of proper channel, but it's really pretty and packs a punch!"

Artorian scratched his eyebrows. "Am I getting too old for this? Also, Dawny only found out her name after she woke up. How did you...?"

It was the Incarnate's turn to break down laughing, though Artorian failed at the moment to see what was so hilarious.

Artorian rumbled. "What?"

Tatum righted himself and dried his face with his sleeve. "Ahh… it's because we're so much older, Sunny. Plus, being an Incarnate changes so much. Whole worlds you never thought real will suddenly be visible, and details people try to hide might as well be a toddler holding a melting cone of ice cream behind their backs. As for Zephyr, I knew about her before the boat incident."

Recovering, he sighed. "If you're worried about things being too complicated, focus on what you know. Then build back out from there. You'll be lost without a good foundation."

Artorian did just that. "Sure. So, body problem one? How do I give my decanted family good lives when it's clearly all going to the abyss in Odin's society?"

The wide grin from the Incarnate made Sunny's nose tingle and grandpa senses spin like a detector. Tatum mused. "Y'know those Pylons we turned off?"

Artorian narrowed his eyes. "…yeah?"

His friend's grin grew. "Wouldn't it just be *swell* if we had some in there that simulated aging?"

Artorian threw his hands up. "You only tell me this *now*? Why the prior preamble? That solves like, half the issues!"

Snickering, Tatum draped himself over the bench. He thought he'd gotten enough amusement in, and should be letting his friendly jabs go about now. "I really wanted to whine about Odin first. The opportunity for a pinch of drama was something I just couldn't let pass me by. We have to make our own entertainment, and I refuse to go the way of the Wisp. Backstabbing little…"

"Talking about me behind my back again?" Tatum sputtered, coughed, and thumped his chest as Grace rounded the corner, her hands pressed to her hips in the classic Dawn style. She seemed serious at first, but the grin spreading on her face betrayed her amusement. Her voice sounded a bit more mature, but that rebellious teenage phase comment was on the copper. "All that drama and I missed out? Tell me you haven't told him about the boss baby yet."

Artorian rounded on his friend. "Wait, there actually *is* one?"

Grace smirked. "Yeah. Odin!"

The three of them shared a moment of raucous laughter, after which the old men made room for Grace to sit between them so they could dote on her like a favorite granddaughter. Grace clearly did not mind the attention as they fixed the bows in her hair, fussing at one another for where part of the ribbon needed to go.

"So cheap shots aside, what were you talking about?" Grace inquired.

Artorian mumbled while slapping Tatum's hand away as he fiddled with one of the knots. "We were... *Fwap*. Will you stop trying to tie that? We were talking about decanting the walls of people we have so we could see them again. Tatum was telling me about difficulties, and how much would be fixed by turning Pylons back on. *Apparently.*"

He shot Tatum a quick look before addressing Grace again. "Also, no Soni or Mittens?"

Grace frowned, puzzled for a moment. "Soni is being chased by the cat. Stay on topic. So we just... turn the Pylons back on? That makes the only limitation... what? That they can't cultivate? Lives as normal will still work, and we have whole banks dedicated to injury and age simulation. Occy, did you leave those turned off just because...?"

The Incarnate smirked. "Of course I *indulged* in keeping them off to muck with Odin! Mainly they're off because many are fried and not having them on will make it easier for Eternium to sync backup with Cal, if not outright required, but it was so good to see Sunny make all those faces!"

Clearing his throat, Occultatum had a moment of real-talk. "As discussed in the last meeting, only critical Pylons are active, and due to the rules, a higher-up Wisp would need to make the decisions per if we turned anything back on or not. Just because I *can* doesn't mean I *will*. So, Grace, as the current highest-ranking Wisp around, if you say to reactivate the batches, I can get that going."

Artorian clapped his hands together, hopeful. "Then, jokes aside, can I see my family? Pull out Don and have him roam about, see if there's approval? He got sicced on me in the early days."

Grace and Tatum shot him matching thumbs up, after which Grace spoke while modifying her romper to add polka dots. "There's no infrastructure of any kind, so whoever you pull out is also going to need to do all the work. Picking a location is easy, getting started is not. On Dad's new planet, everyone starts from square one, and he's *probably* going to wipe the slate clean when he wakes up. So I wouldn't get too attached to what gets built. He had big plans, an ice canopy and all."

Artorian didn't follow. "Ice canopy?"

Grace nodded, a scheming smile on her face. "You'll see. The canopy is part of the world tree project, which he will tell you about when he wakes up. Notes, no matter how extensive, only go so far. Then there's no telling what new ideas he wakes up with. Dad wanted a game, and Eternium will have that covered. For other experiments, there's other Cores, though they're limited by Soul Space size."

She poked Sunny in the chest. "You don't worry about that right now. I'm going to authorize turning the Pylons on until it becomes real obvious that Eternium has enough of his personal abyss together to do a proper reconnect. Then, if we need to, we turn them off and go into a big iteration pause for everyone while we get the space up and running again, after which we unpause when it's all sorted. The cascade crisis is long over, and we should use what we have. We'll do a slow start-up cycle to make sure nothing explodes, but if it can run, I want it running. Personally, I don't think we're going to make any Eternium progress without Dad, and just letting the Soul Space sit still is driving me up the wall."

Artorian squeezed his lips together. "Sooo... I can decant?"

Grace motioned at Tatum. "You'll need Occy for the

bodies, but yup! Just pick a location and you're all set to start. I *do* need to steal him for a while, though. My Wisps, the Gnome Squad, and I will have to do the finer tuning, but those Pylons won't turn themselves on. Some need quality pillow whispering. The beaver-sourced Cores wake up cantankerous."

Brushing the cloth covering his knees, Artorian got up and eased his arms behind his lumbar. "Don't mind one bit. How do I... get back? Do I take the boat? To the other boat?"

Grace clapped her hands twice, opening a plain old portal reminiscent of Cal's early dungeon days. The portal grew from the ground via roots that had no business being conjured in place, but grew fast and full either way without caring for damage to the moonstone floor. Eventually, a ten-by-ten oval teleportation gate occupied the middle of their current room like it had always been there. "Or you could take the quick way. Have fun finding a spot on the planet!"

Artorian rubbed his hands together, then tipped his metaphorical hat at the both of them. "Tatum, great talk. Again soon? Less cheeky drama perhaps. Grace, always lovely to see you. I'll leave you both to it. Toodles!"

With a heave and a ho, Artorian hurled himself through the gate, accompanied by the required *wheeeeee*!

CHAPTER NINETEEN

Artorian wished he'd asked in more specific details concerning where the other end of Grace's portal would deposit him, as falling from the sky without warning put a dent in his excited 'Wheee'ing.

Flailing about for a few seconds before remembering Mages could fly, he dug his heels in against the air and grabbed the Essence in his surroundings like a rope, noisily squeaking to a slow halt as if performing in a comedy act. He then wondered why he hadn't just used normal flight, and did so. "Right. I can just... do that."

Looking up, he saw the last vestiges of the conjured portal wither out of existence before becoming particulates. "She plunked that gate on a cloud and didn't think twice about it."

Looking down, he whisked his fingers through his beard while studying the landscape. Before he could get his rough bearings, the buzz of an insect reached his ears. Cocking his head to locate where that decisively annoying pitch originated from, Artorian spun upside down and clapped his hands together to turn a mosquito into past tense. "Not these things again!"

Peeling his hands apart before cleaning them off, he frowned at the sight. "Something went wrong. This thing has swords for hands. Cal, these were bad enough. They did *not* need improvements."

Artorian was forced to pause his complaints as the buzzing hadn't actually stopped. He closed his eyes, exhaled, and remembered a terrible fact. "These things come in swarms, don't they?"

A nearby cloud had been mistaken for a normal cloud. The floaty anger-management class was instead an angry hive of buzzy-boys. One Artorian swat straight through with a Rail Palm that exploded in the very center of the swarm, turning a buzzing doom-cloud into petered out rusted trumpets. Artorian blew some air over his palm, then extended his pointer finger and *chik-chik'd* his digit like a crossbow with his spare hand. Pointing at survivors, the old man faded them from existence with concentrated thermal rays and improvised sound effects. "Pew pew, pew pew pew!"

Artorian called it a job well done when his digit sizzled hot red and every last mosquito in his vicinity had been added to death's roll call. "Once a janitor, always a janitor. I like a lot of creatures, but mosquitos need to be buried on sight and taken off the census."

Checking to make sure there were no other tiny tormentors in hiding, Artorian decided to take a page out of Ember's play-book and marked each and every visible cloud that so much as looked a little suspicious. A multicolor fireball took out the first hidden swarm with rainbow swirls, a *wub* the second, and just because he didn't want to miss anything after discovering how well these annoyances kept hidden while also creeping up on him, chose the thorough option as a finisher.

Measuring out the rough height where these swarms liked to park, Artorian pulled in some serious aquatic light and applied the Essence attack from the Mountaindale days that had dropped whole fields of undead. The omnidirectional version this time as Artorian raised his hand and compressed the energy to a destructive disk spinning flat above his finger, one that slowly stopped being visible, though not inaudible as the cutting hum grew.

The flattened disk of unseen ultraviolet luminance chose ultraviolence when it was activated with a *wub*, dipping into the Cherenkov glow range. The invisible disk expanded like the edge of a coin, and performed its task like a veteran butler. That being to clean up. Artorian saw his miniature foes perish with sky-spanning pops of aqua-blue light as the wave traveled for an impressive distance before running out of targets. "World's best bug zapper. I should name it Walter."

He once again blew the heat away from his hand, then nodded at a job well done before getting back to figuring out where he was. "Since the attack itself was not in the visible range, all those blue fireworks mean confirmed kills. I'm satisfied."

Inspecting the vague movements of geography below, he discerned his current location. "*Hmmm*, I must be near the equator. Lots of desert under my feet. Not a fan of desert. Not a great place to plunk my people either. Maybe I should go spy first? See what Odin did."

Flying back up for a few minutes, Artorian also cut the planetary poles as possible options from the list. "Too cold. Obvious ice and snow. I'm looking for something more moderate."

Being up so high did let him find one of the clearly visible landmarks. "What was that mountain called again? Olympus? The signs are all gone."

He found Odin's new society smack on the opposite side of the planet, spiraling outward from Olympus. The mountain itself seemed to be for the more well off, while the farther out one went, the less desirable the scene became. Tucked away on the inner halves of bridge-connected canyons, activity resembled an ant's nest for the less fortunate. Whole fields that would be great for farms weren't seeing any use, and land primed for housing was instead pockmarked with lightning-bolt burns.

"Not what I was expecting. Where's the overt luxury? This is a hole in the ground."

Glancing at the mountaintop, he recognized structures that resembled the ostentatious mess Odin had put together in Eternia's Asgard, except that this version was still under construction. "Still has a need to step on someone else to make himself feel better, I see. Would be a *shame* if something were to happen to that mountain. Lake Olympus has a nice ring to it."

Artorian took a closer glance at the canyon society. His stomach did some turns at all the black and red flags, military-looking parades, complete lack of happy faces, and stark living conditions. Noisy individuals stationed on bridges spewed some kind of creed, but he chose not to pay too much attention. A small green-faced marching section dressed in the attire of a Queen's Guard sang something along the lines of "O-Ee-Yah! Eoh-Ah!"

Artorian didn't want to know what was up with these Winkies from Oz. He was already too angry. "A brand new slate, and you go with an imperialist *dictatorship*? Odin, you... *you...*"

Artorian threw his hands in the air, exasperated. "Bah!"

Making a note to himself to set up nowhere near that mountain, he thought to come back when he had the mental energy to do something about Odin and his ways. To begin, he skipped town back to the entire other side of the planet. Sticking to the general region of the equator, he encountered only one major distraction while planning to spend hours narrowing down a place he liked.

The one major distraction was worth the pitstop. He'd found Aiden! "Well, well. Underwater city? Can't wait to hear the story behind that choice. Let's drop by on the quick, I can't see any details with all that water in the way."

Dropping like an Artorian-eor, he hit the water like a pudgy rock and kept sinking until his feet slammed onto the seafloor, which didn't displace as much sand as he expected it would. Rather than swim or fly, Artorian leisurely walked his way to the gates while enjoying the general view, and playing with the incredibly curious fish that kept nipping at his Eternia-exported attire.

His main problem was that his beard kept floating up and obscuring his face, which he sorted by increasing his gait a bit so the beard flowed behind him instead. Before he could get to the underwater city—which was a bubbled-in forest on closer inspection—he received some company.

Some half-wolf, half-fish people swam up to him as a group, each holding spears that looked like scavenged shells with a stick shoved into the back. Perhaps just the best they had to work with for now.

"Hello there!" Artorian's voice resounded through the water, stunning the approaching party and turning a few belly-up. Those who were merely stunned and shaken ceased their approach, but only one of them managed to keep a grip on his... weapon. Sure, the sharp shell could be mistaken as one.

Toning down his volume, as he didn't want to wrench a gate down without even being near one like he had in Eternia's Octopi society, Artorian tried again. "Is this better?"

Most of the advancing party survived the second attempt with only minor shakes, but the whole group had lost all their zeal. The approach was no longer remotely as hostile and confident. Instead, the wolfishian—he was going to need a better name for these—the mer-wolf who had kept a grip on his spear pointed at Artorian, then at the underwater grove behind him.

The old man nodded while keeping his hands near his lumbar, interpreting the motion. "Yes, I do intend to go in. Can't you talk underwater? It's not that difficult."

Scowls formed over all the mer-wolves' facial expressions, which indicated that his statement wasn't so true. Not wanting to kick the crab-nest further, Artorian strolled along in the direction that had been pointed. "I'll just carry on then."

The mer-wolves scattered at his approach, only to reform on his flanks and stalk along. One of them considered charging in for a stab, but was stopped by the larger one with a scar over its face. Experience must have had value, as the others backed off. Flanking instead of charging, they stuck with him until Artorian made it to their equivalent of a door. "A soap bubble?"

Curious, he walked right into it. He pondered its structure, feeling the thin membrane surround him and then close behind him. A mer-wolf followed him, and the fishtail turned back into more familiar werewolf legs once his pursuer passed through. "*Oooh*, partial transformation? Fancy! I like it."

Giving the wolves a moment to file in, Artorian then moseyed along and passed through the other end of the bubble, where fresh air and surprisingly warm temperatures struck him as he entered the forest. Glade? He glanced around and scratched his chin. "Poplar? Interesting choice of tree. How is the atmosphere being kept bubbled in?"

When the wolves spilled out from the soap bubble behind him, they immediately ran for safety, howling to the sky as they fled. Artorian paid the affair no mind, and let them do as they pleased. There wouldn't be much to do until—

"Administrator?"

A gravelly, growling voice sounded from the tree line without having betrayed a hint of approach. Artorian's eyebrows rose at Aiden's sudden appearance. He took a stern look around to figure out the combination of silent approach and stealthy arrival. "Aiden! Good to see you. Incredibly well done stalking like that. If you hadn't spoken, I doubt I'd have noticed you at all."

Aiden smirked and inspected his sizable claws. "Had you not been a familiar face, you never would have. What brings you? This is unexpected."

Equally unexpected was the small furry blur that shot from the canopy. The tiny voice was full of vigor as equally tiny teeth tried to maul Artorian's face. "I got 'im, Grandpa!"

Artorian didn't move an inch as the enthusiastic bundle of claw and fang clashed with his unmoving form. Somewhat amused, he slightly tilted his face to get a better look at this fearless attacker. "Who's this little hellion, Aiden? She's got your fire."

"*Hehehehe.*" Aiden chuckled proudly, his arms crossing as his stance relaxed. "Obaba! You little rascal. Hone your instincts. Your claws are meant for small prey, not sky dragons who do not feel your bite."

"No, I got 'im!" Her reply was full of blind fervor, trying to chew on Artorian's cheek like she was teething. "No escape!"

Artorian turned back to Aiden, who was beaming. "She's adorable. Family of yours?"

Chuckling more intensely at the tiny tyke's antics, he rumbled with a nod. "Little Obaba is from a litter of one of my Chosen. She doesn't yet grasp hunt-gather pack-leader status. Everyone is family this, cousin that. Or food. She thinks you're food."

The old man nodded in understanding, trying not to jostle the small child who refused to give up. "I was told by Grace to find a spot to plunk my people down. Saw Odin's mess and didn't want to be anywhere nearby. Then I saw something odd under the water while looking about, and ran into your people. Love the tails. Very stylish."

At the mention of Odin, Aiden groaned loud. He exhaled through his nose in disgust, and looked away to make a face. "That pest. Were you told he goes by Zeus now? He dares call me Poseidon. What use do I have for a name I did not choose? How dare he attempt to take my agency from me? I will skewer him with my claws one day."

Artorian replied with sagely nodding, while the tyke stopped her assault to catch her breath. Nothing was getting through, and the human wasn't even phased. She pouted and growled. "What are you *made* of? All fall to Obaba's claws!"

Aiden sighed and recovered the feisty child from Artorian's unmarred, pristine face. "This young one needs experience in wisdom, it seems. I hope age can provide these lessons for her, and that one day, she will be a capable pack leader. For now, she is spitfire and rage."

Artorian did his utmost to keep his expression neutral as Aiden tried to wrangle the feisty cat who did not have any intention of being held. She yowled to the high celestials for freedom, hissed with wild abandon, and scampered into the underbrush when Aiden was forced to let her escape because the entire debacle was getting embarrassing.

The old man smirked. "I think she'll be just fine."

Sticking her head out of the brush, Obaba stuck her tongue out at the 'food' that had given her such a hard time, then fussed with little growls as she shot back over to her grandpa to attack Aiden's tail, batting at the moving obstacle of fluff. Two seconds of head scratches from 'Grandpa Aiden' later, and Obaba was a molten pile of happy purring. The entire event of mauling the human was forgotten in favor of getting attention.

Artorian failed to hide his amusement. "How old is that little one?"

Aiden beamed with pride. "Barely a year! Look at her sharpening her teeth on anything that moves. Such a fierce little huntress. She's strides ahead of the rest of the litter—her pack-mates can't even speak yet. Then here comes little Obaba, charging ahead at full speed. Her lineage is long-lived too, so I expect wonders."

Aiden handed the snoring bundle of purring wildcat off to a female wolfman who ran up to fetch her, then paced back and forth since the old administrator was clearly not here to cause him problems. "Have you met any others in the circle? Or are they still trapped?"

Artorian surmised he must have been referring to Henry and Marie. "Dawn got me out. Spent the last little bit with Tatum, in… what did he call it? Asphodel? Strange how travel works by river. Then you. I know Odin's here, but that's it."

"*Bah.*" Aiden scoffed, his nose scrunching to show restrained tolerance. "So Henry is stuck then? A shame, I wished to hash out our differences when he returned. My irritation only seems to grow."

"Would you like to talk about it?" Artorian queried. "Henry's a good lad, but he can be slow and prone to missing details when he's got his head stuck in politics. Hard to notice your friends are upset with you when one's mind is trapped on when and why one should dangle chancellors from the window."

Aiden wanted to stay mad, but that visual image smoothed out his snout and curled up the corner of his lips, and his giggles quickly became barked laughter. "Ha! Hahaha. Old Administrator. That trick is likely one of my favorite traits about you. You can take the painfully serious that eats at the heart, and lighten the burden. Now I cannot stop thinking of the scene. Watching them wriggle! Ha!"

Wiping away a budding tear, the massive wolf got his chuckling under control, then nodded in agreement. "You are also correct. He has always meant well, but he ignores or forgets that relationships require sustaining. We are not all that Eternal Vigil, Erebus. Henry does not visit. We do not enjoy games like in the olden times. We do not spar. Nothing. He merely expects my goodwill, but does not see that he gives nothing in return. I cannot give endlessly, and our sparse meetings are nothing but more requests, or quickly ended events where he must rush off for one thing or another. This has grated on me, and grates on me still. I am now filled with anger towards him. *Only* anger."

Artorian tapped his lips. "I have the thought that when Eternium is available again, you could perhaps pop in and beat him at his own game. His mind is always occupied with statesmanship, so why not best him at it? Then meet him on the field of battle and really let all your feelings and emotions fly, claws first. If he will not listen to how you feel with his ears, then he can taste your feelings instead as you smack him around and introduce him to the dirt. My old disciple was like that, too. Needed to be in the thick of it for any real learning to happen."

"That… pleases my heart to think about. I always knew you were hiding most of your wisdom, old Administrator. Yes. Yes, that idea is most wonderful. My anger feels sated for now, and I shall brood over this. Even if he were to come to this world, I think I would have avoided him. I will instead hunt him on his own turf. His prized little kingdoms in Eternia." Aiden stopped pacing as his mood lightened, his expression turning to surprise as he recalled that Artorian had name-dropped Asphodel earlier. "Hades used my five rivers suggestion?"

Artorian wasn't sure what the large wolfman was referring to. "Five? I saw one and heard of two. The Styx, Lethe, and... the other one had something to do with fire. "

The pack leader puffed out his chest. "The Phlegethon! Along with the rivers Styx, Lethe, Cocytus, and Acheron. Oceanus became the sea, so the original six turned into five. I had that idea! I... I'm surprised it got used. I don't get listened to around here."

Artorian rubbed his chin and neatly filed Aiden's comment away for later. "What's so special about these rivers? Do they do anything special?"

Aiden rubbed his paws together. He never got to gush! "Their names are meant to reflect the emotions associated with death! This was part of my memorial to Bob. I did like that Goblin, even if I never got to tell him. Styx is hatred, Acheron is pain, Lethe is forgetfulness, Cocytus is wailing..."

He paused while counting on his paws, tapping the fifth digit while frowning as if all his thoughts had suddenly blanked out. He couldn't remember what he was doing at all, like his mind had suddenly wandered into another room and mysteriously forgot what it had gone in there for. "The last one is..."

"Yes, it's nice that they have flavorful lore," Artorian cut in softly, noticing that a small crowd was gathering, and they were sniffing the air in confusion as their leader wasn't looking very... leader-y. He wasn't going to be responsible for a coup, so got short with the large wolfman before something could come of the situation. "But do they *do* anything?"

Aiden sulked, pressing his digits together as he deflated. "No..."

"Don't sound so woeful." With barely two steps, Artorian patted the being twice his size on the lower back, smiling that supportive grandfather smile. "Tatum already put them up! So why don't you just do what you said you wanted to, and plan out this lovely budding society you've got going away from it all? I can drop by again, and maybe next time we can talk about trade, or community growth, and the like? When I've got my own wall decanted and a town up and running, I think they'd love freshwater imports and fish. Sounds good?"

Aiden perked up, his ears twitching. "Yes, very good! Return soon. Bring salt! We live under the sea, and yet somehow still can't find any. Oh, and Administrator. Odin *stinks*, and I do not mean of the fishy variety. That would be an insult to the fish. Avoid his attention if you can."

"I will... keep that in mind. Thank you." Artorian had heard him, but was thoroughly distracted by the other details. He found the salt mention odd, because... sea. Maybe there was more to his freshwater mention than he realized? He shrugged and turned, giving the large man a wave on the way out as he planned regional exports. "Salt, sugar, and spice. The complete mix of everything nice."

Aiden's reply was good-natured.

"Ha! If you find any coffee elementals, bring those as well! Nothing like a cup of joe with your mates. Or some salami Sam on your plates." Aiden winked at a few of the gathered beauties, then watched Artorian leave through the bubble. After which he shook his head when the thought of this 'complete list' stuck around, because no, that list wasn't quite complete. "Must include meat on the list. Meat is nicest! *Mmmmm*. Buffalo *Bacon*. Still haven't found one with wings, but I bet they would taste even better with salt, sugar, and spice. I miss dry rubs. It's all so wet down here."

CHAPTER TWENTY

Standing high and dry in the sky once more, Artorian resumed his search. Locations that didn't fit the geographical criteria went ignored, which narrowed down the options considerably. First, water was a necessity. A coastline, preferably two, was ideal. Fresh water rivers that ran between were highly desired. Second, since this world-building attempt was going to be transient, Artorian did not want to instill a sense of complacency. That meant active regions which encouraged moving frequently.

He didn't want to deal with earthquakes if he could help it. Turbulent winds were annoying. Droughts were unacceptable, and extreme climates even more so. "That leaves a few options, but I think I will go with a spot near active volcanoes. That comes with the bonus of fertile land."

He discovered a few decent locations in moderate climate regions nested between the Western Sea and Eastern Ocean, while he stuck to the more central planetary band. His eyes kept returning to coastal areas made up of beaches and mangroves that, as one moved further inland, became mountainous. These mountains averaged a few thousand feet in elevation, though some peaks were much higher.

Where he was currently zipping around, the mountains often ascended into the clouds, creating a cloud-forest habitat. Sky-piercing mountains had a very cultivator vibe to them, and he mentally jotted down the preference. "This has a nice look to it, let's narrow down a more local spot."

The tallest peak in the general region came to about twelve-thousand feet high. He also sniffed out a few volcanoes, but only five remained somewhat active. Those were good numbers as far as he was concerned. Enough to keep one on their toes, but not enough to build a looking-over-the-shoulder habit. There were many streams, rivers, and waterfalls, but only a couple lakes. He would take the lack of lakes to the chin, as so far the two hundred by two hundred mile section he kept going back over continued to capture his interest.

During his zipping about, Artorian blew through twelve distinctions in the climate zone. He didn't even want to count the microclimate pockets. Deciding this chunk of the planet was going to be the next narrowed-down segment, he went on to check temperatures. At sea level, these averaged around the low- to mid-nineties during the day, while night time lows comfortably hovered around the upper-seventies.

He was using the old texts for the measurements, scribed by a scholar named 'Fahren-hide,' who had been in constant debate with his peer 'Celc of Ius' concerning how to determine heat. Both of them were of the agreement, however, that mercury-based devices to measure these accurately were a scam by the wood craftsmen to inflate the prices of the chairs they kept throwing at one another.

Artorian landed near a summit and held out a hand to catch a wayward snowflake. "*Hmmm.* Warm near the sea, colder at higher elevations? That will give people a range to settle in if the coast is too warm for them. I wouldn't be surprised if frost visited many a night on the more extreme elevations. I'm still fond of the tropical and subtropical climates."

He zipped up and down the mountain a few times, stopping in various places to get a measurement of the temperature shifts. A town near the water could be sunny with blue skies, but closer to the cloud forest, just a few miles up the mountain, might be cloudy with misting rain. He surmised that, as a general rule, temperature dropped about four degrees for every one-thousand feet of elevation gained. "Not bad! Not bad at all."

Tapping his chin, he formed a small barrier against the current light shower that had begun to fall, noting it had been pleasantly sunny before. "I've got the feeling this place is only going to have two seasons. Dry and wet."

Narrowing his search further, Artorian discovered a hot springs, plants that considered people food, insects galore, the occasional tiger, and toucans *everywhere*. Also interesting was how some more primal societies had cropped up already. Bananas and 'coffee beans' seemed to be the goods of greatest value, as roving bands of coconut crabs smuggled them away under the searching eyes of all those toucans. There was also a subset of foxes smuggling silkworms? He'd call them silk foxes for now.

Some sniffing about, and he found an encampment that he was going to generally categorize as 'Palm Pirates,' as they appeared to sustain themselves solely on palm-grown resources. He slapped his forehead when his eyes found the little statues and offering areas to... "Oh, who's even surprised anymore? A coffee elemental? *That's* their faith?"

One of the Palm Pirate coconut crabs, draped in elaborate leaves and shells, imbibed some of the beans after they had been processed into a dark liquid. It bubbled to speak, and Artorian froze on the spot as he could *understand* the crab. "That... that's *Aquatic*. From Eternia."

His memory flashed back to when Yvessa had opened his gift box back during his early jaunt through Eternium's underwater world, right before he met Rip and Tear for the first time. The regional language had been one of the options! He was so surprised to have that come in handy now!

Observing, he heard the coconut crab's ritual while rubbing his own chin. Interestingly, the crab counted as a Beast, because when it drank the coffee, Essence was broken down and added to the crab's Core. "Fascinating. That crab just gained temporary Essence Sight even without knowing the skill."

Entranced by the drink, the crab bubbled out its words. "I, Mathew the Magnificent, can smell the colors! All praise the mighty coffee elementals, and their much more harmless brethren, hot cocoa elementals, for their guidance is as sweet as the speedy jitters they provide. May our shimmies ever elude the unshelled ones, their motley feathers be cursed! Host of the Klik-Klak, the brew is ready. *Imbibe! Bibere!* The smell of colors will lead us to the banana halls, where we will recover the most glorious of coconuts from the oppressive toucan overlords!"

Artorian had to look away when the crabs broke into the brew, needing to rub his brows. "Life finds a way, I suppose. They sure reached sapience fast, though. They're... what? D-ranked Beasties? That's way too early for a case of the smarts. Beast intelligence is... Mage-rank equivalents? Or *was*. The proof before my eyes disproves that idea. One day, I'm going to suss out the requirements and markers. Or is this another one of those Spirit-body side effects? Mind not stored in the physical and whatnot."

Leaving the crabs well enough alone, he checked in on the foxes. Why were they smuggling silkworms? He easily discovered that the silk foxes weren't from around these parts. While the coconut crabs were more local, the foxes were making a long trip with their cargo safely wrapped in mulberry leaves. He surmised their path led from somewhere further southeast, to a destination that aimed northwest. To his continued surprise, the foxes could *also* speak while being no more than D-ranked Beasties either.

Unfortunately, Artorian did not know the language this time, leaving him to scrabble together the pattern of their quiet yipping and growling. Based on some adjacency from Baa and

Panda linguistics, he pieced together bits of their conversation, but definitely not all of it.

From the general flow, one fox was explaining to another that there were three main grades of silk, categorized as A, B, and C. Grade A Silk was top grade silk that could be unraveled without the silk floss breaking. When stretched out, a single silk floss could be as long as a thousand foxes each biting the next in the tail. Grade B silk was limited to short floss, and more likely to clump. The Grade C... he couldn't puzzle out the explanation.

The smaller fox asked something that sounded like, 'Why care about different grades of silk?' The response was that, just like eating rabbit, different grades of silk produce different types of products. Which was for... something about spiders.

Artorian didn't follow that part. The mention of spiders made him think Zelia had set something up, because who else would place value on hoarding sewing materials? That or it was new spiders, but that thought brought Artorian severe discomfort as his arachnophobia suddenly spiked. He was good with Zelia and her kin. Some other broods might not be as... friendly. "I suddenly have a craving to learn Fireball."

His copper metaphorically dropped when he looked at his hand, remembering he could just funnel some Mana. A small orb of celestine flame popped into being above his palm seamlessly, which he extinguished by squeezing his hand. "Time in Eternia messed up my perspective on how to live. That must be rectified. When I'm able, I need to go through all the motions again. I'm in no state to be considered a proper Mage, much less fight as one."

His attention was piqued as the calm explanations of the yippy tribe turned frantic, replaced by running and hard breathing as they sped away from... "Oh, hey. A tiger. Abyss, that beasty is *big* in comparison. It's no Decorum... but nothing really matches my boy."

The foxes didn't appear to do a very good job scattering. Their cargo was too precious, and Artorian had to squeeze his own hands behind his back as the tiger acquired itself several meals. He did not like merely being an observer. The tiger, to his dismay, had also stopped eating and was instead playing with his food. A trait that irritated Artorian to no end, even if he couldn't place the cause.

When the tiger began to display behaviors of overt cruelty, the old man had enough. Letting nature play out on nature's course was one thing—watching malice at play, regardless if directed towards an animal or a person, was too much. As the tiger swiped at the last fox of the set and injured a hind leg for sport, Artorian hovered above the scene ominously, looking down in disgust.

If the tiger so much as looked up, he'd be easy to spot. Artorian wasn't exactly hiding. Rather, he was doing the opposite, as the tiger, too, was speaking. The language was lost to him, but the grandstanding, mixed with claw licking and prowling close enough to the fox to give it a fright before 'missing' a swipe, spoke volumes by itself.

The fox replied, but the words were not what Artorian paid attention to. Clutching its one last silkworm to the chest, the fox clawed into the dirt with the other, pulling itself forwards a few inches. Was the fox... *crying*? Artorian's eyes were transfixed on the scene, as the fox gritted its teeth and looked back towards the tiger with eyes full of spark... Artorian saw the heart of fire, and spoke without thinking. "The soul of determination."

Extending his hand, he decided. This. Ended. *Now.*

Mocking the smaller fox, the tiger raised its claw and prepared to swipe. The fox, not wanting to see its end, looked away. When no further pain came, and no sound of a swipe mauled it into a fine paste, the fox dared open an eye. It felt... perplexed. Motion had ceased. Leaves had paused mid-fall, and not a hint of breeze nor tropical shower raindrops disturbed the scene.

Instead there was a shadow. A vast, mobile, undulating shadow cast down from something above. When the fox looked, it nearly dropped its silkworm. A glorious creature hovered overhead. One massive in length, shaped as a curled noodle. It moved on soft fuzzy clouds of its own making while its glowing eyes bore down, gazing directly at the tiny fox.

The dragon looked to the bodies of the fallen, then back to the fox, after which obvious remorse crossed its facial features. Aiming his gathered anger at the tiger, whose malice had brought forth this scene, the dragon *judged*. Because he could. No. Because he *should*. "**Love** does not abide malice."

Fueling his Mana, Artorian did what he thought was fitting. He sapped the might of the tiger. Its prowess, its grace, its strength, the Essence held within its upper D-ranked Core. All of the aspects that had made the supposedly majestic Beast fall to such wanton pride, believing it would never be punished for its acts.

Rather than keep these sapped aspects for himself, the dragon fueled them into the fox. "Essence to Essence, dust to dust."

Keeping his Mana out of the equation so none of it funneled into the fox, he avoided destroying the creature outright. The tiger instead crumbled to dust while the fox's injuries healed, its vigor restored, and abilities magnified at breakneck speeds. The influx was too much for the fox, who passed out from the stress and strain.

Artorian pulled himself back together from his moment of anger, taking the form of a person again, which he had momentarily lost when unleashing his Mana in such a large burst. Turned out, his base form in this world *was* still a dragon, reminding him that throughout the entire adventure of Eternia, he'd been tromping along in the Long-variant which he'd nicked. Tatum's 'new body' route suddenly seemed a whole lot more appealing.

He landed on his feet next to the dust pile and sole survivor, and a hand-motion gathered and brought all the silkworms to him, which he refreshed with a wave of Starlight Aura and bundled in an oversized mulberry leaf. Tucking that into his lap, he activated Dev's telekinesis knowledge and recovered the remaining fox bodies, laying them out in neat rows before placing the survivor on his lap so he could tend to the fox.

With the creature out cold, adjustments and mending were much easier than if the creature were awake. The influx of Essence had patched the small being up, but had done so crudely. Undirected. A slapdash solution. Artorian wasn't going to accept that when a proper mending could be done.

Focusing his Mana, he reflected on the days of the Duskgrove, tending to a tiny sugar glider that ended up becoming the mightiest of blankets. He then reflected on his words to Dawn, and his regrets. He was just going to have to accept it. "I meddle. I change. *Fine*. Then, at the very minimum… as proper starlight, I will *improve*, rather than *erase*."

CHAPTER TWENTY-ONE

Rica woke in the lap of a statue that hadn't been there when the tiger... *Oh abyss, the tiger*! She leapt from the statue's lap in a full panic, every single strand of fur in full-on bristle. She saw no immediate threats aside from the strange place she woke up, a pile of dust, and... the bodies of her troupe. Neatly arrayed in a line? That wasn't something a predator did.

Even as a fresh addition to the Silk Road route, who still needed to be explained many of the basics, Rica knew that wasn't right. This startled her, as her thoughts were usually more sluggish. Like crawling through the muck. Now her thoughts were clearer, sharper, more easily grasped.

Since there was no deadly predator, and the vicinity appeared downright serene, she checked herself. A memory of her hip and leg being shattered flashed before her eyes, but she was in flawless health. There wasn't so much as a scar on her thigh where she clearly remembered those tiger claws cutting in deep.

Looking back, the statue was of a creature she did not know, sitting in some kind of meditative pose. Tapping the object, Rica recognized the material as the expensive trade good opalite, though that was strange, as this material was not naturally occurring, and especially not with this kind of luster and shine to it. The insides even seemed to be swirling with a rainbow-esque energy she couldn't identify. The sight made her hungry? Not that she could do anything about that right now.

The discovery of the ball of well-protected silkworms nested in the statue's lap brought outright elation to her heart. Not all was lost! In fact, when she checked, the silkworms were all well-packed, the leaves fresh, and somehow seemed to be in better health than when she and the troupe had picked them up from the smuggling location.

Neatly putting the bundle back where she found it, because that just seemed to be a good idea, she moved over to the bodies of her fallen troupe. Not all of them were... whole. A small price to pay for getting to give them funeral rites instead of empty words at a lonely fire pit.

Rica buried each and every one, using some twigs to mark the spots. Digging so much made her paws sore, but even when she'd cut one when a sharp stone had come up, the damage was temporary. Being close to the strange statue made the cut heal, as she, like everything else alive in the vicinity, flourished.

When it was night time, the space around the statue felt bright somehow. Bright, healthy, easy to breathe in, and warm. So very warm. Curling up in the spot she'd crawled out of after her self-appointed task was complete, she barely registered that the statue's head moved to look at her before she passed out.

The opalite hand moved over her form, a wave of finely-tuned Mana grazing across her fur like the softest of brushes. Artorian mused to himself, unable to speak while focusing his energies, like Ember had in the forest so long ago. At least this time, there would be no deadly multicolor rays that made Wood Elves play the dodging dance.

Satisfied with the condition and state of the fox's health, Artorian let the girl nap, now that he had learned she was a girl. Important to get the terms right, or else he'd get flashbacks from the Skyspear academy again, where Great Reader Ezben would get on his case for using 'it' when a 'he or she' was required. Couldn't mix them either, that incurred wrath. Very dangerous.

Gently petting her head, Artorian became aware of a possible new problem. A cauldron of bats had moved into the area, but were suspiciously evading the very edge of his compressed Aura field. Why were bats being lurkers? Being fluent in echolocation, Artorian was also not fooled by their poor attempts to hide that they kept checking the fox's location. Unlike Soni, these bats were bad news.

When another screech occurred, he wasn't having it. He sent back a considerably more potent wave that caused the whole hidden lot to fall from the trees they were hanging from. *Let's see where they flee to,* he thought to himself, their movements jerky and rough as the bats recovered. Before flying... southeast?

Interesti—*Abyss, what the celestial feces was that?* As the bats fled, a flying plaid-striped centipede shot from the underbrush and snapped one right out of the sky, before chasing the rest with a buzzing screech. *Okay, new plan! I never want to run into one of those! Sorry, foxy, you need to wake up. It's go time!*

Empowering the Starlight Aura to wipe the fatigue from the fox all in one go, the opalite of his being slowly undid itself, changing back to more flesh and blood colorations as Artorian attuned himself. Turned out not to be that difficult after changing forms often. A-ranked Mana was a must, however. Trying that with B-ranked Mana would have resulted in a goopy mess. The natural rigidity of A-rank Mana did all the heavy lifting.

Rica woke, shot upright, and flicked her ears around as if she knew something was off. Looking behind her, that opalite statue was now far more alive. The being smiled at her, then pointed in the direction of the still-visible flying centipede. Rica's ears slapped flat against her head, the fox scrambling to get the bundle of silkworms under her arms while trying and failing to get a move on.

Deciding a little help wouldn't be out of place, compared to what he'd already done, he picked up the silkworm orb to the yipping panic of the fox, then yipped back in Red Panda since that was going to be the closest match he had to work with. "Let me help. Lead the way."

The fox looked at him funny, like he'd learned the language from a cub and gotten all the inflections wrong. Which, granted, may not have been far from the truth. The fox replied in proper Red Panda, which was easily one of the highlights of Artorian's day. Someone new to talk to! "I am Rica, of the Sodgi merchant tribe. Did you... did you heal me?"

Artorian replied with a nod, which seemed to translate well enough. Rica took one more look at the flying centipede, whose noisy buzzing had attracted *friends*. Her ears re-flattened, and she had to make a snap decision. Friendly statues won out over hungry corpse-feasters any day. Even if this was her first statue encounter. "This way!"

Rica pointed, but rather than her feet finding floor to scrabble forwards on, the statue-man scooped her up and *went*. Flexing her claws, the fox clung for dear life to the hand that had picked her up.

In a matter of strides, statue-man went from ground level, to treetop level, to *flying* over the canopy like a wingless bird. She had never covered ground this fast! In that terrible speech style of his, the statue asked her a question. "Still *that* way?"

Stretching out her arm to point, Rica bit his sleeve for support even if she was in no real danger of falling off. She didn't need to do any talking, and the trip of months was cut down to minutes. When Rica pointed to a cave jutting out from a vast hill, Artorian landed in front of the opening without a sound, or even particularly disturbing the air, which made a few of the moths hanging around look severely perplexed. Artorian tried to put Rica down, but she was latched to his arm real good.

"Do you speak moth?" he asked her gently, not having much

to go on from this point. "Or do I yip at them and hope to interpret the nuance of wing flutters?"

Blinking to regain her senses even if the only real illumination at the moment was moonlight, Rica eased to the ground, then clung to the grass as if she never wanted to leave it again. When the moths realized they had company, activity swirled as great numbers swarmed the area—'great numbers' being roughly the same forty moths that did their best at trying to inflate how dangerous they were, as far as Artorian could tell.

Not very intimidated by rampant fluttering, he eased down to a knee so he could hand the silkworm ball to Rica. Rica, being *very* intimidated by the hostile display, quickly unfurled one to show the moths while making some kind of trilling noise from her throat. Was that moth? Was that how you *spoke* moth? Trilling?

Seeing the silkworm drastically changed the behavior of all the moths. They all made the same fluttering beat with their wings, which summoned forth a somewhat older, grayer moth from the cave. Artorian stood there, doing the equivalent of thumb-twiddling while Rica and the moth got into the trill-equivalent of a heated debate. One which he couldn't remotely understand. How did you interpret wingbeats and trilling?

Rica, apparently, interpreted very well! That or she just spoke moth, which, given that she was a merchant, was the likely option. Sticking his hands in his pockets, he kept placid and passive as Rica occasionally motioned at him with what must have been an explanation as several moths hurried to bring all the silkworms inside of the cave. They all handled the tiny leaf-wrapped creatures with extreme care, as if the silkworms were worth more than the world.

About an hour later, Artorian had a smaller moth perching on his head, all curious about this creature the young moth had never seen before. The two-legs walker didn't appear bothered in the slightest by the probing presence, fluttering off only when chided by a larger moth as the merchant fox bounded up to him.

Artorian replied to the fox's presence with a smile, and a slight forward bend. "Is all well?"

Parsing his question, Rica interpreted his meaning, then nodded before keeping her words simple. "Trade amazing! Very early. More delivered than expected. Very good health. Moths very happy."

Artorian laughed, which made the creatures in his vicinity backpedal before he replied in his Panda variant. "No need to simplify your words. I can't speak well, but I understand flawlessly. You just speak. I will learn."

Rica nervously rubbed her hands while remaining in a hunched position, her ears pinned back. Artorian could tell she was clearly expecting the other shoe to drop. He was a large creature that feared neither tiger nor moth swarm, could fly, and made the trip of months in minutes.

When the facts were processed, Rica felt like she was in over her head. If he demanded something, she was not going to be able to refuse. "Ye… yes. This merchant task, given to my tribe, was the task of smuggling moth-offspring out of the caves of Fear and Loathing in bat-country, bringing them to safety in this new enclave. This moth tribe had to flee from the war."

Artorian slapped his forehead. "*Another* war? What is it with living things and wars? Egil Nolsen *making sense* is not how I want my day to go."

Rica didn't understand the question, but tried her best to keep small. Before she could reply, the large creature noted her discomfort and sat on the ground, which did help her some. "The big-ear bat tribes eat moths. The big-ear bats and the green-fang spiders currently have a tense alliance, because the moths like eating the things that the spiders make, and the spiders enjoy their silk to work with. The moths have also angered a mighty Wisp, which made them need to flee very far, giving rise to the smuggling work for the merchant group as we traverse the Silk Road."

Rica motioned to the cave. "Sortee, the older, gray one, knows the full history. I just work here. We bring protected caterpillar and pupa variants, and return with pearls that the moths can easily get a hold of. The crows value those greatly, and can fend off the spiders and bats well. The hard part is moving through the contested crab and toucan territory, and evading predators. Which… didn't work so well this time."

Artorian nodded in understanding; those details were not difficult to follow. "Easy enough. Are you well enough to return on your own, or do you want the quick trip back home?"

Rica paled at the thought of another flying journey, but the pile of pearls the moths were bringing out was far too big for her to transport on her own. She didn't want to, but she had to take the plunge. "Can we take the goods for the crows before delivering me to my burrow?"

Artorian beamed, even as Rica really started to feel that shoe loom above her head. "Sure!"

She squinted at the statue-man when he didn't… demand anything. Or try to cut a deal. "Just like that?"

Artorian cocked his head in confusion. "Is there supposed to be more to it?"

Rica couldn't contain her curiosity; that shoe needed to drop. Trade didn't work like this. You didn't encounter a profound being randomly. You just didn't! "You don't want anything? No demands?"

The man ran a hand down his beard while he gazed at the moon. "*Hmmm*. Not really? If you're a merchant group, I'd be happy if you could drop by when I get my family installed near the coast of where I found you. Currently, I doubt there's anything in this whole world that I want. Save perhaps to see more demons dead, but that's far above your head and not something to barter for. Gather up your goods—let's get you on your way."

Rica refused to argue. She adamantly stepped on the thought and kept the gift firmly in her paw. Dropping by a society where there were more creatures like this one? Lucrative! The reward she was going to get from the crows alone would guarantee the families in her home burrow would flourish tremendously. Worth!

The next set of events happened like a blur to Rica. She arrived at the Grand Crow's nest and delivered the pearls. Explaining the situation went very smoothly considering the haul, and the palm-leaf pile of dull Beast Cores she got out of the transaction made her eyes bulge. Minutes later, she stood bewildered in front of the entrance of her burrow, a hoard of Cores piled so high next to her that the loot eclipsed her in height.

When one of the family wandered outside to see her standing there with a thousand-yard stare, she was mobbed by the entire family. Each spilled forth a thousand questions. Rica barely heard them, having watched the statue-man *walk into the sky*, and jog off. Her parting act had been a blessing by her one last brain cell.

She'd asked the man's name. "Sunny," he'd said.

Find him near the coast. "Hard to miss," he'd said.

Rica didn't want to miss that trip for all the rabbit legs in the whole world. That evening, her large family mourned, feasted, and rejoiced all in one night. The balance had tipped! Tigers were no longer one of the top three scariest things in the Realm of Green Eternity. Instead, now that top spot was claimed by a new species. The 'human.'

Rica wanted to meet every last one.

CHAPTER TWENTY-TWO

Artorian stood on the coast as the sun rose, wondering why the sand was black. "Volcanic influences? Probably. So, quick tally. Negative rep with green-fang spiders and big-eared bats. Positive rep with silk foxes, razorbeak crows, and limelight moths. I doubt the news about the tiger will get around... No, no I might as well tally negative reputation with all the tigers. Good going, Artorian. You're not even here a day and you've meddled, set up a possible trade route, and gotten on the bad side of at least three species. *Outstanding*."

He thunked his forehead harmlessly against a coconut tree, and caught the coconut as it came down without needing to look. He cracked it open, then downed the contents before groaning at the flavor and looking away with displeasure. "That's terrible! Why is it sour? Why is it *sticky*?"

Choosing not to pursue that line of questioning, he tossed the coconut entirely, using some Aura to clear the flavor away while pacing up and down the coast to find a good spot for a starter village. "Where is some nice open ground to slice in a canal?"

Instead of cutting into the ground, Artorian decided the

natural outlet of a river was a better bet. Walking up along the bank, he found a nice open spot that was nothing but rocky outcroppings. "This could be a nice flat section of smooth rock. What is this stuff?"

Kneeling down, he ran his finger over the stone and gave it a lick. No magical knowledge appeared in his mind, and he was no Dwarven rock hound. "Well, I have no idea! Glad nobody saw that."

He pressed a hand onto the ground and flattened the whole area by fielding his Aura, which dropped the energy like a heavy coat to compress and squish anything around him in a clean, several hundred yard radius. Grass, ground, rock, and trees alike pulverized down to nothing. Then the debris washed outwards from his location as if a common liquid, leaving behind only beautiful, level ground. He picked his Aura back up, and needed to do a physical shimmy to get the coat back on *right*. Then he remembered how difficult this must be for people not used to fine Aura control. "Oh, right. Henry and Marie still struggle with this. Can't say that's a surprise, given the type of skill needed."

He practiced twice more, dropping his Aura only to pick it back up again. This compressed his new floor some more, but that was fine, as the rock attained a glossy surface by being squished repeatedly. "The coat example is very on the nose. If the coat needed to be a perfect, smooth fit when getting your arms back into the sleeves, any loose deviation and the Aura sloughs back off and tries to re-field itself. If those two have been letting it hang all this time, then they might need to use those new bodies just to get a hang of it. Even with the requisite knowledge, the application may be too late now."

Bouncing on his toes a few times, he used the last bounce to fly into the air and hover over his very basic handiwork. That, in hindsight, was some quality application in the art of being a Mage. "I should name this place. Let's see... I met Rica here, and I'm at the coast... the Coast of Rica? Sure!"

Tapping his chin, he frowned and created a ball of Mana.

"Now that I think of it, was this always so easy? I don't recall having such precise control. That's worth a quick experiment."

Shaping the ball into a dancing figure of Dawn, the effort and difficulty quickly made it clear that his hunch was correct. "Alright, that's *considerably* easier. My A-rank Mana is acting with very little input, and is responding to guidance like the energy outright loves me."

A small epiphany struck him. "Didn't I have that as a title in Eternia? Mana Loved, or something? I wonder if that somehow stuck with me as well. In that vein of thinking, what's my current refinement technique?"

He glanced inside by meditating momentarily, and noted the presence of the impossible shape. He turned his attention towards his seed Core, and then checked the box that his solar gyroscope was still chugging along at full force within. "*Hmmm.* Should I try and swap them somehow? Does it... does it even matter if I am going to start all over as another iteration of Merli?"

Rubbing his chin, he shook his head and dismissed the thought. "A problem for later. When it becomes time to consider transferring over, I'll tackle it then and there. That golden Core idea still strikes my fancy... I should tinker when I have the chance."

Clapping his hands together to focus himself, he decided now was as good a time as any. He contacted Occultatum through a forum connection by knocking on the proverbial wall as if it were a door, and Tatum responded by sliding out from the void and physically appearing next to him. His voice lurched. "You raaaaang?"

The Incarnate felt like some of his joy had been stolen when the old man didn't budge. "Not even a smile? A small one?"

Artorian winked. "Was expecting it, ever since you mentioned that you're pranking for fun. Is anything else needed to get the decanting process going? Otherwise, I'd like to start with Don and work my way out from there."

Tatum's face went flat, but instead of quipping, he snapped

his fingers as if he'd been caught. "The Modsognir Dwarf? Yes, we can do that. The testing was all done with Odin's people, though I will admit they're acting a little strange. I expected a raucous society full of noise and spunk. Not whatever they're currently doing. All military, no fun. Just… why?"

The Incarnate shook his head. "Forget it. If he goes the elitist route and builds some kind of oligarchy, everyone else will slap him down. There's work he's good at, but that prideful oaf couldn't rule well even if his precious pride depended on it. He's all orders and no leadership."

Shaking his head in disappointment, Tatum began to weave spellforms instead. "Enough about that. How do you want the Modsognir? Young? Old?"

Artorian tapped his chin. "Any chance we can decant him into the last form he remembers using? Causing the least amount of jarring experiences? Probably the best for everyone, honestly."

Tatum blinked and stared a thousand yards in the distance. "Yes… that is… *so obvious*. We've clearly been doing that this whole time. Yes."

Artorian dropped his hand on his forehead while Tatum experienced metaphorical sweating. "When was the last time you slept?"

Scratching the back of his head, the Incarnate pretended he didn't need sleep, but the look in Artorian's eyes betrayed what he already knew. If Ammy needed sleep, then Occy did too. No matter how much less of it he might need. Artorian fussed like a grandfather. "After decanting, you nap. Those Chosen of yours take very good care of you, and that soup was blessed."

He chuckled, amused. "Heh, soup for the soup god. Alright, old friend, nap after decanting. Grace can tune the rest of the Pylons now that the activation sequence is powering up. Ammy and I can afford to check out for a while with other supervisors here. Eternium is not at risk of an outbreak. Adam does amazing keeping the fear in the demons, so sure. Hades will go hole up in his underworld. Well… moon."

Pulling up his sleeves, Tatum rubbed his hands together before snapping his fingers. A tiny Wisp popped in to help. "Genevieve, dear, the second verse is the same as the first. Get ready to breathe some life into these spellforms as I pull them into being. Ready?"

The vibrantly purple Wisp twirled and landed on his head, already knowing what she needed to do. Shaping was what a purple Wisp excelled at, after all! With a tiny, childlike voice, she chimed in her readiness. "Set!"

Artorian did his part by locating Don's memory Core on his personal wall, and teleporting the gem into his hand while providing the third and last part of the three magic words. "Go!"

The follow-up happened too fast for even Artorian's senses to track. The physical spellform appeared nearby, much like the variant Halcyon had calmed, though the form appeared to be an echoed copy of the original, rather than remaining a set of complicated interlinked runes. The form blobbed into the shape of Big Mo, the Modsognir Don, one of the two great Patriarchs of Dwarvenkind.

Color filled in after the shape settled, which held all of Genevieve's attention. Artorian felt a little awkward, just standing there and watching the shaping occur. Occultatum, on the other hand, needed him to do his part. "Toss the memory Core in!"

Not certain he'd heard his friend right, Artorian jerked and made an incomplete motion, then performed it again to follow through, tossing the memory Core into the still-forming body of Don. That final touch stabilized the entire affair as, with a sucking *pop*, the spellform vanished entirely. Effects, breezy air, warmth and all. Leaving in its place a glaring, scrutinizing, look-ing-for-something-to-be-mad-at Dwarf.

Classic Big Mo.

"Ah. *Just.* Told ya ta make the place as good as ye can… Artorian, why ya lookin' thinner than an exhausted vein o' pyrite? A wayward wind can break ya like a wee dry twig." Not sold on this transaction, the stocky Dwarf searched around. The flattened area didn't look right. "Am gonna wager a whole vat o' brandy that it's been a bit longer for ye than it's been for me. I'll sharpen my axe on yer noggin later. What h—?"

Don's words cut out as a square, glowing prompt caught his eye. He frowned at the hovering panel, pointed in its direction, looked between the other two people present, and found both of them equally dumbfounded by the contents. "A'right. *What?*"

Tatum reached out and tapped the panel, then turned it towards him with a finger so he could read the message properly.

Error: Task failed successfully.

Since the humans were each holding their chin and forehead, respectively, Don figured that the mystical, strange little message was a problem. He just didn't get which kind of problem yet. Therefore, he decided that this new issue wasn't remotely as important as his current predicament. "Oi! Answers! Now!"

Artorian shared a glance with Tatum, who was making successive motions of pressing his hand to his face. Each showing that he was going to say something, then reconsidering every time. When he paused by biting his knuckles, he pointed up at the moon. "I'm just... gonna go see what... *Yeah.* Genevieve, do you have it from here?"

"Sure do!" The Wisp was clearly not at all bothered by either the contents of the message, nor the message having popped up at all. "Have fun!"

Tatum popped out with the sound of a soap bubble breaking, vanishing without any fanfare, while Artorian rubbed his temples and attempted introductions to the new world. "Right. Well. Don, old friend, welcome back once more to Cal's Soul Space, the safe haven we took everyone to in order to survive moonfall. We're at the point where we've gotten a planet together and... can we walk while we talk? This is going to take a bit."

Grunting, the Dwarf fell into step and made a 'come along'

motion as he began pacing across the edge of the decently round, flattened ground. The glossiness of which he momentarily inspected with amazed interest. Listening to Artorian laying a motherload of a vent onto his stocky shoulders, he slowly got the information that he needed to understand the new predicament. Luckily for his human friend, there was nothing the Don could not shoulder. For he was the mountain, and this news was but pebbles.

Genevieve happily bobbed with them, settling on Artorian's head to be along for the ride. She didn't have anything to do until more decanting needed to happen, so made her own entertainment while the lanky one gabbed and the stocky one got his bearings. Artorian was only hit a minimal amount of times, with Don grumbling back grudge-flavored commentary as they circled the space for hours and hours.

When all was said, the Dwarven Patriarch understood the purpose of the nose-bridge squeeze, choosing to perform the action while holding his elbow with the other hand. "A'right. That settles 'er. I'm going to need *two* axes for this pyrite."

CHAPTER TWENTY-THREE

Big Mo raised his hand, starting a count on his fingers while his eyes sternly chastised the willowy human. "A'right. I don't know what'cha had planned, but I'm changing yer plans, and I don't wanna hear no *pish*. First, bring in Hadurin. The new Patriarchs need a huddle. Second, ya said ya flattened this whole area? Stellar. Ya get to do it some more! Walk the perimeter for a wee bit and get ta expanding. Do five laps; I want a nice an' chunky spiraling circle. Three, when you're done, ya stand there on yer wee feet and look mighty pretty 'til I tell ya who and what we need. Four, git!"

Artorian put his hands up and moved his eyes upwards to address the Wisp. "Genevieve, can we recover more individuals without Occy here for the first part of the forming?"

The Wisp gained some momentum via bouncing on his head, then bounded off after gaining enough height so she could fall smoothly right into a chipper hover. "They're all meant for Wisp use. Each of the formations were designed specifically so we could do them in big quantities if we had to. Unlike 'Occy,' I will need the memory Core first if we do it my way. He already knows who you're talking about. I don't."

That was the most Artorian had heard the hovering Wisp speak, and he frowned a moment to point at the spot Tatum had been in. "Did you talk all overtly happy for…?"

"Mhm!" The Wisp sounded pleased-as-punch. "Wisps in my faction have decided we are here to help, and Occultatum has a soft spot for the innocent. It brightens his day when he gets to dote on us, and the Court of Spring is all about causing smiles. You're more of an 'I will carve my own path' person, with a severe helping of 'but I want to know some details of what's going on,' and your actions are already recorded in the Murals of Wisp History that you *can and will* get whatever it is you think you need, so helping you directly is the better choice."

Artorian blinked, pressed a hand to his chest, got a swift glare from Big Mo, and walked away to be less of a problem. "I… *Huh*. Alright then."

Acquiring the memory Core of Hadurin from his wall with minimal effort, he handed the precious item right over to Genevieve, who pulsed bright colors for maybe half a second before the fully formed effigy of Hadurin *whooshed* into being without the addition of an error message. The Dwarf in question blinked his confusion away, then looked around with a solemn question. "Wasn't we… in the middle of a fight?"

Big Mo, the Modsognir Don, slammed into his clan-brother with a hug so fierce that local bears suddenly considered adopting the Wood Elven scoring system. The judge would easily have given an eight out of ten on the hug-slam scale, acceptable even to snooty aware-bear judges.

They shared no words at first, and by the time they did, Artorian had given them privacy by walking to the edge of the current flattened space. He'd chat with both later, knowing well that for them, some family catch-up time came first. He mused out a question for the first. The first of many. "Genevieve, are you going to be alright if I field and start walking?"

She replied by settling back on his head. "Now I will be!"

Nodding, he let his Aura transform and roll out, then began

his meander. "The spellform didn't come into existence when you did it. Hadurin sort of just..."

Genevieve let him trail off. "Occy was being flashy. If you do it *right*, then the spellform doesn't even manifest. Tatum just wants to watch the world learn. Also, if you give me access to your wall, I can handle the transfers better. Then you won't need to teleport the memory Cores in one by one."

Artorian puzzled. "How?"

She giggled. "You just tell me I can. Wisp are... quasi-omnipresent here? It's the social rules and their thousand complications that keep us in line. Since you're going to want to ask, if you want to know about Wisp society, you're going to need to be a Wisp for a while. Other topics are easier to talk about."

"*Hm.* Very well. You have permission." Wandering forwards as his Aura flattened the landscape to true level, since he had little else to do with it, Artorian groomed his beard while compartmentalizing the information and questions. "What happened to the big rule on not sharing information?"

The Wisp beamed with mischief. "The Spring Court's stance on the matter is that the rule is hilarious. Withholding information from the person whose mindset we've modeled our rules around? *Preposterous.*"

The old man closed his eyes and needed to stop. "And... who is this person?"

"You, silly!" Genevieve cackled, supremely amused, as Sunny sighed and kept walking. "The Wisp factions are broken up into the four seasons. Each is a Court. Kind and well mean-ing, but clever and unyielding? Spring Court. We're in cahoots with the Fall court, inspired by Amaterasu, even if on the surface we act like we're opposed. Summer and Winter courts have been around for ages, and they're as they've always been. The whole 'Seelie' and 'Unseelie' division just wasn't working for most of us anymore."

Artorian replied with a raised eyebrow.

She formed a tiny fist just to shake it. "The Seelie were the

Wisps in a good mood because they had dirt on others and were 'winning' the social war. While the opposition was everyone being grumpy and grumbly that they were being stepped on, because those effects can last horrendously long. Not even Wisps are keen to give up an advantage, and a lot of bad apples began to enjoy getting a kick out of 'being better' due to the contrivance. There was a heavy stigma on the Unseelie always being malevolent, but who wouldn't be when you get treated like dirt for *no reason*! Forever! You fail to pick an Essence-lock *one time*, get caught, and the story haunts you until your light fades."

She hissed. "Unless, of course, you can turn it around and find dirt on *them*, turning the tables and starting the whole cycle all over again."

Artorian let her fuss, equally as interested in letting her vent as he was in the finer workings of inner Wisp society. The whole topic reminded him of tangled kelp. He watched the clouds move in the sky while on his lengthy stroll, nodding along to Genevieve, who was doing to him what he'd done to Don. Being a good listener for someone who needed to talk.

He was pulled from his musings by Big Mo's booming voice. "Oi, beansprout! Ya lose track of time? Any more loops and you'll be carvin' a bigger hole in the side of the mountain than that overhang can handle! Pick up yer flattenin' effect and come look pretty. We figured out what we be needin' on Nidavellir!"

Artorian blinked. He hadn't realized he'd been pacing along with Genevieve, who seemed equally surprised at the amount of time which had passed. She settled back on his head after having bounced off to fume, then the duo hopped on Artorian's tiptoes back to the middle. He wanted to know what the new word meant. "What's a Nidavellir?"

Hadurin slammed into Artorian with a Dwarven hug, then jumped up to smash his forehead against the man in greeting. "Say hello first, ya codge—Ow!"

When Hadurin landed back on his feet, he was the one holding his forehead and wobbling about uncertainly, like he'd just stepped off a boat after a long voyage on turbulent waters. "Sweet pemmican and pyrite, what are ye *made* of? Me 'ead feels like a cathedral bell!"

"Ha! Knew ya couldn't stop yerself!" Big Mo bellowed with laughter, throwing his head back. Recovering, he turned to face his old friend. "A'right! I explained what's goin' on, and it don't take no novice tunnel digger to see ya be starting from an empty barrel. The plan goes like this. Pay attention."

He waited a moment for Hadurin to recover, so the second Patriarch could list off what they'd settled on. "My head still sounds strange. Tis good ta see ya, Fringe Myth. In short, we want every Dwarf currently 'Cored.' I'm getting an explainer on that later. All the refugees from Mayev, and any wayward rescue. Every last one ya got. We're naming this place Nidavellir, the new homeland of legend for all Dwarvenkind!"

Both Dwarves stood proud, and Big Mo continued. "Once we've got enough people together, we're going to kick the machinations straight into high gear. This place is so chock-full of Essence that it feels like ya woke me up in a *dream*. The ground under my feet looks to me for direction, and I feel like I can make anything here. Any building! Ah feel it in mah bones. The earth not just be whisperin' here, she be waitin' for us with open arms. Pleadin' for change. She keeps asking for the same thing, over an' over."

Artorian asked with interest, not so attuned with earth Essence. "What does she say?"

Both Dwarves moved their hands together, forming a rainbow motion above their heads while they spoke in unison. "Art. Deco."

Hadurin showed his teeth during his smile. "We're gonna hollow out some mountains. Build labyrinthine underground cities that would leave anyone looking at the surface none the wiser. We'll tap into magma veins for brand new forges, and craft our own hot springs. Then, when we do build structures for all to see, they'll be the kind of constructions that'll go down in myth and history."

Big Mo beamed, his hands rubbing together as his eyes shone with glints of metal. "An' all of it—*all of it*—will be glorious Art Deco. We're gonna make this land so happy! Even now she be givin' us ideas for designs on a silver platter, and they be *beautiful*, Sunny. *So beautiful*. Sumptuous. Elegant. Bold! I don't know what a 'radiator building' is, but I'm making twelve! With... I'm gonna add trains. What are *trains*? Don't care, I'm doin' it! Not the boring ground floor kind either... Skyrails? Definitely skyrails. They can go through the buildings!"

With his two Dwarven friends slowly losing themselves to some kind of 'communing with the earth' trance, Artorian waggled his digit to get the Wisp's attention. Not that he needed to whisper, as the Dwarves barely seemed to notice he existed while the metallic sheen in their eyes intensified. His friends muttered about 'aesthetics' or something. "Genevieve. Do you even need me to be here with access to the wall?"

"Sure don't!" came the chipper response. "I'm looking over it right now. There's only one or two strange Dwarves in here? Who's Tussle, and his missus? Those two have Dwarven shapes, but their base creatures are... hedgehogs? Do I full-Dwarf them?"

Artorian slowly felt a bit of pride rise. "You know what? Yes. Yes, please do give them both full Dwarven forms, and could you pull them in right now? I'd love to finally apologize."

He scratched his chin while Genevieve began to prepare, considering his absorbed-in-thought Dwarven friends. "Perhaps... best not to decant my close family in the vicinity of my old friends. They'll get swept up."

A Nixie Tube lit up above his head. "One moment. Didn't I *wake up* in a copy of the Fringe? Why am I even going around looking for a home when there was one ready and waiting?"

He slapped his forehead, then dropped his hand to recoup his dignity as a familiar old face appeared before him. Easing both his hands behind his back, the thin old man pressed both his arms against his lumbar and smiled. "Hello again, old pal.

I'd love to keep your attention for an explanation, but I'm going to gently request that she goes first."

Pointing at Tussle's missus as her decanting finalized, the dazed and confused Dwarf recognized the old man, then turned to see the life of his heart. Abandoning reason, their arms collapsed around one another, the reunited pair squeezing for dear life before Artorian turned his back to them for a moment of privacy. He didn't wish to intrude on their affirmations and kissing, raising a shimmery field to cause obscurity.

He figured everyone had different priorities immediately upon being decanted, and it wasn't his role to dictate otherwise. Tussle would make time for him when Tussle had the time. A thought struck him. "Genevieve, I modified their memories so they wouldn't remember all the awful things. Right?"

"You sure did!" was the part of her reply that let the old man relax. The part that tensed him up came thereafter. "Shame we had to undo all of that. They remember everything, I'm afraid. Including past lives. My skill in decanting just isn't good enough to allow for cherry picking. I can add, not subtract. I'd... I'd give them a moment. Sorry, Sunny."

Covering his eyes with his hand, he wondered how to make it up to them. Momentarily, he recalled an explanation from Yvessa on creature life in Eternia that felt applicable. "So much for my plan to give the chickens *only* the good chicken life."

A hand pressed to his shoulder, surprising Artorian as he'd been doing his best not to pay attention to the events behind him. Startled and turning, he was caught off guard as Tussle faced him while trying to keep his expression steady, eyes full of waiting tears as the younger Dwarf managed out a broken response. "Thank ye."

Artorian drowned in confusion as his worries swirled, his hand taking Tussle's when he found no better retort "No. I... You. I'm responsible for..."

Genevieve landed on his head, which felt surprisingly calming. "When I said they remember everything, I *did* include that you rushed to save them as soon as you found out."

Artorian couldn't see the Wisp's wink, too focused on shifting his Aura to one of comfort as Tussle's missus slammed into his open side, squeezing him for dear life as well before she hiccupped through her emotions. "Thank ye for bringing him back to me. That means the world. This incomplete life was my favorite, now that I remember them all. I'm so glad I can finish it, with my most favorite person. *Thank ye.*"

At a loss for words, Artorian gently squeezed them both, and didn't ask a thing.

When the two Dwarves were well and good, they talked with the old human, who dropped to a knee to be of even height. Turned out both were mighty pleased with being reunited, not having to return to the Svartalfheim they knew, and getting a fresh clean slate to start from.

The moment they heard the other two stocky powerhouse Dwarves near them were going to build a brand new society, Tussle and Ferra, his missus, excused themselves with sudden burning need. They hustled off to Hadurin and Don to warn them of the past dangers and technology they'd had to deal with, including all the problems those tools had caused. Aether Advancements in particular were not blessings, they were mistakes!

Mistakes that should *not* be repeated.

Artorian smiled at the lot of them, then gave Genevieve a one-finger high five since her hand was so tiny. "I… Thank you, dear. I was so worried, but it seems they were far hardier than I. Will you be alright pulling the rest of their old civilization down?"

Genevieve brightly nodded, putting the old man at ease by flashing red and making a motion as if she were busting through a brick wall. "Oh yeah!"

CHAPTER TWENTY-FOUR

After a swift detour—to inform the Sodgi merchant tribe and extended family that plans had changed—all Artorian managed to do was confirm Rica's tales: that he really could fly, and that the 'Humans' could be found elsewhere, while 'Dwarves' would be taking the earlier spot near the Coast of Rica. The name made half of the fox family faint! They'd gained land? *Land?*

When he arrived in the new version of the Fringe once more, Artorian took two hours pacing up and down the whole place, sniffing out points of interest before realizing he'd left Genevieve with the Patriarchs, and couldn't decant right now. His eyes narrowed. "Or *can* I?"

He steepled his fingers and tapped the tips together, scheming for only a moment before ethics kicked him in the chin and broke him away from those thoughts. "Occy did tell me not to play with the spellforms, and I'm not Dale... I suppose I'll listen this time. *This time.*"

He'd need to wait for either Tatum or Genevieve to be ready, anyway, so he found a nice rock to drop his soul-pillow on, flopped it down, then fell face-first into the soft plush fluff while wondering about the game plan. "I could see about punting a demon? No, Adam's on the case and he's having trouble finding them. Shall I perhaps destabilize Odin's regions? His society looked like a militaristic mess that I really don't want to deal with… but I kind of *should*. Aiden *did* tell me not to garner his attention…"

He rumbled, crossing his arms. "I'm terrible at being a Mage, currently. He'd beat me like a toad trapped in a bag. The likelihood that he's been resting on his laurels is also… minimal. Two centuries head start here, plus however long in Eternia and before?"

He made a sound of discomfort. "That's a lot of experience he has over me, and time is a big factor in—"

Artorian jumped from his pillow when a group of war-geese drum-struck the ground nearby without warning. He'd been drifting away, but his landing calmed to a solemn float as he eased back into his cozy pillow dent, like a feather rather than a rock. Most interested at the sudden interruption, he raised a brow and laced his fingers, watching a flop-eared lapine girl pull a pair of dirty goggles from her face.

Didn't he know this one? "I remember you, my dear. Soup for the soup god, I believe?"

Freeing their war-ladles, the entire group shoved the shiny domes to the sky, repeating the chant before re-sheathing their choice of weaponry, and essentially confirming they were who the old man thought they were. Occy's chosen had done that whole species-shift thing again. Artorian thought he'd been repeating himself lately, but on inspection, those weapons— much like the shells on a stick in Poseidon's faction—were a *choice*.

The half-lapine, half-human wiggled her nose, grooming herself right away when the sensation of being covered in moon-dust got to her. Vanilla spoke just as he recalled her doing in the Elysian Fields. So the voice remained unchanged even as a different kind of being? Interesting. "That's right! You can recognize us even when we're not in the forms you met us in?"

Artorian quietly motioned at the very obvious mode of

transportation. "Hard not to notice the gosling gang. They rumble loudly, like they're all looking for a fight. As for your forms... Alright, first off you're all terribly dirty, let me just—"

Mobilizing his Starlight Aura, he cleaned the lot of them up in one fell swoop. This calmed the geese as well, who shook their wings and tottered about, their source of discomfort removed. "There. Now you're clean. I wasn't expecting to be dropped in on. How did you find me in the middle of nowhere?"

Vanilla shifted to her half-fox, half-human form instead, then smirked a wicked grin. "Turns out someone in our biker gang really wanted to come see you. Refused to take no for an answer! Speaking of, I better signal that we found you."

Sticking her finger into the air, she shot off an air and water Essence firework. Which blew up in an interesting combination of greens and blues.

Artorian didn't follow. "Biker... gang?"

Vanilla chuckled. "Short for *Bickering* gang. We all argue a lot. Even though we're all on the same team when it comes to the matter of those abyssal Full Metal Goats."

Munch stepped forwards, also as a half-fox, while shaking his fist in the air. "We spent a lot of time making those cans! How else are we going to start the soup store? Then they just come in and start chewing on them like wayward grass! We—"

Munch was unceremoniously nudged out of the way as one of the geese pushed right on by, inspecting Artorian for two whole seconds, then flapped up to his lap and bundled in to sit, leaving the group to stare at the goose in abject confusion. Artorian glanced down, shrugged, and pet the goose without a second thought.

He was reminded of his C-ranker days in Morovia, where he'd been informed that wildlife deeply enjoyed his Aura types. Seeing no reason to deny them the small kindness, he let the effect radiate freely. While this flocked the rest of the geese to his side, the old man didn't mind. "Pardon, my boy. You were saying?"

"Watch out beloooooow!" a feminine, mellifluous voice yowled from above as Voltekka, Artorian's Teslasaur from Cal's testing round, slammed into the ground hard enough to bounce and scatter all the freshly-calmed geese, who were now in one honkin' big uproar! An actual roar from the *significantly* larger dinosaur made them reconsider their impending flight of the quackeries, forcing them to scuttle in a hurry.

On Vol's head, another half-fox was holding on for dear life to the improvised reins they'd tried to fasten on the dino. Though, the quality of the reins solidly ranked in the realm of 'an effort had been made,' and appeared like they'd been subject to extreme friction. They just about fell apart in the rider's hands, which removed the last vestiges of her ability to stay mounted.

Scout, an important-looking fox, was thrown off from Voltekka's head when he performed a mighty shake. She landed casually on her feet before berating the beast. "You big feathered lug! What is *with* you?"

Much like that first goose, but with considerably more enthusiasm, Vol slammed the entire top of his head into Artorian's chest, who caught the 'big lug' with ease and doted on him like a long lost son. He even baby-talked the hefty dinosaur without any thought of how embarrassing that looked to those watching him. "You big sweet baby. I'm so glad you're okay! Last I heard, you tried attacking one of Cal's wire-tears like a big doofus. Are you a big sweet doofus? Well, you're definitely big and sweet, aren't you, boy? *Aren't youuuuu?*"

His hands rubbed all over the Teslasaur's plumage-covered head, adoring Vol while molding Aura to give the hefty dinosaur some good and proper back scratches between all those feathers of his. Vol made all sorts of happy dinosaur noises, rolling over several times until he ended up on his back with all his paws in the air, tongue lolling.

Munch pressed a fist to his mouth, then cleared his throat. "I was just saying that the Full Metal Geese, our biker gang, has personal problems with Full Metal Goats. An actual species of goats that lives on the moon. That place was designed entirely for kids! Then, ever since the demons came back, suddenly we had a goat problem. They rudely began eating the place! One of them in particular has our ire, who claims to be the greatest of all time? *Very annoying* bleater, and a particularly nasty keister-biter. Wagner, Mozart, and Beethoven have decreed a symphony order on all their heads. The social insult just could not stand."

Artorian needed to blink and keep his eyes closed far longer than normal as he tried to process what he'd just been told. "I'm... going to need a minute."

Scout brushed her well-fitted cloth and leather attire off, which Artorian noticed matched the rest of the group, including all the members who he didn't know yet. With the second group arriving, the Full Metal Geese easily numbered over two dozen riders.

Scout spoke when she found herself cleaner much sooner than expected. The moon dirt sloughed off her attire like repelled water thanks to the Starlight Aura. "Oy vey. That's the look of a person who walked into a shop too big for his purse. You mind telling me why my ride decided to outright rebel, and is now paw-praising the sun?"

Artorian frowned deeply. "My adopted *son* is not a mere *ride*."

Vol replied with a croaking noise, which made the old man look down. "What, my boy? Do you like this one? She's good to you when not in a bad mood?"

The violent, electric waggle of his tail was retort enough, causing Artorian to drop the growing hostility due to word use. "Alright, alright. I'm just glad to see you again, Voltekka."

The dinosaur whined out long and slow, making the old man resume his adoring rubs. "Hmm? What? No, of course I'm not going anywhere. I'll be here for a while. I've got things to do! Even if I can't recall what those things were supposed to be at this moment."

Vol exhaled hot, static-charged air into Artorian's chest. The old man nodded while all the onlookers watched with confusion. He... Could he speak dinosaur? "Of course, my boy. I'd love to see how fast you've gotten!"

The Teslasaur scrambled to his feet, ran a few excited circles, then stared right down at Artorian as the old man got his affairs in order. He recalled his pillow, made sure his Aura got all the new particles cleaned, and then pressed hands to his hips to look up at the eager saurian. "So. Am I zipping along like last time and following?"

Vol hissed vehemently, and even the half-foxes could tell that his guess had not been what the 'saur wanted. Okay, so he couldn't speak dinosaur? But then... *huh?* Artorian rubbed his long beard, pointing at Tekka's back, an act that made the hissing stop and tail-wagging resume.

He was going to make another comment, but frowned and squinted at Vol's forehead. "Where's your crystal crest mark? Didn't I give you a blessing? You've retained the zappy-zap, but I can't feel a connection with you at a... *Ooooh, right.* You happened during Cal's little nudge back when I needed to make fussy baby Bribri get some shut-eye. That non-iteration. That effect may not have taken place properly. *Hmmmm.*"

"Oh well! No time like the present for a do-over." He clapped his hands together, then considered the pattern so far. "Zelia was... Argent, for silver. Halcyon received Aurum, for gold. Yuki ended up with platinum. That conveniently leaves copper for you! I recall the metal being a great conductor."

"I should tell Frank, if I see him again. Might be a useful idea for his trains, since they keep being mentioned." Hovering up, he touched a finger to Vol's forehead. "Blessing of Aeris!"

The Teslasaur blinked, but felt no different at first. All the physical changes had already been done, but new clarity did build as crackling light in his eyes when **Love**-law connections slowly bloomed into being. Properly this time, as a copper sun formed on Vol's forehead. "There we go! Might take a bit, but maybe we'll see some higher order thought develop. Oooooh, I'm so excited!"

Vol blinked at Artorian, who waited with bated breath only to be met with… silence. Not one change occurred. The old man rubbed his brows, then walked upwards in the air as if it were a solid staircase, sitting on Vol's back as one would a horse. "There, happy?"

The Teslasaur exhaled static air from his massive nose, then crackled with copper-colored lightning, which made the half-foxes in his vicinity scramble for their mounts. They revved the quacks on their geese into gear before shouting in unison. "To the fields! War honks for war crimes. Cry havoc, and let loose the dino-goose of war!"

Artorian wondered why there was so much copper electricity, rather than delving into the meaning of the biker gang's outcry. "Hmm… Isn't this crackly effect what you tended to do shortly before exploding off into the *dista~a~a~ance!*"

His sentence had meant to be a question, but trailed off into an exclamation as Artorian gripped Vol's feathers. The big doofus happily recreated what it had been like for Artorian to run in Eternia. At Mach two.

The old man cackled madly, so terribly proud as they broke the sound barrier with that good ol' boom. "Faster, Vol, *faster!*"

Voltekka replied with a war-honk, which rippled across the landscape and scared off whole leagues of wildlife. His attempt at a goosy cry came out more as an empowered full-bellow roar, but it was the thought that counted! After that, he broke into Mach *three*, utterly trampling anything underfoot as Voltekka became responsible for carving a brand new road through a birch forest, devastating anything else that might have been in his path.

"Oh, I get it," Artorian mused. "*To the fields*. Because he plows!"

CHAPTER TWENTY-FIVE

Artorian sang a happy tune while Voltekka showed off his ludicrous speed. His hands, meanwhile, found which sets of feathers to grip when he wanted the Teslasaur to turn, which became mighty helpful to his newfound urban planning project! "Country roads, take me hoooome! To the plaaace, new roads belooong! From the Fringes, to the Coast of Rica, passing the Dwaa~*a~a*~arves!"

The old man laughed with glee, interrupting his own song as he remembered the need to breathe. He'd not expected the line of geese behind him to so neatly follow along. Each of the war-geese drifted in tow from the speed of the one before it, as Vol trekked along at a very cozy Mach two. The trailing riders were nearly right on top of one another, but not once did a speedy goose step on the feet of the one behind it, or in front of it.

The sight also explained to Artorian their need for goggles. Both for the rider and the goose! Vol, honorary goose who needed no goggles, led the charge and set the speed, allowing the rest of the feathered conga line to power-waddle along. Given that all the riders had huge dirt-eating grins on their faces, Artorian surmised they were all quite enjoying this. "Ha, here I am just carving roads from place to place!"

Paying attention to the dense forest in front of him once more, Artorian grinned and gained some devious ideas. He really *should* be practicing how to be a better Mage while he couldn't do any decanting. He was having a good time making Vol happy, but why not do both? Why not! What was being a Mage even about? Self-control?

Trying to remember the difference between Aura and Presence, he recalled the peculiarities soon enough. Changing your Presence made your perspective expand with it. The space of his Presence *was him,* whereas an Aura was just layering an effect on the edge of his bodily contained Presence, allowing it to radiate indiscriminately.

Artorian adjusted Vol's heading slightly before doing any preliminary testing. Delving into the ways of Magehood while distracted was a great way to get things wrong. "On second thought, I should shelve this for later. Trader foxes were that way."

He glanced over his shoulder again, doing a quick count of the half-foxes in tow behind him. In addition to having found something to do, Artorian had the strange suspicion that all these people—animals? He honestly didn't know their base forms— were all currently choosing to be a fox for some kind of reason. He bet that introducing them to the foxes he knew would definitely score him an easy answer. Straight up asking didn't *feel* right in this instance. So he decided not to press the matter, settling on an older axiom. "Patience is the hardest thing to cultivate!"

With Vol endlessly overjoyed at running through the forest to show off, occasionally snapping up a delicious tiger for a snack, the Teslasaur was not in the slightest bothered at the redirections! He was happy as a hunter to do the dinosaur equivalent of 'look, Dad, no hands!'

Artorian was proud, and Vol could feel that through the connection; a sensation that filled the dinosaur with a vast sense of warmth and accomplishment. When approaching a ravine, or other impassable bit of terrain, Vol jumped, only for the geese behind him to zip right over him, grip some part of him with their paddle-y feet like iron clamps, and keep soaring along in a 'v' formation.

The old man looked around before commenting, rather impressed that Vol, as honorary goose, was getting flight help. "Isn't this a *delta* formation?"

Scout looked down from her temporary mount, positioned conveniently close so she could sketch in more details on a rudimentary map. "*O-ho*? So you know of the fabled delta?"

Artorian quirked a brow. "Yeah?"

The fox smirked, and the old man could smell the mischief when she spoke. "Do you know why one side is longer than the other?"

He didn't know where this was going, so played along. "No?"

"It's because there are more geese on that side," Scout said before her grin broke apart in a set of giggles when Artorian released a mighty groan, needing to close his eyes and cover them with a hand as Scout praised the source. "*Hehehehe*. Praise Cal, master of the one true pun."

That mention snapped Artorian from his pun-inflicted wounds. "One moment. You know of Cal?"

Her giggling died down slowly, amusement replaced by confusion, then consternation. "Oh. Right... We aren't supposed to talk about—"

Squinting one eye, she shot the old man a second glance, then said a word he recognized, but sure didn't like right now. "Inspect."

Artorian felt no different, and while he couldn't see what information Scout currently perused, some quality *hmmm*ing later made her gesture with her paw dismissively. "Well. I guess there's no problem then, though you could have *warned* us you were the fabled, one and only, mythical *Administrator*."

Artorian replied with his own squint. "Didn't I give up that title?"

The fox shrugged, the playfulness clearly vanishing. "That's not what your sheet says, boss! Your screen not only has you tagged as Administrator, but you've got so many more privileges than me that I couldn't even *see* most of your information. You've got a whole slew of multi-colored adjustments in there. Wisp, Gnome, Eternium, and even Cal entries! Here I thought you were just another Dreamer! I'm just glad I didn't get slapped with a surprise audit."

Pressing a hand to his hip, he adjusted his pose to look up more easily. "Explain?"

"Well, I don't think I'm *allowed* to say no, and since rules are everything to us helpers, we tend to stick with being lawful. Or I do, jokes aside." She rubbed her forehead now that the fox was out of the bag. "I'm Jess, and I go by Scout, because my role this time around is being a scout. The last time it was being a Merch-Ant, because I made merchandise."

Opening her jacket, she flashed some kind of badge. "You can think of me as a second-wave of Chosen. I, and most of my kin, are early-entry spellform beings that successfully came into existence during test phases. We're still looking for a good title or designation. Occultatum helped get most of us into the shoes of our new life, since we are all, without exception, the continuation of a person that used to live on someone's personal memory Core wall."

She closed her jacket. "We don't have the same creation story as the Chosen, but we are working with what are essentially nearly identical strengths and weaknesses, so we just went with the naming convention. We're all animal-based at heart, but we've got human souls, and in some cases, a full working copy of the human memory that came with it. We're just not… them. Or at least I'm not."

Checking to see if he was following, Scout was pleasantly surprised to see the old man taking her lecture in stride without much difficulty. So she kept going. "Because we all got the early-bird special, we also became privy to a lot of information we honestly weren't supposed to know. It quickly became easier to just include us, and let us help, than the alternatives. So we were told about the iterations, the multiple game worlds in the other Cores, Cal, Dani, and such. We all made oaths to Cal, and now we're helping out where assigned."

Artorian tapped his lips, suddenly no longer feeling like it was a bad time to ask. "Is that why the entire group went with being foxes?"

Scout released an amused laugh. "Ha! No, we actually have a rule in place that makes us need to adhere to the race of the highest common denominator in the area we plan to be. In this region, that's foxes. We actually came from the rabbit area, in case you saw some of us with lop ears. All of us second-wave Chosen have the equivalent of the game trait 'Shifter,' meaning we can be any race, at any time, so long as the species is in the 'approved' list. Which is a backup Pylon that keeps track of the ten most numerous races. When the numbers shift, so do our options."

The fox pointed up at the moon. "While we're having a good time at the moment, our objective earlier was to bring some order back to the farm, which is the in-joke we have for the moon, since the place is populated by Hel-cows, Hel-geese, Hel-gators, and Hel-goats, rather than the children that place was supposed to hold. *None* of those four species are supposed to be there, but with Hel now being the planet's core, they had to go *somewhere*. We… We have a lot of work to do, and for much of it we need to be very mobile."

Artorian motioned at the geese in response. "Any particular reason?"

Scout grumbled almost incoherently. "Vicious triangle. Geese beats goat, goat beats 'gator, 'gator beats geese. So, y'know. It's a beet farm?"

The Administrator shook his head, not following the joke. "As in, you're growing moon-beets up there. Or, you just really need to get away from these 'gators'?"

Scout nodded viciously at the latter mention. "The cows are the only thing up there not bothering anyone, and even those out-speed us in a footrace. Moon-gators are no joke! The name is short for alligator, though they could be crocodiles and we'd not be able to tell. I've only seen a Deinosuchus once from afar, and I do not want to be anywhere *near* that thing. That massive toothy monstrosity swims through solids like water, but *mmmmm*, the tail's *delicious*."

Artorian thought this an excellent time for a question that just struck his mind. "Did Cal leave any instructions for what to do with the place? Now that his world is a proper planet, I mean?"

The fox made an 'X' with her arms. "Standing orders from the before-times, I'm afraid. Occultatum told me 'just let the place run,' and, 'like iterations, what needs to be replaced will be replaced, and what needs to be kept will be kept.' The Spell-form Attack Squad is here to make sure that iterations keep happening, and nothing gets too horribly out of hand. Like the current case with the moon."

She considered the designation attempt, didn't dislike what she'd just come up with, but still felt it to be lacking. Scout then flashed a merchant's smile, cheekily relaying a thought. "Now, that isn't to say that I'm not interested in not gaining a good reputation with the *esteemed* Administrator. So if there's anything you need help with, the Full Metal Geese would be mighty interested. We've heard tales that the Administrator of myth always wore all the *best* attire, and I for one would love something warm and attractive. It's cold up here."

Artorian noted that, due to his Aura, he wasn't feeling any of the normal regional discomforts that others might. Running a hand down his beard pensively, he nodded. "I believe that could be doable, and yes, given that this iteration is the one where I will be decanting family, I believe some additional trade would not be misplaced. I *was* hoping the existing merchant foxes I met could set up some kind of trade route between the locations where I'm plunking people. Could you perhaps assist with that venture? The route from the Fringe to the Coast of Rica is… admittedly, *pretty far.*"

He then recalled she'd been cheeky. "Also, how about Spell-form Air Superiority Squad? That shortens to *sass*, which is what you're giving me."

"I… *Hmm.* Not bad. Let me confer about that idea, and the other things." Scout leaned over to another rider for some conspiratorial whispering, and Artorian tried real hard to pretend that he couldn't hear every word as if she were shouting across an empty room.

When Scout turned his way again, a most innocent smile was plastered on his face. "Well? Come up with anything?"

Scout glanced back to the group as a whole, who all nodded to the plan they came up with. "The route from the Fringe to the Coast, while almost complete, would be far too long of a trek for the local silk fox group to handle. The S.A.S.S., on the other paw, would be far better suited! We have seen the great fountain of the red bull, and come with wings. How does a five hundred personal reputation investment sound?"

She mused, reconsidering what she'd said. "That double 'S' isn't working out for me. S.A.S. would be far better. We'll work on it."

Artorian had no idea of the value of reputation, and now realized they hadn't been pulling his tail when he'd overheard the whispering earlier. "Is there some kind of chart for what that… means? I've got knowledge of bartering and old world coins, but this reputation thing is new."

Scout procured an intricate, rolled up scroll. The item reminded the old man of his youthful days, where old ancients would scribe upon wall scrolls that hung between sticks of incense.

Unfurling the scroll for some study, Artorian discovered a remarkable plain and simple X to Y conversion. "Let's see here. One hundred reputation to request an item or basic service from an individual. Five hundred for a group. One thousand for a legion. The cost of the deal doubles for each difficulty step above how 'basic' or 'easy' the deal is, and deals cannot last longer than the span of a year, should they entail a duration."

He pondered, rolled the scroll up, and returned it. "The complexity levels were Basic, Advanced, and Difficult, while the ease of action chart ranged along Easy, Complicated, and Impossible. So I take this to mean my request to facilitate trade would count as a basic and easy task, intended for the size of a group. Therefore, five hundred reputation? One hundred, times one, times one, times five."

Scout accepted the scroll, beaming at the Gnomish math knowledge displayed. "So quick! I like you already. That's right! There's two ways to use reputation. 'Request' and 'Requisition.' Requesting happens when a person or group wishes to gain reputation with you, and make a deal. So in this case, we would gain five hundred points of reputation with you, in return for a year-long deal for us to play trader. 'Requisition' allows us to run to you if we have a problem, and return this reputation to you at double cost of whatever task we ask. Except that you *can't* say no. That's what makes 'requisitioning' different. Consider the system 'Commodified Favor.' Also called CFC. The third 'C' means currency. We're considering using just 'Favor.' There's an ongoing debate as to which one we'll stick with."

"I'd just use 'C' for convenience, in reference to the whole idea. Seems easier to say Five hundred C." Artorian puzzled while adding his two coppers, but was fairly certain he'd gotten the system down. "I believe that, if you were to then request this clothing that you would like from me, I would say, calculate it at two hundred reputation? Which means my number would drop from five hundred to three hundred. However, if you requisition the clothing, that two hundred becomes four hundred instead? Leaving you with one hundred Reputation on me."

Scout disagreed with the first part, but agreed with the second. "Almost! If I request the clothing, you would gain two hundred reputation with me, specifically. However, I would still have the five hundred with you. Whereas if I requisition the clothing, you would have no reputation with me, and my reputation with you would drop to one hundred, like you said. Requisitions are enforced, like mini-oaths that won't kill you. Requests are not."

Artorian tapped his fingers together. "Doesn't this mean you could have giant reputation pools with people?"

Scout nodded. "Mhm! That's sort of the point! Occultatum says there were different bonuses for having a high reputation with someone, but the Pylons might not be active? We haven't encountered any yet. Something about 'a high reputation means high cooperation, and goodwill.' Or whatever he means to try. If it doesn't work, we'll discard it and go with something else. Maybe Eternium will try an improved version on some Dwarves."

The old man smirked. "This is *Occy's* currency system?"

The geese riders shared a look, but affirmed with some nods even though they were a bit confused at his sudden inflection. Artorian giggled in response, refusing to believe that Tatum would have implemented this method without some other motivation. "Well, why didn't you say so! Let's give it a test run. I accept. Deal!"

CHAPTER TWENTY-SIX

The S.A.S. arrived with fanfare. Mostly because it was easy for Vol to build up speed, but the same wasn't true for slowing down. This forced them all to circle a few loops around their destination in order to drop their momentum and velocity. When Vol and Artorian managed to come to a standstill, the geese riders were already socializing with the Sodgi.

The third meeting with Rica and her family quickly devolved into barter and trade the moment it became clear that 'all the new foxes,' which the fabled human had shown up with, were an extension of their own profession and responsible for trade routes in regions they'd simply never heard of! This also explained why Rica's elders had not been able to find this 'Fringe' that the human had mentioned on any known cave map.

The matter had almost become a rather heated problem, but the ruckus turned out to be short-lived. Artorian was the only one of the whole lot of them not as subject to the burning needs of water, food, and sleep. His Aura certainly helped, but a two-day power trek on Vol had tuckered out even the copper-feathered dinosaur! The colors of which had come into full swing over the course of the journey.

Given the option was available, Artorian chose to involve himself in the small feast, providing some Mana-powered conveniences. Including the snore-filled siesta that followed. Eating an abundance of good food made everyone tired! *Tubby*, and tired. That and Artorian's Auras may have played a small part in assisting the snore-fest. Shifting them ever so minutely was good practice, after all.

When thinking of what to do about the brand new circle around the Sodgi settlement, he drifted off. He was nudged awake by Scout, who only had to prod him in the arm once for his eye to peek open and look at her. *"Hmmm?"*

Jumping away two whole feet with an outburst of expletives as she fell on her keister, she grumbled, and dusted herself off getting up. "You scared me!"

Doing a hefty stretch, but finding the sensation was lacking as a Mage, Artorian copied her actions and got up as well, as he noted that the sun was out. He'd slept the whole day away, but was going to pretend that had been planned. "Did you need something, dear?"

Finding her composure, Scout stuffed her hands into her pockets. "Oy vey. Yes. Right. We're all wrapped up here, but there's nobody in the Fringe to currently bring any trade or supplies to, so we're sitting on our paws. We're all going back to the moon shortly, and just wanted to fill you in. If you are able to use forum calls, just let me know when you've got your people set up, and we'll come around. Also, your year-length deal is ticking, so if you want to wait a few months to set up, then we will not say no to the free Rep!"

Her teeth shone in the light, but Artorian didn't fall for the cheeky ruse. Instead, he saw the card she played, and upped the ante. "Very good. I'll go get my things settled then, and will call the forum. No senate use?"

Scout scowled, her ears pinning down as she learned the

Administrator held a better hand. "We can't *use* the Senate. We can only be *invited*."

The old man smirked, testing his connection and finding he still had very good access to that function. "Oh? *Unfortunate*. Well, should I open one, you're welcome to attend. I have the feeling I'll be doing so once I'm in the swing of things."

He said nothing when Scout stomped away, aware she'd been trying to show off by implying that she could use the forum feature. He mumbled to himself "To this day and age, those features must be something special. I'll keep that in mind."

Trotting over to give a fast-asleep Vol some well-deserved head rubs, the dinosaur hissed at him from being woken unduly. A quick slathering of sleep Aura, and all those grievances were forgotten right away in favor of some heavy snoring sounds.

Hovering into the air after putting his copper boy to bed, Artorian called his foray into basic road-making good and done. Then he flew off to the Fringe while attempting to open a forum connection. His attempt to contact Tatum was rebuked with static, so Artorian surmised he was either busy, or the Pylons were broken. That newly re-engaged system likely had its fair share of bugs.

Trying again with Genevieve, he had to guess Tatum was merely busy, because the Wisp's voice connected to his mind right away, even if they could not see one another, or exist in the little semi-communal mind space. <Well, this is a meager shell of its former glory. Voice only? For the forum?>

Genevieve sent through her amusement, since her cheeky grin wouldn't transfer unless seen. <I heard the forum feature used to be pretty amazing. I'll add mending those Pylons to Occy's to-do list. I was pleasantly surprised to get a ping! What do you need?>

Artorian beamed at how uplifting she sounded. The lass felt genuinely happy to hear from him? How nice! He could see why Tatum was so fond of the behavior. <Would you happen to

be free for more decanting? I'd like to get my personal family placed in the Fringe. I'll arrive shortly.>

<We finished yesterday. Mo and Hadurin would not take '*stop*' for an answer until *every* Core, holding *any* Dwarf not currently in stasis in Eternia, was decanted in Nidavellir. There's thousands of them, and they already had an entire brandy hall up last night.> Her voice then dropped, suddenly tired. <According to them, it's not 'a good life' unless there's something to drink! Even housing was less important. Then again, there are no real natural threats near them on Caltopia. Other than the decanted, there are no creatures above the D-ranks.>

<Caltopia?> Artorian questioned.

Her reply consisted of a sound that didn't translate well, but the old man took it as confirmation. <There's no official name. Unless you want to go with Zeus' naming convention, who insists the world should be called Gaia.>

Artorian squinted and frowned, his tone questioning. <Was he trying to get into someone's good graces again?>

Genevieve cackled, her mood lifting. <He failed so badly with Amaterasu that he used the Soul Space planet's naming convention as a preventative move. Occy is ticked, but refuses to say anything.>

The old man pondered, landing in the Fringe. <Because Odin came up with it? I doubt he'd be against naming the planet after his sweetheart.>

The Wisp popped in next to him, ending their forum conversation so they could speak more normally. "That's about how it went. I've suggested taking the credit for the naming convention, but if anyone checks the logs even waywardly, they'll know it was Zeus."

Artorian pressed his hands to his hips, turning to face her. "Why Zeus, and not Odin? You keep using the first one."

Genevieve bobbed to shrug. "Officially, we're neutral when it comes to politics between supervisors. So we all use the names people want us to use for them. Unofficially, I would call him potato-face. He's such a *spud*."

The Mage howled with laughter, bending backwards as the purple Wisp smirked, proud as a peacock from her jab being so well received. Waggling his finger while shaking his head, he righted himself to clasp hands together. "I liked that. He was such a meatslab in Eternia. Shall we get started then?"

Genevieve performed a stylistic twist. "All set! Who goes first? I've got access to the entire wall. There's quite a number of people, but they're not organized by importance, and I don't know who is who. I've got them separated by Dwarves, Fringe, Bards, Mountaindale, Skyspear, and Others. The first category is sorted, even if there were side-effects with Rota and Dimi."

Artorian blinked. "What happened with Dimi-tree and Rota? I remember the latter making those explosive dice that scattered the feral version of the Gnomish race. Dimi was responsible for saving my keister on the way out of Ziggurat."

Genevieve tried to create a prompt, surprised when a screen actually popped up. "Oh, that worked? Great!"

The first image in the prompt showed a massive Iron Redwood standing tall and proud right on the edge of that clearing he'd flattened. Artorian found it interesting that, while structures had begun rising from the ground around that plaza, not a thing was being built on the glossy stone clearing he'd flattened. Was that intentional? Had Don just needed a flat open square for something? "Maybe it's a town square. Well, *circle*."

Moving his attention to the topic, he saw what she was pointing out. Leaves of embossed silver, bark streaked with striations of coal, and, according to the notations, the tree had roots of titanium. "What in pyrite's name is *titanium*?"

A label made clear that the tree *was* Dimi, with a little note attached that said: 'Escalated to Supervisor.'

The second image was one of a fine-haired, small-clawed otter sitting on the shoulder of a stocky Stone Dwarf, where both the otter and the Dwarf held the 'flex' pose, arm muscles rippling. To Artorian's amusement, it was the blonde-bellied otter who was labeled 'Rota.' Here he'd expected Rota to be the Stone Dwarf, given his love of exploding rocks. Ah, who was he kidding, otters loved a good rock too!

He wondered how they felt about Wubs.

"Alright then. Should I be able to look at that issue later, I'll see if I don't have access to the to-do log. For now... let me consider decanting order." Artorian simply couldn't choose who should go first. Even after standing in place for five solid minutes straight and inspecting the ground, he came up dry. "I suppose I'll go by the rescue order? First my Wuxius and Lunella. Then Astrea, Grim, and Tychus. Followed by Jiivra and Blanket, Tibs..."

He paused. "Vivi, who else is on this list? I don't suppose you would have a prompt? I like prompts. They're well organized."

The purple Wisp's bobbing ground to a halt, her colors flickering ominously between reds and oranges. She corrected him sternly. "*Genevieve*. Vivi is a nickname attributed to that *slimeball*, Invictus."

Artorian backpedaled in a hurry. "Genevieve it is! You've no desire for something shorter?"

Receiving a glare in retort, her colors restored to their prior hue, returning to her effervescent demeanor as the Wisp calmed down. "I've a preference for something shorter not being used. Touchy subject."

Nodding in understanding, he pressed his arms against his lower back. "That's how it is then."

Satisfied, Genevieve dismissed the prior screens to replace them with a few smaller ones, each positioned next to the other to denote a difference in category. "Here's what I've got."

Category: Bardic College
Kinnan, Pollard, Jillian, Meg, Ash, Maeve, Moza.
Category: Mountaindale
Amber, Ian, Exem, Craig, Snookem Bookem, Emilia Nerys, Father Richard Demonsbane, Raile, Snowball.

Category: Skyspear
Alexandria, Astrea, Jiivra, Blanket, Razor, Ali.
Category: Fringe
Irene, Jin, Tarrean, Tibbins, Lunella, Wuxius, Tychus, Grimaldus, Ra,
Bastet, Hathor, Osiris, Set, Anubis, Ptah, Isis, Ma'at.
Category: Other
Alhambra, Wo'ah, Surtur.

Artorian felt he knew who… most of these people were. "Going to be honest. I don't recognize a few of these, nor do I have any idea how they got on my wall. Abyss, Surtur is one of Dawny's chosen ones! What's she doing in there?!"

The sound of a volcano exploding in the distance pulled him from the prompts. Artorian looked away from the prompts, mesmerized by the heated electrical storm on the horizon that poured into the sky with streaks of red. "I'm sure that's just a coincidence. Well, nothing to see here."

He calmed over a few hours while getting his mental plans in order. He was about ready to move on to enacting plans, but not before something far more important caught his attention.

A pod call from above widened the old man's eyes, his vision shooting skywards to catch the sight of a gorgeous, building-sized, black and gold orca sliding through the sky. The majestic creature barrel-rolled like twisting through a silent sea, then sped right for him.

Artorian smiled broadly, his arms opening wide so that when Halcyon turned into her human form, she could slam into him with wild abandon. The old man didn't feel the smash, but let himself be propelled back by the thundering impact regardless. He came to a stop while still very much on his feet after they dug two line-straight divots through the ground. "Cy! You wonderful darling! It is *so good* to see you!"

Enveloping the eight-foot-tall lady in his oversized construct form to give her a proper hug, Artorian felt elated! In his mirth, he'd missed that something had jumped off her back before his chosen one had cannonballed into him. A thumping sound caught his attention. He peeked his head out from the side of the hug as Hulk, Yuki's favorite Rock Squirrel, slammed into the ground near Genevieve with a three-point hero landing. "You brought a friend! Did your nose tell you I was here?"

Halcyon beamed, then giggled and failed to speak while mushing Artorian into another hug, allowing Hulk to casually stroll up and answer some questions. "Actually, she heard from the Full Metal Geese network that they had just gained Reputation with the Administrator."

Hulk smirked in squirrel, then crossed his arms to embellish the tale. "Our fearless leader over here blinked twice when she was told, then flipped a table while mid-conversation with Dregs and Mu, giving them such a jump scare that they both popped a volcano."

Halcyon made a pleading noise, but that only spurred Hulk on. "She shattered the hinges off of seventy-foot-tall gates, and broke the entire drawbridge getting out of the stronghold because it was raised. There's a suspiciously *Orca-shaped* hole in the middle of the bridge now."

The squirrel shot her serious side-eye. "The only reason I am here is because I was *on the other side of the main-hall door* which Cy smashed through like a Phosgen who'd just smelled cheese. Have you ever seen a three-foot thick steel bend like warm butter? The door didn't even slow her down! Now there's an impossible-to-lift crumpled metal paperweight laying outside our front entrance. Guess who's gonna have to clean *that* up?"

Halcyon flushed and looked away, making the old man think that this tale… may have not been very embellished. This sounded like Halcyon. This sounded *a lot* like Halcyon. His thoughts then turned back to the volcanoes… "Say, those volcanoes you mentioned. They wouldn't be near—*bwoooh*—a new region named Nidavellir?"

Hulk raised an eyebrow at Halcyon, who stoically refused to meet his gaze even the tiniest bit. It was Dreamer time! Yes. She wasn't at all hiding her face in the crook of his neck. This was a hug!

Hulk didn't bite. "I know you can see me looking at you, *echolocation* girl."

Cy puffed up her cheeks, replying with a childish glare when she finally turned her head. Hulk ran his paw down his face, then sat on his massive, fluffy tail before addressing Artorian. "I'll make some forum calls."

"I'd say that when I'm done, my people would call your people… but"—he glanced at Halcyon squeezing her Dreamer tight, and knew the truth—"we *are* your people."

CHAPTER TWENTY-SEVEN

When Halcyon calmed enough to speak, she became a powerful chatterbox. Her hand kept morphing between fingers and a fin from how excited she was, but Artorian kept a fine hold of her regardless, sticking nearby to listen to her talk and talk while Hulk made his calls.

The bulky squirrel's work ended up hampered by Genevieve being *enthralled* with his fluffy tail. When he pressed her on why, the answer had been something along the lines of 'I haven't decided on my first species shift yet' before she continued being enamored by the concept of fluff.

The news from Halcyon was nothing earth-shattering, nor something the Administrator hadn't already found out somewhere else. Spud was being a pain, many inner workings needed attention, a moon war. Just another day in the office, really. He mentally scribed it all down, more interested in Cy's happiness in conferring the news than the news itself. So he of course pretended like it was the first time he'd heard any of this!

The attention and occasional questions made her feel wonderful, and the enthusiasm shone right through her glossy skin. The gold on her gleamed, and he didn't say one word about the endless hand-holding. If Cy wanted to hold his hand to gossip, gush, and gab after not seeing him for a whole iteration, then by the crumbliest of crackers, she'd get to!

Couldn't let those grandpa skills get rusty!

He once again received confirmation that Zelia and Yuki were sleeping the iteration off, and had left explicit directions and orders not to be bothered until they woke up themselves. Artorian knew better than to pull a Loki with those two, and resolved to let them be.

When the topic of Artorian decanting people was brought up, Cy needed a few minutes to compose herself. The anticipation of meeting her Dreamer's family made her bubble over into a full Orca form, and she needed several sky-swimming laps to calm down. When she landed, Cy managed to fix everything except her tail.

She wiggled her behind, then again with more gusto to it, but the tail wouldn't budge. Pressing her hands into her sides, she looked behind to frown at her behind. "Great for hip-checking my enemies through walls. Terrible for fitting through tight corridors."

Artorian tilted his head to glance, then looked back up at her. "I'm not seeing the problem, dear."

Cy pointed at her tail. "That's not supposed to be there in my human form."

"I wonder if I can still use Astral Celerity's Restoration feature." Artorian rubbed his chin as he pulled his Presence back into his previous, lanky old-man form. He poked the end of her tail and gave it a whirl. "[Restoration.]"

He hadn't expected the bracket speech, or to drop down to A-rank five, but Halcyon promptly glowed! She grew a whole foot in height, lost the tail, and felt a whole lot better. She gave a massive, toothy smile that reminded the old man of Rip and Tear.

Cy felt elated, and the mirth shone in her voice. "That's *such* an improvement! I didn't even realize I was a whole foot shorter than I should have been!"

Artorian copied her toothy smile, and when he looked up at her now, he saw flashes of Tychus from the Ziggurat days, posing in that equally massive, infernal-Essence freight-train frame of his. Halcyon did a little jig, and Artorian recognized it as the dance all the way back from when Yuki was still too shy to be in the original Jotunheim pagoda with them. What a splendid lightshow of a party that had been.

Regardless, his thoughts wrenched right back to his Fringe Sproutlings, and that must have shown clearly on his features as Halcyon's demeanor changed from a bouncing youth to a knowing matron without any warning. Her hands pressed to his shoulders, taking a knee so her nose could bump the top of his head. "Your face looks haunted, my Dreamer. What troubles you?"

Artorian touched his own cheek, then looked up. "Is it that obvious? Here I thought I had my feelings under control. It's… it's the decanting, dear. I have been so looking forward to this moment, yet have been forced to put it off so many times, that now I am dreading the event."

He turned to look at Hulk, who was running away at full speed on all fours, from a very demanding purple orb who was 'gently requesting' he gave up some of his tail fluff for 'study.' "Don warned me. Make the place as safe as it can be. As real as it can be. Am I supposed to ignore that little hole in the ground Spud is putting together? Do I blind myself to the knowledge of just how many demons I failed to lance out in space? Even with Adam hunting zealously, I know they're out there, somewhere. Scheming. Biding."

He squeezed his own hands. "Now here I stand with the knowledge that it's decanting time, or bad things happen to Cal. Given I have a direct deal with him that's… going to last for far longer than I thought it did, I don't know whether to feel like I ran out of time, or that I didn't do enough of what I could with the time I did have."

Halcyon laid her chin on his head, which didn't bother the old man in the slightest. Not even when she spoke. "You have done the best you could with the time you've had. Which, subjectively, hasn't even been twenty years for you. Subjective time has been far, *far more* sporadic and lengthy for others. I will turn five hundred in a few weeks."

Artorian observed her in shock as she lifted her head, but said nothing. "Yuki has at least double my time, and she refuses to be out of the action when Odin is active. This iteration the timing simply didn't work out. Her rest was a necessity for her health. Yuki did take great pride in the fact that she is now able to say someone 'is a thousand years too early to face her.' She got a chuckle out of the saying."

He tried to bite his tongue, but failed. "…Zelia?"

Cy provided her hands to squeeze. Since she seemed to believe he would need it, Artorian did not fight, and accepted them when she spoke. "Zelia… without dungeon Core memories, is about… twenty-thousand-ish? As a dungeon Core base, her perception and ability to live without deviating from who she is, is far stronger than ours. If you were not aware before, my Dreamer, that is one of the ways we have been carefully rationing our waking time."

Artorian choked on air and needed to press a hand to his chest. "Twenty th—that's *without* dungeon Core memories? Never mind, I should have listened to Occy's advice and just not asked. It was a mistake. I don't want to know."

On the plus side, the surprising trivia fact had knocked him out of his unpleasant mood. "You're right, Cy. I did what I could with what I had, and now it's just… time. My thoughts on who to decant first are all scrambled again."

Halcyon soothed her Dreamer, trying to be helpful. "Well. It would likely be best if you only had to explain this world once, and then trust that person to relay that news to everyone else who comes after. Do you have anyone like that?"

"Lunella." Artorian had no hesitation. "Irene would keep her feet under her as well, and not budge. She's a Morovian woman. They stare down ligers, slap them, and say 'bad kitty' without flinching."

Halcyon laughed heartily, a sound that was very welcome. She swatted him on the back, and supported him with an enthused smile. "Do that then!"

"Genevieve?" Artorian loved some clear guidance, and called the Wisp right away. "Do you have a moment?"

The purple Wisp appeared at his side, a basket of packed fur hovering nearby. Further away, Hulk looked savaged, his lower lip quivering as half of his tail had been plucked. He kept repeating assurances to himself. "It'll grow back. It'll grow back."

"Ready!" a chipper Genevieve replied. "Who first?"

Artorian decided not to address the basket. "Lunella and Irene first, please."

The old man gripped Cy's hand tight as the people appeared before him, now that the Wisp knew who was who thanks to having wall access. Genevieve was efficient, and additional practice only seemed to make her faster. When the adult Lunella, Matron of the Fringe, blinked her eyes open only to realize who was standing in front of her, she said nothing. Instead, Lu firmly stepped forwards to squeeze the air from his lungs as hard as she could.

That she didn't get anywhere with the attempt was not important. Artorian gently copied her hug, and let her decide when it was time to let go. Granny Irene, on the other hand, had no such heart-wrenching needs. Her eyes instead locked on the woman twice her height, sporting arms thicker than trees. When Cy attempted to say hello with a handshake, Irene stared her down, then used her entire hand to shake one of the Chosen's digits.

It hadn't occurred to Artorian beforehand just how massive Cy was in comparison to 'normal' people, but the view really hammered the concept home. He'd been using his Aura constructs to compensate for the size difference, but that wasn't an option for a non-Mage like Irene. Not that the woman seemed bothered? Irene instead had the feeling of a large cat about her, looking at an equally large toy that she was definitely going to attack and roll around.

When Lunella let go, she took one big breath, then knew this place wasn't her home. The area looked like it, sure, but she *knew*. The details just weren't right, and she understood the Fringe salt crystal by salt crystal. The scent of which was sorely missing from the general area. Instead, she focused on what was important. "I have *missed you*, grandfather."

Artorian tried to keep his face from streaming tears, because this was going to be a long set of reunions. "Likewise, my dear Lunella. It has been so... so very long."

She looked him up and down, then her watery eyes and weak smile slowly bled away to a frown. "Have you been forgetting to *eat*? You're skin and bones!"

"Ha!" He wiped his face with the back of his hand. "I'm a Mage... well. You're still a non-cultivator, so that won't make much sense. Yes, I suppose I could do with a proper meal."

Artorian turned, amused at Irene's antics when she started to growl. "Irene. Trying to glower Halcyon down into a corner isn't going to work. I may have gotten you over a wall with my original rail-palm, but Cy will hurl you across the continent and make it look easy."

Irene's eyebrows shot right up, and only when she turned did Artorian notice she looked like a granny. A D-ranked cultivator granny, but an elderly lady nonetheless. "So? I know prayers that look to have more bite to them than this small smooth-skinned mountain. Am I supposed to back down just because she's large? Did you forget where we came from? I've seen taller bluegrass. You..." Irene rounded on him, then prodded him right in the chest with a stern finger. Though, rather than commence one celestial lecture, she fell silent as her eyes twinkled. "You're a Mage? An actual... honest to the scriptures *Mage*?"

Given Artorian didn't see her spill a non-existent lunch all over the floor, he surmised there was a way for other cultivators to tell without Essence cycling, and aforementioned side-effects.

"Good eye! So you don't feel too bad, I'm significantly older than I look, and I have *much* to explain. A-rank six, by the way. You can stop squinting."

Irene sputtered. "A Vicar? You're at Vicar-rank?"

Needing to repeat himself, Artorian just nodded, then left Irene to stare off into the distance to cope as he returned his attention to Lunella. She had questions, just not the same ones that Irene had. "I don't know much of anything about the cultivation nonsense, no matter how much Grim and Ty swear by it. Can I expect them to be with us shortly?"

The old man smiled, then sighed proudly. "Always knew you kids were something special. Indeed you can, your own little ones included. Come sit with me by the bonfire. I have a lot to explain, and would prefer you both managed to explain it to the others as Genevieve and I bring them in."

When his mention of the Wisp was met with silence, rather than the quip he expected, he looked around to see both Hulk and the Wisp missing. A glance at Halcyon and her expression was enough to be reminded that Wisps had rules, and Artorian was an exception to many such otherwise hard lines. He was sure she'd be back shortly, and would ignore more of those lines, springing some shenanigans. *"Pah!* Spring Court indeed."

When they all sat, Halcyon and Artorian spent so long explaining that Lunella and Irene needed to sleep for the night, and resume in the morning. Cy procured them all breakfast, but Irene cooked it, rebuking all attempts to help as she claimed that she felt 'sore,' and that the activity would limber her up.

Neither of them chose to say anything about Irene having shot up two ranks in a single night from the purity of Essence in Cal's Soul Space, with D-rank nine clicking in during the middle of her cooking preparations. She wasn't even actively cultivating! Wasn't that supposed to *not* be a thing, or did Cal's approval have some sort of safeguards? He'd need to delve into it later.

She served the stew with bewilderment in her eyes, all her Morovian-inspired hostility with Cy forgotten in favor of news, information, and secrets. Because where the *abyss* had that bedridden old man brought them? Were they all dead? Was this the celestial plane? Even the grass she lay on was a goldmine for her cultivation.

Breakfast had threatened to throw her into C-rank zero! She was gazing off at the clouds, holding her meal rather than eating it after finishing but half. Her voice was a whisper. "I'm not even using *chants*."

Between mouthfuls of stew, Artorian managed to speak. "*Mm!* Those won't work here, by the way. Or, you may not have to use them if the Heavenlies eventually show up. Still working out how I need to handle that bucket of venison when I've got time to chew on the topic."

Irene blinked at him, holding her forehead, and squeaking out a very discouraged reply. "*What?* Show up? Why wasn't that a lie? I would have felt so much better had that been a *lie*. My head hurts."

Artorian waved a hand, removing the headache with some basic Aura. "There you go."

Irene looked at him like she was about to throw her breakfast at his head, then at Lunella. "I am so, *so glad*, that you are the village Matron, and not me. I think I would have just asked to go back into the stone."

CHAPTER TWENTY-EIGHT

Lunella declared she'd gotten the gist of the matter and situation during her third morning of breakfast. Meanwhile, Irene broke into C-rank zero with some helpful guidance, and her first act had been to completely ditch the old-lady look in favor of something that made her feel more lean and liger-like. Even if the change took all her reserves down to nothing, she was most pleased with the investment.

What Artorian found interesting was that, one, looking younger was possible before the B-ranks. Two, Irene apparently knew how. But most interestingly, three, he'd watched the entire process in detail, and now knew how as well. "Irene, do you have a name for that technique?"

Irene couldn't be bothered to reflect on the matter after she told Lunella about the side-effects of the attempt going awry, causing her to fuss. With her refinement intake what it was, and the local Essence this plentiful, she estimated recovery time to last but a single day.

She was right, too.

The young adult Morovian smirked when she replied, her voice surprisingly unchanged. "Morovian Revivification. Look younger, feel younger, no real internal changes. Does wonders for the outlook on life, though. Great for Cultivators who use Essence to keep ticking, but you need C-rank reserves to pull it off. You never studied the scriptures of the homeland? Looks like this Keeper has a thing or two to teach you yet!"

A noisy *pop* made them all turn to look at a very obvious purple Wisp, who sped over to the old man before settling onto his head. She relaxed with a sigh when she did, like sinking into the coziest puddle. "*Ahhh*, pillow Aura is the *best*."

After a short primer about Wisps to his immediate circle, and informing them that some Courts had a stick the size of a tall tree stuck in dark places when it came to the topic of secrecy, Irene and Lunella calmed. Genevieve had received more of a shock response than Halcyon, who still appeared human, though an attempt was made at explaining Chosen anyway.

Which went… alright.

When Lunella received access to Artorian's lists, she declared that the next people to be 'let out' would be Jin, Tarrean, Tibbins, Wuxius, Tychus, Grimaldus, Astrea, Jiivra, and Blanket. The musical chairs brigade could wait since they didn't have a good spot to be. She did not want to tango with anyone from the Mountaindale category. When it was explained who and *what* lurked in the 'Other' category, she wanted nothing to do with the whole section.

Artorian did not… fully agree. Still, he let her do her thing.

Lunella did not want Alexandria out and about without something to invest herself in or the poor girl would go stir crazy, and since she learned her children would suffer no ill side-effects from remaining rocks for a while, she made it clear that they could *stay* rocks for a while. When Cy asked why, Lunella's reply was terse. "Darling, I have nine children. *Nine*. I was just told I could have a vacation with zero repercussions, and be able to get this place working spick and span before they'd ever need to wake up. *I'm taking it*."

Halcyon didn't see what was so difficult about herding a

meager nine podlings, but didn't comment further. As an ex-Daimyo of an entire realm, her perspective of the matter felt somewhat different in scope.

Wux, as one of the few other non-cultivators on the list, was pulled in first. He was overjoyed to see Lunella, then fell over himself when Artorian made a quip about his early days fawning all over her. Wux attempted to tackle the old man, but Artorian forgot to let himself fall backwards, resulting in Wux slamming his face into a proverbial wall.

"Grandfather!" Wux managed before ignoring the injury to his face, copying Lunella's rib-squeezing technique. Since Artorian had forgotten to allow himself to be moved, he *oof'ed* loudly as compensation.

"*Ha-haa*! Still the strong one, I see!" said Artorian, teasing the man. He let Wux jab him in the shoulder, only to see the man howl and hold his own fingers from having done so much too hard. "You didn't change a single hair, did you, my boy?"

Lunella promptly removed her largest baby to chastise him, before shoving a bowl of food into his hands so she could keep them busy. Irene and Lunella locked eyes, and silently agreed that idle husbands with idle hands frequently found themselves to be up to no good.

Tychus, Grimaldus, and Astrea were decanted as a bundle. Artorian, expecting to get mobbed, plopped his soul-item pillow on some open grass. This way, he could sit on his throne of plush, and rely on the pillow to handle the physics as his three remaining Fringe-kids barreled into him. Tychus wept, Grim had a thousand questions, and Astrea just wanted to be held and never let go.

A small helping of sleep Aura was needed to calm the three of them so Lunella and Irene could pry the trio from the oversized pillow. The sight of which instantly sent Lunella into a full on tirade while she hauled Grim away over her shoulder. "You carry one of those puffy monstrosities with you everywhere you go? Was leaving one plunked in the Fringe not enough for you? We're going to have words later!"

This was, of course, more than enough for Artorian to resolve plunking another twelve by twelve fluffy 'monstrosity' in some inconvenient location. In fact, why limit such schemes to *one* fluffy monstrosity? His face adopted foxlike features as his hands rubbed together, eyes hunting around for additions to this wonderful new side quest. *"Let the games begin."*

Jin and Tarrean followed in the decanting order, only to instantly have Irene grip her son and husband by the ear and drag them away to one of the A-frame homes. When Tibbins appeared, Irene somehow knew. Her Keeper senses outright tingled when he stumbled around like a lost rabbit. She yelled for him the moment he popped into being, making Tibbins turn his face towards the noise and bounce off in that direction before having the chance to greet anyone. One did not keep Irene waiting. "Coming!"

That Tibbins had been the official Head Cleric back in the real Fringe didn't matter all that much. The true hierarchy never relied on titles. One simply *knew*. With Tibbins back out and about, only Lun's nine kids were still Cored under the Fringe section. Since she'd requested that status quo remain for a while, the prompt was dismissed as she went to check on the troublesome trio.

Lunella being away for the moment allowed the C'towl to play.

"Genevieve." Artorian raised his arm to wave at Halcyon, physically motioning for her to come attend. "Surtur next please."

The purple Wisp bobbed in agreement, but a long moment of silence followed, without the expected **fwop** noise. The Wisp seemed to be concentrating, which gave Cy enough time to close the distance and speak. "My Dreamer?"

Artorian leaned to her slightly. "Surtur is on my wall for some reason, so we're decanting her. Could you bring her home, or wherever she's supposed to be?"

Halcyon assented with a nod, her smile full of teeth at the thought of getting her old playmate back! Age, it seemed, did not deter individuals from being playful. Artorian chuckled at his own thoughts. As if he wasn't the walking example.

"So that's where she was! That makes sense now, I suppose." Cy, having realized something, eased her pose. Not having her tail changed how she needed to balance. "I haven't seen Surtur since her evolution. I can't wait!"

When her Dreamer quirked an eyebrow at her, Cy explained. "I overheard the other Dreamers speaking about 'cultivation limitations' one time? The Fire Dreamer mentioned to the Void Dreamer that Cal had given 'your wall' something called 'carte blanche' when it came to 'being allowed to culti-vate.' Can't say I understood it all, but when Irene managed to cultivate like Yuki did, it must mean that anyone kept on your wall was also allowed to keep growing in power. Surtur said she got stuck at a threshold last I saw her. Her body demanded more resources than the world was willing to give her. I just didn't get it at the time."

Artorian considered this, then frowned, but swiftly eased as he moved a hand to summon the prompts closer. When they came whizzing in front of him, he held his beard while reading them over. "That could explain *some* of these names, but I feel my nose tingle when I look at some others, and have this suspi-cion that Occy was involved in strategically placing some entries in there."

He pointed sternly at the Mountaindale prompt like a person he needed to scold. "This entire list is *suspect*."

When a heavy violet lightwave pulsed from Genevieve as a wall of illusionary fire, they stopped their inspections of the prompts to pay attention instead. The environment darkened, a shadow falling over the whole village. Artorian looked to his left and right, but saw no Surtur, even as the Wisp proudly exclaimed her job being well done. "Sorted! Took me a bit, but turns out all I needed was more energy than normal."

Halcyon squealed excitedly, and since Artorian felt at a loss, he glanced at her. She was looking up? Peering upwards himself, both his eyebrows rose in unison as a quietly burning Dalamadur with a person's scale-covered upper torso, arms, and head, where normally the mouth of the snake should have been, filled the air. The enormous monster blotted out some sun as Surtur coiled in on herself, waking up slowly as her sporadic tufts of flame dissolved into wispy fog.

"That explains why it got dark. Well, she certainly grew up!" He inhaled a firm breath, then bellowed to the sky. "Mornin' Surty!"

Snapping her eyes open, the floating Dalamadur blinked a few times before looking down. After which she frantically clawed at the air as if she had no control over her movements. Artorian recognized the problem right away. "Crackers, she's using bonescripting to fly. That's a *mess*. Cy, come up with me. She's going to need a handhold or we're going to have some Surtur-craters shortly. I know from personal experience how much the ground wants its hugs."

Her Dreamer shot upwards without a jump or bounce, shifting straight to flight while Halcyon took a few deft steps before leaping. Her transformation felt seamless. Flawless. Smooth. *Natural*. Whatever trick or technique her Dreamer had used hadn't just fixed some minor irritation. His method had evolved her, restored her very being to the apex of what it was supposed to have been all along. While Cy certainly felt proud of her personal accomplishments in growth, her attempts up to now felt limited in comparison to the scope of freedom she could feel in her fingertips. She felt *right*. Not only correct, but with the distinct sensation that, if she wanted to, she could change details of herself at leisure.

Halcyon bubbled in delight, putting those plans in action as she got right to fiddling with her colors like a fast-acting chameleon. Her gold colorations remained in place, but the black of her orca form pulsed like a strobe light, flashing a cavalcade of party colors!

Artorian laughed at the sight, thinking to add some bass and Wubs to match each pulse. Rather than fly upwards as normal, he instead made his light platforms appear as footholds. Each time he stepped on one as leverage to gain altitude, the plate released a thick *wub*, the sequence of which he timed to form a solid rhythm. Something a person could really bop and bob their head to.

At the minimum, it made everyone currently looking out of a window gawk. Their old man was crazy! Why was he going *towards* the abyss-off giant sky-snake? Plus, how was that fish flying? Where did it even come from, and why did it look like Hal—*ooooh*.

"Genevieve!" He exploded into a puffy cloud to take on his Long form, which would make it easier to help Surtur, since he'd have more direct feedback ready. Bonescripting difficulties were no joke. "Decant Jiivra and Blanket, and send them to Astrea. Then pull out our bards! It's party time. Make them a fun spot a bit away from the village!"

"Can do!" The Wisp caused visible violet soundwaves to ripple upwards. She felt like she'd just been given permission to put on a show! She would *capitalize*! Zipping over to the bottom of a hill, she borrowed some power to let it roll out across the local landscape. Then she cast a rune spell using the old ways. "[Odeum]!"

The ground rippled where she cast the rune, the chipper Wisp feeling thoroughly in her element as she did what purple Wisps were gifted at doing. Design, aesthetics, and *creation*. The malleable Essence of Caltopia responded to Genevieve's will, each particle pulling free a metaphorical glow stick as the section of land she was affecting lit up like bioluminescent fire-works. Positively scintillating with colors to match the show in the sky!

Since there was no corruption or immalleable Essence in Cal's Soul Space, aside from what was being kept deeper under-ground for stability, the surface was entirely up for grabs when it came to formation. Especially in the artistic hands of skilled formers such as Dwarves, or Wisps.

The land dipped as particles of earth and grass reformed to make stone, the visual effect leading to that of a whole building rising up out of a muddy lake. Loose Essence gushed like water down the effigy as it rose, either adding to the building itself or pouring across the zone of its foundation. The hills next to the location rippled less, but moved regardless as stairs carved into their slopes, followed by horizontal slabs of stone seating.

Particles began to run dry the higher on the hill this went, so Genevieve focused on making the small theater itself—the Odeum—look as nice as she could in the limited time her rune remained active, then allowed the rest of the Essence to roll over the scene and smooth the entire building like a sandpaper scrub.

Delighted at the permanent new fixture, she gave the monument a moment to cool off as she zipped to decant Jiivra and Blanket like she was supposed to, landing them both right on the pile with Astrea, Grim, and Tychus. They all woke from the sudden new weight before sputtering into bouts of laughter. Blanket 'chirped' out in panic, gathering them all up in his arms and protecting them by bundling them into his fluff to the complaints of Lunella, who still happened to be nearby when the house-sized sugar glider snatched her up. He absconded her to safety while the rest of the family stared at the sky and hills, utterly baffled at the spectacle all around them.

A few hundred feet away, the chipper purple Wisp cackled in delight as hosts of instruments began to appear in the middle of the half-circle stage, pulled from storage to finally see use again! Zipping above the altar afterwards, she did the second portion of what she was asked to, and brought back the bards all in one go so they appeared in a dramatic poof of glittery smoke upon the stage.

Rather than question their new surroundings, it was the persistent thumping thud of bass in the sky and roving light show that stole their attention. That there was a Dalamadur hovering up there wasn't remotely important. Some *percussionist* was trying to show them up! They declared their feelings on the matter in flawless unison. "Oh, *abyss* no!"

Kinnan, Pollard, Jillian, Meg, Ash, Maeve, and Moza

looked up at the source, then around at all the instruments ready for their beck and call. Instruments that swiftly found their way into the hands and fingers of slighted artists, who were not going to let some *thumpy-boi* show them up like that. Fueled with the power of spite, one of them knocked some sticks together to set the pace, allowing Meg to break in the gorgeous piano she'd sped to, while Maeve broke into a melodic, powerful opening with her gift of a voice as she claimed a viola.

Her chant was directly in tune with the thumping in the sky, even if she was oblivious to the irony of the contents. Her voice resounded as she put Essence into her words, causing stars to show up on all the rocks in her vicinity. "I can show you what love's supposed to feel like. I can show you what love's supposed to be!"

CHAPTER TWENTY-NINE

The Fringe turned into a madhouse of a party, which was what the S.A.S. chose to call it when they came by to check on their fearless leader. Cy hadn't returned to the moon as expected. Not that they could blame her for the daily visitations.

They arrived to a fight between a musical dragon trying to teach a Dalamadur how to fly using some kind of Dance Dance Revolution method, and a group of refusing-to-quit bards in a brand new Odeum that saw the percussive thumping as some kind of insult. The geese riders decided to land and join in on the gawking.

It wasn't like they could catch up to Halcyon and her brand of swim-flight anyway. Cy managed to be both very thick and very graceful at the same time, all while finely controlling her speed and momentum, like a hunter gliding seamlessly through ocean waters. Scout, Munch, Vanilla, and company chose to take this time to go around and make introductions while looking like humans.

A loophole they adored, since the racial options in their quiver were entirely limited by location. In the new Fringe, there just wasn't that much wildlife. This meant that the trader's introduction went smoothly! Though that was, in part, attributed to the... other distractions around. That they came down on geese just seemed so... mundane in comparison. Lunella didn't even feel like fussing when she freed herself from Blanket's fuzzy protections.

She felt like this was going to be a new 'now' that she'd have to get accustomed to. Her grandfather had just turned into a sky-snake! To help another sky-snake! Along with a fish bigger than her house. She instead shook her fist at the sky. "Old man, I did not decant my children so I could have a few days of peace and quiet. This better be temporary!"

'Temporary' turned into a whole day, but unlike Artorian, Surtur was gifted. Bonescripting had taken him a lot of effort to get the hang of, but Surtur was a natural master of 'the wiggle.' She got her full three-dimensional axis movement under control in just a few hours. The rest was practice, play, and ending up a better flyer than Artorian in his dragon form.

A fact that left him just a teensy bit sore, no matter how much Surtur deflected with praise that it was all because of his teaching.

When she had her movement under control, Artorian didn't want to be in the air for a bit. He landed in a big puffy cloud, then slammed into the ground like Hulk's three point landing, having resumed his human form on the way down. He'd shaped his body first, then turned his existing one into mist that swirled to fill it. If he was going to get beaten out in performance, he would *ham up* his performance to compensate! A victory that lasted a solid five seconds before the bards mobbed him. Because of course they did.

The bardic victory also only lasted about five seconds, because Blanket decided it was Blanket time! Thieving Artorian right out of their bundle, he ran away with the old man's cloak in his mouth. He chirped loudly, chittering in defiance until he sat on a hill and bundled himself all around the familiar smell.

When Halcyon landed nearby, also having retaken her human form, the house-sized sugar glider hissed at her! Cy replied by grabbing his mouth faster than Blanket could react, keeping his maw closed with two fingers. She growled back with a tone only Beasts and Mages were able to hear.

Blanket quickly found his chill with the sudden establishment of hierarchy, and allowed Artorian to crawl free and gasp for air once he'd spelunked free from the rolling dunes of poof. "Freedom! Oh, hello again, dear. Meet Blanket! He's a sweetie."

"An overprotective sweetie, but he means well." She reached out a hand, which Artorian used to pull himself up. "Are you well after that strenuous flight?"

"Thank you, dear." Brushing himself off as he flopped back on Blanket's leg, he sprawled for comfort. "*Ahh*. Much better now that I'm on the ground."

Artorian looked back at the protective puff-blanket. "I'm surprised he didn't try to attack you."

"He considered it." Cy shot the sugar glider some powerful side eye before plopping herself down in the fuzzy space as well. "Then he learned how that would end, and *re*-considered it. Beast hierarchy is really easy and straightforward. He's a very darling low B-rank, I'm the equivalent of A-rank five. One level below my Dreamer, following the new Beast rules. So to be challenged would be... funny."

Blanket replied with a rolling coo, laying his head on Artorian's. This allowed the old man to scritch the glider under the chin, eliciting a bundle of happy noises from the fluffbutt. The Mage then rolled out his Aura, letting it radiate the good stuff from the olden times.

Cozy, cozy, Starlight Aura.

The effects freshened everyone nearby right up, though made the bards feel like they just drank seven cups of espresso as a side-effect. Their Essence channels did not play the nicest with his Aura, as their infernal channels felt like they tingled with live sparks, jittering like a sleeping limb that woke up far too slowly for anyone's comfort.

Specifically theirs!

"Is there a reason why you're a rank below me, dear? I

know nothing about these new rules." He shifted some Mana to pet Blanket's head. "Last I remember was some mention about everyone being A-rank nine already, and I think that was ages ago, timewise. Is Yuki an Incarnate?"

Halcyon shook her head, and clearly didn't want to talk about the rules she was abiding by right now. It would be a topic for later. "Nobody can Incarnate in Cal at the moment. I can temporarily boost my rank higher, but it will drop back down to where it's stable once the food digests. Yuki and Zelia are both, officially, at A-rank nine. Yuki's a proper cultivator, and Zelia's a walking dungeon. I'm the only one with a special restriction, or else we end up with more edge cases like Wagner. Zelia's rank... technically fluctuates? She tried explaining to me that her **Law** can be finicky. I don't have a **Law**."

Halcyon paused, making a face and then making quotation marks with her fingers. "Officially, I just have an Essence combination in my Beast Core, so I can't understand too well when she says her rank doesn't follow the rules."

Artorian nodded, adding a mental note to ask for clarifications later. Perhaps the topic was not something she wanted to speak on publicly. He changed the tone and flow of the conversation. "Speaking of, I want to talk to you about my golden Core idea one day. Adapted Beast Cores as refinement centers for normal cultivators. For now, though, since Blanket isn't going to haul me off again..."

He reached up with his other hand and smushed the glider's head softly between two big copies of oversized Mana-hands, before rubbing his face nice and good. "You're protective, aren't ya, you attention-demanding fluff-wall? Let's go see Jii!"

Blanket, his face thoroughly ruffled, chirped. He was about to bite Sunny's cloak again for a drag-and-run, but just barely didn't when he caught sight of the look Cy was giving him. He politely closed his mouth without a bite, then sulked while padding along behind them.

Halcyon ended up patting the glider's head when they got

back to town. "You're a sweet child, Blanket. Smarter than you look, despite how much sway your Beast side has over you."

Right when Artorian thought things were looking up, Surtur discovered the ground's love for hugs as she slammed into the packed dirt, nary fourteen feet from the edge of the active bonfire. He supposed they now had room for a second one, given the small crater that whined out a crooked and measly 'ow.'

"Did the bonescripting get you, Surty?"

The crater whined back. "I did the thing you told me not to do."

Artorian figured as much. "And how's that treating you?"

After a pause from the crater, the hole once again replied, "Ow."

Making sure his Aura reached her, with a bit of fiddling, Surtur snaked her way out of the hole in the Lamia form that they were all familiar with. Well, everyone but the Fringe's new —old?—inhabitants. Artorian reigned himself in at their looks of confusion. "Looks like I get to do more 'splainin'! Alright, party's over. Onwards to tomorrow."

During the evening's meal, the New Fringe had already become rowdy. There was easily enough housing for everyone, but there was little in the way of things to do. Acquiring food wasn't exactly difficult, and once Tibbins, Tarrean, and Jin did their round of meetings, they stormed the kitchens to claim it.

Everyone save for Tibbins ended up dragged back out by Irene, who was calling a huddle with her boys and Jiivra. They were all in the same boat of sucking up local Essence without the normal need for chants. Tarrean and Irene were having an especially difficult time with this, being older-school cultivators.

Jiivra thrived, but wasn't making automatic gains like the others were. She was, on the other hand, feeling pretty cozy and stable with her energy supply. Once Blanket returned to her side, they both began to cultivate, seeing the progress of months happen in hours as they caused the local temperature to plummet. They both needed to stop because they were reeling from the influx, and the complaints of everyone huddling ever closer to the bonfire.

Jiivra and her kin were all used to very slow, difficult, laborious Essence intake. Essence needed refining, corruption needed purging, absorption was slow, and cultivation needed the correct conditions. Even joint-cultivation with a Beast only did so much in the grand scheme of things. Just because one improved their energy intake did not mean it improved the rate at which they could build themselves up.

Their knowledge of cultivating told them the process was akin to fine alchemy. Instead, they were tripping on finished potions just by breathing. When Artorian and Lunella gathered people up for the midnight bonfire, they had a discussion on the topic, even if Wuxius and Lunella felt more adamant than ever about not wanting to do this cultivation stuff. To them, it sounded painful, horrible, and impossible to raise their family during.

Wux shrugged, not buying the goods Tychus and Grim were trying to peddle. "No, no, and a thousand times no, brothers. Grandfather checked me already. I have none of this 'corruption' in me, I feel downright fantastic, the crick in my back feels like a faded dream, and I do not want to spend hours and hours of my time 'making a cultivation technique.' I do not care about these supposed benefits."

Lunella agreed vehemently, copying the retort to Astrea. "No matter how much better or stronger such tricks might make me, sister, I have children to raise, and my time must go to them. Not losing days and days of time sitting in a rigid lotus position."

Astrea tried her best, gesticulating with her hands like her grandfather as she spoke. "Being a cultivator will make it so much easier to handle your kids! You can till whole fields in hours rather than days, and the Essence gain is automatic here!"

Lunella shot her the stink eye. "Sister, I will not hear it! Grandfather already told us that 'this place' is a temporary refuge, and I vividly remember the journey it took in order to get here. We will one day need to 'ditch' these temporary bodies, no matter how convenient, and start over as children if we wish to live true and proper lives in the real world. Instead of this fantasy."

"Yes, but if you learn how *now*, then it will be easier *later*. When the kids are all grown up!" Astrea pleaded, with Grim and Tychus furiously nodding. "You'll be free from most illnesses, disease will be a faded dream, you'll see the sunrise for... *hundreds of years!*"

Wuxius replied with a pained smile. "But... sister, I don't want that. I don't want that at all. I want a normal, simple, easy life with my Lunella. I don't want to feel the pain twice, even if feeling it once makes the second time easier. I honestly don't even want to feel what you've been describing *once* at all."

Lunella nodded. "I don't want to live for hundreds of years. I just want a life. A life away from raiders, people fond of switches, and madwomen who steal children for sport. I want *none* of it. I want to run my little village, grow old with my Wux, and fade when it's my time. No amount of us having a doting, mad grandfather for family makes me want to change that."

She swallowed. "He looks *so old* now, sister. He's so frail, and thin, and looks at us with nothing but love and pride in his eyes. But he has suffered. He has lost. He has been through seas of pain to claw and drag himself to where he is now. No amount of sweet, supportive whispers that 'he had it pretty easy' in comparison will make me look away from his efforts."

She spoke with her hands as well now, the trait solidly part of the family. "Because from where I'm sitting, the history sounds horrible, the process sounds horrible, and while I won't take the choice from my kids if they decide that's the path in life they want to tread. I. Don't. Want. It."

Astrea hung her head, and gave up. She cast one more pleading look at Tychus and Grimaldus, but her brothers seemed to have accepted the same kind of cold resignation that currently lay like a lead weight on her own heart. "I... I don't want to see you die, sister."

Wux hugged Astrea, who was starting to have emotional difficulties. Like the father he was, he had learned what to do. "Everyone will one day fade, sister. It is the privilege of those who are well off to choose how. How would we end, if not with a smile on our wrinkly faces? Would you see us on the field of battle? Would you see us 'starving' from this Essence-deprivation we heard about, if conditions aren't what we think they are in the real world?"

He squeezed, but Astrea could take it. She was a proper C-ranker, not that this helped with her rampaging emotions any. Wux continued. "Now that we've heard the full story of what happened to the three of you, the Ziggurat, the cultivation, losing your natural Essence channels to the infernal channel, being restored when grandfather finally got to you, Lun and I know that we're not meant for that life."

Astrea just burrowed her face into his clothing, and he said nothing more. Grim and Tychus rubbed her back, aware they'd failed to convince two members of their family to pick up cultivating with them. Not that they could naysay the outcome. Not cultivating was... an easier life. A normal, painless-in-comparison life. A warm and fuzzy thing, with hard work most days, and the laughter of children in the background.

Artorian sat with them, and hugged the lot. "We make the choices we can live with. There's nothing more to it than that."

CHAPTER THIRTY

Over the course of the next few days, the Fringe found its flow. Lunella resumed the mantle of village elder, lapis robe included. Whether that was because nobody wanted the job, or nobody wanted to fight her for it was swept under the rug. Exactly *how* Lunella had wrestled a wild bear to the ground, *and* dragged it back home all by herself from the birch forest was a topic that confused many of the actual cultivators.

Stew was amazing that night, though!

The news that Wuxius and Lunella refused to walk the path of Essence was a tough pill for many to swallow. Artorian did his grandfatherly best to help people come to terms with the choice, but some injuries could only be mended with time.

Wux chose the path of a miller. It was high time he stepped up to the responsibility of that building. As a minor bonus, this one was brand new! Not one tear in any of the sails! Were they called sails? He was going to call them sails, make a few people groan until he could slap down a right proper dad joke.

Lunella was helped by Irene, who resumed being a Keeper like a person consumed by ledgers. Or she was when the S.A.S. came by to trade, which was where the great majority of the bear stew went—courtesy of Master Chef Tibbins, and his special sauces! Tibbins was asked to cook for everyone. "Even if nobody had asked, my life belongs to the cooking fire."

He took the house right next to the kitchen building, since in this version of the Fringe it remained unoccupied. Tarrean busied himself with the bees, having found a passion for the apiary and its tiny inhabitants. Bees they would not have had if curious noses did not go looking for information on where Lunella wrestled down the bear, only to upset a nest of the tiny yellow monsters, after which they ran for their lives from the buzzing swarm, which they claimed up and down the whole stream counted several thousand members strong.

Jin treated Ty's 'wounds' with only minimal mockery and sass, then went into the woods himself to check the validity of their tale. He nonchalantly returned with a fist covered in swarming bees, having 'casually' captured a queen. Because that was clearly something you could do to F-ranked bees. Tarrean had excitedly led his son to one of the hives he'd been making with all this spare time he had, then could not be distinguished from a worker bee for the rest of the day himself.

The ex-head cleric, looking rather aged himself, didn't seem to mind in the slightest. He had a project! That, or a craving for pie and confection. In his own words: "There *will* be honey."

Everyone knew it was for the pie.

Jin, on realizing what this meant, decided he was ditching his prior village requirements. He was no longer a church figure of any kind, as there was no church! Cultivating in Caltopia required no chants, and he could afford to play around with Essence in his free time since the excess intake was literally sloughing off his skin as a fine mist.

This left him completely free to pick up a new profession. "I think I am going to take up brewing. With honey in the works, we should have everything we need locally for some quality mead."

Jiivra and Blanket decided that the town needed guards, especially if bears were barely a hop, skip, and jump away from where everyone slept. As a joint-cultivation set, this also primed them both to receive and send off the S.A.S. as Blanket could speak to the geese without any trouble, and Jiivra could handle all the ins and outs of trade so long as she had a primer from the local Keeper.

A few short chats with Irene later, and a basic filing system was set and ready to go. Jiivra did not mind taking up the additional position of head trader. Being the town guard would also let her find oddities and interests in the general region. Little things that she could bring to the attention of others. Spices for Tibbins, for example. Or how the Salt Flats copy next to the village most certainly *did* have salt in it. "I have no idea who did this, or how they copied the tides, but they added some *detail*. Well, we have salt!"

That news ended up being most welcome, and also allowed Tychus, Grimaldus, and Astrea to puzzle out what they were doing. Astrea was of course going to spend some time helping Jiivra out, as best friends did, then went ahead and made the call that she was going to room with her and Blanket as well. There was no saying *no* to that lush, plush fur, and she got cold easy. They went with one of the houses that could be easily insulated.

Otherwise, Astrea decided she was going to learn music from the bards, who had collectively decided that the longhouse was both their nook and cranny. A few had pleaded that they take one of the easily insulated homes as well, purely for noise protection, and the health of everyone else's ears. Unfortunately, the troupe refused to hear it. Kinnan, Pollard, and Jillian each made a matching hand motion as they spoke the magic word related to their obstinance. "Acoustics."

Grimaldus rubbed his temples, retorting with a plan and simple answer that seemed to solve everyone's problem. "Why not just *live* in the Odeum?"

For some reason, the bards had not thought that was an option. To Lunella's vast relief, they packed up and moved locations right away, returning her precious longhouse to blissful peace and quiet until she discovered that the Odeum was still a single hill too close to the village for them not to hear the practice sessions. Lunella chased the lot of them through their own stone halls with a rolling pin and promptly assigned them fishing work. "You can stay, but you have to contribute!"

When not accompanied by Astrea, Grim and Tychus chose to be full-time cultivators. Until Lunella got ahold of them and gave them the same treatment as the bards. They quickly turned into part-time cultivators and part-time farmers. Luckily for them, they tilled and took care of fields like they were each worth thirty full-grown people. Otherwise known as D-rank three.

They had to trade for seeds with the S.A.S. in order to have anything to plant, which was when the new currency system came up. There were minor gripes when 'Requisition' was explained to them. Especially with Grim, with whom the whole idea sat very poorly after his Ziggurat days. Still, they made the trades, otherwise there would be no fields to work on. To lessen the sour taste, they indulged in some cultivation goodness.

Before throwing themselves into the deep end, they checked with grandfather first, who mumbled a little about the state of their cultivation techniques. Artorian otherwise didn't stop them. "If that's the path you want to walk, I'll help, of course. Those core techniques swirling in your chest could use some polish, but that does not need to be rushed when Essence is so easily gathered."

Artorian, in simple, clean clothing that Halcyon had brought by, checked on his adopted family to explore their difficulties in more detail. His own soft lapis attire was proudly emblazoned with an Arachne insignia on the chest. This both told the old man how Cy had gotten a hold of finished clothing so easily, and why they were so celestially cozy! Stain resistant too. Zelia had apparently left him an entire warehouse, allowing him to provide a steady stream of Sage-quality clothing to the entire village!

Zelia had wanted her wardrobe to be worn by all, after all.

He'd make it so! "No reason to hoard an entire *warehouse* all to myself. Let the Fringe be clothed in quality! Plus we look celestially good, even if there needs to be some sleeve-tucking here and there. They wash like a charm, and they retain heat *just* right."

Tychus and Grim, both wearing green and red outfits of the same kind, strongly agreed. Tychus pulled on his sleeve to show his robe off. "Stretches well!"

Grimaldus fixed his belt, then rolled his arms. "Doesn't chafe."

Artorian chuckled, pleased as punch when Astrea arrived in yellow. "That's number three. Alright, so we patched up your Essence channels last time, but all that told you is that you escaped the grasp of the infernal, not what you ended up with. I'm sure the three of you already know, but humor me as I go over this. We will also be skipping cultivation techniques, because we're improving what you have regardless."

They nodded, and Artorian motioned at his kids one at a time. "Ty, my boy, you've got a single, weak Earth affinity. Astrea, weak Air affinity. Grim, weak Water affinity. All singles. Which, granted, is pretty normal. Being reset after a life of sporting a strong infernal channel likely did not give you a lot of time to align yourself with the Essences."

Artorian rolled his arms, his three students hanging on his words with rapt attention. "I think I've got good news on how to do something about that. There's some graduates from the Skyspear Academy that I can decant who have your current channels. Opening new channels comes from you aligning yourself to the ideals of the Essence in question. Usually that means big life changes or traumatic events. We will delve deeper into the nuances of this topic when time permits, because there's some newly discovered downsides about having multiple channels that you didn't gain naturally."

Grim cautiously moved his hand into the air. "So, having all our channels opened to perfect quality is off the table?"

Artorian nodded, deflating his grandson. "For now, I'm

afraid so. Gain what you can naturally, while studying the effects of what happens when you do. In the event the choice in the matter is revoked, and I have to open everyone's channels, I want people to know what they're in for. So it's not a surprise, everyone in the bardic college has, at minimum, an infernal channel. Air is pretty common as well."

Astrea voiced a thought. "Do Wux and Lun have channels?"

Artorian paced, and answered without much thought to why the question was asked. "They sure do. Wux has a minor earth channel, and Lunella, to nobody's surprise, has a strong fire channel. Since we're on the topic, Jiivra has a strong celestial channel, while Jin and Tibbins have a weak one. Tarrean has two strong channels: celestial and air... I mean earth. Celestial and earth. I was distracted by a memory of his early days in the Fringe. He was a total windbag!"

They laughed, and Grimaldus picked out a name that was missing. "You didn't include Irene?"

Artorian paused, then ran a hand over his bald head. "*Uh, promise not to tell Tarrean?*"

This tidbit instantly got the trio's full attention, gleaming, toothy smiles and all. Like children, they chanted a 'we promise' in unison that even a first-day mother wouldn't believe. Artorian sighed, knowing the C'towl was out of the bag already. "Celestial, fire, and earth. All minor channels. She hid it well, and I'm fairly certain she gained the latter two later in life. When I met her, I think she was a celestial monotype."

Astrea motioned to the sky. "What about the sky snake?"

Artorian needed a moment. "Surtur? She's a Dalamadur, not a sky-snake. She even stuck to a Lamia form for everyone else's convenience. That brings us into the topic of the differences between Cultivators, Beasts, and dungeon Cores. Surtur is a Beast, and affinity-wise she matches the one who blessed her. So in Dawny's case, that's fire and celestial. It's also why Halcyon ended up with all six."

The trio stopped cold, as Tychus blurted out what they were

all thinking. "Wait, you have *six*? Last we heard from Irene, you had four!"

Their grandfather cackled. "Oh, that's just... so precious. They've missed so much. No, it's been six perfect channels for me ever since my deal with Cal. Let me assure you that it hasn't been all sunshine and roses, no matter how much it maddeningly increased my ability to quaff Essence. Though it *has* been the sole reason why I can down Dwarven spirits and not blink an eye. Those poor, stocky pyrite-delvers, drinking their brew like weak water baffles them every time!"

Wiping away a tear of good cheer, he shook his head. "I'll explain all that during one of the upcoming bonfire gatherings. There's still so much I need to put in words. I expect I need to explain my dragon form as well, but that brings us into Eternium territory and *sweet crackers*, am I not ready to explain any of that hutzpah! That's begging for headaches."

He needed to drink, so Grim handed him a waterskin filled with spring water. A small gulp later, and Artorian felt like he could continue. Before speaking more, he looked up to see Halcyon and Surtur fly overhead in a race, arriving at the gates that Jiivra was starting to put up. Cy had once again brought several merchant carts worth of goodies, and Artorian would not be surprised if she would ask to set up an outpost near their village soon.

"Halcyon looks so happy." He sighed, watching her laugh in the distance as Blanket ran around her in circles. "I live for smiles and laughs like that."

The trio let their old man have his warm and fuzzy moment. He was back with them soon enough. Grim had his hand raised and ready, so Artorian addressed it. "Yes, my boy?"

"Who are these people from the Academy you want us to meet? Astrea only ever tells me about Jiivra when it comes to stories from those days." Grim looked hopeful for more possible friends to talk cultivation-shop with.

"From Skyspear?" Artorian held his beard, waywardly playing with it as he recollected the information. "Razor and

Ali are the graduates. Proper C-rankers with earth and fire channels. Ian and Exem… were but students in the infernal wing. Oh! *Craig*!"

The old man felt like he could slap himself. "He was Dale's original guild teacher. If he had the patience to deal with Dale, he'd be wonderful here! We should go do that right away! We've got the clothing, food, living space, and Lunella *definitely* has a need for more people to do some work. Come along!"

Artorian sped away, leaving the three adults to scramble in his wake in order to give chase. "Do I have anyone for air and water? *Snookem and Nerys*! Perfect! I best run it by Lunella first, or I'll get scolded."

Realizing that last part a bit late, he detoured to the village center instead, ecstatic to relay his ideas! He had such plans! Even when Lunella launched into a tirade after being told, as she'd just finished getting everyone already here properly settled, Artorian couldn't stop smiling.

This place was starting to feel like home.

CHAPTER THIRTY-ONE

"These people of yours can come, *if*, and only if, they contribute. A village falls over when half the people in it laze about!" Lunella dictated imperiously while pacing circles around the scolded old man. Her finger was stuck high in the air, and she went on and on while walking ever deeper divots into the ground. "I still want my vacation, and until the answer to 'is this place dangerous' becomes a no, my children will safely remain a hardy pile of rocks! Can these people of yours help make the village safer, *Dad*?"

Artorian felt touched at the naming convention, then beamed in response. After all, that hadn't been a no! "Of course! They will need the breakdown of recent history that's gone around the bonfire a few times, but the people we're considering now are all cultivators, and adults! Well, except Ian and Exem. Those are children, so perhaps I best lump them in with Ra. Give our tykes some more friends to grow up with."

Lunella approved of that latter idea. "I like playmates for my babies. Keep those little ones safe, and call on your Wisp friend tomorrow, when the midday meal is ready. Decanting leaves one very hungry, and shoveling food in your face makes you very receptive to other explanations going on."

"I'd be delighted!" Artorian purred out the words, then slowed. "Say, where *is* Genevieve lately? I've seen her zip about now and again, but without decanting tasks, I actually don't know what she's up to."

Lunella proudly informed him. "Helping me out. Almost everyone that knows you is falling over themselves to do things for us. It's both very creepy, and very endearing. She asked if she could make a place to stay, since she expects you'd be here often. That's the third request of that type I've gotten, by the way. They must all love you to bits."

Artorian laughed, playing off his sudden bout of nervousness. "*Ha-haa!* They're all just enthusiastic. I bet most of the people coming to you, I've helped a little in the past. That's all."

"M*hmm,*" Lunella hummed, feeling her nose tingle. "Well, they're friendly and, more importantly, helping. Genevieve is a chipper little sweetheart that responds well when I'm straight and direct with her. If you haven't taken a stroll recently, go do so. She has been growing willow trees. Four of them, to be exact. One in each cardinal direction. She mentioned something about 'court-homes' that I didn't follow, and that she will be staying in the 'spring' one. Explain that to me at the bonfire later."

Artorian nodded, helping her fold some clothing, and had gotten her humming tune stuck in his head before heading out the door. The trio awaited him. Given what they'd heard inside, they had decided not to enter their sister's home like a cow tossed through the window by a hurricane, as had been the initial plan. They chose to wait outside instead. That had been the better choice.

He was about to speak, but Astrea raised her hand. "Tomorrow at midday, we heard. She told you to take a walk. We will find something to do."

One group hug later, they split to attend to their chosen tasks. Pressing his arms against his lower back, Artorian went on his mandated stroll. The New Fringe was already looking different from the home he knew. He just hadn't noticed how the small additions had been piling up already. "It's barely been a week, how does the place change so fast?"

He attributed the changes to all the new people rolling in, and there being an entirely new host of circumstances that needed attending. Also, Hadurin wasn't here to throw his weight around and start impossible cathedral-sized building projects in the middle of a lake. So that certainly helped.

Should he start his stroll at the center, or at the edge? Flipping a mental coin, he chose the center. Waddling his way around in a town starting to get its bearings, his first concern was that there was beginning to be a bit of a *smell*. That, and the grass under his feet had been walked away to muddy paths. "That's... a bit more pressing."

He considered taking care of those issues himself, but realized he knew nothing of tunnel digging, making roads, or how to make good architecture. "My Dwarves, maybe?"

He tried a quick forum connection to Don, but slammed it shut when all he got back was a giggling, manic, hyper-enthused babbling. <Suspension bridges *define* the Art Deco period. Hadurin, *more cable*! I want the whole thing covered in a thin sheet of labradorite.>

"I'm gonna call that a *noooo*." Artorian was a bit... concerned about his friends. They'd be fine? "They'll be fiiiiine."

"Elongating your words makes them a lie." Vol padded up to his side, Scout on his back as she teased in a comment. The S.A.S. was in town. The dino's face affectionately shoved right into the old man's chest, followed by a set of truly adoring noises when Artorian scratched between his head feathers with Mana, getting all those hard to reach spots that normal claws just could not do justice. "Don't look so surprised. He misses you all the time. Jiivra sent me to Irene, who sent me to you. Anything the village needs that sensible people would not have put on a scroll already?"

The old man glanced around, but came up blank. "Sensible people likely have it in the bag. Unless you know of any moles with spare time? Or… material. Maybe all we need is material. If Alexandria is coming, we're going to need a library."

Scout pressed her hand to her hip, considering it. "Raw material? I don't see why you couldn't just ask the bored out of her mind Wisp loafing around? Normal people and most Mages may have to craft building bricks the hard way, but you have Wisps. All of Caltopia is malleable. A hill could be a block of stone if you needed it to be. Tatum was careful with organizing the redesign. The whole place is made from Cal's unaligned Essence that counts as all affinity types. I don't see how I could bring you what's already here."

Artorian grumbled. "Ah… I see. That escaped me, or I just didn't internalize the detail. Then no, dear. I'm afraid there's nothing for me this time."

Scout nodded, then turned a very uncooperative Vol away to head back out. He whined deeply the entire walk out of the village, dragging his feet like a sulking teenager.

Continuing the stroll, he figured he'd ask Genevieve about the project when he found her. First, the village center. Turned out that was the bonfire, with the new addition of a barbeque pit, as they'd had to repurpose Surtur's crash crater. "Wasn't the center supposed to be the longhouse? *Bah*, the big fire's just as well."

Around the bonfire was a big open space with places to sit and eat, the seats of which hadn't left since they'd gotten here. One circle out, and the big buildings were the longhouse, the kitchens, a warehouse that was being put together, his house— which was likely going to get repurposed—and then a bunch of open spaces. Including where Tibbins' house was supposed to be. He'd call this space the first ring or inner ring, since that's roughly how the layout was set up with the place changing.

When he looked for any information on where Tibbins' house had gone, he found makeshift signs in the inner ring for a market, tavern, and something labeled 'monument.'

Extending his walk, he found all the homes in the second ring were all being repurposed, since nobody wanted to sleep near the biggest source of noise: the people who liked evening-bonfire time. Based on the little signs, these were going to become the new blacksmith, woodcutter, charcoal maker, baker, furrier, carpenter, tailor, cobbler, barber, and mason. Each with room for expansion! "We certainly have the space."

Doing a little backtracking, Artorian did his best at land-size calculations without any sort of device. Seeing him struggle and backpedal a few times, measuring by taking big steps, Irene broke from her Keeper tasks and prodded him in the shoulder. When an embarrassed Artorian explained he was trying to figure out distances, Irene's lips curled up with a slight smile.

"Easy." She was the person responsible for the changes. "In the old Fringe, we had some recurring problems because of the layout. Since we can start fresh, all the existing buildings are just materials. The old Fringe got very… *cramped*. Choir camps are designed with protection in mind, not expansion."

Irene's discomfort bled through on her face, as she'd yearned for a good personal garden in her prior life. "So this time around, we're measuring by acres. Each major feature or building gets one, with some wiggle-waggle hand motions for the exactness. The bonfire, as an example, is in the middle, but we don't actually know how to measure a circle… so we're handwaving."

The Keeper, wearing a very lovely flowing orange robe with Zelia's insignia on it, then pointed at the Longhouse. "We used the plot of land where we're going to put the great hall as a basis. If we pretend the whole layout is made from squares."

She mumbled under her breath, cutting off an argument before it could come back up for a third time. "I know it looks like circles, don't say anything. The design was nice and was Lunella's idea, even if she heard it from Wux and we're all pretending."

Artorian snickered. Some in-village politics were already budding. He said nothing and let her continue.

"If the bonfire is the central square, we've got eight squares of land around it if you're looking at a top-down grid, meaning we've got room for eight buildings. In the 'circle' around that, there's sixteen plots of land. In the circle around that, twenty-four plots of land. Makes a neat square, but with our handwaving, it makes a neat circle instead."

Artorian nodded. "Would that last set be the village bounds, then?"

"That's the idea! The A-frame homes were always too small. The plan is as follows." Irene smiled wide, counting on her fingers. "Buildings of social importance, first circle. Buildings for crafting and village sustaining, second circle. Homes and other needs for non-cultivators, third circle. Homes and other needs for cultivators, fourth circle. That way the people most at risk in the case of a rogue bear, or similar, are defended. The bear would have to get through the cultivators first."

Irene then pointed at a willow tree in the distance. "At each cardinal direction, in what would have been the fifth circle had we not planned to put up a wall and towers, Genevieve *grew* very pretty trees. Jiivra is using them as markers for where to place the gates. The colors of the willow leaves are also the only denotation we have for what the directions actually are."

She explained without pause, Artorian paying firm attention. "The cycle goes blue, to green, to yellow, to red, then back to blue. The willow with arctic blue leaves is at the gate we now understand to be north, which represents winter. The willow with normal-looking soft green leaves is east, representing spring. The willow with golden leaves stands at the south gate, and represents summer. Finally, the willow with the deep russet leaves stands in the west, and represents fall."

Artorian nodded, then pointed east. "I suppose I need to head that way then. Thank you for the explanation, Keeper."

"Oh, we're using our made-up titles? Very well. You're welcome, *Elder*." The old man cringed, but didn't get to quip a reply as Irene walked off while cackling. She knew exactly what she'd done. "Dinner at sundown!"

Trying out new expletives under his breath such as baguette, bagel, and croissant, Artorian finished his walkabout to find Irene's explanation pretty much confirmed. When he got to the green-leaf willow, he didn't see Genevieve, so knocked on the bark. "Anyone home?"

"Sunny!" Her chipper voice popped from below the roots, ascending slowly as the purple Wisp made herself visible. She was *covered* in dirt. "I was just playing with the rivers since I didn't have much to do. Is there more to decant? Anything that needs artistry? I'm *so bored*."

Artorian didn't understand why. "Is there a hiccup with what you normally do?"

"Sort of." She sighed while landing on his head. "Can't go to the moon; my slack was already picked up by others. I'm assigned to the spellform decanting project, but that means I'm sitting on my keister-light until that actually needs doing. A purple Wisp might be good at shaping, but with nothing to shape, we get antsy."

Artorian's Aura cleaned them, and the general area, in one swoop. "That's unfortunate, dear. Still I'll count my blessings, I have a complicated construction project I'm not sure what to do with. Would you happen to be any good at making proper streets, or sewers? We need something underground so make sure the, uh, *smell* doesn't accumulate. I understand if you don't—"

"Can I make it *fancy*?" The sense of need in her voice hushed Artorian, who instead smiled widely, then nodded. "*Yesss*! Something to do for a couple of weeks. What do you want the streets made out of? How many layers deep underground do I need to go? Do you want pipes? I can do pipes!"

Artorian was at a complete loss. "Uhh... I would... Ask Irene and Lunella about details like that. I'm just happy to have someone with the skill to actually do it."

Before he could continue, the purple ball zipped away in a line of light straight to the longhouse. She bowled over Tibbins, who looked confused as all abyss as to what had flicked him from his feet. The sight made Artorian think of the chicken event from Eternium again, then slapped his forehead. "Chickens! I should have asked Scout to bring chickens!"

He quickly opened a forum connection, but was thinking so fast he used the animal's sound instead of the animal's name. "Scout, I thought of something. Can you get me a *buh-gawk*? You know, a *boc*. With some *cluck-clucks*?"

CHAPTER THIRTY-TWO

Craig had the easiest time adapting after being decanted. A hot bowl of food in his hands, and plenty of people eager to talk over one another and be the one to explain what was going on this time. He fit in so smoothly that he was cracking jokes with Tychus not even two hours in.

Ali and Razor both needed more time to find their footing, but were happy to hear that housing had been pre-planned for them. Ali decided that she would help grow herbs and spices, since salt wasn't quite what made her palate happy. Razor decided to learn how to work a blacksmithing forge. Otherwise, they both strongly agreed with the cultivation-improvement route. Both were incredibly happy to meet the others, and discover how much their Skyspear classes were going to be prized! The fire part of their dual affinities wasn't going to help much, but the other one sure would.

Craig—with his single strong earth affinity—was equally interested in comparing how guild methods and Skyspear methods clashed, joining the huddle when the conversation came up. Snookem and Nerys' decanting had to be momentarily delayed, because Genevieve shot out of the ground as a harsh, shivering, yellow light. *"Ugh. Ash Bugs."*

Artorian put down his bowl and hopped over, letting a wave of Aura wash over her to clean the awfulness of her muddled light. "Are you alright, my dear?"

She needed a moment to compose herself, but everyone released their collectively held breath when her color resumed being a soft violet. Matters that made the old man jump up were treated with severity. "I'll be alright. I need... I need some cultivator help. I broke into a nest while making tunnels, and those beetles are hungry for anything that gives off light and heat."

While that was concerning news, all the cultivators put their bowls down and stood up, a sudden sharpness in their gazes. Jiivra, being a Mage, got to Genevieve the fastest, a hungry grin on her face as she spoke. "Where is the entrance to this tunnel network? We have all been *itching* to burn off this rapid Essence intake."

Genevieve led the way while Lunella tasked Artorian to stay behind to protect the topside in case anything went awry, as the majority of the village delved into the depths of the darkest dungeon. The cultivators were all tingling with an over-abundant Essence pool that was roiling from their fingertips, more than merely metaphorically for the few who didn't have their Aura under control. Which, interestingly, was almost all the bards.

Lunella and Wuxius sat next to their old man when it was just them remaining at the fire. Artorian laid his arms across both their shoulders, tugging them in a bit. "It'll be alright."

Wux softly shrugged. "It makes me think I may have made the wrong choice. I feel like I'm missing out from that rumbling beneath my feet. I swear I can *hear* them fighting. That or everyone is laughing at the bards as they try to play in the dark."

Artorian rubbed his back, impressed that a non-cultivator could hear them at all. "You made the choice you were happy with, my boy. Should you ever decide otherwise, just know that so long as we're in Caltopia, it's an option. You can't get some of the more dangerous side effects here. So if you ever change your mind, just let me know. Otherwise, you just be happy, my boy. I want you both *happy*."

He looked to Lunella, who said nothing, and instead had her face scrunched while chewing on her cheek. She was clearly thinking of something complicated. Nobody prodded her, allowing Lunella to chime in when she felt like it was the right moment. "Is it bad that I like this? Peaceful. Quiet. Soft. Warm. What bothers me about the entire cultivation thing the most is how much time it would take away from my kids, when I have them back in my arms."

Genevieve returned by herself, silently grumbly about the walking noise complaints who were preventing her from doing excavation work. Taking a break from being a cavelight amidst that underground Essence firework-show, she settled on Artorian's head with a huff. Since she didn't speak, the grandfather shook his head slowly in reply to Lunella. "No, that's just fine. Should I find something for the latter problem, I'll let you know."

Blanket, who hadn't gone with the big group, took this opportunity to bundle in behind them. This gave them all the wonderful idea to fall backwards. Lying in soft fluff was a big improvement compared to sitting on a hard log. Blanket, equally, was mighty happy when they did. Blanket felt important! He chirped loudly and croaked, even though nobody understood.

The following silence allowed Artorian to mentally query Genevieve for the Mountaindale prompt. When Lu and Wu untangled themselves to go cuddle up and have a whispered conversation, Artorian stroked his beard and poked a name on the screen. "Who is 'Amber'?"

Genevieve mumbled from a position of comfort. "From what I gathered, Amber is a portal Mage. She makes portals that connect from one place to another. The stable, long-term, permanent kind. She helped make the portal that led from Mayev's Spire to Mountaindale. Spent easily two hundred years in the guild, so she might be one of the difficult ones."

Nodding, he poked the next name. "Father Richard…"

He paused, thinking it over. "I think I have only ever heard this name in relation to something else. There was… I was walking to the Academy in Mountaindale on the first day. When I arrived there, I overheard this name. I don't recall liking what I heard too much, which must be why this 'demonsbane' affix became part of the entry. I like me some demonsbane, but it's too early to start announcing ourselves, and we definitely want the trouble to start elsewhere."

Artorian momentarily wondered about Spud's society again. "I'm starting to get suspicious that there was a second meaning to Adam's little mention. Or to the information tidbit about them gathering there. Was that something we *wanted* to happen?"

He considered what he would do if Odin allowed a demon to ride along, then determined that the face-punching extravaganza would end up being pretty much the same. He threw some shadow-punches in the air, and immediately felt lacking. Not only had he looked silly, but his punches were no good. "Maybe it's just because I'm lying at an angle?"

There was no reason to lie to himself. He sucked. "No, no, I just need to practice. I feel all wrong; the Eternia vibes are still running through me, and I'm missing the *flow*. Unlike my family, I am not automatically absorbing the Essence here. Must be a below-Mage-ranked feature?"

He shifted into active cultivation to see if he could, only to hit the ground hard and get knocked right out of the attempt as the fluffy floor vanished from under him. Rubbing his butt, he looked over to see a wild-eyed sugar glider holding Lu, Wu, and an upset violet Wisp tight in his wing.

"Blanket?" Artorian questioned. "Why are you hiding behind the longhouse?"

A firm *thud* nearby made Artorian look over his shoulder,

spotting an alert Halcyon who was hurriedly looking around for something. When she didn't find what she was looking for, she turned to him. "My Dreamer, was that you?"

"Was *what* me?" He asked in confusion. "All I tried to do was shift into active cultivation. I'm…"

He paused, frowned, and realized that he wasn't looking at Blanket or Halcyon from the expected ground level. He was in some kind of a hole. A crater? He prodded the ground, but it felt like ordinary ground. There was simply a big chunk missing. Getting up, he walked out of the hole where his seat used to be, then scratched his head. "How did this dent form?"

Halcyon looked at Blanket, who swiftly chirped out the story. "Ah, I see. Blanket says you did that. In your location, all Essence suddenly refined, flooding into you at speed. He says you did what Jiivra does during her part of cultivation."

Artorian threw his arms in the air. "I barely even…"

The copper dropped.

"Oh. I… *Oh.*" He looked at the ground. "*Everything* is made of Essence, and my intake, in combination with the **Law** I have, with the cultivation technique I'm rolling with, makes me a hungry boy! My absorption is so strong that I literally tear the world apart by cultivating even a *teensy* bit. No cultivating for me on Caltopia then. One technique from me and a mountain will vanish to fuel my invocation. Or the village, if I'm not careful. My tricks are *wasteful*. Good thing I've been so focused on practicing with Aura."

Halcyon did her best to be helpful. "I heard you once had access to runes that allowed you to be both powerful *and* efficient? Do you not still have those?"

Artorian recalled what she meant when he thought of his testing days, when he was clearing out that ant's nest. "I suppose I do still have access, if those Pylons exist. That's just it though, dear, I used Pylons. External help. I don't actually know those runes myself. I think if I tried it again, my output would be better because I roughly recall what it felt like the first time, but certainly not as potent."

She tapped her chin. "Would learning them help? I could introduce you to The Thunk Squad. We play Speedball, and that will teach you to be good with your techniques *quickly.*"

Artorian glanced at the hole, then at Blanket. "Are you hurt at all, my boy?"

Blanket chirped to the negative, finally letting Lu and Wu down as Genevieve escaped the fluffy confines. She flew a wide circle around him before bashing downwards on his head a few times, flashing angry reds and oranges while little steam-puffs fumed out of her. No longer wanting to be here, she loudly exclaimed her plans before zipping away. "I'm checking on the underground expedition!"

Artorian was worried about his family, but the non-cultivators were shrieking with laughter, already picking each other up to get back to the bonfire. Lunella explained through her smile. "That's just going to be another normal occurrence from now on, isn't it?"

Artorian looked sheepish. "I'll do my best not to take accidental chunks out of the landscape, and will find elsewhere to be when I need to practice. Doing it here will, uh, not be good for the village."

Blanket bounced over to Halcyon to make noise, easing his head down so she could easily pet him. He did a good! She amusedly gave him attention, then turned to her Dreamer when he chirped up a storm. "Blanket says he can protect the village just fine on his own."

Looking at the ground after, she cocked her head for a moment, then guffawed. "How one-sided. Your village found a nest of F- to D-ranked beetles. There's a Mage down there, so that's as good as won. Looks like she's letting everyone else get practice in, and slapping any bugs that are too smart for their own good. Your adopted family is having a... *hmm?*"

Artorian walked up to her. "Yes, dear?"

"Who is the one with the earth affinity, in the trio between the water and air one?" She pointed at the ground, which made Artorian remember that, if he wanted to, he could look *through* solid matter. Shifting his sight configuration to do just that by thinking about it, he recoiled and needed to rebalance, ending up in a hover for stability. Depth perception became an entirely different game when matter and opacity were more of a suggestion.

It took him a minute to get the combination right, until he could see skeletons fight... foggy shells? No, that still wasn't quite right. Another minute of back and forth adaptations, and he found a good enough mixture. "There they are! That would be Tychus. What about him?"

Halcyon pointed with a digit, keeping track herself. "He fights like he is significantly larger than he actually is. He feels... too small for what he is trying to do. Like, he thinks he's my size? The water one keeps trying to summon things, and it's clearly not working. The third one is keeping them both out of danger."

Artorian understood. "Tychus used to have an infernal channel, and was actually about the size of you. He was not given a wealth of time to come to terms with normality. I will not be surprised if he attempts to return to being a small titan. Grimaldus went the way of a necromancer in a past life, while my Astrea used to be known as 'the nightmare.' I still worry if I took more from them than I gave back. Without that channel, many of their abilities will be out of reach for them."

Cy did not follow. "What's so wrong with having an infernal channel? I have one. You have one."

Artorian was at a loss for words for a moment. "Whennn... people gain infernal channels, it eats all their other channels, unless those channels are of the strong variety. An infernal channel also has a tendency to make you pay attention to one thing, at the cost of... most everything else. If you're not careful."

Swaying a little, she still didn't see the problem. "I'm pretty sure they can handle that? They grew up with it. Besides, can't you give that channel to them without it consuming the others?"

Artorian rubbed his hands over one another. "I... I suppose

I could. I haven't actually asked them. I should do that. That seems the right thing to do."

Halcyon nodded, pressing her advantage. "It also looks like you need to get your mind onto something else for a while. Why not come with me for a bit? Do some combat training."

Artorian just wasn't sure, but Lu and Wu made it easy for him. Wux nodded while Lunella spoke. "Go! Get your ground-eating habits under control, then come back to decant the rest of those people you were talking about. We're waiting for the children regardless, and I want a nice foundation up and running before Irene and I need to do more paperwork."

He resigned himself and nodded. "Alright, alright. I'll be back soon, then. Anyone you're planning on bringing into the village I should be aware of?"

Wuxius smirked. "Only the entire Spring Court. No biggie! We need some specialized work around the village that we just can't do on our own, and Genevieve said she knew some newlights."

"*Ha!*" Artorian chuckled, his mood quickly restored thanks to the little jab. "Well, good luck with that! I'll be back soon. Have Genevieve forum-call me when the trio comes back up; I need to ask them about restoring a channel. She'll know what you mean."

Halcyon changed into her Orca form and took to the sky when the conversation seemed finished, prompting Lu and Wu to start waving as Artorian eased into the air. He appreciated their support, and tried not to make too big of a bang when launching himself straight up into the sky.

When they were gone, Wuxius walked to the new hole to see how deep it was, with Lunella hanging off his shoulder. "Well. This is convenient. You did ask where the bonfire and barbeque ashes needed to go. Now we have a pit! I'ma call it the ash pit. Because Ash Beetles live around here. Maybe they have a use?"

The Matron agreed that having ash storage would be useful. "Good for the fields, and even better for lye. Which means we can finally make soap. We are in *dire* need of soap."

The loud chitter of a sugar glider scooping them up paused their conversation. The house-sized puffball huffed loud, then bathed the dirty children the animal way. With a big, wet, messy tongue. In response to their complaints, the unstoppable bathing only intensified.

When the glider was done, Wux could only laugh at Lun's sour expression. He finally thought of something good to say, and grinned out the wise words. "Blanket defends. Blanket protects."

CHAPTER THIRTY-THREE

Artorian received the forum call mid-flight to Moonbase Alpha —which was surely only called that for innocuous reasons. Genevieve connected them in a group, and Artorian felt the need to be cheeky. <Yoo-hoo, fresh pastries and honey-cakes hotline. What sugary confection can Air-Artorian get you today?>

Astrea replied without missing a single beat. <Three infernal cherries with the channels on top!>

They laughed heartily. It was good to be silly and make jokes. Artorian needed to hit his chest a few times to get a hold of himself. <Ah, you're a hoot. I've missed you lot! There's very few others who can hear me get on a tangent and jump right on the merchant cart with me, peddling our madness.>

Astrea snickered. <Listen, old man, the time under the Skyspear may taste foul in my mouth, but dropping that sick beat on the blight's head? That is one of the grand highlights topping all my accomplishments. Mad plans are mad fun, and us Fringe kids don't stop until the party is dead on their feet and the fight is won!>

Artorian could see why she wanted to hang out with the

bards. <Splendid! Well, I'm halfway to where I need to be, I take it you all want those channels back open then? Do I need to hurry back?>

Grimaldus chuckled, adding to the conversation with that telltale family-friendly smarm in his words. <No, Grandpa. You go get *dragged* through the mud for a while. The change of pace sounds healthy. Irene has been telling the tales of your early training with this massive grin on her face. We all want the channels, but we've decided to train and practice with what we have first. We know how to use our infernal side, but the channels we currently have are... going to need some getting used to.>

Tychus cut in, refusing to be left out, even if he wasn't ready to talk. <Especially since we'd like the channel in addition to our current one, and not an... uh, r*eplacement,* like last time. I... kinda...>

Grim was blunt for his struggling brother. <We think we want *all* the channels, like the family-lineage troublemakers we are. Also, I wanted to know how you felt about summoning? I miss Sarcopenia, but the stories about how the demons are an even bigger problem now are difficult to ignore, and she definitely is one.>

Their old man needed a moment, mulling it over. When he came up with an answer, he decided that he needed some kind of arbiter. Lucky for him, he knew a good one. <I'm going to give that a solid maybe. There's someone I'd like the immediate family to meet when I get back. I have... an addition I'd like to introduce.>

The mention made the trio mighty curious.

<Otherwise...> He sighed. <Ask Genevieve for Adam, and consult him on the topic. He's a bit of a character judge expert, so if you tell him what you know, and he replies kindly, well, there's a quicker answer. If he replies poorly, on the other hand, same difference, just the other way.>

Then the old man had a terrible thought. <Actually, no,

scratch that. Do not call for Adam. If any of our old church people see him, they'll have an aneurysm from sheer shock.>

Tychus could be felt blinking in confusion through the connection, speaking for the three of them. <Who's Adam?>

Momentarily, Artorian regretted not having kept his mouth shut. Still, the C'towl was out of the bag again. One day he really needed to invest in better bags. <Adam is a Celestial. Full, honest to the above planar being. We get along. He's keeping the Silverwood tree safe from our demon problem, plus this and that.>

Astrea promptly changed her mind. <Can we get a celestial channel instead? Infernal suddenly sounds like a *really* bad idea.>

Her grandfather could not help but relapse into weak laughter. <*Ah... aha...* no, no, my dear, it doesn't work like that. Having the channel is fine, and at worst he'll grumble. It's far more important that you go with what works for you. The opinions and views of others be abyssed.>

Grim smirked, Artorian just knew it when the boy spoke. <Pretty sure that some people who do that get the *smite!*>

The grandfather fussed, and it was the trio's turn to break down into a heap of weak laughter. They loved pulling one over on him. Artorian's mumbles only grew louder. <Yes, well, it's not my fault that some people choose to be complete abyssalites with their choices. Sometimes, you just need to punch a fool. Particularly if that fool believes that someone else doesn't deserve what they have themselves. Or really anyone that doesn't treat people like people. That might just be my personal bone to pick with humanity though.>

<Humanity? Not, like, High Elves of all kinds?> Astrea was somewhat interested in the specification. <Can't just be the humans who have your goat.>

<My goat?> Artorian mumbled back, trying to find the joke. <My sheep, maybe. I do speak Baa. Wait, no, now that I think of it, goats speak a dialect of Baa. Though it's more of a *Beh-h-h*.>

The goat noise made Astra crack up and dismiss her question entirely. <Alright, alright! I was just being funny.>

<I was as well!> Artorian mused. <Though, no, High Elves and the rest aren't exactly exempt, but I've got some extra annoyance on my shoulders when it's my own kind. I abyss-well know that they could do better. In short, injustice is everywhere, and just because a law somewhere says something is allowed and alright doesn't mean that it is *either*. Crackers, now I want to go back to my philosophy scrolls and write a book on the matter. Alas, I have to go play Speedball. I'm gonna get *rolled* is what's going to happen.>

The defeatism was unlike their old man, causing Tychus to prod. <Grandpa, you never give up before getting started. What gives?>

The insight made Artorian honest to celestials stop dead in his tracks mid-flight, making Halcyon loop around and double back to check on him. She found him holding his chin in the thinker pose, floating through space as he puzzled. <Y'know... that is a *fantastic* question. Why *do* I feel so down?>

The trio gave him some silence, but after half a minute they were getting antsy. Grim decided to call the end of the conversation. <Grandpa, listen. We're worried about you, but we're also sure that you're going to figure this out. You always do. So, we believe in you, and you go feel better. When there's time, we'll be where you left us, doing what we do.>

Tychus became distracted by a prior thought, thinking he was answering his brother. <Meditating on how legality is not a guide for morality?>

Astrea snickered. <Causing trouble, you goof! Lunella doesn't have remotely enough gray hairs, and without her children around, we need to step up to the plate. Seriously though, Grandfather. Grim's right. Remember that we love you, and come home soon. Or, y'know, send stories of you getting *rolled*.>

Artorian managed a, <Why you little—> before the connection cut from their end, and he held his forehead. "Insightful *brats*."

<My Dreamer?> Halcyon nudged, her massive, soft orca nose bumping him as she opened her own forum channel now that he was available. <Did the talk you were in not go well?>

He reached out to rub her nose, and shook his head. <No, quite the opposite. Dear, have I been down, or dawdling? I feel out of it for some reason, and have for a while. I can't shake it and can't seem to find where it's coming from.>

<Is... it not obvious, my Dreamer? It's been obvious to any Chosen or Beast. Even Blanket saw the problem right away.> She smoothly swam along his side and nudged him along with one of her fins, like he was a common podling, guiding him back on track with the grace and skill of a practiced leader.

<You think too much, and act too little. You worried about your problem, but you didn't do anything about it. You're so enamored with wanting to return to the nest, to experience daily life with family, that you have forgotten to hunt and provide for yourself. That is why I stressed so directly for you to come along with me. To me, what you need is very clear. You need *action*.>

Another guiding nudge, and he was flying again, following in Halcyon's starry, golden wake. <In Eternia, your life was 'go, go, go.' There was no stopping unless you were forced to, and no slowing down unless it was needed for some kind of plan, ploy, or setup. You faced an Incarnate and won, as a Mage! That would get anyone's blood pumping, no matter whether you did it in Eternia or not. Nobody will fuss that the task would not have been possible in Cal. It was *done*.>

Letting him pass, Cy adjusted his heading. She nudged her Dreamer more affectionately this time, unwittingly making him match her speed and keep up as they rebuilt momentum, neatly allowing them both to surf the wave of her wake in tandem. <Exiting Eternia, you've done nothing but see new places, and meet old souls you've sorely missed. That is a pleasant life, but a *slow* one. One not currently suitable for Administrators who are needed to tackle larger problems. No matter how badly I wish to join that pond and look the other way.>

A quick placement of a fin, and they were outpacing her glow, streaming along the stars on a clear trajectory to the moon as she spoke from experience. <Being in Eternia puts this... coating? over the body. This layer of rust that needs to be ground back off the hard way. Not quite needing to know how to walk again, but nothing feels quite... *right*. Eternia is the biggest convenience. The system makes you comfortable. *Complacent*. Eternium wants you to fit in a neat little box, whether he intends it or not. Once you fit even a little, that fitting feels like the new *right*.>

She bumped her nose on his head for being good as he listened. <Then, when you exit back into Cal, it all feels so horribly, horribly *wrong*. Like the world is raw, and frayed at the edges. There is more to sense, more to feel, more to smell, and more tiny details that grate. I've experienced it a few times, and each time the transition became more noticeable. The welcoming ease of Eternia, then the more realistic rawness of Cal, who, I'm told, is but a pale copy of the even harsher world out there.>

Halcyon eased her rapidly building temperature, her colorations cooling back down from a blazing red heat. The difference between worlds was an irritation to her. <When that coating sensation returns, that rust, all one can feel is unease. During my first return, I could not shake the oddity either. The unpleasantness stuck with me, the knowledge and feeling of *wrongness*. My actions were the same, but they felt different. Incomplete. Skills executed with thoughtless ease in Eternia became truly difficult to replicate in Cal. The knowledge was still in my head, yet it was so hard to reach. So difficult to make the motions. Like Eternia was this half-life where I could coast on by, because the world I lived in intended for me not to be bothered by certain things.>

Artorian could only nod. That all sounded right on the money, down to the coated feeling of 'something is stuck' that not even his Aura could scrub from his skin. The problem wasn't skin deep at all, he realized. The problem, like Tychus had pointed out, was rooted entirely in his perception.

He inspected his own hands mid-flight for a reason he wasn't quite sure about, mentally speaking while Cy took a breather. <Then you're back in Cal, and the ease of it all is gone. Some tricks come with you, but there's certain conveniences you get used to in Tim's world really, *really fast*. The mana regeneration for one, the half-physics, the sensations being tied to numbers. Yes, I... I think I understand. Our bodies become accustomed to the convenient truth, rather than what's real.>

He squeezed his hands shut, frowning as he considered her mention that compared Cal to the outside world. A world she'd never seen. <Except that in this case, the location of where one is *changes* what is real. Both worlds are real, but both still operate using the best facsimiles they have access to. This body... this body should be so much harder to control if it were my true one. I should leak Mana like a sieve, and I have no true bearing for personal Mana capacities either. I just know roughly where I'm at, but I know I don't have the same limitations here as I would out in the real.>

His vision sharpened, eyes locking onto the moon as he concluded his mumbles. They made sense to him, and for now, that was enough. <Yes, 'raw' versus 'constructed.' A very apt comparison.>

Artorian finished with a stern nod. <Halcyon, my dear. I think you're right. I'm covered in rust, and need to change what I consider normal.>

He turned his head, smiling sweetly as a thank you for all her kind help. She made the pod call in reply, the energy of which rolled over him as a measure of understanding, and soothing comfort. She was delighted to have helped.

Given her elation, Artorian thought to ask one more thing. <Halcyon?>

<Hmm?> She was suddenly suspicious of a podling who was regaining confidence too fast for his own good.

Artorian sped past her, regaining some of his cheek. <Teach me this Speedball.>

The Orca's reply was to surprise him right away by out-accelerating him, and hip-checking the cheeky podling so hard that he didn't see the strike coming. With a swipe of her tail, he was sent off towards the moon at double-speed with a very noteworthy and obvious *thunk*!

<Sure thing!> She laughed, matching his prior pep. <Speedball is all about throwing your weight around. Welcome to the Thunk Squad! I am its *captain*. Lesson one, *everyone* is the ball.>

Appearing next to him again with an acceleration that surprised the old man for a second time, he suddenly realized that Halcyon was using the same acceleration ability he'd had such fun with in Eternia. Not that it helped him react in time when she twisted on her axis, that large Orca tail coming at him again with another *thunk*!

<Lesson two!> Artorian scrambled to right himself without a handhold, successfully dodging the third smackdown as the massive Orca zipped past. <The goal is to *not* be the ball.>

Thinking this game was considerably wilder than assumed, Artorian could suddenly feel the difference between a state of readiness, and the cramped limitations that distinctly felt like rust covering his skin. The need for sudden, instant, rapid high-energy movements caused an epiphany, and a purpose of the game was revealed to him.

When Halcyon zipped towards him with her fourth tail-swipe coming down from above, her Dreamer straight-up caught her tail and stopped it, causing a golden shockwave to ripple away from his hand. Or he thought he stopped it, as Halcyon grinned at his quick uptake, then completed the other half of her movement anyway to violently send him flying again. <Very good! That brings us right into lesson three.>

Artorian tensed, forgetting to correct his heading in favor of assuming a defensive posture. The unexpected follow-through from Cy had knocked him out of his concentration, the silly old man having dropped his readiness. He'd failed entirely to get into the proper flow of things, as that sensation of rust felt impossible to ignore while it clung to him. Now that he was aware of the rust, Artorian couldn't get his mind off it. He didn't understand. He'd been such a fantastic fighter in Eternia, why was he freezing up completely?

<Lesson three!> Instead of smacking him a fifth time, Halcyon stopped right in front of his path, having shifted fully into her large humanoid form on the way. Catching her Dreamer, she patted him on the head while he fixed his vertigo and regained an idea of which direction 'down' was. <Remember that no matter how intensely we play, it's a game, and all we're trying to do is knock the other away. Which will make a lot more sense when you see the Thunk Arenas. Or as we call the big one in orbit up here, 'The Orb.'>

Feeling his tension fade, only now did Artorian realize that his flight had ended as a jarring memory of being chased by mozzarella balls temporarily haunted him. That snapped him out of his funk real fast, and at a good time too! They had reached their destination.

With his bearings regained, and the heart-pounding sudden introduction over, he held on to Cy while looking around. Which was all that was needed for her to beam a toothy smile at him, and swing her arm out to introduce the structure in question.

Floating a few miles above the bastion-style stronghold on the moon that unfurled beautifully like a lotus flower—doubling as the ground Artorian had needed to orient himself—hung a massive, oversized version of the soap bubble 'door' that led into Aiden's underwater ocean forest. The first location of many that Halcyon was very happy to show off, as she spoke with gusto. <Welcome to version three of my Daimyo castle, and *The Oooorb*!>

CHAPTER THIRTY-FOUR

While it was the orbital arena that Halcyon wanted to bring attention to, the point of interest holding Artorian's gaze was the crumpled chunk of metal slag that once used to be a proud door. The folded-in bulwark—very much embedded in the ground far outside the front gate—appeared like it belonged there. The accidental monument served as a front-entrance statue, as it was the only landmark he could find that would indicate any sort of 'front' on Cy's fortress.

The structure did not look like he'd thought it would based on prior description. Shaped as an actual lotus flower that was in process of blooming, the center was taken up entirely by a truly *thick* multi-tiered pagoda with a sundry of well-designed golden detailing. The flower itself was more for art, rather than function, though the design did hide the actual two-tiered fortress lurking beneath.

He saw the star-shaped fortifications, recognized a few dead zones, and noted the entire structure was positioned on a high hill compared to the surrounding flatlands, laid out in a radial pattern within polygonal fortifications and extensive outer earthworks. He blew out air between his lips as he immediately thought about how to assail it. "*Pfff*. That's a tough nut to crack."

Some movement caught his eye, pulling his gaze from the moonside structure.

Hulk, muscle-squirrel extraordinaire, was failing to move the lawn ornament even a little bit. Looking distinctly red in the face while leveraging himself against the obstacle, it was clear he was putting his back into the effort, all for minimal progress. Or *no* progress! To the great amusement of Artorian, for whom it was equally clear that Halcyon's cultural monument to 'rushing out' was also going to become a permanent new fixture.

That bulwark was simply not budging.

When she cleared her throat hard, Artorian turned and *oooooh'd* at the soap bubble, nodding like he was impressed. Halcyon's arm dropped as she released a heavy sigh. She knew she'd lost him. <Okay, so the door is hard to ignore, and I haven't particularly wanted to go move it.>

Artorian looked back down, now that Hulk's resistance training tool was the proper subject of the conversation. He decided a joke would be well placed. <Honestly, dear? I rather like it. The broken door gives some much welcomed directional aesthetic to that otherwise very organic building down there. The roundness of the bulwark matches the roundness of the Orb, and that does something for me in the artistic sense. Smooth above, blocky in the middle, smooth below.>

He motioned at the art piece with a grin, knowing full well that the only blockiness here was in the fortifications. <Hulk's thrashing has also cleared out some space around the metal chunk, and the view from up here reminds me of one of those sand gardens that you make look nice with a tiny rake. Out of curiosity, *can* that thing be moved?>

Halcyon ground her teeth together, silently vowing to make fortress version four anything but angular. Rather than fuss, Cy knew that she wasn't going to get to give her tour any other way. <If *I* do it, yes. I think the only other people who could so much as budge that thing would be Dreamers. I just... I haven't wanted to go near it. Because I broke that door in a rush, it's become the topic of some giggles among the S.A.S. and their ilk. If I go and put it back, they'll come watch, and for some reason, the idea that *they will* causes me intense discomfort.>

Artorian squeezed one of her digits with his hand. <Cy? You know I can tell when you're hiding something, right? I'm not going to pry if you don't want to talk about it, but I do want you to know that what you just mentioned felt like a symptom. Not a cause. I also don't know you to be concerned over such small trifles. Can I help at all? You did just help me pretty effectively.>

An unpleasant train of thought crossed Halcyon's thoughts, but she shared it without preamble. If there was someone she could tell her worries and problems to, then it was certainly her Dreamer. <Well, much like rust feels bad on the skin, I've got this flavor stuck in my mouth that's causing me discomfort. Like bad icing on a cake, or the sour taste of lemon.>

Crossing her legs under her so she could sit in space, Artorian moved to copy her pose, also sitting cross legged before scooting onto her ankle. To be nearby. <It's Odin's little patch of defiance against you, his wounded pride on equally proud display. Just like everyone else who's seen it. The sight of that place sickened me, and even now it's difficult not to think of that slab of meat and not feel the hunger to *do* something. But the truth bites me in the tail first, because I know I can do *nothing*. Nothing except *lose* if I were to engage.>

Halcyon's face scrunched up, her feelings complicated. <Knowing that you are guaranteed to lose against another creature is both a blessing, and this... intensely terrible sensation. On the one fin, my nature tells me where not to engage. On the other, Odin has caused us such grievance in the past that the *inability* to do something about it makes me furious.>

Artorian let his Aura roll out, assisting with the comfort so Cy could feel welcome to get this off her chest. He expected everyone would have something that bothered them, after all. Keeping pleasantly silent, he used his Mana construct to rub along her back.

Halcyon bumped her nose to the top of his head in reply, then spoke in their private forum connection. <This one thing that should be tiny is breaking off into other small discomforts that should not be bothering me, but they do. I could go fight Odin, but because my innate senses tell me that I will lose, and I should back away... I know that I will not be able to fight him properly. I will keep shifting to be on the defensive, which is partially why we developed Speedball.>

Seeing that Artorian's brow rose, and his interest piqued, Halcyon explained. <What I showed you before are aspects of the game. What I tell you now is more the inner truth of it. Speedball is about aggression. Hunting. Taking initiative and focusing on positioning in order to get in the best strike. Against Odin, I had the thought that *one* strike would be all I'd have before the bestial inclinations kicked in. Inclinations I simply can't ignore, or pretend aren't there, no matter how good I made my humanization.>

He nodded, so she continued. <Because of this one-strike idea, the second wave of the Chosen got together, and we collectively came up with Speedball. Getting the rust off is best done by being forced into highly explosive, sudden changes in movement and activity. By forcing your body and energy into a state where it *has* to react, it isn't allowed the complacency that it so badly wants to keep returning to—freezing up like you did earlier, my Dreamer, is actually rather common for people freshly out of Eternia. On the same fin, because playing defensive will only make you lose the game of Speedball, you *must* take initiative and strike first.>

Halcyon motioned to the bubble, and this time her Dreamer paid proper attention, inspecting the soap bubble. He saw more than just a copy of Aiden's front door, as Artorian could now detect that crystalline gyrosphere wheels turned steadily around the outside. They were massive rings keeping the bubble together that held seating where a crowd could sit. The crystal structures were see-through, which told him how he'd missed them the first time. The bubble's supports just blended in against the background.

Halcyon finally felt the pride she was hoping to feel as she took in her Dreamer mumbling about little details, pointing out small tidbits as his eyes darted from one feature to another. When he realized that one of the more solid metallic rings looked rather familiar, he snapped his fingers. <No wonder I recognize the design; those are modeled after Cal's first sun project. The big outer rings are support struts!>

Artorian felt some of Cy's tension wane, successfully being brushed away by his Aura. Her comfort rose, easing her reactions. <*Mhm*! They are what keeps the bubble intact at the size it is, which is how we keep that advanced arena in one piece. The goal of Speedball is to knock all other players out of the ring, and be the last one still inside. This is why playing defensive is no good, you'll just get hip-checked or tail-slapped out.>

Rubbing his beard, he pondered a detail. <Say, is it called the Thunk Squad purely due to the noise your tail makes when it hits something? That sound can't be specific to just me.>

Halcyon beamed. <My Dreamer. I love your ability of insight. That's exactly it, and is why my team is named the Thunk Squad. When my tail smacks one of the bodies people use here, for some reason the impact always makes that sound. There's a betting pool in the stronghold below on why, but nobody has an answer yet.>

What Artorian was actually happy about was that Halcyon's tension and concerns had bled away. He nodded, and felt confident that he could tap the issue and see what else was going on. <So, because Odin is being a spud, and he's likely very strong, you're uncomfortable because you want to slap him halfway across the moon, but can't. Because you can't—but want to—

other, smaller things have been starting to get to you. Like what public opinion might be over a lawn ornament. That's… Dear, that's honestly very reasonable.>

Halcyon jerked her head up, surprised. <It is?>

<Oh yes!> Artorian nodded sagely. <Why wouldn't it be? Little irritations make other irritations even when you don't mean for them to, and the same is true for discomforts. I bet that as soon as Odin isn't a problem anymore, all your worries will suddenly vanish at once, since they all actually only stemmed from one thing. When we have slapped that wall of meat down, you're suddenly going to look at that bulwark and wonder why you were ever concerned at all. That piece of slag won't bother you any further, and you'll be able to laugh the event off and recount the story as some fond old memory of past times. I promise that it'll all be alright.>

Artorian patted her with tender care as she squeezed him, and didn't fuss one iota over her crushing strength. <Worries only seem difficult to handle on the surface. The hard part is figuring out what the actual concern or irritation is. Frequently, what you feel is the issue is, in reality, only the side effect of something else happening. When you know what the real issue is, then you can tackle it, or at minimum plan for it. Even if you can't do anything about the problem, knowing what the specific case and cause of the problem is, by itself, will help you deal with it.>

Artorian continued being supportive—always here for his most favored few. <We now know that Thundy, and what he's doing, is a problem for more than just me and mine. We also know that you'd like to do something about it, and while you've moved ahead admirably with some key ideas—because you're still bothered—it means that the current efforts aren't quite enough. That means the next step is quite clear.>

Halcyon's eyes sparkled with hope. <Which is?>

Artorian showed his teeth as he smiled. <We get all this rust off, put the small things out of mind, and go thunk Spud out of his precious gilded castle. All this whinging about me not feeling

quite right as a Mage now makes a lot of sense, and I want to get into the flow of things. So we can swim in there and get right to swinging!>

Halcyon was feeling the hype, and punched her fist upwards. <Yeah!>

CHAPTER THIRTY-FIVE

With a smile on her face, Halcyon thought about a topic she was supposed to return to from the earlier conversation in the New Fringe. There was one more thing she wanted to vent about before returning home. <Slight detour. Do you remember when I was talking about **Laws**, and had to awkwardly pause?>

He nodded, rolling his wrist to ask her to continue.

<So, Beasts may only have Beast Cores, but the story is a little different for Chosen. Your blessings did more than just... saying some fancy words to give us a boost.>

Artorian sat up straight, his arms crossing while his face positively glowed with a desire to know more. <This I *must* hear.>

Halcyon wasn't sure how to explain the next part, so she moved away from her Dreamer a tiny bit and shifted into her Orca form. They both re-engaged their flight, but Cy motioned for a loop around The Orb first. They were forum-speaking anyway. <So, the common rule is that Beast Cores are located in the head or the heart. Mine is in my head. Could you look at

it rather carefully? It has something that it's not supposed to have.>

Doing as requested, Artorian spent a few minutes getting his eyes to look at what they were supposed to. When he located her frankly gorgeous icosahedron Beast Core, he released a loud 'Ha!' <It's a golden Core! That's, like, one of the projects I was going to look into. You had it all along? I'm intensely amused.>

Halcyon nodded, but that wasn't what she'd hoped he'd see. <That it is, but they're all supposed to be gems. *Crystals*. Beast Cores aren't *metallic*. I think mine might actually *be* gold.>

That detail made Artorian hush, lacing his fingers as he began his inspection from the beginning. <Is that so? Interesting. Well then, I was looking at the wrong aspect, wasn't I? Let's... *Hmm*? That's odd. No, I'm fairly certain your Core is a gem. It's just... affected by something. Why am I getting the sympathy-connection feeling that you are tied to some kind of **Law**? Do you mind if I delve deeper?>

<I would greatly prefer it if you did.> Halcyon wanted her own suspicions confirmed, or thoroughly squashed.

With new permissions, Artorian looked deeper, this time allowing his Mana to flow freely from his being. The effort made him look like a localized pink supernova that flew small circles around the orbital arena.

Tapping into his own **Law** so the energy could brush over Halcyon's Core, he mentally jotted down that the act felt effortless. He also noted that some of the free energy was absorbed, as Beast Cores were known to do, but some shot off *elsewhere*.

A clue!

Sending out a second pulse, his Mana allowed the image of the Tower to bloom in his mind's eye, complete with an uncountable number of connector cables that looked horribly disorganized. Artorian's nose tingled with the firm belief that he'd just stumbled across some of Cal's homework. A piece of behind the scenes kludge that the dungeon had thought nobody was going to see. Nothing was even labeled! <When Cal is back, we're going to need to talk about cable management.>

Not wanting to plink each connection manually, he sent out another pulse of Mana to do the heavy lifting. One of the connections in question felt significantly more potent than the rest as his Mana traversed it, providing him a guideline.

Following that line with ease, Artorian mentally stood in front of the **Law** dedicated to the concept of gold in Cal's kludge tower. **Aurum**. Cal clearly still had a lot of work to do on this project. He'd gotten it functional, but the exact workings were a mystery to all but the creator. Artorian did find a loose end or two that definitely told the story that Cal had still been working on this before the big bonk, so he dropped his fussing and inspected the **Aurum** node instead.

<Well, I'll be. That's interesting.> Tracing a few connective lines afterwards, he pressed his mental hand to his chest. <Oh! I think I get how your consciousness jumped levels in sapience now! I am tied to Cal's **Acme** law rather than the Tower directly, and this tether connects my **Love** Law to your **Aurum** node. This gives you easy access to the cultivation track, and all the requisite sympathy connections that allow energy from *me* to flow to *you*.>

He was enthralled. That was one intricate little trick Cal had devised, terrible cable management aside. <You have both a Beast Core *and* an… *indirect* **Law** connection? Yes, indirect. I'm acting as an intermediary. This sympathy tether allows you to easily identify me, allows my memories to flow to you—which would certainly help with the sapience categories—and comes with a slew of minor bonuses, one being limited **Law** access.>

Retreating a layer, Artorian searched Halcyon's golden Core over again. <That must also be why your Beast Core is gold instead of crystalline. The blessing I applied to you is, in actuality, a pseudo-connection to a **Law.** One that exists in a Tier somewhere under mine in the Tower. I want to say… seventy-nine?>

A momentary headache joined the words 'atomic number' as both flashed through his mind. He kept that to himself since it was another one of those intrusive word-thoughts he didn't have a spot for. He filed it away and returned to telling Halcyon about his findings. <I think this was done either to keep the **Laws** in the tower more active, or to speedily get another entity up to par. Unless Cal had secret plans in the works that I was simply never privy to. Was this perhaps one of the steps needed to bring Mages back?>

He tapped his chin. <Either way, this nixes my prior assumption. Your golden Core, and the one I had in mind, are completely different. The idea I had was to form a Beast Core as a human, and use that physical marble as a replacement for an otherwise very mental refinement technique. To the back-burner this idea returns.>

Removing himself fully, Artorian blinked to reset his vision as Halcyon adopted her humanized form once again. She exhaled in relief, feeling much better about the strangeness concerning her Core. <That's far less worrying than what I thought was going on. So my Beast Core being different is good, then?>

Artorian nodded powerfully. <Very much so! Your Core has clearly been doing all the things Beast Cores are supposed to do, but is now... *more*. As a truly wonderful addition, you're walking proof that my idea to cross progression tracks isn't just viable, but outright possible! I'm now having a wonderful day.>

Halcyon, too, felt considerably better after getting prized one-on-one time, and having vented. <Thank you, my Dreamer. That removes a considerable weight from my heart. Shall we go down? I don't think the bulwark is bothering me anymore. All I can think of now is making Yuki proud.>

Artorian could hang his coat on that statement, and got into gear, slowly descending towards the moon as he followed Halcyon to the front gates. <A story to make Yuki proud!>

For the sake of maximum dramatics, Artorian and Halcyon both copied Hulk's three-point landing. Right next to him! Jump-scaring the oversized squirrel right out of his fur. He replied by tackling Artorian to the ground, grabbing the man by the foot, and slamming him around in any and every direction he could. "You think that's funny? You puny Dreamer! I will paint the ground with your face!"

He whirled the old man above his head a few times, and tossed Artorian right through the hole in the drawbridge Halcyon had created on her way out. Another landscape feature which had been retained for 'cultural importance.' The moment that Artorian flailed through the opening, moon-crabs shot out from under the gray rocks, each holding up a plain slate with a number on it.

Hulk fumed when he saw his scores, stamping his foot. "That's *it*? A six, two threes, a seven, and a two? A *two*? That was a Dreamer I just tossed. I deserve bonus points! *Sartre*, you just have it out for me, you coffee-lover!"

The drab, equally grayscale crab holding up the panel with the 'two' on it, took a strong puff from his rolled up coffee leaf. Blowing out the beige cloud, the existential crab resumed a war of words that had been ongoing between them. The large-pincered crustacean replied in an accent that was decidedly nasal. Impressive for a creature without a nose. "*Mon ami*, zat is vat you get for voting against me concerning ze measurement of time!"

Hulk shook his quartz-coated knuckles at the opinionated walking seafood dish. "We need a system. One grounded, and trackable, in order to measure the proper passage of time! We can't just *float along*. There's schedules that need keeping."

"We have already tried zis!" Sartre the crab chuckled, tapping his rolled leaf to get the ashes off before gesturing with it. "To have ze concept of ze week, it means we must have ze weekend. You wished to make her a day of rest as well, *non*?" The crab launched into dramatics. "Ah, ze weekend. She is beautiful, no? And yet, she can never be yours. For when you feel zat she will stay with you forever, alas, she is already gone." He waggled his rolled leaf. "You see? Ze idea is absurd. Just like your rigidity on ze discussions of language. Words are *flexible*. Zat is ze point!"

Hulk stomped the ground and formed stone, fuming in

disagreement. "No! Words are like bricks. Words with one correct spelling have only one correct meaning! I despise this watery approach to *meaning*. If what you say doesn't intend what you *mean*, then you said nothing worth saying! Language should make *sense*. Lobsters should be part of a lob, but they're not. It's a *pod* of lobsters for some reason. Definitely not a *risk* of lobsters —that word doesn't exist with that connotation."

Sartre waved his leaf around, releasing a bubbly laugh. "Ha! A risk of lobsters is still more likely; have you seen those claws? Besides, nut-breaker, you are once again wrong with that stony view of yours. As someone who studied linguistics, I will never not laugh when someone says 'that word doesn't exist.' Zat is folly! If a word is regularly used by a certain number of people, then it exists. If it has its own grammatical rules, then it's perfectly valid, you 'ardboiled egg."

Hulk wasn't having it. "It's a made up word!"

Sartre bubbled loudly in response, supremely amused. "Fluff-tail, or what's left of it—see the truth! *All words are made up*. Linguistics didn't just bubble up from the seas. Nobody excavated ze world of ze ancients and went '*behold, vocabulary!*' Even if zey did, a record of language is but zat. A record. Not a rulebook. A language that doesn't adapt to an ever-changing society is bound to be lost, because, eventually, it won't be able to keep up with social progress. Feel free to feel at *risk*, petit Hulky."

Hulk stared down the crab who was currently bubbling menacingly, ignoring that Halcyon was speeding into the fortress after the Dreamer he'd chucked like yesterday's newspaper. "Crabby, if we weren't on the same team, I would be having your coffee-loving claws as a snack. But I've had enough of your drivel. I challenge you to a thunk-down!"

Putting out his coffee-leaf in the dirt, Sartre scoffed. "Ze only claws you vill be having are ze imprints that vill be left behind on your face! To ze arena! When I win, I demand you fetch me a latte from ze iced-coffee elemental on ze coldest of Caltopia mountaintops."

From the sidelines, freshly-arrived S.A.S. cheered with

popcorn already in hand, having left the fortress for some fresh air. They had paused their own discussion on the way by, but now that the crab and squirrel were both making their way to the pits, resumed talks. The leader of the group, an air Essence squirrel, now clearly in a rush to get back inside, hurried along his words. "Alright, I need alternatives to ladies and gentlemen. Us announcers have been using that for too long, and need a shake-up."

The rest of the group chimed in with ideas. 'Guys, gals, and pals.' 'Beloved friends and tolerated acquaintances.' 'Entities of interest.' 'Wagner's least and most wanted.' Then finally, 'Ladies, gentlemen, and those of us who know better,' since they were mostly all something other than what they appeared to be.

Assured that they found something good to pick between, the S.A.S. sped inside to watch the showdown while munching on their snacks. Trade with the corn-cultivating raccoons was going incredibly well! A shame that negotiations had broken down with the desert deer. At least they could still get good quality antler bags.

These events halted when the S.A.S. smacked into the back of Sartre, who smacked into the back of Hulk, who was staunchly holding his ground in order not to stumble forwards and smack into the mountain that was Halcyon.

A steaming Cy loudly boomed very pointed words at Wagner, who currently had Artorian half-swallowed down one of his many metallic mouths. The distinct look of being chastised was present on all his faces as he honk-whined out a very recognizable '*but Moooom*' in response to Halcyon.

"I don't want to hear it, young man!" She exploded back at the gargantuan, multi-headed, Iridium hydra-goose. "You spit him out in one piece, this instant! Or I will not bring you *any* of the good snacks. For a *week*."

Wagner spit Artorian forth from his metallic bill dejectedly, who fell on his butt while covered in the most... undesirable of juices. The old man's face remained entirely scrunched, expression stuck in the most obvious example of 'ew' the S.A.S. had ever seen. His arms were raised and held like a T-rex, with his posture hunched in on itself.

Remembering he could solve that dilemma, Artorian rolled out his cleaning Aura and refused to move a single Mana-muscle until the very last vestige of the aforementioned 'ew' was gone. He wondered for a moment how he'd ended up like this.

When he'd been tossed like a sack of grain through the broken opening, he'd done a truly majestic tuck and roll. His momentum careened him right into a proper and honestly regal standing pose, where he stood triumphant. Unfortunately, his only witnesses were Wagner's many heads, who all blinked in confusion before recognizing the face of the old adversary who'd trampled over the ol' homestead.

All Artorian managed was a rather sullen and bear-y, "Oh, bother," after which the goose attempted to eat him, only to be promptly and succinctly shut down by Halcyon. Even with Beast-rules what they were, there was an even more potent rule at play that allowed mothers to circumvent them entirely. Halcyon, being a Mage-ranked Beast, told Wagner, very much an Incarnate-class creature, what to do with heat and fervor.

"Thank you, dear," Artorian said as he got up, watching a very fussy goose sulk away to his room under the judgmental glare of Halcyon. "How…?"

Halcyon's stride had not lost any steam, and her reply boomed appropriately. "I'm their mother, my Dreamer. I have been ever since the first spellform geese were let loose upon the Soul Space. Although, in truth, you were entirely responsible for the *first* one. Don't think I didn't find out that you cast the Rune behind your back, you sly fox."

Artorian looked away with a whistle, then saw some kind of dirt-covered oval arena through one of the open doors. A dust cloud within obscured the activities, but it seemed like such a great location to escape to! With such a convenient distraction directly in view, he power-walked to it without missing a beat. "Oh look, what's that over there! Looks so interesting!"

Crossing the threshold suddenly changed Artorian's entire

vibe.

Where it had been peacefully quiet in the main hall—his almost being eaten notwithstanding—Artorian became acutely aware that he'd passed through a membrane of air.

On the other side, there was only cacophony.

The striking notes of violas clashed with the pounding of drums. The arching stands were full of shouting creatures that came in all varieties. Commentary was hurled from anywhere like-dressed people were seated, insults aimed at a side of opposing colors. He heard the words 'upset,' 'line of scrimmage,' and 'yellow card' hurled with wild abandon as he came to a stop. As he stood on the other side of the now shattered Seventh-Tier Air-Barrier that he'd casually strolled on through, the importance and intricacy of that protective ward was lost on him entirely as he took in the sights.

When Artorian looked over his shoulder, it quickly became clear to him that everyone had expected him to walk smack into that solid wall of well-shaped air Essence and be stopped cold. Halcyon's berating paused, her expression telling him that she was in the same boat of having expected him to be unable to enter an *active* Speedball Arena.

She'd not stopped him, convinced he'd smash into the shield, waddle away in confusion, and then return for the rest of her tour like a good podling who'd been appropriately chastised from his own mistakes. Instead, she slapped her forehead. "Of course *my* Dreamer finds great trouble in record time. *Of course.* Well, he did want a crash course. He's *got one* now."

The roaring sound of an announcer drowned them all out, the noise originating from a moose wearing a truly spectacular set of shades. "Ladies and gentlemen! This match has been a royal rumble with all the rule-breaking, but if everyone could divert their gazes to the south gate. We have a late entry and *neeeew contestant*! We're already bucking all the conventions in this feud-fest of a match, so what's one more! Welcome, new player, to the least forgiving game type in all of Speedball. The Crown Game!"

CHAPTER THIRTY-SIX

Artorian raised his finger in the hopes for an explanation, but a Grackle—one of the contestants currently breaking rules in the arena for a greater cut of the seed—squawked out an attack. "Imperious piercing finger!"

Charging in a straight line with a feather extended towards Artorian, the man badly wanted to ask if the Grackle had meant 'imperious piercing feather' instead, as that would have made more sense. When Artorian turned—like a fool—in order to question an approaching Halcyon as to just what was going on, the dark bird succeeded with his dastardly strike, aimed right at a vulnerable keister.

"I have you now!" the bird croaked, before a noisy *snap* turned the loud *hay-aaah*! of the charge into an *ai-ai-ai-ai-ai* of pain. Holding his own hand, which Artorian noted was just covered in feathers, the Grackle heaved loud, deep breaths between repressed tears. "What are you *wheeze* made of?"

To Artorian, the attack had been negligible. Barely an inconvenience. To the crowd, who'd been wildly cheering for one of their favorites to cause yet another upset by using paralyzation techniques, the spectacle only added to their enjoyment.

William the Grackle waddled uncertainly away as the technique backfired horribly. Coating oneself in paralytics was one thing, but the discharge—much like the pointy end of the stick —was supposed to go *into the other guy*. Instead of properly delivering, the Essence had impacted the old man, promptly betrayed their owner, jumped ship, and then boarded the original vessel for a straight-on mutiny, electrocuting William well enough to jar him right out of whatever he was doing with jerky little motions.

The crowd on the opposing bleachers jeered at him. "What's wrong, Mr. Three Legs? You're not even balancing on one!"

William attempted to reply with a rude gesture, but wasn't able to make the motion. He just couldn't get his arm up before collapsing like a twitching mess into the coarse sand of the arena. This received hollered chants from both sides. "Ring. Out! Toss. Him. Out! Ring. Out! Toss. Him. Out!"

Halcyon leaned in the doorway, but shrugged silently at Artorian's pleading visual questions. "Aren't you supposedly very good at this, my Dreamer? A natural, I was told."

Artorian motioned at the twitching oversized bird on the ground. "What story did you hear that made you think I would be good at this? I do not make it a habit to randomly walk into Arenas!"

"Chasuble." Halcyon's response was curt, before raising an eyebrow to make a general motion at the location he'd waltzed in to. "Or perhaps Ziggurat? What was that about walking into arenas again?"

Adopting the patented Tibbins expression, the flat-faced old man turned on his heel, grabbed William by his, and promptly tossed the bird over what he surmised counted as the edge of the ring in this arena: the large sandy oval surrounded by tiny flags. A wild cheer broke out from the crowd, and they picked up a new chant while Artorian walked back to the door. "Crown. Game! Crown. Game! Crown. Game!"

The Moose announcer stood, lifted a small metal crown from an official-looking chest, and tossed it from the box seat he occupied straight into the middle of the oval arena. "The people have spoken! Since the crown was destroyed in the first game, we have ourselves a round two! Fight!"

A Tapir, Mongoose, Elephant, Cougar, Marmoset, and Buffalo all charged the center from outside of the flag line. When they crossed that threshold, they each adopted their more human forms like it was some kind of rule, and then they all beelined right for the item on the ground. The Tapir countered the Elephant by tackling him right in the face, causing both to stumble and veer into the path of the Marmoset, who was currently favored according to the noise from his colors of the crowd.

The announcer-Moose provided context to a scene that Artorian considered comical. "*Oooh*, a nasty tackle from team blue's Stan the Tea Tapir, breaking the wild charge of team red's Earl Elephant, Gray! Team yellow's Mimosa Marmoset discovered a sudden crushing defeat between the combined weights of team blue and team red. This season's rivalry is so strenuous that they have ignored the crown altogether to continue their tiff that began in round one! Someone better call the medical bakers, because they need to scrape the pancake that is team yellow's contestant from the floor. He's *doooone!*"

Artorian watched with his mouth agape from the non-active side of the flags. "The only thing 'done' are my expectations. They've got some oomph, but no clue how to use it. No wonder I found this comical. Those critters have never been in a real fight."

He wanted to turn back to Halcyon, but a glance revealed that she'd removed herself from the door before she could be properly recognized. Instead, a well-dressed man in a clean suit walked down the wall while fully ignoring gravity. His brooding appearance and deeply pigmented skin reminded Artorian of a

Dark Elf, until the spider insignia on his breast came into clear view.

Once within handshake distance, rather than offer his gloved grip for shaking, the man bowed with a hand pressed over the blood-red rose pinned to his Modsognir suit lapel. He spoke with an accent that Artorian likened to Shaka's. "A great honor to meet you directly, mighty Dreamer of my most esteemed mother. Long has it been since the months spent in the previous Daimyo castle, when Dreamers gathered freely and my mother's mood was anything but blue. It was never polite to introduce myself in those times, and I am thankful to do so now. I am named Anansi, son of Zelia, Elector Count in the Autarchy of Administration."

A moment of discomfort crossed Anansi's face when he rose. "If that branch of my mother's Autarchy still properly exists. The information between the Main Branch and our outpost in the Soul Space has not strummed as a web should. I am one of the chosen sons responsible for greater thought and hub-administrating in her dearly missed absence. May I offer my services to you, great Dreamer?"

Artorian cocked his head to convey that it would be best if Anansi dropped the 'mighty' and 'great' qualifiers. 'Dreamer' was just fine. The arachnid man in human guise made a sideways motion with his head to signal understanding, after which Artorian pointed at the Buffalo currently chasing down the fleeing Cougar, who had the crown in hand. "A primer, if you would be so kind? A small one would be great."

Anansi looked like he'd be delighted. "Of course. Speedball is about playing king of the hill. The last one remaining in the ring wins. Crown Game is a variant of speedball where you not only have to remain in the ring, but cannot win unless one also wears the crown. When one wears the crown, they become the only target anyone else is allowed to attack. Attacking anyone who does not wear the crown incurs penalty points, unless nobody has put on the crown yet. Anything goes, so long as you do not kill anyone from the opposing teams. The point and purpose is to use all your skills, tricks, and capabilities in order to win. Do not hold back. Nobody else will either."

When Anansi paused in order to break into the second half of the explanation, William the Grackle sprang upright from the medical cot and crowed loudly. He took a stance, only to jolt and fall right over—to the great laughter of the crowd. He then marched right towards the duo. Interrupting the arachnid, he slapped his wing against the wall next to them for effect. "You are at fault for this! My technique is ruined! It won't charge!"

Artorian shrugged, not exactly feeling remorseful. Anansi, on the other claw, did not take kindly to being interrupted, his accent bleeding through much harder. "Not 'is fault you can't get it up. Perhaps you only have yourself to blame for your impotence?"

With a squawk, William adopted his prior fighting pose, his balled hands making fisticuff motions, though the attempt very much appeared… lacking. Incomplete.

Anansi took that as an opportunity to verbally skewer the bird. "Go ahead, raise your arms if you want a fight that badly. *I'll wait.*"

William turned red and puffed up his feathers and cheeks, only for his arms to tremble as he couldn't quite get there. A feat that made Anansi grin devilishly. "If you can't even get your arms up, then the blame for your faltering technique can likely be found in the mirror. Unless that's *too hard* for you as well?"

William, having more than enough of being insulted, attempted to swing regardless. His attack reached as far as the floor, which he found himself pressed down against full-force. The Grackle's entire body squished to the sands while popping and groaning, an incredible weight laid upon his frame.

Artorian was in no mood for childish antics. He was honestly surprised to see the crushing effect his directed fielding was having, as he chided the bird like a tired parent. "Sit. *Down.*"

William ceased his noisy chirping, which ended the additional gravity that was slowly making him become one with the ground. He coughed out a wordless apology, then remained silent when the medical bakers came to collect another pancake.

The warm, amused, gruff voice from one of the bakers chimed as the Grackle was dragged away. "You best behave, feathers. Any more of that, and you'll be a pastry. With how flat and layered your feathers are getting, I could make a mille feuille!"

The crowd laughed, then paid attention to the action once more as someone appeared to be explaining the rules to the newcomer. An event far less interesting than Carl the Caramel Cougar using the Tea Tapir as a blunt instrument to fend off a truly upset Mint Mongoose, who currently had the crown in his mouth.

With the distraction gone, Anansi swung right back into explanations. "Speedball points determine a clan's ranking within this haphazard society we've got going. I... best explain that."

Procuring a few colored tokens, he handed the animal-shaped cutouts in different colors to Artorian for inspection. Each appeared to indicate allegiance or affiliation to some kind of clan. A word that was right on the copper as Anansi pointed to the mint-colored Mongoose emblem. "A clan is a group of people united by actual or perceived kinship and descent. Even if lineage details are unknown, clan members are organized around a founding member. In this case, the M.M. wearing this badge not only shows affiliation, but is what allows you to gain points at all. Otherwise you're just playing around."

Anansi took the tokens back, then procured a chart that had some of the insignia's grouped together. "Several clans united make a sept. A sept is a division of a family, and in this case that comes down to who considers who family. Septs choose a champion or representative for their family, and they are always considered to be wearing an insignia, even when they do not. Champions are also the people who play in Crown Games, rather than normal Speedball. The septs currently competing are not the top of the food chain, but they are still champions. The top contenders are instead handling 'gators, goats, geese and the like."

The arena rumble brought itself dangerously close to Anansi and Artorian, who both shot scathing looks in the direction of the wayward Essence techniques being thrown out by the contestants. Some had eschewed common combat and instead upped the ante to the 'tricks' level. Dodging a sawblade of compressed earth, Anansi clicked at the Arena in irritation. "While the moon's best of the best are dutiful, being a Champion sadly does not mean they are upstanding, or just. How I abhor injustice. I swear, there are but two types of people."

Artorian quirked a brow, interested in an Arachnid's perspective of that particular saying. Anansi noticed the Dreamer's interest, and motioned at the contestants caring nothing for anyone they might be injuring in the bleachers or boxes as they haphazardly threw out their techniques. "Those who believe in doing what's best for everyone even if it means personal sacrifice, and those who see their own inconvenience as unacceptable no matter what."

"Both in combat and politics, Champions, for a reason no spider can fathom, have distinct problems seeing past themselves." A foul look crossed Anansi's face. "As someone who has had to keep tabs on the politics of Olympus in addition to this, I am so *sick* of the latter."

Artorian considered Halcyon's prior words, a sudden smile gracing his features. He recognized Anansi had referred to the people who saw inconvenience as unacceptable, but had a wonderful thought for brightening the mood. "Sick of politics, you say? My boy, that sounds like a terrible affliction. I believe I've been informed enough to join this fray. Allow me to provide you a good show, and some sweet, sweet medicine in the days to come. I've the most wondrous events ready in the timeline for you, and need only to mix the ingredients with mortar and pestle."

With a scheming wink, the A-rank six Mage pressed his

right hand to his left shoulder, rolling his arm while crossing the line of flags with a massive grin on his face as Anansi observed the Dreamer with keen interest. "Anything goes, huh? Oh, I have *such* ideas. No time like the present to remember what it means to be a *Mage*."

CHAPTER THIRTY-SEVEN

A frail old man entering the Arena caused as much fanfare as expected. About none. A frail old man reaching his hand out to the crown, only for the object to wrench itself free from Mongoose's mouth and snap right into his extended grasp however, earned him a mighty and incredulous roar from both the crowd and players.

When he had cleaned the crown of spittle with a flick of his Aura, the metal object shone like it was the piece's first day out of the shop. More than just a pretty ornament, Artorian received both animosity and crowd favor when he plunked it on his head with minimal effort. Thinking it would be hilarious to stir the pot, he adjusted the item with a finger so it was ever so slightly off-tilt, causing great discomfort to anyone who really needed that item to be level.

Snapping his fingers for attention, he then sternly pointed at the arena's orchestra without facing them directly. The local musicians had been using music to fight with each other more than fit the setting or match, but the sudden wave of Mana that rolled over them fuzzed their senses and jerked them all to their feet.

Artorian spoke, gathering attention like the drop of a beat. "Maestro!"

Exhaling firmly, Artorian pulled his Aura in close, then decided it would look much more interesting on fire. Exploding in a small localized blaze, he raised his hand to the open air as the crowd gasped, requesting what he wanted from the Oriole conductor and Painted Bunting orchestral pit. "Music! Give me, *The Crown Game!*"

The previously tweet-happy viola section stopped harping with the violin section, layering their sounds as the bass-viola titmouse got their instruments set to actually get involved. The horns opened with a rolling introduction, then went quiet as the string instruments played along with one very enthusiastic Starling, whose vigor on the instrument informed everyone that she was a teensy bit salty at not having been placed on the drums.

Shaking out his sleeves, Artorian hopped on his toes a few times to find his groove. Exchanging breaths as the music began, he found a good rhythm when the contestants understood what was going on and came for him. He was now the only valid target!

With the musical beat finding a spot in his heart, Artorian snapped his mind into a state of clarity before allowing that passion to burn rampant. His Fire affinity channel was raring to *go*. "No more rust. No more *lethargy*. Release the corruption, and embrace the unity. I am a *Mage* of six perfect affinities. Like all steps, we must begin with the basics. When I move, I move with meaning. First, a baby step. Then, *Acceleration*."

With a hot spark of flaming lightning, Artorian took a blitzing step. One that began from one extreme end of the arena, only to end at the other in a flash of light and glimmering plasma. A persistent line of light left in his wake served as the only indication he hadn't moved via teleportation, showing his sharp, but careful, angled movements that slipped between the charging contestants. The lines lasted mere seconds before clearing away as more reasonable physics demanded attention.

The air had burst into liquid flames when he'd come to a standstill, unable to cope with the friction he'd caused as the expelled Mana became kerosine which clung to him for sustenance. The corruptive, rust-scented material licked his skin before sloughing to the ground like sweat rolling down summer cheeks. Artorian dismissed its clingy, corruptive presence entirely by performing a haka, powerfully stomping his foot down as he adopted a wide, stable horse stance.

He needed to remember what he actually was. How he squared up against literally everything else. How he was not the commonplace average.

It was good and well to be *the* grandfather. To be the kind soul who did not stand on the rank and file. To be the powerhouse one only saw as a friendly face, whose knee was but a bouncy horse for Sproutlings, rather than a deadly weapon to pull free from a demon's face.

A fate he was sure he would be recounting soon enough.

Artorian knew with certainty that the words and feedback he'd been given were correct. He'd been dawdling. There could be no more dawdling. There could be no more leisure for the moment. He'd been over the moon and filled with delight at seeing the smiles and long-awaited faces of his family.

He could afford to be an indulgent irregular no further. Thundy would no doubt be taking notice soon enough, if that sly wall of meat hadn't already. The mentions were coming from all over the place now, making the thorn in his thigh too recurring to ignore. No matter how much he wanted to build with crazed fervor like his Dwarves. No matter how much he wanted to live an endless amount of days next to that bonfire at home. No matter where he was or who he was with. Odin's foul machinations kept sneaking into the conversation.

He, like Anansi, who was hurrying back to his box seat, was *sick of it*.

As if right on cue to assist with the release of steam, his opponents were on him. Artorian's actions responded in kind, inner fire blazing as he was beset.

Rising up, his left foot slid back, tripping the Caramel Cougar in a motion as fluid as water taking the bend of a river. With an arm swivel, he weaved his wrist between earth-Essence-laced claws while imbued with the freedom of air. Redirecting the blow in what felt like slow motion, even if dilation was still not something they could control in Cal, Artorian negated the claw strike. Gripping the tripped Cougar by its own wrist, he twisted to complete the original motion along a new path in order to allow momentum to do what momentum did. To continue the spiritual journey of face meets wall, physically.

In a flash, Carl was knocked out cold via direct and unceremonious impact against the inner arena structure. A human-shaped outline crumbled from the impact zone as the Cougar forcibly reverted to his animal shape due to unconsciousness, only to fall right into the webbed paws of well-positioned medical bakers.

Having changed shifts with the Bread Beavers, this group of medics was composed entirely of adorable Orange Otters each wearing tiny chef aprons. Some had brought cherry potion pies in advance, to restore health in the event of injury. Crown Games were known to get rowdy, and today was no exception. What most of the fallen contestants got to look forward to during their shift was the Otters' famous orange juice, for it was both sweet and delicious, with minimal pulp.

Carl had one such poultice dumped down his throat, waking him just enough to become aware of the burning handprint plastered to the middle of his chest. A mark that had burned right through the colored jersey and bitten deep into his otherwise stalwart and stony fur. Carl was known for being a defensive heavy slammer, and he had the weight to back it up, so the sight made him wheeze. "That old man burned my rock fur? I've never been burned in my life!"

Artorian moved slowly after the redirection, acting with purpose, flowing with feeling. Instead of denying the accumulating layers of rust clinging to his skin, he focused on the sensation, sought the restrictions out, and isolated the hampering irritants to expel them as additional kerosine from his skin.

Halcyon was to be trusted on the subject. The solution was swift, sudden, explosive movements. That was what his acceleration had been for. The fire couldn't hurt him, and his Mana kept his attire thoroughly untarnished. All that was left was the difference between how he wanted to move, and how his body *thought* it should move. The latter was… wrong.

A wrongness he would correct as his sympathy connection to **Acceleration** deepened, a bond forming like a hand being pressed to his shoulder. He greeted the node in a kind whisper. "Hello, my new friend on Tier thirty."

With the Marmoset and Cougar out of the game, Stan and Earl both decided that their house rivalry could wait. The Crown Game was in full swing! Someone was actually *wearing* the crown, rather than waiting until the end to put it on as was custom, and the new contender was a *newcomer*. Some new blood could not be allowed to steal a sept's points! No matter who they were!

The announcer Moose thought this was wild, scrambling to hold a large rock before commentating like a living megaphone as the music lulled to let him. The orchestra's eyes were sharp, poised on the action as their senses trained to observe the field. The slightest hint of grand action, and their work would swell to match the energy!

First, they wanted to hear the exposition.

"Wagner's least and most wanted, what a crackling turn of events! Before I get into the match, I'd like to welcome my co-announcer back from his popcorn-fetching break, Bullwinkle! Who catalogued and provided us this lovely new saying. Bullwinkle, buddy, what do you have to say to today's crowd?"

The air Essence squirrel from before took the stone from his co-announcer that allowed the megaphone effect, sliding right into his role. "It's great to be back, and why I tell ya, Rocky, I saw this new contestant arrive and, *ooooooh* boy, wait until I tell you who he was *with!* I've got some juicy gossip for you all today, my darling bees and birds, so stick around and find out all the new green moolah on Moonbase Alpha. My news isn't just green, it's supergreen!"

Rocky snatched the rock. "This segues to a commercial for Ruby Rhod! Who would like to welcome everyone to the wonderful new world of *Flotsaaaaaam Paradiiiise*! Opening in a dungeon Core near you next iteration, so make sure to bring your multipass!"

Bullwinkle quickly took the stone back, cutting the commercial short as events were getting spicy! "Now back to the show, because I am seeing some *action*! The newcomer must have heard us because he is looking *fo-res-tyyyyy*!"

Artorian was indeed in the thick of it. With the Cougar and Marmoset out of the picture, and a clear visual effect remaining on the former's chest indicating just how potent the newcomer was, the remaining four had teamed up. They attacked with their individual elements in tandem, since it would be impossible to defend, deflect, or cancel out their effects all in one go! One of their elements would get through, and bring the newcomer low.

Instead, Artorian made like a tree and channeled some of Chandra's wisdom, canceling out intent with intent against their joint attacks as he adopted a Wood Elven fighting stance. He assumed a defensive position with both his arms as he prevented his Mana from automatically stopping the energy coming at him.

He wanted this to be purposeful. A task of skill. Keeping his eyes firmly closed, he saw with Essence instead as the energy of the world sprang to life in his senses.

Four entities were attacking him with matched timing, each sporting a different idea and Essence channel as their assault bore down. To the crowd, these resolved in instants. To Artorian, they were but a slow dance.

Stan, Tea Tapir of team blue, attacked with a water-infused tongue lash. Artorian sensed the motif, and felt it fine to name the particular combination of 'strike and catch' coming at him

'Toad Style.' The kerosine heat coating his skin was going to sort that attack without him needing to do anything.

Gray, Earl Elephant of team red, attacked with a fire-tusked charge meant to 'pin and push.' Artorian was reminded of a Corundum Rhinoceros, and thus filtered the attack into the mental checklist of 'Rhino Style.' Though, against this strike too, he would need to do little. Stance alone was sufficient, and the fire coming his way was… lesser.

Marvin, Martian Mongoose of team green, was coming at him from below with an earth Essence burrow attack. Except that was a clever ruse, as the movement technique and the attack technique shared an Essence type, thus obscuring the other. The actual strike was concentrated on the venom coating his claws and fangs, which reminded Artorian of snakes. Thus, since Marvin's intent was to 'pierce and debilitate,' that went into the 'Snake Style' bucket.

Branson, Bacon Buffalo of team orange, was attacking him with the secret 'Buffalo Wing' air Essence technique—a trick that did not appear to be intent-laden, and was the most straightforward Essence-to-face forehead bash he'd ever seen. This baffled Artorian somewhat, both because for some unknown reason he considered the buffalo delicious, and because he felt the urge to place the technique in the 'Buffalo Style' box, even though they didn't normally have wings? He could sort out the problem later, and taste the Essence now.

A much better plan!

"Being a Mage, Core Curriculum." Artorian narrated to himself, as he doubted the attackers were paying much attention to anything other than their strikes. "Mana is composed of all Essences, but listens to what you want to make of it. Since we're getting into the habit of naming our tricks, I welcome you all to class. Lessons are now in session."

In his defensive stance, the image of a sturdy, multicolored oak exploded from him, his Aura deactivating as he shifted over to Presence to put it to good use. More than merely shaping himself as a tree with Mana, he could feel a growing kinship with the concept as he aligned his Presence to the ideals and affinities of **Nature**. To use one's Presence over and above mere shaping was to become something more. It would no doubt become a topic of great amusement amongst the other supervisors that the first 'other thing' Artorian actually chose to be was a pyrite-blasted *tree*.

He wondered how that was going to stack up against Ember's 'candle.' What he knew for sure, on the other hand, was that his Wood Elves were going to be in a tizzy when they found out.

As Decorum gave new life to the name of Adamz, so would his brother make noble fagaceae stand proud once more. Fueling the four basic affinities to match the ratios of **Nature** —which he'd seen Chandra do aplenty—Artorian canceled out all four incoming elements simultaneously. The physical blows he could stop due to the solidity of the haka's stance, but the new sensation of energetic roots growing out from the bottom of his feet made him feel that there was more to it.

A flash of insight from Eternia brought skill tiers to the forefront of his mind, providing fuel for a stroke of genius. Shifting the weight on his left foot ever so imperceptibly, he rebuked the incoming offensive intent by applying a brand new idea he derived from watching Hulk struggle against the unmovable bulwark.

Channeling what he considered a higher tier defensive intent compared to the ideas of the attacks coming at him, he mentally moved his adapted **Nature** Mana and invoked the concept of immobile imperviousness. In response, the image of the tree around him tensed, gaining both strength and solidity.

"Arbor Style, Stance of the Onerous Oak."

CHAPTER THIRTY-EIGHT

Artorian's mind whisked away to olden times as the aligned direction of his Presence pulled him towards **Nature**'s ideals. His thoughts swirled to reflect on the age of falling spiders, his early forays into Magehood, and the moment where the Wood Elves of old had gifted him all their knowledge. All these techniques of 'utility' were refined and trained by a people driven by a focus on skill, rather than power.

Dedication that would now be, in turn, saving him.

One with the tree, a pulse from the energy roots under his feet showed him more of the world than could be seen with the eyes. Each nearby step was a sounding board of life and color. Each grain of sand became akin to a drop of water settled in the ocean, individually discernible. He could see them with uncanny clarity as the drops shifted, moved, and settled onto the ground anew.

He saw with waves as he instinctively pulsed more of them from his feet, feeling the exact dimensions of the arena rather than guess them. Nature revealed itself to him, bringing light to all that was life, and layers of gray to all that was still. Roots of

Mana sank deeper into the ground, and when the blows of the enemy fell, Artorian did not budge.

For they were leaves of grass pushing a mountain.

Against such insignificant forces, a mountain did not move.

All four attackers bounced off, rebuked by the dense image of an oak tree before the protections shimmered out of being when Artorian released his mental focus on the defensive concepts. One could not win a Crown Game through defending, so much like Ember's lessons that he was trying his darndest to recall, he shifted to the offensive and opened the box of Wood Elven goodies. Which, to his most intense amusement, were all designed to inflict *insult* more than actual combat resolution.

"Foot of the Furious Fern." In a snap kick that happened so fast that onlookers could only see the aftereffect, Gray shot to the sky. Crossing his eyes, the elephant released a nasal *pwaaaap* tuned like a rusty, bent trumpet. His head smashed into the ceiling after he'd been power-punted right in the jewels, and by the time his body returned to the ground, this round of the Crown Game was over.

"Elbow of the Erratic Elm." Marvin spiraled out of control upon being thunked, landing right in the stands with a dust-plume crash. He never even knew what hit him, seeing only images of his mother dance before his eyes as he was scolded for digging yet another hole. He also saw a ring of birds fly around his head, but those were real as he'd broken their perches on impact.

"Backhand of Boisterous Bamboo." Stan the Tapir's cheek burned red hot as he was educated on keeping his tongue to himself, team blue's representative becoming a crumpled heap on the ground after skidding across the sands like a skipped stone. Still, twenty bounces! Good score.

Branson, the Bacon Buffalo, received an actual directed lesson. He'd been the sole champion to throw out a strike without intent plastered on, making it terribly lacking. While Artorian spoke, Mr. Buffalo Wings was the only one who could hear him, the short conversation whispered in the passing wind. "Air-based techniques are invisible, and that is a strength. *Intend your strength. Like this. Impact of the Insidious Inula.*"

A blow that Branson was entirely unable to discern the origin of punched him right in the stomach from below, with all the grace of feeling like he'd tried to catch a hurled brick with his belly. Foaming at the mouth and making a truly awkward noise while bending over himself, the twitching buffalo craved one monster of an energy drink to get back on his feet.

Reflecting on how his energy moved, Artorian pinned down a personal weakness.

He wound his hands together, weaving an intricate pattern with his fingers as he drew the light pattern outline of a butterfly in the air. He'd done this before, and pleasantly reminisced about an early conversation with his Gnomish friend, Dev. "I… I shape, fuel, intend, and let go. I do not squeeze juice into the mold of a pattern, and do not find it comfortable to do so. I move my Essence as it was intended to, as it desires. It seeks to be given identity and purpose, then be let loose upon the world. The freedom gives unique properties to the effects I produce and create, allowing them to be altered, shuttered, skewed, and bent with limited difficulty."

Artorian finally opened his eyes after all this time, and released his adapted **Nature** Mana. "My weaknesses are my lack of molds."

Hearing his parting words, the **Nature** Mana saluted, and promptly became a sturdy wheel of blue cheese. Covering itself in a sealed coating of red wax, the wheel rolled itself right to Anansi's left leg before stilling. All remaining vestiges of autonomy left the wheel, but Anansi felt pressed to poke the red wax a few times, just to confirm that the wheel was neither alive, nor sentient. Sure enough, *now* it was nothing more than what it looked like.

Anansi chuckled, then bowed to the arena as he was humbled. "Anything goes, he says. I feel chastised for believing the Great Dreamer would provide that which one expects.

Anansi gives thanks for parm-mission to partake in this lesson of mental flexibility. The ideas of the creators are truly as incomprehensible as they are wise, may they age well, and not grate the senses."

The pugilist Grackle *boo'd* Anansi from the sidelines, but only caused the spider to smirk. "Another illness? You should inform the bakers that you are laugh-tose intolerant. Run along now, I'm sure someone made the mistake that it was gouda to see you. I'm certain we'll all swiss you when you're away, but since you insist on being such a stinker, I'm equally sure I'll brie you soon. Or smell? Probably smell."

"You're not funny." The Grackle's voice was flat, his face twisted with distaste at the platter of poor jokes. "None of that was cutting."

Anansi was on a roll now. "Of course not. This is rochefort, not sharp cheddar. My insults were rather blunt. To this, I cannot dissa-brie."

The bird doubled over due to psychological injury. "I *can't even* with you. At least make it a different one you haven't done before."

"Brie-ten up, birdy!" the spider replied. "The de-brie of your shambled pride is something you'll eventually scrape up from the floor. You really need to learn how to brighten up, or you'll be forever prov-alone."

That was all the relief team could take as the Orange Otters burst into tears of laughter. When the Grackle looked back at them to plead for pity, they waved him off. The one in charge wasn't having any of the bird's lip, but kept polite about it. "Excuse me, but I think you are mistaking me for a Beaver who builds a dam. I'm only here to dunk on those who need the juice, with juice."

He then enthusiastically motioned to the glass jars to adver-tise them, since he had the attention of a good portion of the crowd. "It's the juice! Now with a complimentary smooth rock accompanying every bulk order."

That got a chuckle out of those watching, the eyes of which

redirected when the Elephant hit the deck. All those who had been paying serious attention either burst out into wild cheering, or silently grumbled with crossed arms. Both Artorian and Anansi took instant note of the latter, as more than a few looked like they were about to jump in and shout justification for doing so.

Artorian already knew that he welcomed the interruption.

Sure, the game was cute, but he was here to brush up and *lift*. He was scrawny and needed to regain those gains! Opening and closing a hand, he considered the difference between B-rank and A-rank Mana. If he did not apply intent and identity to A-rank mana, shaping the end result, then the product would be firm, uncontrollable, and rough as all abyss. He'd noticed this when trying to channel air Essence with Mana, as that impact really had hit like a brick.

A-rank Mana solidity was no joke! The effort had also taken a good chunk more energy than expected, and again he was reminded of part of a conversation with Dev.

In the Gnome's voice, he heard the memory as he replayed it. "Even a perfect mold cannot always make a perfect arrow, but an imbued identity will always make the arrow act as an arrow, even if it looks like a rock. It's a matter of where you put the cost. Your issues stem from working with functions that are so far removed from the basics that you're overlooking them entirely. I know it might be difficult, and I can tell that your body isn't great for learning the limitations. But unfortunately, my friend, that's going to be the next step for you: figuring out the 'molds.' I'm convinced that you will start slinging flawless techniques if you can accomplish that, since what you're pouring into a non-existent mold already accomplishes what a technique should."

So smart. So insightful! Dev really had known from the beginning, except that now, after all this time, a key component was different. Artorian no longer suffered from limited affinity channels. His earth channel was now part of him, and sitting to study some runes was no longer an idea that fled from his brain the moment it arrived. As a Mage, and especially with the boon that was his body, he also did not suffer in health to the point where he'd be unable to do so.

He had both the means and the capacities to turn his weaknesses around, and all it would take was some direly missed, well-managed studying. Though, he was going to have to climb up to Magehood a second time. How would he make these runes as a fresh-start cultivator after he learned them? Currently, unless bunny-hopping via use of a Pylon, a Mage traced and formed the pattern of a rune inside of their own body to complete it. A feat only possible due to having the Mana body in question.

A flash of genius struck him again. "Perhaps I could... make them external? Some kind of... *ritual circle*, perhaps? No, that's more Tatum's thing. However..."

That entirely new method of thought felt so much more grounded than what he was used to that he was glad to still be standing in a sturdy pose. Artorian distinctly felt like he was now looking at the topic from the angle of a C-ranked *body* cultivator, rather than the path he'd originally walked as the external variant. "If I knew the pattern, I could form the design with energy directly for but an *instant*. Then, funnel the fuel through that external construct rather than through myself; *then* complete the technique at a fraction of the cost, with easily a magnitude worth in increased output and efficiency."

He tapped his chin. "Not quite incantations? Those are based on inscriptions. I could use the pattern quality of a Rune, rather than an inscription, focused as an incantation? Flashy rune-development for instant technique deployment? Would be good for my 'Mage-quality *oomph* output when I'm a non-Mage' problem."

A moment of prescience and insight struck him with the right word. "*Flashrunes*! Oh, oh yes. *Me likey*. Sounds like I've got myself a project!"

The idea had never struck Artorian before, and when he wondered why, he came upon the thought of *how* he'd initially built his Aura. The topic he'd focused on over and above his body rebuilding and technique designs. "My focus was elsewhere."

An Aura could be expressed as a great many things, and much of its shape and use had to do with how he thought of it. How one conceived their Aura guided how they built and infused it, causing personally created limitations in the functions of what it would be able to do in the future.

Thanks to watching Dale, Cal's help, and a natural gift to see the inanimate as something alive, Artorian had rebuilt his Aura as a neural network before becoming a Mage. Much like the brain functioned, connected, and transferred information, so too had the inner structure of his Aura. Even now, when he took a quick glance, this structure appeared to be in place, which was most interesting since Artorian simply could not fathom how something complicated like that could follow along when transferring bodies.

Credit to Tatum and his 'dendrites' for that one, in all likelihood.

Artorian thought of his Aura as a part of him that adapted, responded, and behaved symbiotically with him. He didn't think of his Aura as a shield, or second skin, or something to merely pour Essence combinations into—which was a truly terrible idea as that was how you got rogue Essence constructs —and he really wasn't of the mind to try throwing random Essence combinations around with A-ranked Mana.

Considering that, did he know the proper difference between shaped Mana, and an Aura construct? Oh, yes. Yes, he did. In addition to using it for Halcyon hugs, he'd verified it with the luminous owl wings on many a descent. The difference was that the effect could be accomplished with either method, but the one he was more proficient in happened to be easier. Inner, or body, cultivators were going to have a smoother time with direct Mana manipulation. They could, after all, count the units of investment. He, as their opposite, found it easier to shape the Aura instead, eschewing any sort of counting to throw a mixture of wisdom and gut feeling into the mix.

Content with these thoughts, Artorian returned his attention to the task. With the current Champions out of the running, other septs were beginning to jump into the arena. As expected, they were speaking loudly to convince the crowd of their justification. As planned prior, that just wasn't important.

Instead, Artorian responded to their threats by tilting the crown the other way just to infuriate them—choosing to goad them into action. He included some last minute shadow boxing in their general direction while he deployed his Presence, preparing a surprise to any who blindly charged in. "Come at me, you whippersnappers! Show me what you've got. It's time for lesson two!"

CHAPTER THIRTY-NINE

Several champions turned their fur red at his proclamation, but none immediately fell for his trap. Most turned to the stands for more speechcraft.

Of all the turmoil in the stands, Artorian grasped only some of the shouting. He really needed to find whoever had replaced Translation Bob, as this was getting out of hand. Luckily, he could narrow his focus down to the few who had descended and would be participating. The part concerning 'the outsider should not win,' he'd understood fine. Even if he hadn't, the wild posturing was more than giving the new champions' intentions away with their body language alone.

Except for the fish, he supposed. He had no idea what that floating Koi was doing with her fins and tail. Bless Eternium for giving him the chance to pick up Aquan, or this would have been a mud show. Still, he noticed some rather interesting social hierarchy at play as he watched the interactions. "Intriguing. The Crown Game I walked into must have been for the bottom-rung champions, divided by their single-channel natures. The second wave appears to be dual-channel critters, as the Koi's Beast Core possesses a mixture of water and air."

His suspicions were confirmed when the Koi fish, accompanied by an earth and celestial mix Chinchilla, strolled into the ring's boundaries. Though, that was as far as they got before being plastered face-first down into the sand. Surely they hadn't expected he was just going to let them keep posturing, right? "Did you all miss the part where I mentioned lesson two? I know they're mostly for myself, but I sincerely did hope you'd learn something here. I'm specifically using—"

A dearly missed line of predictive light populated in his vision.

As he ever so faintly dodged his head to the left, a quillspine shot past where his head used to be. Artorian promptly backhanded the interloper in the stands who didn't even have the decency to enter the ring with him. The effect resounded with a *wub* since he didn't move from where he was standing.

The deep sound smacked the Crested Porcupine right out of his seat as the Mana in the air transferred Artorian's backhand. "Now, now. You can either play the game with me, and we all learn. Or you can be cheeky, and I'll see fit to spank the unruly."

A second threatening wave from the back of his hand drove his point home. Shaping his Presence, he picked up the Koi and Chinchilla cosplaying as Ostriches to casually toss them right back out of the ring. "Try again."

The sept Champions of three channels observed this, silenced their claims to the crowd, and gathered for a quick huddle while the heaving dual-channel champions were both hauled off to be given some orange juice. Artorian let them, so much more interested in how the Koi was doing any of the things it was doing. "Air and water... sky swimming? Like Cy? What was she breathing? Maybe that's not as big of a problem as I think it is. Alright then, back to Mage lessons."

Deploying and retracting his Presence several times to get a good feel for the differences, Artorian chose to pull it back in and conform the energy and perspective to his human shape. Yes, his Presence was potent and powerful, but he was already versed in its use. Thus, he wasn't going to learn what he wanted to if he just let it crush the opposition down to the ground.

He really *should* be using techniques. He did sort of know a few, Wood Elven repertoire not counted? The Pylons he'd used in the first iteration had spellforms that he mostly remembered, particularly the ones he'd played around with on old Jotunheim for fun. "I likely remember them *because* I was having fun."

A thought struck him that most Mages did not bother to perfect techniques. Instead, they focused on learning how to push more power out, rather than getting good at what they did. Which seemed like such a strange topic to focus on, since Mana would be taken from the Mage regardless in order to fuel the effect they wanted to. Trying to force more juice out of the container would just cause strain if you didn't have the Mana in the first place, and... Actually, why had he not encountered this problem?

He spent entire *ranks* of Mana when throwing out invocations. "*Hmm...* On second thought, I can't rightly call my invocations 'techniques.' Maybe I'm thinking of this wrong, and what they're actually doing is trying to get more juice out of a pre-existing technique?"

He reeled his idea back, and tested some quick basics.

"Walking as a Mage." Taking a step forward, he compared and contrasted the rusty feeling of the C-ranker Eternia body, and his current movement. His gait felt the same, but there was an uncanny, intrinsic difference in how the world reacted to his footfalls. He, in turn, felt like he was automatically compensating for this change as a secondary response. "I cross the same distance I would, when that's the distance I want to cross. Yet, if I wanted to cross this arena in a single step..."

With a discordant boom, Artorian moved from one end of the Arena to the other by applying the kind of physics a Mage body could exert. With dilation not a factor he needed to account for—because he couldn't while in Cal—Artorian was surprised to find out that movement worked very much the same, with the significant caveat that the kinds of forces he could exert upon the world were blasphemously more potent.

A look over his shoulder revealed a small crater where he'd begun, and a silenced crowd covered in a sheet of sand and moon dust. A wave of his Aura apologetically cleaned them all right up. "Terribly sorry."

The announcers went wild, and to Artorian's irritation, they were not using the prior language. Rocky and Bullwinkle were having a blast up in their booth, and he felt a little sore about not knowing what they were spouting. The topic was *obviously* about him.

He grumbled, and considered tapping into his **Love Law** to see if he could understand them anyway. "*Mmmno.* It's a touch invasive, and I suppose I don't need to comprehend them just yet. I've got other things to try until the triple-channel hiding-in-a-corner champions over there find their brass marbles."

Testing Mage speed just to be sure he did not have dilation access, he instantly learned that a greater force was outright stopping him from even getting started. Like the potential energy was being taken from him. The name Frank crossed his mind for some reason, but Artorian didn't want to bother that train aficionado right now.

Wait, no, he couldn't! Frank the Wisp was stuck in Eternia. He could swear that Wisp was, for some reason, bound to the **Law** of Potential Energy. Momentum? No, not quite. Eternia fuddled up the whole sensory perception experience. "Where's Invictus when I need him? I've got another piece of information I want to finagle out of him."

Trying a second time, he found that the effort did cause a bit of feedback to bounce back through his current body, making him acutely aware that there was something odd with his legs. Like... fractured streaks were running through the insides? "Isn't that where Dawn fixed my burnout damage? That's what that feels like? Mighty unpleasant."

When he funneled energy into that feeling with some 'hey, fix that' intent, and a good helping of Mana that he made sure contained all six of his affinities, the discomfort swiftly faded. That old lesson that Mages could not be healed with single Essences had been most important to learn. Shame he could no longer do it with just celestial, but that was part of the cost of Magehood. "Burnout seems to comprise different kinds of effects that are all lumped in under the same name. Overload burnout and out-of-Mana burnout are distinctly different. I'm going to have to rename the variants one day, if I'm ever to be clinical with the subject or need to know how to mend that kind of damage."

He was pulled from his thoughts when two new champions in the upper B-type Beast ranks—evidenced by their immaculate Cores—crossed the flag line.

An Arid Termite, possessing earth, fire, and infernal channels, was joined by an Arctic Penguin, possessing water, air, and celestial channels. Artorian could see their affinity connections and Beast Core qualities plain as day, reminding himself that most people couldn't just *do that*. In Eternia, the matter may have been confused, but in Cal? *Ha*! In Cal, now that he actually wanted to see, he saw it all.

Ever since doing his deeper inspection on Halcyon, what he saw had been tweaked. On any Beast he'd seen so far, the quality of their Core and associated channels were an open book. On a Mage, their **Law**, channel strengths, and Essence types may as well have been on a museum display with little tags attached. With **Love**, nothing was hidden from him. Even the Mana in the air around him felt like it quite literally adored him to pieces, still partying from the earlier *wub*.

A sensation with a most interesting side effect that he did not have time to delve into, as one of the champions took the initiative and engaged.

The Arctic Penguin used a technique that reminded Artorian of his Liger mouth-cannon equivalent, save that the attack was an empowered line of compressed water with a piercing quality, instead of disintegrating light. A thought that was paused as the water beam nearly struck him in the forehead.

"Well, *that's* interesting." A theory was one thing, and a feeling another, but seeing the attack quite decisively *shatter* right in front of his eyes because the Mana around him… what, decided it liked him more? That was an *experience*. By all rights, that beam should have hit him. But no! To his baffled amazement, the Mana Loved feature from Eternia must have followed him here as well, because he could see the technique visibly unravel inches from his eyes.

The process was spectacular.

When the attack seemed to realize that it was going to successfully strike, it dug its heels in. The assaulting Mana instantly had a change of heart, and began taking itself apart on a fundamental level. The intent of the attack was thrown out of the window like an unwanted chamber pot.

The identity of the attack quickly followed, immediately chased by the factors of shape and size as luminous fractals peeled off from the incoming line. This changed the attack from a beam meant to do harm and push him out of the ring to more of an… ineffectual sprinkler.

Once the water beam near him was more of a fine mist, the mold it had been contained in fractured and came apart like a block of sugar dissolving in hot water. With the mold no longer a factor, the skill it had been applied with was sent packing by the rebellious Mana, forced to carry both of its suitcases while being evicted from the premises. With the skill invested made unwelcome, the control of the Penguin's technique wavered, faltered, apologized for arriving in such a state of undress, then swiftly fled in search of a towel.

With the technique stripped down to its power investment, channel types, and Mana quality, the rank of the technique dropped from 'honestly pretty good' all the way down to 'why did you even get out of bed this morning?'

In the case of a Mage, rather than a Beast, a Mana Tier and Theme would have been present in this step of the equation. Given the Penguin was on the Beast track and had a Beast Core instead of a **Law** connection to a node in the Tower, this was not the case here. This reaffirmed to Artorian that he would be spending a few months of time with Halcyon to make sure the dual-track she was currently on wasn't going to cause any adverse effects.

A fascinating component of seeing the water beam technique come apart was that Artorian could now also clearly see some self-imposed limitations the Penguin had applied to himself. Though, those did not seem to be willing or desired limitations. The perceived limitations that the Penguin had were causing power blocks that prevented the full breadth of the power investment the technique could take.

Having seen the pattern come apart in detail, Artorian named this technique 'Waterjet Cutter,' as that properly comprised all the components when put together in the right order. "Strange how the champion is using maybe... sixty percent? of the total 'oomph' Waterjet Cutter could provide. *Oh*, is this why Mages try to pump more juice in? Because they know the technique isn't giving them the full breadth of what another could do?"

What a revelation that the crux of the matter laid in the realm of self-confidence, rather than how long and hard one could scream and grunt. A road to constipation, that. Definitely not recommended.

With the technique equation down to power investment, channel types, and Mana quality, Artorian noted that the investment and quality really only determined how much Essence all the Mana in the attack was breaking down to. In the case of the Penguin, the Mana broke down into refined particles of water, air, and celestial Essences. Oh hey, those were exactly that Beast's affinities! "Coincidence? I think *not!*"

On realizing he was doing flipper-all, the Arctic Penguin stopped his attack. Then blinked, then slowly gawked. Because the target he'd intended to shoot out of the ring in one easy motion was gazing at the sky while doing some pensive beard stroking, mumbling over something that sounded painfully philosophical in nature while the shattered Essence in the air filtered clean and smooth into his refinement center. With the Essence needing no further refining as he gathered it up without really meaning to, Artorian was contemplating what this meant. "So it *doesn't* all always go back to Cal? I'm confused."

Turning to the Arid Termite, the Penguin strongly motioned a 'did he just?' before throwing both his flippers to the air and waddling out of the ring. The Termite, not as easily daunted with this new knowledge, decided to flip the script and charge in while condensing his Mana nice and close against his carapace. If long-range wasn't viable, he wouldn't use it! *Bite the bug's head off! Like they do it back in the hive! Chomp chomp!*

The Termite did not understand what happened shortly after the old man spoke. "An Ant? Wait, I remember this rune! I used it during my first iteration. Here goes the *Bugzapper*! Hit me, crawly! I don't remember how to control the range."

CHAPTER FORTY

Kpop! The Arid Termite sailed out of the ring in a smoldering, smoking arc of deep gamboge-colored **Lightning**. The arcs of electricity followed along the entire path of the Termite's axis, ending when the bug hit the ground and all the energy grounded.

Artorian tapped his foot and held his chin, watching the culmination. "*Hmmm*, note to self. Using a proper rune inside one's own body as an A-ranked Mage is mentally tiring rather than physically draining. Initial guesswork says that too much of this will lead to mental exhaustion. Hypothesis: the more complex the rune or spell, the bigger drain this will cause. Frequent use of lesser versions may have other, differing adverse side effects. I don't dabble in the ground-up version all that much. I don't have this problem with invocations, but they're also vastly more expensive in comparison to what it just took to fuel Bugzapper. I didn't even *notice* a Mana loss. Definitely noticing that pain in my head, though."

Pressing his hands together, he considered a mental topic and momentarily monologued to himself. "Y'know, old boy, you wouldn't have been able to do that at all if you weren't a Mage.

As a non-cultivator, keeping as many details of that spellform Pylon pattern in mind as I did is not feasible. I know I didn't get them all and almost abyssed that up and got the range completely wrong."

That would need to be accounted for, so he counted on his fingers. "Let's make a small chart. Mentally holding on to the full pattern in one of the Pylons would be outright impossible as a non-cultivator, a cute idea before the C-ranks, and somewhat plausible when starting the B-ranks. The jumps in brain capacity and processing intellect really, *really matter* when attempting to use some of these more complete, and potent tools without Cal's help. This comes down to the Pylons being Spells, I suppose. They're just too intricate and complicated. I need to backpedal my thresholds; I'm jumping the crossbow. If I knew the *rune* version rather than the Pylon version, I think that would be riiiight about where I'm at in terms of competence."

He nodded at that deduction. "Even as an A-ranker, with *my* head, spellforms go right over the noggin. Even inscriptions are all three-dimensional and multifaceted. At this stage, getting all those additional details spot on is going to require some external help, or… honestly, Incarnating would likely do it. Shame I'm nowhere near. External help it is, since I'm probably going to find the spellforms lying around, but not the runes."

Artorian mentally added a second tally mark next to the flashrunes idea. "Cal wouldn't abide that kind of inefficiency."

He shuddered momentarily. "As if I would ever forget that he made my walls drool when back in Mountaindale while we were on the topic. Ah well, needs must."

Bouncing on his toes for a moment, he reminisced on keeping Mana in his body versus his Aura. "Next topic. Grumpy old Moon Elf instructor said the right way to Mage was to keep one's Mana going at full tilt, at all times. What was the problem here? Right, adding Mana to your Mana body immediately changes the state of time dilation experienced. That's not a factor here, so I wonder if there's a skill pertaining to keeping Mana in the body, *without* triggering that dilation effect? Seems plausible."

Looking at the arena when impact sounds hit the ground after new creatures came flying down through the new hole in the ceiling, Artorian figured he had a bit longer now that the four-channel beasts had arrived. Interesting how their Cores were all still of Immaculate quality.

Shifting his Mana around, he pulled from his Aura and added the energy to his body. Then he stood there wondering why nothing happened. "Aren't I supposed to feel different? I'm experiencing a whole lot of nothing."

Adding several more ranks of Mana to his body from his Aura, he rubbed his bald head afterwards, wondering what he was doing wrong. "Alright, I firmly remember something about maximum storage, and vaguely something about how an Aura can't hold more energy than one rank over the Mage's maximum. Or… was that pertaining to my fondness of pulling from Mana Storms, since that all wasn't exactly my energy? Or maybe it was about B-rank limitations? *Bah*! I'll ask when I can, let's just test and see what's going on."

Artorian evened out his Mana.

As an A-rank six, he moved half his ranks to his body, and half to his Aura. Right when he did, a sensation of *comfort* washed over him. "*Wow*! Wow, hello there, that feels nice. Equilibrium is good stuff! Right away, this feels like a fantastic baseline, so I'm going to call it just that. 'The base.' This distinctly feels like a natural state, one of balance. Going to start recommending this, or at least put it in a book. Now what about extremes?"

Shifting his balance, he moved five ranks to his Aura, while keeping one in his body. Now that he had an average to compare the difference to, he *could* feel the changes. "See, I *knew* something was missing before. I just didn't have the right measuring stick."

A four-channel Lynx champion took this distraction as the opportunity to pounce. He got as close as ten feet from his target before Artorian's Aura formed a blinding Liger-claw construct made from solid light. Not a moment after the blinding creation, the gleaming talons took a swipe. The Lynx nimbly dodged by rolling beneath the strike, but aborted his chance to attack in doing so. In an awkward set of stumbles, the Lynx came to a standstill on his back with all four paws in the air, positioned right under Artorian's nose! He scampered away when the old man made a sharp nose motion for him to *shoo* and try again.

Watching the champion flee, Artorian mentally notated his findings. "More Mana in the Aura means faster assembled, stronger quality, more potent constructs. My body feels significantly more vulnerable in comparison, while my Aura is a robust wall. Damaging my Aura in this configuration feels possible, but more difficult to do. Damaging my body... An A-rank two Mage may have a very easy time ripping my legs off. The rank difference, if I don't tally Tier, is quite noticeable now that I have a feel for the difference."

Measuring the ring's distance by inspecting the line he'd dug into the sand from his Mage step, he nodded. "I would not have been able to cause such devastation with only one rank of Mana in my body. That crater would have been much smaller, as the amount of energy I'd be able to impart on the world would have been lesser. Speaking of, reminder to self that the baseline quality of matter on the moon starts at B-rank one. This is some sturdy ground in comparison to Caltopia. If I'd Mage-stepped in the Fringe, *all* of the Fringe would be a smoldering crater. The *region*, not the village."

Shifting his Mana to the other extreme, Artorian watched himself physically lose control of the claw construct. The large, solid claw dissipated as his Aura was no longer able to uphold the kind of energetic quality necessary for it to remain. "Other way around, body with five ranks in it, and an Aura with one rank in it. Celestials above, what a blasted *difference*."

Artorian could scarcely believe how... *significant* of an alteration this was. "I must have been subconsciously moving my ranks back and forth as needed, without really thinking of how many ranks I put where. This is astounding. I am an untouchable castle with such density and force in my frame!"

He looked down, making his eyebrows metaphorically break another hole in the ceiling. Swole-torian was *back*. He was a massive, muscled, heaving hulk of a bodybuilder. Much like the powerful frame he'd thrown around in Eternia. "I don't... How? I thought bodies stayed the same and did not reflect investiture. I was a frail, thin old man. Surely I would have stayed the same, and not physically changed just because I moved some Mana around? Mana bodies don't..."

The copper dropped. "Right. This is a Spirit body *mimicking* a Mana body. This is probably a compensation feature of some kind. If I intend to... could I return to being a thin stick of a man while keeping this much Mana in my body?"

Giving it a basic test, he saw his perspective shorten and shift as he reduced in size. When he inspected himself again, the Mana had helped him attain his prior form. His body was still at A-rank five worth of investment. "Yup. Looks like intent and identity are a core feature. If I had done the Mage-step with this amount of body investment..."

He mentally calculated the damage. "Arena would be rubble. Yup. All of it would have been gone."

Walking to the middle, he looked around the crowd before making dramatic martial arts poses just for the hilarity of it. Halcyon saw the spectacle when she entered after there was enough distraction to warrant doing so, saddling up next to Anansi. They shared cordial greetings, after which Anansi filled Cy in on the few things she'd missed while doing some quick administrative work, including a mediation between Hulk and Sartre, who were both guarding the door while shooting the other grumbly glances. The crab started up a brand new coffee leaf, but kept his peace while learning from the spectacle.

There was language in expression.

There were hidden gems worth of lessons here!

What Artorian was actually doing amounted to getting a

feel for a highly invested Mana body while it wasn't affected by any of the dilation side effects. He made swift, explosive, sudden movements as ever more kerosine poured from his form, catching flame while the old man rolled through old Phoenix Kingdom weapon maneuvers and stances. With a heavily invested body, his movements were smoother, crisper, sharper. Faster?

Faster may have been inaccurate, but he performed his militant dance better than he would if his investment ranks were reversed. He knew that for certain. "I think I understand. Like I needed to be underwater for my dragon form to have sensory data, more ranks in one aspect over the other provides additional empirical information as stimulant feedback. I feel more, so I understand more, and can refine my outcomes with increased potency."

The champions were all having a noisy debate in the corner rather than engaging him, as the more they learned about the crown-wearer, the less inclined they became to keep attacking. Especially since so far the rebukes had been horrendously damaging to their social status, and served as a buffet of jokes and laughter for the announcers and gossip train. The Lynx was even considering hanging up his champion hat altogether. Ending up paws-up under an opponent only to be chastised? The humiliation made him feel like he should become a hermit, and the shrieking laughter from the stands wasn't helping any.

The orchestra, on the other wing, was having a blast keeping up with all of Artorian's antics. Thumping action when he moved, to soft and steady low-fi until it was time for more entertainment. The birds were incensed, enthralled, and invigorated. They felt connected to each other like they never had before, as the soft pink luminosity pulsing out of the crown-wearer was visible only to them. The energy sang to them like a kalimba, setting the tone and rhythm of upcoming actions. The glow spread, searched them out, surrounded them, infused them, all to sync them up with one another to allow for a performance like they'd never done before.

The brass section felt like they could read the Maestro's thoughts, while those with the strings conversed without words. Their music evolved from pristine and old school, the correct way of using their instruments, to something new and emotional. Sliding the bow down the strings incorrectly caused a deeper, dirtier sound. Yet when they all did this together, the melody harmonized into something that only *sounded* dirty, yet resulted in music both guttural and good. Like they were pouring their hearts into their songs; playing for fun. Even if it made their music more synthetic than natural, that was just the flow they followed as the pink glow head-bobbed along with their improvised creations of sound.

The Maestro called this creation 'White Steel Eel.' The feeling was powerful. The feeling was beautiful. The feeling was inspiring. The feeling was **Love**.

When Artorian sprang to action, they dropped the beat.

A charging neigh-bear was stopped cold. The powerful swipe of its claw redirected at the wrist by a dancing, frail, thin, old-looking long beard. The redirection caused all of the neigh-bear's momentum to shift, ending with the creature slamming face-first into the sand before being made to roll like a wheel. The neigh-bear crossed the flag-line to end against the wall with a loud *wham*!

The finale was performed with a flourish, Artorian moving with the music rather than the other way around, as he too was starting to feel the influences of his Law. **Love** adored music and musicians! She lived for a good party and good cheer. So in the middle of the arena, like a fool blind to all the eyes watching, Artorian performed an energetic shuffle. The fire-clad *bon vivant* danced with wild abandon. The purpose of the Crown Game was lost already, and the intent to learn about being a Mage was mixing in with a powerful desire for fun.

Fun made for that good learning!

Tuning some of his Aura, the music from the orchestra exploded out of the arena as Artorian turned himself into a living amplifier, trading his billowing flame effects out for it.

This caused raucous cheering from the crowd as they got up to applaud, scream for more, and began attempting to copy the crown-wearer's dances. He had been upgraded from unwanted interloper to most entertaining guest. The announcers could simply not get enough of all the antics. Rocky called out through the megaphone rock. "The newcomer moves to only *one* speed! His *ooooown!*"

The four-channel champions all said 'abyss with this' and charged him en masse. Not interested in being so thoroughly outshined, they led the charge of the three- and two-channel variants from the other septs, which followed in their wake.

Had Artorian felt like being hostile, this would have been a slaughter. So he had determined that, unless they were particularly clever or inventive, the B-ranks of Beasts were not going to pose a challenge. Hulk, with his Immaculate middle A-rank Core was far more potent than all those sept champions, and that squirrel had but a single earth affinity channel.

"Most interesting how affinity count, channel type, rank, and Tier all interplay." Artorian grinned, welcoming more contestants to this improvised Crown Game. He was so happy to have more volunteers, because he had so much more he needed to test! "About time! Onwards then, to lesson three!"

CHAPTER FORTY-ONE

So far, Artorian had been mindful about the Tier of **Law** he used, specifically channeling Tower nodes on lower floors to keep on par with his opponents. **Lightning** and **Nature** had been excellent test beds, since that kept his need to keep the Tier difference against the other contestants somewhat out of mind. Now, that luxury would need to be shelved. He needed to refresh himself on how rank and Tier properly played ball.

He'd always somewhat noticed that everyone's Mana looked and behaved differently, even within the same **Law**, complicated by the tidbit that some **Laws** had Essence combinations that looked identical on the surface, but differed in composition.

That's how one got the difference between **Swamp** and **Gemstone**, which Cataphron had explained to him in the Skyspear days. Both were derived from earth, water, and infernal Essences. He surmised that everyone learned how to handle their Mana a little differently due to these subtle differences, making structural lessons difficult, and Dale's 'flying by the seat of his pants' learning method more effective in the end.

Even if it made the boy look like he lived in a tumbler.

Having tapped into **Nature**, he now grasped that the **Law** one was tied to altered their entire perspective of the world. Yet… perhaps not *because* they were tied to their Law? More the other way around? He, himself, was aligning himself to the ideals and view of **Love** because that was simply how he wanted to live his life. Those concepts and ways of thinking were how he wanted to act, how he *wanted* to shape his pattern. The repeated actions that made up the determination of his soul were not derived from his **Law**, they were derived from the path he was choosing to take. That those ideals so strongly lined up with his **Law** was more of an… amplification. A comfort that another had walked this path before, and was willing to share their views.

This made him think that all those who wanted to outline the paths in the Tower, and all its options, were performing an act of folly. The point wasn't to have a map and then to choose based on the options available. The point was to move oneself, and create a place for those ideals in the Tower. You moved to create purpose. Not to select a purpose from some list and then arbitrarily move to action. That kind of thinking couldn't support hanging a coat, much less a soul.

Had Artorian been on anything other than the Tribulations track, he would have bumped up a Mage rank just now. He felt the surge of Mana well up inside of him, only for the treat to be whisked away by Scilla as she hung out on the ceiling in his bonfire space. He could feel her shaking her head 'no,' snapping two of her fingers from her eyes to his to indicate she was watching.

The relaxation time in his bonfire space was doing her well, and his miniature Silverwood in there seemed to be pulsing with colors, matching luminance to the music he was being an amplifier for. The leaves, after all, reflected his emotional state and reacted to sound. Currently, his space was a dark night filled with stars, the tree acting as a disco ball.

Scilla made an attentive motion. He needed to stop paying attention to his inner worlds, so Artorian got back to being accosted on the moon.

Artorian cracked a joke, his energy surging. "Time to move up a few Tiers. **Acceptance**, how have you been? Oh, that's right, kicked to the curb like the snoot you were. Should have gone to see a wise bearded one for some acceptance and commitment training. Goodbye **Acceptance**, and hello, my most darling **Sun**!"

The air in the entire room changed.

All the B-ranked Beasts within the confines of the flag ring had their approach cut short, slammed to the ground from the sudden, intense, and unopposable spike in heat, gravity, and power-density. The pressure of which continued to rise in a slow, but steady fashion.

An unsurprising side-effect when the Tier-quality in Artorian's Aura shot up from around five to five hundred and fifty-five. The only reason none of them were crushed to paste was because he specifically did not want them to be.

Outside of the flag ring, few fared much better. Hulk, Sartre, Anansi, and Halcyon remained unaffected and stood firm. Mostly due to their Immaculate A-rank Cores. The orchestra cut to a wheeze. Most of the crowd became glued to their seats as the farther they were from Artorian, the less his effect touched them. He was specifically trying to reel it all in and keep the effects contained, as jumping to the **Sun Law** had forcibly made his Aura spill out regardless of whether he wanted to or not.

Even *he* was not a flawless master of all things Aura, and had much more to learn.

When he got the effect back to being skin-tight, he could begin the fun. Or, he supposed, could find new opponents to test things against as all his current ones were fleeing like a pack of lemmings who had just seen a mountain get up and declare it was hungry.

He actually did not know how **Law** Tier and Beast Core interactions worked. Not properly. In Dawn's chat with Shaka, the Beast tower had but seven Tiers. As he'd been operating under the assumption that a Law below the seventh floor would be manageable for his opponents here, he'd been sticking to those. Could he equate that somehow, now that he had more clues? Most Mages in his time weren't over Tower Tier four, and the Beasts were seen as vastly more powerful in most cases, if his scrolls were anything to go by.

His voice squeaked on helium as he spoke. "Let's set that as a hypothesis to test for now. The highest Beast Tier is seven, determined by affinity count."

Blinking at hearing his own voice, he broke down laughing and slapped his knee a few times, slowly reeling those effects back in as well. He knocked on his chest a few times to test his voice with some noises, speaking when it was back to normal. "I'm just going to have to accept that there's more effects to changing Tiers than meet the eye. Booting side-effects comes with the territory."

On a larger scale, Artorian wondered what would have happened to any Mages tied to **Acceptance** when the **Law** was booted out, then had the distinct sensation they'd go back to being untethered C-rankers. He didn't have any concrete proof for this, so shelved the thought.

Instead, his mind once again turned to the new language Rocky was using. He didn't understand it. Would or could that have any effect on the Tower when it came to the concepts in there? He felt that… no. Language would not be a barrier when it came to a specific idea. The words to describe the concept might be different, but a chair was a chair no matter how it was said, so long as both parties agreed they were talking about a chair.

As he shook more kerosine off his skin, the material burned up in a flash now that he was attuned to the **Sun** law. The feedback was overbearing, in a way. The **Law** nudged him to be all-encompassing, an eternal engine of roiling energy; the *beginning* of a cycle.

Artorian replied by patting the feeling on the head, like a child. The feeling phased out after that, working with him rather than against him. The **Sun** Mana filled him, channeling from his center to his fingertips as his skin tones gave way to the tapestry of the milky way. His eyes shone as twin suns against the backdrop of the cosmos, just like his followers had seen him in Eternia.

A conversation with Dale as a fresh Mage came to the forefront of his mind. Artorian had said: "The important piece of information that will be useful to learn is that we don't generate Mana, we channel it. If you can't control yourself, your Mana will destroy you long before an enemy will. Have you had time to consider why it is so important to refine techniques? Become precisely skilled at them? This is because, as a Mage, any flaw in the technique is patched by Mana. Where common Essence users suffer either backlash or technique failure, a Mage instead has the requisite energy siphoned from them to successfully complete the intended effect."

Controlling himself to return his skin tones to the more human pigments, he rolled his shoulders and flexed his hands. The more aspects of being a Mage he tested, the more questions he had that he felt like he needed to write about. Being a Mage was going to take entire collegiate courses in order to do right. 'Right' meaning to act in a manner and fashion that does not hurt the student, or those in their surroundings just from the Mage being the kind of creature it was. "A third project, next to Aura constructs and flashrunes, perhaps?"

Seeing that he currently had no playmates within the ring of flags, he raised both his hands and let some Mana roll over his form. In his left hand, a block of solar light solidified. In his right, a hexagon of light liquified. When he pulled them apart, a triangle of luminous air swirled within the confines of its assigned shape between them. "First, a quick primer on Mana types pertaining to states of matter. This is easier to do at higher Tiers, or so it feels. Particularly, at this Tier, I feel like I could…"

Slapping his hands together, he combined all three states into a single one. A pulse of light and a wave of pressure burst out from his location. When he took his fingers back apart, a mass of incandescent gas became trapped in a spherical furnace. Contained heat flashed bright, fusion commencing as an orb of radiant plasma quickly roiled in place of its components.

The orb of solar plasma floated between his hands as he kept the sustained effect steady on the smallest possible scale. It swirled like it was alive, and the ground beneath his feet turned to glass from the sheer energy still spilling free. "Incredible, this is *eating* through my Mana supply. This state of matter is so much more unstable, yet so much more intense and powerful than the other three."

A throb of discomfort pulled him back to reality. "Upkeeping the effect is increasing my headache, slowly but steadily."

Awe dawned on the arena as they watched the spectacle of all that Artorian was making, even as they needed to shield their eyes from the oppressive light and heat. They couldn't turn their attention away, enamored with this philosopher of the Essences. This madman of cultivation. This mythical smith of the elements.

He was magnificent.

Holding the radiant globe up above his upturned palm, Artorian studied the microsun. Reeling and basking in the power it contained, he slowed the glassing effect, preventing it from spreading too far. After a twenty foot radius spread of glassification, he got a hold of the output for about a second before the internal fuel contained within the orb expended itself. The microsun first increased in size and turned red, then condensed to become bright white. Like some kind of dwarf sun? "White dwarf? Seems like such a fitting name."

Absorbing most of the remaining energy back into himself, he took a few minutes to do so, studying the pattern of this white dwarf compared to the one he'd given to Cal, since he had the time. Thinking of it, the pattern of the Sun counted as a rune, did it not? Though with the complexity... it should class as a spell, if not something higher still. "Wouldn't it also serve as a pretty fantastic refinement technique?"

A shame he couldn't find out the latter. The former, on the other hand, was perhaps not out of reach.

Looking at his feet, he took stock of the glassed ground. "It's not quite a Mana construct, but if I carve this up *just right*, could I maybe manage an inscription? I don't have enough for a rune, but a flat-plane inscription might just do me. I'll just have to pretend there's stacked panes of glass for the third axis of the details, rather than a single sheet."

A sharp look from Halcyon made him put this experimentation on quick pause. She could hear him, and she knew abyss-well that he could hear her when she cleared her throat. He swiftly recalled that inscriptions and runes, when done incorrectly... uh, *exploded*. Maybe in the midst of a busy public arena wasn't the right place to do this. No, that wouldn't be proper and ethical, would it?

He sighed, and absorbed the remnant of the solar plasma rather than delve into the depths of scholarly pursuits. The scent of doing so registered as hot bark, or the balmy fragrance of an old tome. "Celestials above, I miss books, parchment, vellum, and the smells of fresh pages."

He slapped his hands onto his cheeks for focus.

"I'm not going to make any headway if I keep letting myself be distracted. I'll test the prior thought, and drop myself to a Tier seven **Law**." He did so right away, missing his mark and ending up in the celestial and water node of **Disenchantment**. "Oops, that was too far! That's what I get for sliding along on the strongest sympathies. *Why* does this have such a strong sympathy? The pattern is fairly simple. Downright novice-quality, if I needed to set some kind of scale. What does this even do? Blank-slate disenchanting and identity stripping? Oh wow, am I glad I'm not in any water right now. I'm radiating the active effect; let's stop that!"

Fiddling with his output, he deactivated the blanket effect, then took a good look at the connection. "There we go, now why the link? Feels like... someone I know used this effect last? What a strange detail to discover. I wonder who did..."

Artorian paused and blinked when the answer came to him. "*Dale?* Was my old disciple supposed to end up as a **Disenchantment** Mage had it not been for Cal? The boy did strike me as someone who would be happy as a clam with the mundane. Running Mountaindale as *Baron* Dale did not appear to make him happy. Farmer Dale? Now *there's* a thought, *hah!*"

Everyone, save for the four A-ranked Beasts, breathed more easily when the pressure pouring off the crown-wearer lifted. The announcers once more exploded with commentary the moment they were able. The duo quipped first at the addition of a fresh new tan, then how all the reptiles in the room looked divinely invigorated. A tidbit that Artorian caught when a whole group of skinks tore their shirts off to flex proudly, having gained visible muscle mass in the wake of his solar explorations. Skink wasn't quite the right species anymore. The word 'Iguana' fit this new evolution better. Artorian noted that exposure to certain **Laws** could have drastic effects on individuals.

He snapped at himself. "Focus! No hocus pocus."

Attempting to navigate the turbulent seas of the Tower once more, Artorian slowly went up and up until his **Love** sympathy connections felt like they were on Tier seven. A most intriguing set of Essence mixtures and concepts made their homes here. **Calibration. Barrier. Disease. Metrology. Corrosion**... Artorian frowned at the last and middle one. "**Disease** distinctly feels like it fell from grace recently and used to be much higher up. More importantly, is someone playing some kind of practical joke? There's a **Law** of **Onion**? Why is there an Ogre in the center? Do... Do I want to find out? *Mnnnnnn.* Ni. No. And Nu. I'm calling this the N7 Tier, because I'm going to need to find a fellow who can do some calibrations on this level. This floor gets a big ol' no from me. I bet the person who straightens this out will be called Garrus, or something. Sounds fitting."

Ignoring half of the **Law** connections outright, Artorian saw nothing particularly viable to keep on keeping on with the Crown Game. That was, if anyone still wanted to participate.

"Well… if I borrow **Barrier**, I'm technically on the defensive. That might put some fire in their step if they think I'm only going to block or parry. What's the combination? Looks like earth, water, and celestial. *Celestial?* Interesting. I would have put my silvers down on the third one being infernal for the more physical barriers. Or… is this version not *for* physical protection? Oh, well now I *must* know. Saddle up, **Barrier**, you're with me!"

Artorian left his half-meditation state as the edges and outline of his body looked like they were becoming esoterically impenetrable. "Neat!"

Before the announcers could indulge with commentary, the entire arena had to momentarily look away as they all heard a very intrusive, and unwelcome:

Caw!

Crashing through the ceiling, Huginn and Muninn crashed the party.

CHAPTER FORTY-TWO

Artorian observed the two newcomers thinking this was likely no big deal, but the angry sounds from the stands and silence from the announcers told him two things. These two were bad news, and the game was thoroughly over. Glancing over to the orchestra, he could see the Maestro fume with rage. His feathers all bristled while the conducting stick trembled in his grip. The first seat of the violin section was doing her best to calm him.

The old human faintly overheard the first chair speaking, a small detail that quickly solidified his negative perspective on the swaggering duo. "It'll be alright, Conductor Penkins, they'll get thrown out."

One glance at Halcyon informed him that she was sending Anansi to get her weapons, while Sartre was already holding Hulk back from charging the two dark Crows. Ravens? Artorian narrowed his gaze at the rune-coated birds, each feather inscribed like it was jewelry to be adorned. A species name didn't pop into his mind until the smell hit him, along with words of warning from Aiden.

"They *stink*. I know that rot. They're Hraesvelgr! Corpse tearers, or corpse swallowers. Eagle-sized gluttons and pesky annoyances. Didn't I smack one in Eternia's Muspelheim with a piece of a building?"

Artorian crossed his arms, no longer mumbling to himself as he cleared his voice to get nice and loud. "What do you two want?"

Not a moment after Artorian asked did he notice an oddity. There were only two entities in front of him, right? So why was he sensing four? Two of which felt far more familiar than Odin's ravens, but he just couldn't put his finger on why. Or he couldn't until Huginn and Muninn adopted their human forms: Asgardians of old.

Right down to the stubby omni-men mustache detail.

In addition to that form, a tarry black mass surged over and around them both, covering them in a thick mesh like some kind of venomous symbiote. Both Hraesvelgr smiled cruelly at him, and when the symbiotes spoke, the clues clicked in Artorian's mind. His gaze darkened, tone dropping to acidic as his mood soured.

"*Pencil and Hanekawa.* Well, isn't that just the answer to the universe, life, and everything." Artorian spoke, seething, a towel composed of **Barrier** Mana forming in his hand as a lot of little hints and details were suddenly making a whole lot of sense. He considered his lesson plan, and spun the towel. "We must have skipped chapter forty-two, because it's spankin' time for you."

The tarry voices, which altered to match the tones that Artorian remembered from Eternia, laughed at him in unison. Pencil pointed at him with a black arm that molded out from Muninn's back. "Tier *Seven*? All that misery you caused, and this whole time you were a measly Tower Tier seven? *Haaaahahaha.* We were preparing for nothing!"

Hanekawa's face formed in the black mass resting on Huginn's shoulder, curling into that self-righteous crooked smirk. His voice was just as spot on drained as it had been in Eternia. "Told you he couldn't have done any of it without help. I bet that towel he's holding is his *real* soul item, and the pillow was just the Eternia equivalent. Insulting, but *harmless*."

Artorian spun the towel. "Yes. That's right. You've found me out, boys! Good job! I'm a measly Tier seven **Barrier** mage. Who knew! That's still more than enough to whip your second-tier **Lightning** node hosts."

Artorian didn't like that he was having severe trouble discerning what the **Laws** of the demons were. Or their Tiers, for that matter. That didn't bode well, and smelled of preparation.

The old man's slow, steady advance caused the two to shriek in amusement. Pencil fully covered his host, gaining control. "Not used to demon-possessed Mages, are you, old man? We're stronger than we would be alone! Demons of rank are almost always cultivators, as well! You're not facing a mere B-rank four **Lightning** Mage, but one who is amplifying a mighty A-rank three **Corrosion** Supplicant!"

Artorian blinked several times. Well, if they were just going to *tell him*, he wasn't going to complain about it!

Hanekawa covered his own host, performing an over-dramatic bow before speaking like he was already tired of the engagement. "Plus an A-rank three **Disease** Supplicant. A true shame that I can't just watch you waste away, but alas, I'm feeling scorned after our last meeting. A *true shame* that we are not the ones who will get to delight in your suffering."

Artorian frowned, the towel defensively wrapped about his left arm. This smelled like a setup. "Explain."

A third impact in the shape of a Bifrost beam broke through the smaller holes in the ceiling, creating a far bigger entrance as the big cheese himself filled the entire arena with a truly foul odor. Even the wax-covered wheel of blue cheese spontaneously resurrected, evolved into gorgonzola, then needed to regain momentary sentience just to wheeze and fall over dead.

Wearing a toga that both covered enough to look important, and not enough to hide a meatwall of a physique, Odin strolled out from his Bifrost beam before the effect ended, a Cheshire grin on his face. "Well, thanks to you tapping into my old **Lightning Law**, tracking you down was much easier! Two hundred years spent fine tuning plans to trap you in the snare that was my city, like you did to all those poor demons back in Solar Gate. Then you go and announce yourself while you're still… what? Re-learning how to be a Mage? Did you truly think I was going to *give you* the opportunity to buff up? To prepare?"

Artorian didn't like what he was seeing. Odin was also roiling with black tar, but before he could address that, he needed to come to terms with the new elephant in the room. "**Revelry**. Your Law is **Revelry**? Not **Zeal**, or **Annoyance**?"

"I, the great Zeus…" Odin took a wider dramatic stance as he curled his wrist to press fingers to his chest. "Am not bound by such mere trifles!"

Artorian poured on his sunlight Aura, seeing no reason not to start chipping away at the demons if big and square over there was going to press for a monologue. He frowned when the terrible smell cleared up, but the demons seemed to be… entirely unharmed. His eyebrows slowly climbed up his face when he realized that the Auras from the host cultivators were *protecting* them. This likely had something to do with the demons manifesting externally as tarry goop, rather than hiding inside the cultivators as he knew they had a tendency to do.

He'd seen other variants before. One where the demon hid in the cultivator, and one where the demon had taken over the cultivator entirely. This new half-and-half business was new, like it was geared entirely to get around… *him.*

This was going to be a problem.

"I, most magnanimous of all the supervisors, the great Zeus! Of course, understand that a wounded, soon-to-be-crippled crafter such as yourself, Hephaestus, requires such trifles to get through your day!"

Since Odin pointed at Artorian, the old man felt he understood who the new name was for. What this one meant, he didn't know yet.

Amplifying his Aura in an attempt to overpower Huginn and Muninn's protections, he frowned when all he seemed to accomplish was everyone else being refreshed while the general area continued to be cleaned up. His efforts were noticed, as Pencil and Kawa both pointed to laugh, causing a vein of irritation to appear on Artorian's forehead.

As he rubbed at it, his fingers pushed at the crown that he'd forgotten was on his head. Taking it off, he twirled the object between his fingers while an idea sprang to life behind his eyes. Only *he* was on the backfoot here. "If you're so magnanimous, Odin, then why do *I* have the crown?"

"It's Zeus, you cretin!" Odin's speech pattern immediately dropped the booming nature once even the most minor instance of annoyance crept in. No longer acting over the top for the crowd, his face twisted into a mesh of apathy before breaking with cracks of distasteful anger. "You've been nothing but a thorn in my side. A roadblock on my path to greatness. A stain in my most illustrious stories and records. In Eternia, you were a schemer who stole my thunder. You took from me what was rightfully mine. The victory over the greatest foe! You only managed it with cunning and trickery, but I, most poetic and valiant of all, would have brought Barry low with my overbearing might!"

He pointed a fat, accusatory finger at Artorian. "I had hundreds of years of Magehood on you before we began, and two hundred after! What schemes do you think will save you from me now? Now that I have learned your weaknesses, your strengths! Your foes are my allies, and your allies are my foes. Eternia's numbers were all that allowed you a most momentary edge over me, but now I am here to settle the score! What's more, I've brought some of your old friends to ensure that it won't be a bore."

Artorian changed tactics and pulled in his sunlight Aura, funneling Mana to the **Barrier** law he was upholding instead as a terrible feeling crawled over his skin. Though it was the tar crawling over Odin's skin that proved to be the source.

Just like the other two, a demon roiled its mass across the High Mageous's skin, forming a symbiotic mass as the unmistakable face of Ghreziz replaced the one he'd been speaking to. "Well, look what the dragon of the darkness flame dragged in! Demons never quit. How many times do I need to teach you this lesson, old man? You should have chosen to break! Your life would have been much easier when focused on service to your betters."

Artorian stood with his hands held behind his back, chest up and shoulders square. His eyes flicked planetside, taking stock of the situation now that he knew a few things for certain. First, Adam was at the Silverwood tree, in full defense mode. Good. Second, the areas where he'd decanted people were currently unmolested and unharmed. No demonic incursion activity to speak of. Good. That meant he could focus on the here and now.

He flicked the crown with a finger from behind his back, the round object landing on his bald head to hide the motion that he also flicked a marble of pink energy to Halcyon. The crown landed on its side, spun a few times, then flopped into place while Artorian addressed Odin with an eyes-over-glasses look. "All this for a tiny grudge? I know children with more clout than you. All that posturing and puffing. You got beat by Barry, *boy*."

Ghreziz barked. "Don't you dare ignore me, mortal!"

The demon did not have a chance to continue as the synergy between the host and demon fractured. "You will not tell such blatant lies about me, Loki!"

Artorian pressed his advantage, addressing Thundy rather than Gri-gri. "So we're using our made up names again? Is Hephaestus suddenly no good? Can't make up your mind? Might need to see someone about that, boy. Too much time as a meat-brick must have affected your ability to reason. Making deals with demons… *Appalling*. My Grim and Ty had no choice, but you, *you* of all people should have known better. Don't tell me that entire planetside society of yours are all mistakes like you? I bet Hephaestus means janitor, with all these messes of yours I seem to need to clean up."

Zeus was three whole feet taller than Artorian when they stood the equivalent of nose-to-nose. His face was red, the steam almost visibly coming out of his ears. "You know nothing of me, feeble old man. You know nothing of my grievances with our jailor overlord, Cal. What would you know of my history and plights? Did you know that our jailor armed a Dworc named Evan with a special pickaxe? That this Dworc then infiltrated deep beneath my ancestral home, and struck ley lines created by this very dungeon? The entire history of Clan Azguardia exploded in my face, and while nailed to the sky, the Mana storms composed of my fallen friends and family molded me. Remade me. Improved me to something more. Something *better*. I am a living legacy."

He lowered his head so he could whisper right into Artorian's ear. "You're the one who postures, fallen Administrator. You never had power. You only had status, and a responsibility that you shirked. I am the one who became a *god*, to my Valkyries and *real* people. A true *divine* to my Asgard in Eternia. I am the one blessed with an elemental channel of air, reborn to lead all that is left to true, eternal **Glory**. The likes that even Marie can't hope to attain with that lesser **Law** of hers. Not even Henry, with all his **Valor**, can match up to *me*."

He grinned wide. "You have *nothing* on me. I am a better, more experienced Mage. I am *two*, while you are but one. My allies have been most forthcoming about all your tricks, pillow man. I have literal hundreds of years of practice and experience over you, with skills and techniques you couldn't dream of. Then, as a cherry on top, I am a true genius in the arts of battle. A prodigy. A *natural*. I remember you struggling to get anything other than the sleep effect under your belt during first iteration training! All your students exceeded you by leagues, and left you in the dust. To be left alone and forgotten to the sands of time. What do you think you actually have on *me*, old man? Save for that little trinket that will soon no longer be on your head."

Artorian cracked the tiniest smile. He inhaled slowly, replying in a whisper as well. "The risk you took was calculated, but oh boy, are you bad at math, *Jasper*."

Zeus roared, exploding with rage as he punched Artorian right out of the arena with a crackling uppercut. The crown spun in place as the person attached to it broke the moon's orbit not one second after the air-rupturing impact. Electricity poured in waves from his fist, breaking like arcs of water as the energy rolled over the ground to snap, crackle, and pop.

Too irritated to speak, he lashed out with a hand to snatch the crown, which was rightfully his. Rather than grasp it as expected, the object evaded his grip, smacked him in the face, and used the counter momentum gain to flip through the air and land right onto Halcyon's head, covering her in an esoteric coating of **Barrier** Mana that manifested in ultramarine flames.

"That's mine!" A thunderous moment later, Zeus backhanded Cy right across her face. The crown went flying before she'd fully realized it was there, but her feet didn't move a millimeter from the sand she was standing in. The ultramarine field coating her shattered, but that was all that broke. Her face had moved due to the kinetics of the impact, but aside from a red mark on her cheek, the look in her eyes as she turned back to Zeus was pure predator.

Zeus snatched the crown with Mana as it flew away, sighing in delighted relief once the metal object was again between his fingers. He wasn't even paying attention to the animals in people form around him. They were all beneath him. "Finally, we begin approaching what is right. That I am not merely a god, but a god-king! I—"

He was interrupted by Sartre slamming a crab claw into his knee. The gray crustacean looked up at the vastly more powerful entity like he did not have a care in the world, long resigned to his end as he blew out a cloud of ashen coffee-leaf smoke into the meatwall's face. The source of which he put out with a tiny sizzle, right down on Zeus's foot as his other claw pressed down.

Zeus snapped out his words as he punted Sartre away with a devastating crunch. "Enough! You are, all of you, beneath me! I am a god, you dull creature, and I shall not be bullied by—"

Hulk grabbed Zeus by the exposed ankle, the opening Sartre had generated for him. With significantly less effort than it took to move the broken bulwark outside of the Moonbase's front door, he loudly and violently slammed Zeus around like a rag doll, leaving him face-up on the floor in the cracked crater left behind before adding his own insult. "Puny Dreamer."

Huginn and Muninn rushed to Zeus's aid, but Halcyon made a sharp motion with her fin. Rather than make it, the duo was beset by every single attendee and champion in the arena. All of them had been holding back rage. All of them on a hair trigger to do *something*. But Beast-rule was absolute, so when the highest echelon dropped the hammer and declared war, their only restraint broke like a weak shackle.

Halcyon mentally heard her Dreamer's voice as Zeus got up to backhand Hulk away, along with a powerful influx of pink energy that bulged her muscles and primed her for action as the marble she'd caught fueled her. Her guardians had bought her the needed time. She felt invigorated, empowered, and most of all, could taste the building **Acceleration** fed from the leftovers of her Dreamer's spare **Love** Mana. <One shot. One opportunity. Seize everything you ever wanted. Capture it. Don't let it slip. *Go.*>

CHAPTER FORTY-THREE

Halcyon telekinetically picked up the crown from the ground, and in the moment before Zeus's confusion cleared up, the crit-fishing Daimyo struck. Turning with enough torque and force to create a powerful gale, Halcyon released her humanization to adopt her full and proper onyx and gold Orca form. The spin of her attack culminated with her tail aimed squarely at Zeus's chest as he got to his feet.

Applying the **Acceleration** Mana gifted by her Dreamer, she shunted the effect to her tail, improving her strike from an already rather potent A-rank five impact to one amplified by a bonus forty-thousand meters per second of solid **oomph**. During the exact moment of the strike, Halcyon shone a luminous **Aurum**.

THUNK!

The actual impact deafened all, and a sharp ringing in the ears was all anyone could hear for several minutes as the space around Cy's tail caught fire, formed golden plasma, and displaced matter in a violent enough manner to blow the entire ceiling away, plus a few bonus walls. Physics did not play kindly with **Acceleration** without appropriate cost, and this wasn't Eternia.

When the dust settled, Zeus was gone.

Countless lay twitching on the ground while holding their heads, the arena a complete wreck. Only six got back up. Huginn and Muninn stood on one end, with Sartre, Hulk, and Anansi rising on the other as they each stared the other down like they were in a dusty standoff.

Halcyon closed her eyes and took a breath, feeling uncannily liberated. A primal restraint ran down her senses like water, leaving her behind as she had overcome the Beast limitation. "The shackle. It's broken. I am *free*."

Crackling with energy, Halcyon found herself elsewhere.

The room was crystalline, small, and hexagonal. Six nodes hovered in a circle around her. The basic Essences, one orb representing each affinity.

A slow clap originating from behind her startled the Orca, and she found the image of a man when she turned. His voice was outright jovial. "'Ello! My name is Shaka. Welcome to the Tower of Ascension, even if you are here only as a formality. I am so happy to be getting so much company. It feels like just yesterday where I spoke to Ammy about crossing the streams. Welcome, Halcyon. I am your humble guide, and **Aurum** cannot wait to meet you. Floor seventy-nine is eager for your presence."

Halcyon looked up, seeing the Tower become fully transparent, save for a single floor that was burgeoning brightly both with golden light, and the pod call used by her Orca family. Halcyon was there in no time at all, her arms squeezing around a very welcoming and familiar feeling. To Halcyon, the Tower trip was anything but short. To those looking on in reality, the change she underwent appeared instant.

Her eyes snapped open in the arena, glowing gold as she re-adopted her humanization. Unlike last time when it had been just the body and basic clothing, this time Halcyon's Eternia armor came with her. Anansi was there in the same moment, and provided her with the latest graviton Iridium tonfas, the weapons he'd gone to fetch earlier. She gripped the hardened handle-straps, then twirled both for comfort as the pressure she exerted increased.

Comfort found, she put her foot forwards in the settled sand as her solar sigil blazed with new metallic light, unsettling her two opponents as the other three pulled their own armaments out of hammerspace with a glowing shimmer. The Beast-only version of Cal's lunar warehouses.

Adding the crown to the top of her head, Cy rolled her shoulders. "Tag in."

She then vanished from her position, caused another gale, and introduced Pencil to the glowing blunt stick. The dull *ph'nock*! cratered in the side of Muninn's face, sending the symbiotic duo crashing through the wall while the other three descended upon Huginn.

Hanekawa groaned. "Why do *I* have to deal with three of them?"

"I don't want to hear it, Kawa!" Pencil spat back from the opposite side of the dust cloud. "You're not the one getting clocked by what killed you in Eternia!"

Managing another languished groan before he was beset, Moonbase Alpha turned into a warzone as the Full Metal Goats chose that exact time to invade. There were delicious soup cans to be eaten!

While the majority of residents got back to their senses and feet, Halcyon pummeled Pencil while the other three gave Hanekawa a strong reason to care about short term survival. No amount of truth in 'death just means being re-Cored' made the demon feel like that fate was a worthwhile venture.

Both demons hoped that their glorious leaders would return to help them, but the shattered *Oooorb* Arena in the sky told them otherwise, when Zeus chose to instead launch himself planetside, chasing a glowing dot that was considerably faster than him, had a head start, and was already almost back on Caltopia. That blasted geezer had planned to get hit!

Pencil scoffed in irritation. "Abyss it! It's just us, Kawa! Kill those three and get over here to assist me!"

"You kill that Orca and come assist *me*!" Kawa spat back. He was pushed into a corner as it was. "Think with portals! Call reinforcements!"

Taking a brutal hit from Halcyon's right hook in order to get a Horn of Calling out, he managed to blow the instrument in the nick of time. Unfortunately for the ever-degrading state of his face, the follow-up left hook broke the instrument and mashed the shrapnel into his mouth. A mouth that grinned an evil smile before he was sent flying.

Call of the Savant activated with a stark green glow as the sickening borealis filled the sky. Standing up from the bludgeoned stands while wiping the leaking Mana from his face, Pencil grinned wider before laughing. He believed he had now won, because more demons would be coming. "The tides, how they turn!"

The green borealis gathered into a single spot above the moonbase, tearing open a portal that formed into a smooth circle. The gate solidified, then unceremoniously popped like an overinflated balloon after making a truly unfortunate wrenching sound. When the effect dissipated, only a single demon appeared to have walked out of the hijacked portal.

The tiny bat stuck his paws into his pockets, whistling as he pretended to be impressed.

"You know what, Pencil?" Soni grinned as his voice carried down to the unbelieving Savant. "I never liked you."

Removing his tiny paws from his pockets, he slapped them together, causing the borealis in the sky to reappear. Except now it was colored a marbled azure blue instead of a drab green. An identical portal opened as he wove the energy like a fine tapestry, allowing Valkyrie rebels, rather than demons, to swarm from the stable gate. After a host counting one hundred strong poured through in but moments, Valhalla herself stepped across the threshold last before the gate closed smoothly.

"*That's* how you think with portals." Soni blew some nonexistent dirt from his claws when the force counting one-hundred and one strong brandished their tridents in unison. "Cheers, Love! The cavalry's 'ere!"

———

Artorian would have laughed had he been able when shaped like a mote of light. So when he resumed his human shape and slammed feet-first down in the region of the whistling mountains—the one's he'd blown holes through with Dawn's Damocles bow before entering Eternia—he did just that. "Soni, I've been so curious if you were alright or not! Good to see ya, buddy! Cheers!"

That the bat was a moon's distance away and couldn't hear him fell by the wayside for now. Artorian's attuned Mage vision caught sight that Odin was speeding his way, which made him press his hands into his hips and firmly exhale. *"Pffff.* Alright, now what? I need to pull back up in Tiers, **Barrier** got me off the moon unscathed, but she's not going to cut it now and I already lost my towel. Adapting between Tiers takes a bit more mental focus than I'm willing to admit. I gave the Cy the **Love** Mana I was holding on to, and this sensation of being shaken is making it hard on me. Still, needs must. Spud's going to be here in… give or take thirty minutes? He's fast, but not light-mote fast."

Part of the mountain range rumbled. Artorian looked left, meeting the face of a very surprised Dalamadur as Surtur got up from her nap. Her voice was kind, but her size made her sound larger than she was from all the air displaced. A fact she realized only after speaking. "Dreamer?"

Artorian pressed his hands over his ears and blinked a few times. *"Fhwooo,* girl, you have lungs! Moza would have been jealous. Being able to articulate so clearly at that size is an art!"

Letting her bonescripting do the heavy lifting, Surtur advanced and coiled in around his position while reducing her size. When she was back in the more common Lamia-shape about a minute later, they could talk properly. Even if it was going to be a hurried chat. "Dreamer? You look tense, and shaky. Can I help?"

Artorian wrenched his hands together, eyes on the sky. "I hope so, Surty. I'm on a countdown to a world of hurt, and I'm very much not slated to win the engagement. Odin found me and cut short my session to get a good grip on myself. I mean *basic* functions; I am nowhere near combat readiness. Channeling the **Sun** law burned off a lot of Eternia rust, but he's in it to win it, and we're both so mad at one another that thinking straight is taking more than an effort of will. I rarely have trouble here, but since I can't focus enough to fix my Tier yet, I'm currently looking at a most unfavorable engagement. I'm D.O.A. if he gets here and I'm still like this. All shaky."

Surtur sat on her tail, not grasping the urgency from still waking up. Yawning wide, she used the back of her hand to rub at her eyes, and thought of how her own Dreamer solved problems like this. "Do you need more weapons?"

Artorian perked up. "Do we have any? I'd love some Mage-quality weapons that aren't the backups stored in my spatial ring. Those two have nasty side effects, and nothing else in there is going to be of any help."

"Why am I so *tired*?" Surtur popped her neck, stretched, and hovered upwards with her bonescripting. "I know of at least one weapon that my Dreamer put aside in case of an emergency. This sounds like it applies. I'll go fetch it and return it to you."

"That… that would help bunches. Thank you, dear." Relaxing a tiny bit at the news, Artorian nodded. He looked at Surtur properly, noticing she was in some rather interesting clothing. "I love your new leathers, by the way. So stylish!"

Smirking a teensy bit, she shared its origins. "Thank you, I made it out of a male of my species who seduced and then betrayed me. It's surprisingly comfortable; so far this has been the most useful he's ever been." Artorian's fallen face made her laugh. "*Ah-ha*, I love the expression I get when I tell people."

"I don't know if I'm bothered to be aware that you weren't lying…" Artorian interjected, composing himself. "Or proud."

"Be proud. He was a no-good Lamia, and without societal laws, we've all gone back to doing things the old way. It works." Another heavy yawn followed as she shook herself to get a move on. "I swear it feels like my Dreamer is asleep, and that's just…"

A third massive yawn broke her speech. "So infectious."

Artorian thought she might actually be on to something. He observed his shaking hands, felt his trembling insides, and just couldn't understand what had him so stirred up. He waved as she snaked off into the sky, then pulled free his soul item pillow and plopped it down.

"I need to shake this dread. Feeling like this is preventing focus." He threw himself down on top of it while his eyes remained locked on the sky, then closed them to focus on his breathing. "Accept the fear, old boy. Let it flow over you. Through you. You need to be calm to rise back up the Tiers. When the fear is gone, only you will remain. Only what's important. Only what's held dear. Only **Love**. Approach this heart-pounding threat like all others. Think of the flowing sands in Socorro."

Sal'ha'din, the Sha of Socorro, whispered through his memories as the sound of tents fluttering and winds breezing by was all he heard for a while. Over time, the warmth of the desert snuck into his icy, trembling hands. "May your heart find peace."

When the Sha left his tent, the dread went with the man. Afterwards, Artorian was once more alone on his pillow. The fear was fading. The trembling was leaving. Panic subsided, his two hearts calmed, and his breathing eased. Odin was coming regardless of what he did, so even if it had taken twenty minutes of lying there with his eyes closed, he was now at peace.

Both with himself, and his situation.

Others might have prepared more vigorously, but not Artorian.

To the old man, mental clarity and ease of mind were far more important than rushed defenses and shaky confidence. "If you know the enemy and you know yourself, your victory will not stand in doubt."

When his eyes opened again, Scilla was sitting next to him in her adult clothing, her own gaze on the sky. "How ya feeling?"

"Every battle is won before it is fought." Artorian spoke calmly, patterns and puzzles still flashing before his eyes as complex battle plans were made, broken, and remade as new ideas and situations presented themselves now that he had the clarity of mind to conjure them. "This one is no different. Though there may be a greater cost than my usual fights."

Scilla's face said she didn't believe him.

"You don't like engaging unless you know… mostly for certain? That you're going to win." She shook her head at the absurdity, recalling his past engagements with combat that mattered. "Who can actually do that? You've just been extremely lucky. That's all."

A tiny smile played on the old man's features. "Yet S still equals one-one-seven, and luck suddenly has less to do with any given event than one might think."

Scilla rolled her eyes, waving her hands in a playful, spooky fashion before sinking back into his shadow. "Alright. Sure. Keep your secrets. So mysterious. Now what's the *plan*? The details I could discern looked like a *gamble*."

Artorian sighed, closing his eyes for another minute. "The path to victory is the path you're on. It becomes a path to victory the moment you decide it does. Step one. Place one's hopes in dreams. Step two. Forward unto dawn. Three. Run the clock."

He wobbled his hand, making a sound that confirmed Scilla's concern. "Alright, so it's pretty much a gamble, but it's my best shot. Here I go."

With his eyes closed, Artorian expended whole ranks of Mana as he let one of his invocations fly. Rather than cause a visual spectacle, the energy released from his form instead seemed to… ebb away, filtering through other layers rather than the one he was on as the lingering dream Essence that Tatum had told him about was expended.

Feeling a connection build, he whispered the message, adding it to the waves. "Sweet dreams are made of these. Hold to hope and reach your seas. The lighthouse shines, and the buoy is down. One foot in front of the other, let your heart resound. Step hard, and listen with your feet to the ground. From one-one-seven, to one, the timer is wound."

Artorian slid off his pillow and stood, an extended hand retrieving his soul item before his feet hovered inches off the ground. He'd found his determination. He'd made his plans. He'd put his chips on the table. Now, all that was left was execution. He opened his eyes and shot into the sky, ending the message with a final sigh. "Run, boy, run."

CHAPTER FORTY-FOUR

Zeus expected to arrive on Caltopia to meet some hastily-organized defense. None of that was to be found. Instead, he found a reason to put the brakes on his approach as he discovered the aging brat in the center of an Essence... hole?

Sliding to a halt on a cloud, Zeus watched suspiciously as Loki remained at a standstill in low orbit. Well, standing wasn't quite right if the rigid lotus position was anything to go by. The old man was cultivating, but what kind of cultivation sucked every drop and particle of Essence from the environment in a radius of three point fourteen leagues around a man? He was taking Mana as fast as the energy could pour back into the vacant space!

Ghreziz commented by forming a second head on Zeus's shoulder. "Reminds me of the Demon's Maw technique in a way. Not the same in practice, but his **Law** isn't as conveniently low Tier as it was. I'm feeling distinct... **Greed**?"

Zeus shook his head with a minor motion, as his target wasn't worth the effort of a full head shake. "No, **Greed** is on Tier thirteen, with the other *miserables*. The weakest denominator of Barry's *real* **Law**. I passed this one on my way up from the **Lightning** node. That rotten leaf of a codger. Here I thought he was going to skyrocket back up, and he goes and hangs around the most *insulting* tier in the entire tower. That's not **Greed**, that's the Law of **Cultivation**. Tier six."

Ghreziz raised a brow at his host. "The nodes have moved since my time, but surely someone wasn't as pedantic as to put an actual node of **Cultivation** in there?"

Zeus stuck his tongue out in disgust, the nodes had been moving around much more lately. "You've got some sick irony, partner. **Cultivation** *is* on the same tier as **Pedantry**. Quick information, somewhere before the fall of the metallic-referenced ages such as gold, silver, and whatnot. Tower climbs stifled. Few to no Mages climbed above the fourth tier, but that I believe in part has to do with the *insult* waiting for you on tiers five and six."

Ghreziz did not interrupt, as he greatly desired this knowledge for himself. Zeus had instantly gotten a reputation as a man who loved talking. Specifically about himself. Anything involving explanations where he could cut into a conversation and abscond with the spotlight was prized. Ghreziz called it monologuing, and he knew that all the wretched should ensure to grow their skill in this particular category.

"I'll show you the easy way, from what I recall during my last ascent." Zeus huffed, forming some letters of lightning above his hand in a mockery of both Nixie Tubes and prompt screens. Mockery or not, his Mana formed surprisingly high-quality images in the vein of Eternia's prompts. "It surprised me to see **Nature** on the fourth Tier instead of the third, but that's not what bothered me."

Tower Tier Four
Nature
Portals
Ice
Shadows
Darkness

Light

Zeus pulled his nose up, his tone hasty and angry. "Seems like quality stuff, doesn't it? Then, someone in the past must have been a true spear between the cheeks. Because, then, *suddenly*, we get *this*."

Tower Tier Five
Annoyance
Ambiguity
Recursion
Sardonicism
Argumentation
Contradiction

"One of these Tiers is not like the other!" Zeus broke into a mocking sing-song voice. "Or so I thought until I kept climbing. Normally Mages forget the **Laws** they've passed, as Tiers you abandon turn into a drunken haze. The Tower doesn't want you to remember. Lucky for me that I've such vast experience with these matters. It allowed me to get properly upset at *this*."

Tower Tier Six
Pedantry
Pride
Snark
Spite
Laws
Cultivation

The man fumed. "Mages in the past became so *backwards* that two entire Tower tiers got twisted, and turned into that disgusting brew of a drink. Come on, the **Law** of **Laws**? How much arguing do people need to do for that to end up an actual concept that demands room? Not even as a secondary meaning in a node either! Those are front and center!"

Ghreziz now felt curious. "What made Tier thirteen the 'miserables' if these are already such a mess?"

Zeus spat and changed the information. "Just look at this atrocity! Life during the era where this Tier was prevalent must have been truly awful."

Tower Tier Thirteen
Hunger
Bone
Violence
Sand
Annoyance
Greed

Ghreziz prepared to comment on this having been one of his favorite eras to be summoned into, but was interrupted by something he considered significantly more foul. Words from the pillow-man.

"Problem up there, Spud?"

Zeus and Ghreziz looked down, not having noticed when the Mana and Essence in the air evened out as the sucking pull ended. The toga-wearer twitched, and didn't fall for the ruse. Using lightning as a foothold, Zeus cannonballed himself right towards Artorian, as the latter was climbing tiers at a sickening speed.

Revelry beat out **Acceleration**, the **Law** Artorian had adapted to before nimbly dodging out of the way. Without dilation, unfortunately, this meant that Artorian was faster due to its inherent properties, even if Zeus's own **Law** was of a higher tier.

"I'm not playing this game with you, Loki," Zeus snapped. The lightning around his form solidified as he summoned advanced armor and weaponry from his own spatial rings, going through a short but potent transformation sequence which made Artorian feel thoroughly out of his league; he visibly paled when Zeus spoke further. "Ghreziz, symbiote me."

Those last few words only worsened the feeling, as even with **Acceleration**, Artorian failed entirely to dodge the follow up strike. A move that was both calculated and intensely painful as he broke the sound barrier, then flew through every single hole in the whistling mountains. A feat that amused the demon greatly. "Ha! Hole in one! That's it for any defenses he might have had up. The show is all yours, host. Blast him!"

"*Ha-haa!*" Zeus laughed, his hands pressing palm out towards the spinning Mage trying to right himself and stop careening into high orbit. "I've been so looking forward to this!"

Powering up with a frightening amount of popping lightning, Zeus unleashed a technique he'd been working on all century long, as he knew well that Artorian's true form was a Long. He thundered out his words, naming the attack. "Dragon-Piercing Nova Doom-Cannon!"

The cloud layer split, the whistling mountains turned to rubble, and an energy beam that could have easily cracked Cal's moon into tiny fragments punched into Artorian head-on. Zeus laughed maniacally along with Ghreziz. The duo, who both despised him, relished in what was more than likely an instant victory and vaporization. There wouldn't even be particles left when the blast culminated, not with the pillow-man's Tier so low!

Ghreziz smiled while barking out some insults. "Suffer, ingrate! For all the 'good' you've dared to do me and my entire kind! Over all these realms I've had to chase you through!"

The beam wasn't even half done discharging when a voice, clear as day, replied to them from above. "What a name. Did you mean lesser formation of the limp noodle? I've seen soup contents with more rigidity to them! C'mon, Spuddy! A collaboration with Gri-Gri and this is the best you've got? That's no better than some friar standing on a dais to meekly lecture to a sleeping congregation! If Traviticus of Baldree was here to see this, he'd slap you silly."

The flabbergasted duo choked on their responses.

The beam was cut short, revealing Artorian doing a little

shimmy before turning his rear towards them and giving it an insulting slap. "Dragon-Piercing? Ha! Was that supposed to scare me? That's not how you do '*scary*.'"

Zeus cursed, charging the sky-dancing old man as his **Law** Tier once again began to rise. A factor far worse than most other things the annoyance could do at the moment. Fortunately for Zeus, having a bond with the A-ranked Savant-class demon put significant extra pep in his step, allowing him to arrive at melee range much sooner than Artorian had expected.

When he punched the longbeard with enough force to cause a tidal wave, Artorian cratered the old mountain range's remains on impact.

Feeling mighty unpleasant being buried in the ground, Artorian released a short, singular, "Ow."

Too discombobulated to keep climbing Tiers, he also knew that staying put was only going to make him an easy target. Not wanting to be a sitting duck, he considered his options. Down meant Odin would be breaking Caltopia, and he did not want to be even slightly responsible for that when the Incarnates woke up. Up meant he was going to get trashed. "That 'one option coming out to none' thing is biting me in the keister. I need to get back into orbit; he doesn't care at all about planetary damage."

He sighed, forced to pick the painful option.

"Welp, if I'm gonna get socked in the cheek anyway..." Collapsing his hands together, he formed a fire bee and held it tight as—just like he'd expected—Zeus ignored concepts such as 'solid ground.' He moved through rock fast enough to displace a whole ravine and punt him right out from what the brick wall of meat considered a hiding place.

Taking that kick to the ribs did not do Artorian good, but it did get him high into the sky enough for him to release the bee. He needed backup. He needed it badly. Surtur was currently nowhere to be seen, and his saving grace at the moment was that Odin seemed to be changing outfits. That or the military outfit covering Ghreziz's tar form wa—*Wait just a darn second.* That was his outfit! From one of the first meetings!

Screeching to a halt in the sky, he held his ribs with one hand as they recovered, while pointing an accusatory finger at the suit. "Odin! What? Explain! What are you doing stealing Zelia's designs? That's not yours. At all!"

Ghreziz raised his brow again, smirking as he smoothed out the details, down to the frilly tassel hanging from the shoulder. The tar moved, giving way to a knight's helmet with the face-plate down, which seemed to allow Zeus to speak. So was that an outfit, on a demon symbiote, on full, highly enchanted armor, on a Mage's frame?

Artorian **pfff'd** at seeing what he needed to deal with. At least absorbing all the Mana from that heavy technique Odin had thrown out nearly topped him back up. The cultivation in Caltopia's low orbit had not been nearly as helpful as he'd hoped. Some interesting tidbits were gained, sure. Nothing like having a costly technique shatter on your face and getting to absorb it all, though! Eternium just saved his bacon with that title! He'd never been happier to have speedrun that dumb game.

Zeus sounded downright chipper in his response. "As ruler and future king of all Caltopia, one must fit the part! A topic you've never understood, Administrator."

"Oh my word, you think you've won." Artorian blinked back, his voice full of disbelief. "You think that just because I need to manually hop between nodes, rather than return to where I belong because I can't sympathy channel them, you just win the battle for free?"

"Of course I've won!" The large, shining white smile beamed back from behind the visor. "Forget your silly Tiers. I've halted your progress. More importantly, you've just now noticed my gear, didn't you? I bet you've seen its properties. The enchantments. The powers and protections it grants! It's nearly as good as my end-game Eternia equivalent, except far more useful. Or did you see my mighty blade, Calibur! I made it out of a parrot, you know. The mocking little copycat. Now she's an ex-parrot!"

Brandishing the longsword, which could be mistaken for a hand-and-a-half sword or some kind of awkward gladius, Zeus posed like he was king of the world. Likely because, in his mind, he was. "You have once again pulled one over on me, but don't believe that I will be throwing such a big technique out twice! I have decades of practice against Auras and Presence. I have battled and trained against constructs and formations. All you have left is to face me in close quarters, for which I am far better trained, equipped, and mastered in the field."

Artorian pressed his fingers to his forehead, sharply dropping them back towards Odin. "Are you mad? Just what qualities do you think you have that would make you a good leader? Or even a good king? Did you not see how much Henry and Marie have struggled with the topic? They've been trying for centuries! What do you think you have?"

To Artorian's instant delight, Odin took the bait.

Given precious moments to recoup himself and try to return to a state of mental clarity where he could continue to Tier up, Artorian pretended to listen as Zeus began monologuing with glee.

CHAPTER FORTY-FIVE

Artorian ran through his tally of Odin's weaknesses while the wall of meat lauded himself with some epic ode. Currently, all he could think of was what Tatum had said, mouthing the words to himself sotto voce. "Odin loves being cliche and contrived. He wants the show more than the result. He wants the big villain speech, the scripted showdown, and the triumphant tales. Not having that infuriates him, the vindictive eel."

Given Spud's penchant for tapping into his old **Lightning Law** with the frequency he did, that seemed apt. When he found himself to be steady enough to skyrocket up the Tiers, a lance of lightning smashed into him in the center of his chest. The effect was wrapped around a metal rod, which, unlike the electric bolt itself, didn't shatter when it struck him. One shattered technique and Odin *already* had a counter? Big oof.

Groaning as far more of the damage got through than Artorian expected, Zeus boomed. "Pay attention! If I notice your density increasing, there will be more of those!"

"Density?" Artorian held his chest with a groan, the cloth he'd been protecting with his Mana no longer able to safeguard the material, as a large round hole now exposed part of his chest. His chest was unharmed... mostly, but the clothing was meant for the rag-pile. "Right, Mage Tiers increase a Mana's density, rather than the direct amount when comparing one to the other. The whole bucket example from ages ago."

Righting himself, Artorian quickly got back to a place of clarity where he could try to zip up the Tiers again. He hesitated. Spud was clearly paying attention, big speech or no, though he doubted that Odin understood the actual weaknesses with the Tier-hopping he was doing.

Artorian had two basic choices when it came to emulating a **Law** that was lower in the Tiers than **Love**. One, he could be on **Love**'s Tier and node, and channel Mana from another **Law**, if and only if that other **Law** had a strong sympathy connection to his own. Such as **Sun**, **Acceleration**, **Light**, and the like.

Two, if the node he wanted to channel had a weak connection, or worse, then he needed to descend in Tiers and adapt his Mana to the ideals and concepts of that particular **Law**. This allowed him to use that node in full effect, but had the downside of limiting him to that **Law's** Tier and Mana quality. Or Mana density. Same thing.

He could hold on to a limited amount of **Love** Mana if he had to take option two, via his Aura. He'd expended that backup reservoir because he'd prioritized Halcyon's wellbeing over his own. "An investment well made. No regrets."

Going back *up* the Tiers was a different story. If someone else were to do this, they would have needed to contend with the problem that they needed enough raw Mana to be condensed into a higher form.

As a quick, and extremely general note to self, he added some numbers. If a Tier five **Law** needed five units of Tier one Mana to make one unit of Tier five Mana, then a Tier fifty **Law** would need fifty units of Tier one Mana, to make one equivalent Tier fifty unit. Reality had told him there was a far more intense curve at play, but he needed to dismiss that in order to keep his math simple. Even if it made his math wrong.

So a person who had one hundred units of Tier one Mana, could go, at maximum, back up to Tier one hundred. They could not, however, climb back up to one hundred and one due to a raw Mana deficiency. Artorian would never have this problem given that his 'maximum capacity' for holding Mana was always going to be set at the highest Tier he'd ever gotten to, that being the **Love** Tier. Combined with his frankly insane Essence intake, this whole part of the equation went out the window.

The difficult portion was that he had to go up the way he came down. Either by bouncing between footholds, those being **Laws** with a strong sympathy connection, or having enough raw Mana in the reserves to shoot back home all in one go. The big downside? This took concentration, and *time*.

Shooting back up to seven-twenty just wasn't happening. Going down was easy in comparison. So to succeed, he'd have to leapfrog between nodes of strong sympathy, and that caused him a big problem. Because between Tiers thirty and two hundred and four, there was *nothing* for him to stand on. Higher and lower he had a few options, but that gap in the middle, which he'd initially dismissed, now looked like an oppressive chasm. "There can't be nothing. There *must* be something I missed."

Next problem.

Zeus was subtly attacking his Aura and Presence.

Artorian would have praised the man for his subterfuge, but the idea made him sick. The attacks were pinpricks, prodding and testing his Auric defenses. Needles pretended to be bugs while Zeus distracted from it all with his dramatics. What interested Artorian was the same thing he accidentally fumbled on and spoke out loud. "Why does that feel like being prodded by Henry or Marie?"

Zeus paused his tale mid-pose, needing to scrunch his face and groan with a painful sigh. "Future interruptions will be *punished*, Administrator. I'm going to need to divide my up thematic ideas into different periods eventually, but since answers are known to shut you up, I will *indulge* you."

Adopting a politician's oratory pose, he began. "Measured by the festivals of Saturnalia, two's a company, three's a crowd, and ten is a party for those who are hardy. From there, you keep on adding pie until ravishing sparks fly. At thirty-one point four, **Celebration** is at your door! At ninety-eight point five, **Revelry** is *live*."

Artorian's eyes widened, the puzzle pieces aligning with what he saw in Odin, saying the words with matter of fact surprise. "Your **Law** is Tier ninety-eight!"

Zeus smirked. "Along with **Valor** and **Glory**, yes. A fact I found most interesting is just how many supervisors ended up on this Tier! Aiden's **Law**—I mean, Poseidon's—now rests with ours as well. He went rather primal with it, and he's using an older, secondary denomination, but that warrior playing at being a druid and shaman is with '**Berserkr.**' How good the gifts of Cal were, when they kept on giving. Now that your eyebrows have climbed up on your forehead, be silent until it is your turn to lose in the performance of this play."

Artorian was prevented from having his face caved in with repeated punches when his snappy comeback was stopped cold. A mental nudge pushed at his mind. He had a forum call! Accepting the link, he could not feel more delighted at hearing a demon's voice.

Soni's tone was victorious. <Hello! Moon's secure. No longer haunted! The dastardly duo was made to flee right onto Goose territory, and had to deal with Wagner, Beethoven, Mozart, and Weird Al Goosovitch all in one go. Not even plumage remains. The last Goose boss wasn't around to join in on the fun, but I thought I'd give you a call. Strategy's easier when you know it all.>

Artorian sighed and hung his head, making a motion for Spud to please continue while he hung there and kept pretending to listen. He was still primed to play Tier-leapfrog, but maybe he could get some new information this way.

While his face remained the picture of neutrality, his mental voice filled with joy. <Soni! Good to hear from you. I was aware you went to help, but this helps take a load off. I would normally ask if you could portal some reinforcements to me, but it pains me to admit that unless we get one of the Incarnates involved, or I find some angle, Odin is currently the most powerful cultivator in the Soul Space. Especially while bonded to that sassy Savant, Ghreziz. Is there anyone there who might have any key knowledge on Odin? Anything will do.>

Soni was quiet for a long beat. <Yes. Valhalla is here. She's very unhappy with her Dreamer, and will likely tell you anything you want. Let me close this connection and tell Halcyon. She's the only reason I could make a direct connection with you from all the way up here.>

The forum connection faded. Artorian ignored Spud's new pin-needle prodding of the literal fortress that was his Aura, and accepted the new connection when it came in. <Hello there, is this Valhalla?>

Valhalla, now sounding far more world-weary, replied. <It is, respectable Dreamer. I heard you needed some of my... You needed information. How can I help?>

Artorian got right to the point. <Weaknesses. Flaws. Anything.>

Valhalla felt vindicated, and unloaded on the Dreamer. <He is incredibly stubborn, proud, doesn't want to redo tasks, prefers lording knowledge, and will refuse to do something twice. He plays at being a relentless seeker and giver of wisdom, but in truth has little regard for communal values such as justice, fairness, or any respect for law and convention.>

Taking a breath, as she was saying the words out loud in addition to mentally, she continued. <He wants to be portrayed as an eminently honorable ruler and battlefield commander, not to mention an impossibly muscular one. But he's nothing of the sort. He incites strife between peaceful people with what I can

only describe as sinister glee. There's a saying about how just reasoning can justify war, the means to an end thing? To him, it's flipped. War is the justification for any reasoning he feels like employing. That only got worse after he abandoned all reason and made a bonding deal with that… *thing*. He's consumed by vengeance against a minor inconvenience he's never been able to do anything about.>

Artorian could hear her grinding her teeth. <We had such a good start going with our society. Proud warriors all, powerful cultivators, geniuses and gifted powerhouses. It's all he could see. He refuses to concern himself with average warriors, preferring instead to lavish his 'blessings' only on those whom he deems to be worthy of them.>

Valhalla's tone soured. <When I was offered the blessing, and found out what it was… I felt appalled.>

Artorian sighed. <Let me guess, it was demons?>

<It was demons. He had many convinced that they're 'special' and now won't see reason like some blind herd, or have foolishly surrendered themselves to their demon, thinking there were no downsides. Most are husks controlled by tar.> Valhalla confirmed for him. <He has eyes only for the elite of society, but that's really not the source of the problem. He likes to stand on top of that pile by causing conflict. He's never concerned about the reasons for the conflict, or even the outcome. Instead, he can't tear his eyes away from the chaotic frenzy the struggle causes. He lives to see someone climb to the top and shout to the sky. Then he flashes with jealousy, and reminds them that they're still beneath him.>

Valhalla turned apologetic. <He despises you, respected Dreamer. I am sorry. This has been broiling, and now the pot has boiled over.>

Artorian physically nodded. <Worry not, dear child. You've told me far more than I was hoping, and it appears that I will have friendly company shortly.>

Valhalla didn't understand, but smiled toothily as the Dreamer sent through the visual image of Surtur bee-lining towards him. The tactician in her understood that he was going to need to be active in the next few moments, and saw herself out, feeling much better after being told she'd helped. She kept it short, her voice full of confidence. <Success to you, respected Dreamer. Punt that pompous ultracrepidarian!>

CHAPTER FORTY-SIX

Artorian needed to severely rack his noggin at Valhalla's word use. He'd never heard that one before. His face strongly reflected these feelings, as they had contorted into a baffled squint that peered into the distance.

"Alright, enough. What part of my well-detailed tale are you so terribly stuck on?" Zeus interrupted his train of thought. "I've been thorough, and you're not known to be easy to fool. So what has your knickers twisted into a jar?"

"Twisted into a…?" Artorian blinked. "Wha…?"

Now that he was actually confused, playing his earlier facial expression off became quite easy. He babbled on, handing his confusion right over to the grand orator. "I just… I mean. You've been going and going, but did I miss the part where we have an epic fight? Or is that still to come? Is it because I didn't have a weapon? Was the stage wrong? I can go stand on the ocean down there if your story needs the concept of a floor, because it was getting really hard to follow. You've repeated yourself four times on some details that I can't, for the life of me, understand to be important, and while I've been trying to follow your narrative, it doesn't actually show off that you're…

better? The method by which you've been describing yourself is like you're a candle on a cake, that's flexing. Were you trying to go for grandeur? You're just a *smidge* off."

For not having paid attention to a single word, Artorian must have hit a few marks, as Zeus quickly broke down into talks with Ghreziz, who had been bored out of his mind listening to the wall of meat do his speech. Ghreziz, unlike Artorian, did not have as easy a time concealing that he'd simply not been paying attention. Mostly because he didn't bother concealing any of it at all, and instantly broke into argument with his symbiotic host. It wasn't Ghreziz's fault that Spuddy was so abyss-blasted wordy!

The argument between them increased ever more in volume and expletives as Artorian hovered there, twiddling his thumbs while humming a little tune to himself as he roughly calculated when Surtur would reach him, adding it to his existing countdown tally. She seemed to be experiencing delays, as another **Lightning** wielder was on her tail and slowing her down with sporadic attacks. Given the annoyed look on Surtur's face, her chaser was also someone who did not appear to be able to shut up.

From the sound of it, an Amazonian woman? He could hear her all the way from here. "I am Tyrian of Zeus! Face me honorably, for the glory of El Dorado!"

Chasing right behind this Tyrian was a tiny bird person, who clearly had opposing opinions. His equally tiny male voice sounded hesitant and unsure. *"Oh... T... Tyri. I dunno about that... oh... That doesn't look like a good idea!"*

Artorian pulled himself away.

"Hey, big guy. I'm uh... I'm gonna go stand on the ocean until you're all sorted, alright?" Artorian spoke softly, knowing full well they could hear him with how much spare attention they had on his Mana tier. "You look like you need a minute."

Dropping after the warning that neither Zeus nor Ghreziz believed, Artorian also dodged the lightning bolt sent hurtling towards him. He'd expected it. All he had to dodge was the metal rod acting as tether and conductor. Or was that anchor and conductor? Semantics! The metal rod missed him, and the residual effect shattered on the way by. "Free snack!"

As Zeus cursed, the timing of Artorian's plan clicked into place like clockwork.

True to the information Artorian had been provided, Odin took to being ignored like a snail to a pile of salt. Throwing another arc-lightning-infused bolt, he missed again, though this time because he was the one who'd made a mistake. For some reason, Zeus had believed Loki, the trickster, when the man had said he would be landing *on* the water. "Abyss!"

With no choice but to quickly give chase for an up-close and personal brawl to drag the old annoyance back out of the wet realm where electricity was useless, he re-coated with Ghreziz's tar as the demon snarled in delight. The symbiote had noticed a detail that Zeus had not. "He made a mistake!"

While both Zeus and his bonded demon shot towards Artorian and plunged underwater, the former noticed that, while the old man's Tier had flared, it was not going up. Instead, to what must have been the Administrator's horror, his Tier was going *down*. Loki *had* made a mistake! Zeus felt vindicated when it came to his reports on the old Mage; he barely had any skill! Of course the fool would flub.

"I have you now!" Zeus gripped Artorian by the burned hole opening at the front of his robe, then felt a dawning sense of terror as a significant portion of his senses blacked out while deep underwater. He'd been swallowed up in Artorian's expanded Presence!

"You do indeed. Remember that 'being scary' thing?" Artorian retorted sinisterly, his next word one that gave Odin all the dread he'd previously held.

"**Disenchantment**."

Laying down the **Law** with the drop of a hammer, all the water in Artorian's immediate vicinity became permeated by the channeled effect. Artorian's ring crumbled to pieces before all the gear and items contained within spilled forth and came apart. Only two appeared immune to the effects washing over them. Surviving the hostile brush with a **Disenchantment** effect so strong that it returned enhanced equipment to the very particles they were made of, the blades of **Sorrow** and **Compassion** both sank to the bottom of the sea.

Artorian could live with the temporary loss.

Zeus, on the other hand, could not. All his equipment. All his items. His tools. His toys. His hoarded weapons and carefully procured armories in his many rings. All of it crumbled save for his own blade, Calibur, as it was the only item in his possession to have a soul. Odin's own, twisted attempt at Artifacting. With the item temporarily not in Odin's grip, Artorian could feel the mind held within. Flashes of a parrot's life washed over him, with a single, short, truth.

All Polly had ever wanted was a cracker.

The poor bird had been taken against its will, and the trampling of Polly's agency enraged Artorian when more details of the story came to bear. When Artorian was socked in the face and sent downwards through the water by a furious, gear-stripped Zeus, he had the opportunity to snatch one of the three blades.

His hand squeezed around Polly's grip, ignoring the porcelain cracks that had formed on his right cheek. They represented real, actual damage. When his feet pressed to the seafloor, he didn't need to look up to know that the bonded pair was coming right at him for a quick and painful follow-up. Both were seething, but in the span of time it took for Zeus to get to him, he'd managed to connect with Polly, the Calibur.

The conversation had been short. Spoken in feelings more than words, the battered parrot's spirit lit up from their dull and downtrodden state. She was Polly. Now an ex-parrot, she was no more than a silent sword. Yet when the new energy gripped her bladed form, there was no oppression. There had been a question, and a gifting of energy. Polly, feeling alive from the momentary rush, answered it in kind.

What are parrots? Easy.

Parrots were intelligent, playful, and possessive. In the memories shown, Polly proved herself to possess mixtures of a short attention span, lots of energy, and dramatic displays. In addition to being highly empathic, Polly revealed that her behavior and mood tended to reflect who she was around, which made it all the more interesting to Artorian that when Polly had copied Odin, he had despised the bird for it, turning her into a tool.

With the first question answered, a second came. This one tested Polly's weathered spirit. The gut reaction that the Parrot's soul provided, rather than the uncertainty strangled beneath piles of fear, was what Artorian accepted.

Zeus was rushing, but his foe was shooting up the Tiers again, having traded taking actual damage for precious time. He felt Loki lock into Tier six, and hurried to make his next strike. He could not let the old man climb! That would be his *one* downfall if it happened. The only edge that the ex-Administrator could lord over him in order to win.

Artorian's stop at Tier six had been purposeful. It was where he needed to be in order to ask Polly the third question. The last question. <Do you wish it returned, ex-parrot? Your playfulness. Your warmth to the world. Your **Pride**?>

Polly replied with the equivalent feeling of gritted teeth, strained neck muscles, and tears that ran down her cheeks. It was the moment Artorian learned she'd managed to complete her humanization on the same day that it had been taken from her. This newly-learned fact caused the fury in Artorian's soul to make Zeus's rage look like a measly toddler's tantrum.

His bonfire space turned frozen and dark, carnation-colored ice and rain coiled along the leaves of the Silverwood copy at its center. Artorian only wrenched himself from the space because Polly had given him an answer. Without hesitation, he replied in kind. <Then be **Proud**, for you have found strength and strength has found you. We may not win this battle this day, but I promise you, Polly, that we will reforge you. By the tip of your blade, there will be an end to this menace and demon parade.

Escape today, and win tomorrow. Will you show this world just what an ex-parrot can do? Will you show it that *ex* stands for *extraordinary*?>

The overwhelmingly positive waves of emotion screaming back at him were all the confirmation he would ever need.

Artorian did not hesitate. *<Blessing of Gloria.>*

Taking the second hit from Zeus, he hurled the blade skywards to remove Polly from the theater of war. Her time was not now. Her time would come later. <Gather your power, break free from this oversized lake, and fly!>

The business end of Calibur shot straight upwards as she was hurled towards freedom, cutting Odin along his right eye and giving him pause as the blessing imbued Polly. It suffused her just like it had Zelia, Yuki, Halcyon, and Vol. Tying the ex-parrot with renewed vigor to the **Law** of **Pride**, he bit the arrow on the additional setback in favor of doing this small act that had become far more important to him.

Porcelain cracks formed across his right ribs, Artorian once again sent flying when Zeus finished his attack. Artorian's last act after the hurled launch had been to prepare for the blow, which he did by leaning into it purely so that his redirected momentum allowed his hands to snatch the hilts of **Sorrow** and **Compassion**.

Artorian regained control over himself before Ghreziz was in range to perform the third strike, the tar covering Zeus's arm reformed into an oversized executioner's axe blade. The demon must have expected him to block, but instead, Artorian ran.

Flew was the more accurate description, even if done underwater. Except that Zeus and Ghreziz were having some difficulty moving at higher speeds because the counter pressure they faced seemed to increase the faster they tried to go. Artorian was having no such difficulties as he pulled his Presence to safety and put it to good use, cutting through ocean waters like a sailfish.

When Artorian burst onto the beach, he stumbled and had to stab both his swords into the sands as counter leverage so he could drop to a jog and come to a halt. The drained colors slowly returned to his gray hands. "Holding both of those swords... has... *costs*."

He chose not to think about the investment price to connect Polly to the Tower node, instead accepting that he would never have chosen to do otherwise regardless. He was not the Ascended of **Love** for nothing.

"Dreamer!" A booming call from above quickly got his attention as Surtur found her target, and hurled an item towards him. She had to quickly move on, because now there was more than simply one demon-symbiote Mage on her tail. The initial one, on the other hand, was now fighting with her supposed compatriots rather than chasing the Dalamadur. One of the symbiote hosts had punched the tiny bird, and Tyrian had taken extreme exception to that while Pim, the tiny bird, pecked the celestial feces out of the demon in question.

Surtur called him to action before fleeing. "Catch!"

The cloth-covered item struck Artorian's open palm as Zeus burst from the shore waters. Upheaving many tons of liquid, he howled in rage as he hit the sands hard enough to shake and fracture the entire island they found themselves on. Not particularly surprising for an A-rank seven putting his might into something.

If anything, Artorian had to give the island credit for not being a misty wreck right now.

"You took everything!" Zeus howled, Ghreziz roiling across his form, trying to re-establish himself. "First, my stories with that ice-witch. Then everyone's respect with that squirrel. Then my honor in Eternia. Now you take my weapons and tools? I am going to beat you with my bare hands until you're a fine powder. Then, to make sure there's nothing left of you, Ghreziz and I are going to take a trip up to that shiny silver tree in the background, and break. Your. Core."

Now *that* was a threat.

One Artorian capitalized on.

"Fine. Odin. *Fine*." Pulling the veil from the weapon Surtur had brought him, the mighty blade Dawn had set aside for emergencies, Artorian let his Tier rocket upwards as he found a new foothold on Tier Fifty-five. The moment he did and found stability, flecks of phosphorus instantly began to coat and then flake off from his skin.

The weapon provided him a strong sympathy, now that it was in his hands. Much to his surprise, he knew it well, and even held the Mage related to it close to his heart.

For she was family.

"For the last time. It's Zeus!" The tar-covered man bellowed, advancing at speed as he reached his hand out for one of the swords stabbed into the sands. "You will call me as I see fit, Hephaestus! While I cripple you, and ensure that you fit yours. As my *broken* court crafter."

The old man narrowed his gaze. "You don't deserve it, Spud. Others? Sure. It's a kindness I gladly indulge. A comfort freely given that I see only benefit in, with no harm."

Artorian fully unsheathed the weapon, feeling its weight as the long blade gleamed in the sunlight. While the spirit within was technically already gone, he could still feel the lingering pattern of the soul left behind lay supportive hands on his shoulders.

The grounded strength. The certainty of confidence. "You, though? You are a child in dire need of reprimanding. This is not the place for the hands of a kind parent. This? This demands only the finest of truth-speakers, who will do what must be done against a brat such as yourself."

As the last of the rust burned away in favor of even more phosphorus that was starting to ignite, Artorian steadied his breathing. Ancient Elven lessons crept back into his fighting style. "Feel honored, Spud, for you are in the presence of a true leader."

Holding the weapon above his head, he aimed the business end aggressively towards his enemy as Artorian fully settled into the node where he was planted. In a flash of energy, waves of nitroglycerin poured free in clouds of barely contained steam from an Assault Nagamaki, whose very design screamed that it was meant to reap honor.

"Kneel, brat. For you are in the presence of Ephira Mayev Stonequeen, Grandest Matron of all Dwarven history!" Right on its edge, the sharp glow flickered and brightened, as if coming to life. Artorian's Aura popped and crackled, his gaze made of steel. "Come. Face *Gran'mama*, the **Explosion**."

CHAPTER FORTY-SEVEN

Zeus bristled at the provocation. His emotions utterly clouded his sense and judgement as he came in range to grab a sword handle.

Ghreziz, paying plenty of attention, recoiled from the cotton-candy colored blade. The katana on the other hand... Oh. He shuddered in pleasurable delight, his voice constipated. "*Ohh-hh-hh*. The dark blade, partner, *take the dark one*. The oppression on Garuda's soul. The *twisting*."

Not in any state of mind to consider why that might not have been the best advice to follow, Odin's hand squeezed **Sorrow**'s hilt. His regret was instant, and profound. Ghreziz, on the other hand, spiked in the completely opposite direction as he made a truly unacceptable face. While the human suffered, the demon drowned in pleasure.

Rather than a slow seeping drain of color, their clothing, body, and Aura all filtered down to different, subtle shades of gray in an instant. In fact, aside from the laughably minuscule flicker of pink flame at the very tip of the blade that even a nearly dead match could outperform, Odin seemed frozen in a mixture of wide-eyed existential agony and like he'd just taken crush damage straight to the orbs.

No flame at all sourced from Ghreziz. Artorian wasn't surprised. Only euphoria filled the demon, who seemed to gain in strength and might at the speed Odin lost it. Silent, horrified tears ran in carved channels down the Asgardian's cheeks, the scenes of whatever he was seeing destroying him from within before his quaking fingers managed to release the blade.

Sorrow fell to the sands with a dull *fwop*.

When Odin's eyes fell to observe the blade, he viscerally recoiled in fear, falling backwards only to be caught by Ghreziz, who usurped bodily control and coated his host entirely. "Ohhh… That's just… *Nrhm*."

Reaching his tarry claws for the blade, the **Synergy** effect keeping them bound flared in disagreement. Ghreziz's arm turned into a tarry slop. His claw lost all cohesion as the black material was forced to return to Zeus's chest. Even Artorian could tell that whatever amount of desire Ghreziz had to pick the sword up, Odin had an equal and opposite desire to be as far away from it as possible.

So they couldn't do or take an action they did not both agree on? *An edge.* Artorian thought it most interesting that the blade had affected each of them individually. Seeing the incredible effects of opposing **Law** concepts interacting and putting Spuddy in such a wrecked state, a fantastic idea bloomed behind his eyes. The fight against Odin was still looking questionable, but as the board of Kings and Castles formed mentally beneath their feet, Artorian saw a way to remove a demon piece from the board.

"Ha! What's wrong, host? A little **Sorrow** not good for your **Revelry**?" The Savant giggled in a state of relish while Zeus remained placid, entirely unable to reply. Stretching, crackling, and popping his features, Ghreziz noticed that the undersea chase had removed his favored odor. No matter. His scent would soon be replaced by the sweet delicacy of Mageblood! Speaking of the source, what was Pillow Man doing? All that mumbling and muttering under his breath. Numbers? Was his opponent doing *math*?

In addition to doing math, Artorian had cashed in on the unexpected faltering. A little bit of cultivation went a long way! Even if he had to be slow and sneaky with it to not rouse suspicion. He hadn't used the upwards-cone cultivation alteration since... the Fringe days? It still worked!

The extra moments Spuddy had spent frozen in terror from touching **Sorrow**, rather than instantly letting go like the old man had expected, he had spent patching himself up internally. The porcelain cracks were still visible on his face, but the hidden damage was now taken care of.

The math he'd been doing was some experimental madness, formatted as a neat prompt in his mind. He'd been trying to find an angle of victory for his current situation that didn't rely on the main plan. Mulling between several aspects of Mana, he'd excluded psychological changes since that card was played, tallied opposing concepts as particularly effective, and considered the following list:

Rank
Tier
Opposing **Laws**
Opposing Concepts
Soul Space Items
Identity
Patterns

Artorian had to dodge out of the way of a black-flame fireball that turned the landscape behind him into a scene he didn't want to look at, positioning himself in a place optimal for attack. He attempted to fuel prediction lines, but they sputtered out right away, pushing him back to the grounded approach.

"Damaging a Mage, given my injuries and past experience, may just be as simple as hitting object A with a more dense object B. So, if I just..." Artorian shunted five ranks of his A-class Mana to his body, leaving one for his Aura. "Five ranks of A-class Mana, times my current Tier of fifty five. Two-hundred seventy-five? Sure, let's test that number. Since I don't know what Ephi's Mage rank was, I'll lowball the weapon and assume it provides an additional fifty-five. For a total of three hundred and thirty."

Eyeballing his opponent, he measured Ghreziz to be about on par with Spuddy. A-rank seven. He was only able to detect Odin's **Revelry** Law, slated to be on Tier ninety-eight. "If I guesstimate Gri-gri to be on par, then three ranks times ninety-eight is two hundred ninety-four, but four ranks comes out to three hundred ninety-two. So if I hit him when he's at three ranks invested, I do damage. If I hit him at four ranks invested... I don't? Could it be that simple?"

He put the theorizing down and shot forward into the testing phase. "I bet there's more if I consider the column for expending Mana, but let's get this party started! Mayev style!"

Ghreziz formed his axe with a roar of laughter, replacing his right arm with the executioner's blade since he had proprietary control of the body for a while. His attention was stripped away when he swung, missing his opponent because the old man had dodged instead of attacked. Then he felt horrible as the awful, cringy, purifying sensation of a Sunlight Aura bathed over him with radiant light.

Screeching as Zeus's Aura was not currently able to **Synergize** and protect him, Ghreziz lost visible chunks of his tar before realizing that he was not, in fact, going to get indulgent playtime. Forced to heal Odin and quickly retreat behind the protective barrier of his host's Aura when it strengthened and flickered back to life, Ghreziz was also forced to protect the man during his recovery as the pillow warrior brought the hot-edged cavalry slayer to bear in a swing that could cleave the heads off a thousand men.

With the power of a full naval broadside, Artorian carved into his opponent with a mighty yell. The words spoken puzzled

Ghreziz to no end, whereas the violent nitroglycerin explosion wasn't a problem at all. "Consider the coconuts!"

The demon blocked the blow with his very being, preventing the damage rather than the physics as the vast *boom* sent him flying skywards. With his host in such a poor state, the demon was forced to expend resources so his unique connection didn't break. If it did, this would become an entirely different fight. They had already lost the edge of all their gear and equipment, and since giving the pillow man any breathing room whatsoever over long periods of time would spell their guaranteed defeat, he had to be snappy about decisions.

No matter how much he wanted to avoid putting in effort.

Artorian's eyes flashed with the beginnings of an emerald green spiral as he absorbed the information. He learned that **Synergy** forced the pair to move their ranks at the same time in the same places, and that it *averaged* their Law Tiers. When Spuddy pumped up his Aura to block out Artorian's Sunlight effect, Gri-gri was forced to follow suit.

Able to inspect the details of their unholy union, Artorian classed their combined **Law** tier as a solid eighty-two. Meaning that Gri-gri's **Law** was on... level sixty-six? "Yes. Sixty-six. That's where you are. What *is* your **Law**, Ghreziz? Is it actually **Synergy**? I can't help but feel like it's a ruse. Why do you hide it from me?"

Shooting into the sky after them, neither the demon nor the Asgardian believed it when the opponent weaker than them dared to challenge them so openly, the old man's sword already coming down on them! Slicing vertically as he appeared to maneuver with controlled explosions that blotted all hearing. Every step was a *boom*, every motion a *pif*, every swing a *kla-kow*!

Ghreziz dodged or blocked what he could, flabbergasted at where all this mystery skill was coming from as sky-breaking explosive slashes violated his sensibilities. Every fight with the pillow man prior to this, he'd had the fiend on the ropes! He'd always been more powerful than this nuisance! It wasn't allowed to—

An unwelcome sensation made Ghreziz leap away.

Looking down, his mouth gaped in disbelief. "A… a *wound?*"

Artorian grinned like a fool. "Oh my word. It *is* that simple!"

The old man had been doing more math. A tier of eighty-two meant that if his opponents were not pulling any special tricks, or expending Mana, then four ranks of their A-class Mana would bring them up to three hundred twenty-eight. Which was *two* points shy of matching his current output of three-hundred and thirty. When Zeus and Ghreziz had been at five ranks body and two ranks Aura, he'd done zip-all. The demon had been able to completely negate all the raw damage dealt.

When he'd cleverly forced them to change that ratio around, on the other hand… Well.

Ghreziz bled *green*.

"Oh no you *Le Didn't.*" The demon spat, his gaze snapping from his wound to Artorian in a mixture of wonder and fury. "*Now* I see why your Aura suddenly stopped flaring after our retreat. You think I am so prideful that I will let myself be defeated by your trickery? I am far older and more skilled than *you*, accursed pillow man!"

To Artorian's dismay, Ghreziz then vanished under Odin's skin. No hint of the demon was in any way visible, and that… bothered the old man. Zeus shivered and snapped to it, flexing with a groan before rolling his arms. "That took me out of it for a moment, but **Revelry** is live! That horrible little trick could never keep me down for long. Not me. Never me. So! If we don't use Auric protections, you'll fry my helper. However, if we lower our density too much, then your attacks start being useful? Oh, we *can't* have that! Now can we?"

Zeus's stride was interrupted when Artorian appeared right in front of him with some sick **Acceleration.** Like his partner before him, it was the words that Artorian used, rather than the aftereffects, that puzzled him. Artorian growled under his breath, channeling the might of the slipper as this was probably his last shot to do any sort of physical overpowering. Angling his strike so the blade would bisect that stubby moustache, he fulfilled what was requested of him as the annihilating energy building up was directed right at Spuddy's schnozz. Might as well make it spicy, and praise Gran'mama as he borrowed some of Shaka's words.

"El Kabum!"

The sound-breaking, cloud-shattering, sky-immolating environmental catastrophe of explosive impact was so powerful that Artorian lost control of the Assault Nagamaki entirely. Zeus fared no better, if not outright worse on the receiving end, before he had a chance to change where his ranks were stored. Blasted with enough force to circumnavigate Caltopia thrice over, Odin went on a spiritual journey while the backblast smacked Artorian planetside like a poorly-tossed pancake.

Groaning as he pulled himself out of yet another crater, he drew a deep, stern breath before apologizing to the very ground he was laying on. "Sorry Cal. Looks like I might need a bit more after all."

The ground Artorian lay on vanished as he slipped into hover mode. With the weapon no longer in his hands, he lost all footing of his current Tier. He was either going to crash down back to Tower Tier seven somewhere, which would spell defeat, or he needed to pump the jam and pump it up right now. *Right now.* Exhaling, he opened the full breadth of his cultivation draw as he momentarily lost hold of his old man form and turned full Swole-torian. "Three, two, one. Hoist! Up with the swoletariat, down with the bencheoisie!"

Vast sections of landmass granulated to particles in every direction around Artorian. His draw sucked energy in as if he were an endless vortex, bathing him in light and colors from all the Essence and Mana rushing into him. Using Gran'mama's **Law**... invocation? The word used when using the **Law** itself.

It was costly! "Crackers and toast! No wonder you don't just throw that out willy nilly."

He'd risen to about Tier ninety-seven when Zeus appeared to clock him in the right knee. Artorian had first thought the man might have missed. Though that was before he realized that the thing missing turned out to be his lower right leg.

CHAPTER FORTY-EIGHT

Pain Artorian did not know how to describe surged through his being. More intense than burnout. More acute than being stabbed. More overarching than hard water pressure or being burned all over. He could feel where his leg was supposed to be, and then felt where it wasn't, as bloody Mana poured from the ripped-away right knee.

His attempt at a scream didn't get past the breath stage as Odin punched him across the skies. He was kicked into orbit, slapped out of it, and thrown through mountains and clouds in what felt like moments. He saw glimpses of the Fringe far below, then the Dwarven territories. Where Gran'mama's blade seemed to have neatly stabbed into the exact center of that flattened ground he'd made. Then he saw Olympus, then a flash of something that could have been the Skyspear, then an up close and personal greeting with beach sand.

By the time Artorian could deduce how much damage he'd taken, he looked like a cracked porcelain doll from bald head to... well, both broken legs now. He was missing everything beneath both knees, and his left arm wasn't responding like it should, even if that was still attached.

What had he just been hit by?

"Now we are back where we should be." Zeus spoke matter-of-factly as he clapped his hands together and fixed his toga, watching the broken wreck slowly push up with his remaining good arm. Zeus had even been magnanimous! They were back at the exact place where they'd properly started. He'd even punched Artorian to be right next to the cotton-candy colored sword. How kind of him. "Now, as I was saying…"

Artorian was oblivious to any sort of talking Odin did after that tiny bit. He felt the extent of the damage, the cracks, the tears, and the painful Mana loss pouring from both his legs. Oddly enough, it didn't feel like his Mana reserves were so much as dipping? He was sloughing off waves of Mana, but it was all coming back?

That wasn't right—extra Mana went to Cal.

The copper dropped when he realized that people could cultivate, therefore must have a breach point where the static pull of Cal was exceeded. Otherwise nobody would ever get any Essence. Was his passive gain higher than Cal's threshold, so all the loss was going back to him? Unlike before, he now *wanted* to draw in Essence. That difference of intent resonated with the Mana that loved him, pushing his passive draw over and above the upper bound Cal had planned for Mages. Had he never lost his legs to feel the sensation so viscerally, he'd never have made the realization.

Focusing on more important matters, he felt at the portion of his Mana he'd made function as a timer. Fifteen? That was too far off still, and he was in this state? Well… desperate times called for desperate measures. There was no hint of Dawn to be seen. He'd lost… well, returned Gran'mama to his friends, and had specifically asked his backup not to come. Given the trouncing he'd just gone through, that still seemed… like the better move.

He pressed his good hand down onto **Compassion's** hilt, and propped himself up more as he attempted to keep gathering Mana. What was Spuddy gonna do? Hit him some more?

Zeus spoke with a bored tone. "You shouldn't try to climb, Hephaestus. Any more exertion and you'll leak to death, and death by burnout makes a poor tale."

Did Odin not know he was recouping his losses? No, no, that would be unthinkable unless one really looked and happened to be in Artorian's exact situation. Odin was back to thinking he was on top of the world; victorious. "How... How did you just... do that?"

"How did I defeat you so soundly?" Zeus laughed, fists pressing to his hips. "You finally want me to repeat myself? I'm better than you! All it took was realizing that so long as I had enough physical might, you'd never be a threat! My partner hid in me to act as a booster, even if he despised doing so. Meanwhile, the great *me* shifted my focus! All seven ranks condensed and squeezed into my body! I was already provided exceedingly mighty velocity, so I put that to good use! You never saw it coming."

"Knight took my bishop?" Artorian didn't believe it. He'd struck Spuddy *before* the rank allocation changed, right? Something was up. Unfortunately, getting up was an issue he seemed to be having a considerably greater problem with right now. "H... ha. I'm... not done yet! It's my move. Here, watch this!"

Zeus raised an eyebrow as Artorian made a comedy show of himself. He appeared to barely even manage lifting **Compassion.** Pulled tip first from the sands, the weapon was tossed so weakly and casually towards him with a **nyeh**, hilt first no less, that Zeus barked with laughter. The blade whistled as it moved, but that detail went ignored.

He extended his hand, and Ghreziz rushed to his thoughts with utmost haste. "No! Do not! *Do not cat—*"

Odin ignored the demon, remembering the insults the last time that monster he called a partner had so casually suggested for him to pick up that horrorshow of a katana. The things he felt when holding that blade were going to scar him for life... and his cultivation as well, if he wasn't careful to spend a few hundred years mending the damage that black sword had done to his cultivation technique.

Odin caught **Compassion**, and felt an entirely different kind of terrible.

The poofening.

First, Ghreziz shrieked in his mind, then vanished in a celestine bubble-pop **poof**, like he'd never existed at all. Leaving behind only a faint smell of honey, all traces of Ghreziz were erased outright. His extermination caused a cascade, whole waves of unseen minions losing their tethers as they were hurled into storage Cores. When the celestine poof passed and the smell cleared away moments later, the demon was… gone.

Gone.

Synergy failed on a Soul-Space-wide scale as the demon responsible for upholding the power died permanently. The culmination of Artorian's clever Kings and Castles move played out.

The damaged, downed man coughed out his sandy retort with a bloody smile as he watched two become but one. "Pawn takes Queen."

Second, more silent tears ran down Odin's cheeks as he was subjected to the full force of the sword's concept. Unlike her fondness for Artorian, she had no such gentleness for the callous-handed brute currently squeezing her grip, so not a single sound came from her staff inscription as musical notes flared down the blade's five equidistant lines.

The effect vanished as quickly as it appeared.

When Odin was able to let his trembling fingers release the blade, he heaved in a breath and squeezed his heart with his left hand, stumbling along the sands like a confused foal. He ignored the fallen foe when Artorian spoke. "Pawn takes Castle."

Zeus, in his frazzled state, was then forced to contend with his fallen foe trying to do the exact thing he knew was likely to kill the Administrator outright. Artorian prepared to climb the

Tiers. A strong, emerald green spiral spun in his eyes as he defiantly locked gazes with Odin.

The staggering wall of meat pointed at the fallen man, though whether his words were a threat or a warning was difficult to discern. "You will die!"

Artorian had only one response for him, showing a wide-mouthed stare on his face as he flared his Mana and began the skyrocket. "Cowabunga it is, then!"

Zeus couldn't let this happen.

No matter the damage he'd taken—or the turmoil currently surging inside that none but him could feel or see, after he was exposed to both concepts blades individually—he couldn't let the Administrator win *again*. Starting his stride, he made it two powerful steps before the tip of a yacht caught him off guard. The entire vessel slammed with pinpoint accuracy right into his eye.

The ship broke to pieces with cracking sounds, but the half-second distraction was enough to throw Zeus completely off his game. He looked behind him, seeing the ship skid over the sand and pull itself together. Condensing to the size and shape of a person, his rage exploded when Zephyr's bloody smile peered up at him from her prone position. "Told you I'd get your other eye."

Zeus's eye wasn't actually damaged, given the differences in quality between himself and the inferior specimen. He wanted to scream and shout at the girl, pound her into the stratosphere, and slap her back down into the middle of the ocean, but he had other problems. Turning as fast as he could, he made it to Artorian just in time to hear the man whispering. "I knew there couldn't have been *nothing*. Thank you, Halcyon, for a foothold on the way up. Pierce the heavens! Ulam **Spiral**!"

Howling a heave of effort as he shot forwards with a percussive rupture, Artorian named his own attack. "*Giga. Drill. Pillow!*"

Artorian's glowing, emerald-green-coated soul item spun like a drill over his fist. A fist that connected with Odin's chest while resounding with the prime number ninety-seven. Glowing with verdant might, the law of the **Spiral** stuck the unsuspecting warrior. Because who expected a counter-attack from a fallen foe on his last legs when they had no more legs?

The soul item knocked Zeus both out of the park and the planet's orbit, with a surprisingly dull and gentle **pdumpf** sound. The damage on Zeus's chest was anything but dull and gentle as the emerald green drill launched the foe. With vast acceleration, the energy-drill caused a shrieking noise reminiscent of metal cutting metal until both left the planet-contained bubble of air.

Artorian slumped afterwards, quickly stowing his frazzled pillow as that had not been good for it. He would fix it, if he lived. No, no ifs! No take. Only throw! Pushing himself up with his only good arm, he shook his head until his vision cleared and he could see Zephyr lying motionless on the sands. She moved her head to make eye contact, but clearly wasn't able to speak any further with all that red coming out of her mouth.

Remembering forum connections existed, he tapped into one. The communication line opened without any resistance. <Zephy, you managing?>

The neon Elf mentally shook her head no, glad she didn't need to physically speak. <Ammy couldn't come. More… important…>

The connection broke when Zephyr passed out. For a cultivator at such a low rank who'd gotten serious revenge on an A-ranker, she was lucky that she would probably live to tell the tale after some serious medical attention. For now, she was out cold, and that was the end of it.

The news, even if only a few words, made Artorian feel both dread and hope. He checked his timer. "Six? Six is… too long still. He's going to be back before then."

Temporary bonus from his soul item or not, Artorian knew that he hadn't hit Odin with nearly enough force or power to remove him from the fight. He'd caused a delay, and that was it. Not being able to see all the true damage Odin had taken bothered him a bit, but that bother could take a number and get in the queue, because it was a very long line right now.

Artorian balanced his ranks and skipped Aura use, shifting straight to Presence while also abandoning the human form. It was just flipping a lever… right? Relief washed over him as his undamaged Dragon form replaced his wrecked human one. Floating right over Zephyr, he molded his Presence to include her, then patched her up to the point where her life wasn't in critical danger. A feat he managed to complete just before Zeus graced him with a return visit, his toga looking significantly worse for wear.

"So it was true!" Odin spat. "You were a monster in disguise this entire time! A mere Beast playing at being more than what you deserve to be."

Artorian didn't quite understand what Spuddy was on about. Did he hit the man too hard? Thundy clearly knew about his dragon form with the whole Nova Cannon attack. Perhaps his swords had done some internal damage? No reason to dwell on it. Still, that reasoning revealed some truly problematic prospects if that was a mindset at play on Caltopia. He also didn't understand why Odin himself looked *pristine*. There wasn't a *scratch* on him. Extremely suspicious. "Why the pale abyss aren't you hurt? Do you have any idea how hard I hit you?"

"Not hard enough for it to matter, noodle boy." Zeus's follow up was to grab Artorian by the end of his tail and give him a repeat of Hulk's special ground-sweeping services, ending by throwing him across the sea. Zeus rolled his shoulders, then spat on the sand when he saw the unconscious Zephyr. "You're not off the hook. I'll be back for you, *future sword*."

CHAPTER FORTY-NINE

Zeus clapped Dragon-torian through the sky with consecutive backhands. Each attempt at Aura manipulation was met with an opposing strike that forced him to turn it off. Each molding of Presence was smacked as if Odin hit him with a lead brick. Each attempt at a construct made the warrior rip the half-finished effort away and discard the creation to the waters below.

The lauding self-portrayal had, unfortunately, not been a lie. When Artorian used old tricks, or attempted to, he was beaten instantly with the counter. Just like Odin had practiced.

Wood Elven techniques were burned, known fighting styles made moot or outright countered when Artorian barely managed to do something other than heal and defend, and each attempt at Tier-increasing was turned into something of a recurring gag. Since Zeus punched him in the throat every time he tried.

The blasted Asgardian was faster than him. Stronger, too. Normally, Artorian would have defaulted to his Auras and Presence skills, but the baguette-snapped **Revelry** Mage knew how to injure those directly when he exposed them for use. Artorian may have pulled a fast one under the sea, but now there was no place to hide tricks. Odin was even laughing as he beat poor Artorian into a tenderized fillet.

Laughing, like he was having the best time in the world *reveling*.

Artorian considered another round of pillow use, but no. His soul item wasn't meant to be an offensive item. No matter how he sliced it, even layering the item with the spiral drill effect hadn't appeared to do anything. A fact that was really eating away at the battered and bruised old man, because he just couldn't put his talon on why.

He also couldn't focus on the question long enough with Zeus using him as a punching bag. When he was finally punted planetside and crumpled into a heap on the ground, no attack following up after causing a few seconds of silence made Artorian actually uncoil to see where he was.

The sight did not do him good.

"Nice village you've got going on here, Administrator! Oooh, look at all those vengeful little glares from those vengeful little people. What have you got, *one* Mage? Two, if I count the Beasties? They're not even A-rankers! What were you hoping to accomplish here? A happily bustling little village for you to live with your happy little sept. *Tsk tsk.* All you did was give me the workforce I've been looking for, for two-hundred years!" Odin looked mighty proud of himself. "Do you have any idea how difficult it is to make cultivators do any sort of real work? Roads? Cooking food? I mean, it's all beneath *me*, but it shouldn't have been beneath them. Now, that problem is sorted! All these workers will make for fantastic fodder!"

A notification prodded Artorian, and he hoped to Cal it was accurate. "Three."

Zeus's ear twitched when the Administrator said something strange. It was never good when the old loon said something strange. He picked the Administrator up by his face and slapped him back and forth while hollering out laughter after each strike. Eventually he dropped the dragon when its face was so battered that Artorian was forced to change back to his human form because it had *less* damage.

Slumping to the ground, he groaned and pulled his Mana in as tight as he could. He was doing his best to heal himself, but the damage was looking fairly catastrophic on all fronts at this point.

"Well, anything to say for yourself before I crush you underfoot and call it a day? I've been dreaming of the day Caltopia became mine! I'm still thinking of calling it Gaia. It's just such a good name for a planet, y'know?" Odin clasped his hands together, but faltered in his step and nearly fell over before catching himself.

That detail finally told Artorian what was going on with all of Odin's damage. Spuddy had most certainly taken a beating! Not as badly as himself, but the damage was definitely there. On the *inside*. Hidden from view. Where Artorian had healed up his inner damage, allowing the porcelain breaks to remain, Odin had done entirely the opposite, patching up his looks first, so it *appeared* like he was unharmed. Clever.

"No? Nothing? All that wordy flapping out of you normally, and now nothing?" His mouth flashed a row of pearly white teeth. "I'm still blowing up your seed Core, you know. I'm so sick of you. In fact! I think from this angle I could do both at the same time!"

Jiivra and Blanket rushed the man, but he knocked them off their approach vector with a spear of lightning that appeared from his hand like it was hidden in his sleeve. They fell hard, clutching their stomachs as their insides crackled with ominous, alcohol-scented electricity. What a... strange detail.

Everyone else looked mad, but seemed to realize they weren't going to be of any help here. Artorian could see Genevieve and a few other Wisps hiding in the cardinal direction trees, but they were equally trying their best not to be noticed.

Artorian mentally tried to connect with her, regardless,

asking his most important question right away when the link went through. <Can you get Tatum?>

Her response felt like it was going to be a *no* before Zeus sliced through the air with his electric spear, looking thoroughly confused. "What was that just now? I could swear I cut something. Trying more tricks, Loki? Don't be too concerned! You were supposed to become my crippled crafter, but removing you entirely will also remove all those bothersome little worries. Like this tiny child!"

Turning on a copper, Odin raised his weapon and brought it down onto Astrea's head. Or would have, but a pink hand from her shadow gripped the weapon mid-swing and stopped it cold. Zeus's eyebrows raised high as Scilla slid forth fully, snapping the construct weapon in her hand and forcing it to dissipate.

"*Oho*! And who are *you*?" Making a brand new lightning spear like it was nothing, Zeus pointed the bolt right at her. "You don't look like a fighter. You don't look like much of anything."

"Two," Artorian replied.

The complete topic flip made Odin ignore the being covered in a soft pink glow. She may have stopped his strike, but he just couldn't view her as any sort of threat. Like he knew she wasn't going to attack. Whether she wouldn't or couldn't didn't matter too much to the lightning-wielder, as he was far more annoyed at what this abyssal countdown was about. "Explain, Administrator. Or you get to watch them die before I take you."

Artorian replied with a gaze of steel.

Bleeding Mana, battered, and missing some legs, he raised his trembling arm. The hand on it formed a fist, as if in defiance. A fist clearly part of a martial pose to indicate combat readiness. Even lying on his side on the ground, Artorian issued his challenge. He wasn't done. He wasn't going to quit. "Come pry it out of me, Jasper."

"Where *did* you learn that name? No matter. There won't be any witnesses." Zeus frowned and empowered his weapon, but stopped advancing after two steps as a detail bothered him. That was it? That was all? No further quips. No clever words?

There was just the look in his eye, giving Odin pause until Artorian exhaled a barely audible: "One."

Thinking the real ruse to this ruse was that there was no ruse, Odin raged mindlessly, wanting this over with. Charging a blow meant to take out the broken Artorian and his seed Core as the tip of his spear cracked with more of that alcohol-scented lightning, the Asgardian showed off all his muscle and prowess as the energy morphed to coat his fist.

Without any regard for matter, ground, or the space in between him and Artorian, his launch turned the budding pasture behind him into mud and rubble. With physics paid its dues, Zeus' fist tore through the ground, determined to uppercut the ex-Administrator out of existence.

The impact discharged waves of electricity that roiled across the ground and caused everyone's hair to stand upright. None other than the combatants did anything but hold their breath. Even if the sight revealed to their eyes was not one they could believe when the view cleared.

Zeus had carved a river in a straight line from the initial power of his movement alone, but what captivated all their gazes was the surprisingly plain and simple person holding his fist, who had stopped the entire attack with the ease and difficulty of plucking a falling leaf out of the air.

"*Zero*. Somebody called for a Cal Ex Machina?"

Artorian squinted up at the new man. A man who he could recognize from his early Fringe days again. The lad that had become the prolific writer, his works spread across all the lands. "Scholar D. Kota?"

"Hey, buddy. Miss me?" The plain-looking fellow spoke before winking. "No, not him. It's Cal! I do like the look, though. This model was the quickest thing I could ease into to get here faster."

Odin blinked, eyes locked on his punch as all his Mana felt

locked up. He wasn't able to use it, bend it. Nothing. Heck, he couldn't move! "Who d—"

Odin fully locked up when Cal turned, giving him a cold look. "I woke up to a busted Soul Space, pure anarchy, and my worst supervisor beating up my best Administrator. I'm not in a good mood, Jaspy. Why don't you go spend some time in your seed Core?"

Before the man could even think of a retort, Cal fractured him like dusty plywood.

"Much better!" Cal mused, clapping his hands together as his eyes followed the soul returning to the Silverwood, after which he waved at an individual none of them could see. "Hello there! I've been so looking forward to meeting you!"

"Cal…" Artorian wheezed. "A *tiny* bit of help? Please?"

"*Hmmm?* Oh, wowza! You're in terrible shape. I'll fix the basics, but I am sorely needed everywhere else." With a motion, Artorian's Mana leakage stopped pouring from his limbs. He was still missing his legs, but he could now feel both his arms again, and a wooziness he hadn't noticed cleared up. "There you go, buddy. Now, excuse me for a moment. I'll thank you later for helping me wake up, Mr. Lighthouse."

Cal shot his arms to the air as Amaterasu and Occultatum slid into the space behind him. Tatum already had an unconscious Zephyr in his hands, while Ammy entered with several weapons floating in a delta behind her. Two of his among them. The Incarnates hurried over to the people to help, with Tatum splitting off for Scilla and the village, while Ammy rushed straight to her boy to pick him up, getting Artorian right into her arms. "I've got you."

Those words had never brought Artorian such relief as they did in that moment. He weakly replied, managing the hint of a smile as his head collapsed against her shoulder. "I've been got."

"Anything broken?" She rubbed his back.

"Only some cookies," he replied, exhausted.

Cal clapped as the heavens brightened, welcoming the new

arrival with wide arms. "Hi! What did you think of my Cal Ex Machina, *hmmm?*"

Fluff rained from above, only to vanish as it touched the ground while Adam descended from the sky, matching Cal's pose. With a serene smile, the celestial spoke, like welcoming someone home. "Hello there, my dear old friend. Very well timed, indeed, but just a touch *inexact.* Can I interest you in the good word of Acyrologia?"

EPILOGUE

A battered, bruised, unconscious Artorian was placed in bed in the structure next to the New Fringe's prime bonfire. It had been vacated for this purpose as soon as the residents saw the old man being carted in. When their favorite old man began snoring through solid oak logs mere moments after being swaddled and tucked in, the whole village breathed a sigh of intense relief. Relief that didn't fully set in, as the bonfire gathering that evening was one of hushed conversations and sideways glances toward the source of the superior snores.

Cal and Adam had immediately gallivanted off, leaving Amaterasu and Occultatum to pick up the torch. When the two caretakers finally stepped away from the building, the entire town was on their feet at the same moment; attention fully on the incarnates as they took swift strides towards the main fire. Lunella was the first to approach, and Ammy motioned her toward her fellow while she herself waltzed straight into the middle of the bonfire—standing in the heavy flames like it was a hot shower after a long day and releasing a sigh of comfort.

The flame contorted about her, forming variations in the oranges and reds that danced about as Ammy's weaponry took formation around the flame; gathering in a wide circle as she guided them with mere thought. The blades, mighty entities each, answered to her like loyal inner disciples dutifully responding to a Grand Elder of a Sect: with poise, respect, and profound deference. Each of the weapons were, after all, capable of far more than what the sleeping old man had been able to draw out of them.

No amount of majesty glinting from the weapons—which reflected the bonfire light with their own spectacular effects— drew a single iota of attention from the villagers. Every bit of their focus currently lay on Lunella as the Matron stood before Tatum, their concern clear. The incarnate wore a complicated expression but looked up to meet her gaze and answered one of her questions before she needed to voice the matter.

"He will pull through." Tatum began, watching many sets of shoulders lose some stiffness. "Moreso, he will likely make a full recovery, in the way only he is able. Artorian has never been known to sit on his laurels, so we have no concerns that this may impact his mentality either. The legs are… admittedly, going to be a challenge. Should it come down to it, I have no doubt that the old fox could tie twelve squirrels together and sled out of there at a velocity that would make the very air complain if he needed to do so."

Wuxius stepped up next to Lunella; his arm holding her side to provide not only physical, but emotional stability. The news so far had been good, and the jesting from the incarnate went appreciated, but there were other burning questions in need of answering.

"Is it all finally over?" Wu just about *demanded*; his gaze leveled on the incarnate that was worlds beyond him in so many ways. "Are we done needing to look over our shoulders for threats like Odin? Our lives were difficult, but manageable. Then turned very grim when grandfather was thrown down from the sky. We're all very tense. So… is it over? With Cal back, are we in the clear?"

"No." Tatum tiredly replied, his resigned attitude turning

resolute as he straightened his back. The concerns of the New Fringe were clear from that one question. They were concerns that he himself had encountered, only to have his hopes dashed with a serving of cold reality. "No, this is just a new beginning. Cal being back is not the answer, or some perfect solution, that everyone may have been hoping for."

That was not the answer anyone had been hoping to hear. Several sat down heavily as mugs of honey-based drink started to make the rounds.

"There is an incredible laundry list of problems that still need to be tackled. For many of them, we're going to need Artorian." Tatum stated clearly. "To that effect, it does not escape me that the people he cares for need to be in the best shape they can be. We're going to add a few silent protections to the area; and there are many counter-offensive plans I would like to share in case some other *thing* tries to break the village in half."

Learning to protect themselves better was a necessary concession, as far as the people were concerned. Jiivra was almost in as bad of a shape as their old man, and she had only taken a single blow. That single blow had completely put her out of commission, even if the incarnates had already assured them that she too would be making a full recovery.

"We don't exactly have other Mages in town to stand up against problems that are Mage-quality." Tatum muttered as he fiddled with his inner sleeves. Lunella moved to take some scrolls from him when they were retrieved and offered. "These are for her when she wakes. They contain ancient knowledge from the Old World. Very compatible with her skills, while also allowing the entire village to meaningfully contribute to a defense. Cultivator, or not."

That perked some ears up.

Refolding his arms into his sleeves, Tatum's fingers traced the plague doctor's mask on his hip. "You're all hardy people. You'll wake up tomorrow, stick your nose in Artorian's window, see he's alright, and then need something to do. You don't need me, or someone like me, to give you guidance on that. You already know what you want to do, and carrying on like you have, is what's going to help. Your old man *is* going to wake. He is going to see what you've been up to. He's going to prance around like nothing happened, check in with everyone he can, and sneakily attempt to wiggle the new ways of the world out of you—all while being completely invested in the smallest detail of your wellbeing."

Perked ears turned into chuckles and smirks. Now, many people were nodding, and drinks were sipped for the enjoyment of it, rather than the act of coping. Tatum was not about to stop a lecture when the embers of good cheer were starting to glow. "Cal being back will not fix all our issues. By that I mean: not all in one go. There are going to be stages of progress, and each time we meet a marker, we should celebrate. The entire world we live on, with all its strange rules, effects that change, and calamities so common that we could dig ditches around them to ward off newcomers… we honestly have everything we need to thrive."

That got a few 'here-here's' from the back of the crowd, several mugs raised as the people found their spirits. Tatum did not care if that was because they found it in the spirits of their mugs, or the spirits within themselves. Only the morale mattered.

He raised his voice to match the mood. "Plans are roughly as such: the entire soul space, that being Caltopia, needs work. Ammy and I put in a lot of hours, but we have the exact same problems Cal did when it was just his old one. That's our part to continue tackling, while you build up here and prepare to live a long life. If we get to a point where we can exit Cal? Great! If not? Let's make it matter, and let's make it count. Our world-"

"Has holes in it!" Tarrean shouted from the left, Irene moving to grab him before he went off. "Biggun's!"

She squeezed his hand and drew his attention with a look.

"What?" He questioned when his significant other got to him. "There are! We got one right in the backyard next to the

Apiary. You wouldn't believe the size of the bees down there. They're bee-hemoths!"

Tatum chuckled. Massive underground caverns were just the start of it. There was an entire hollow that spun and weaved through Caltopia, able to hold who knows what, of proportions that would make Jotunheim natives develop agoraphobia. He wasn't going to bother Tarrean with that right now.

His own thoughts were that Cal was going to see it, gasp, and squeak out an overexcited 'New Dungeon!'. Probably with a pun. That would be a very Cal-like thing to do.

A 'Pungeon'.

Tatum picked that thought up and then hurled it out of the proverbial window before speaking again. He must never tell Cal of such thoughts. The results would be Cal-amitous. "We're expecting the existing civilizations on Caltopia to go through extreme cycles of development. Whole new groups are supposed to form and settle. We're going to have dozens of announcements on changes in the coming days; updates on Cultivation, Pylons, Trade, and more. I want to give the heads up that it's incredibly likely we're going to be encountering a few 'redo' events in the coming weeks to months. Cal has already informed me of a frankly ludicrous series of tests that we're going to run, so... perhaps make more of that honey mead!"

That got solid belly laughs out of the town, the drink very happily one that was enjoyed. The level of positive cheer was also enough for the Wisps to come out from their trees and start hanging around the area, filling the air above them with a multicolor luminance that changed the atmosphere from a somber gathering, to one of a party.

"Plus honey pie!" Lunella yelled from the crowd, only to be greeted by raucous cheers and howls of agreement. That did much to brighten her mood. Her full smile was a breath of fresh air to Tatum especially. If the Matron was going to pull through, then everyone was going to pull through. The rest was time, effort, and... another loud snore ripped through the center of the village, turning the unamused Incarnate's gaze to Artorian's abode and eliciting a mad cackle from Ammy.

Tatum grumbled, "Perhaps *earmuffs*."

Blanket heard these words and decided it to be the exact moment that absolutely everyone needed hugs. At the same time. 'Absconding them to safety' within his fluff. He chirped loud!

That was the cue for the bards not in Blanket's grasp to pick up their instruments, playing a tune while following the Glider's chirps as they began a one-four-five chord. Rather than whine as the last time the house sized glider had 'absconded' with them, the bundled people of the New Fringe roared back in approval. They were going to be just fine: they weren't going to be caught unaware like this a second time. They were a hardy people! A salt people!

"Be prepared, everyone. Much, *much* more is yet to come." Tatum called out, only slightly muffled by fur as he'd willingly gotten swept along. "You know how it is: as soon as Artorian is back on his feet... that is... when he's awake... there will be work to do, and enemies to fend off."

"Enough, Tatum. We get it. We're going to be fine. You say we don't have Mages to protect us? You're forgetting..." Lunella had decided right then that she agreed with Wu's initial verdict. They'd been worrying too much, and had all the help in the world; plus one fluffy monstrosity that loved them all to pieces. The cuddle from the overprotective sugar glider really was doing wonders. Her words rang out, pulling smiles onto the faces of her people.

"*Blanket* is a Mage. Blanket defends. Blanket protects."

ABOUT DENNIS VANDERKERKEN

Hello all! I'm Dennis, but feel free to call me Floof. Credit of the name now being accumulated by the vast and powerfully cultivated viking beard, that grows ever more in potency. I'm now counting my writing experience in years, so let me say it is my great pleasure that you are reading this, and welcome back to the goodness!

I have been the designer, plotter, and writer of Artorian's Archives since its inception, and look forward to gracing your eyes with ever more volumes of the story. Indulging my dear readers in secrets otherwise forever obscure.

If you have any questions, or would like to chat, I live on the Eternium discord server. Feel free to come say hi anytime! I will keep you entertained for years to come!

Connect with Dennis:
Discord.gg/mdp
Patreon.com/FloofWorks

ABOUT DAKOTA KROUT

Associated Press best-selling author, Dakota has been a top 5 bestseller on Amazon, a top 6 bestseller on Audible, and his first book, Dungeon Born, was chosen as one of Audible's top 5 fantasy picks in 2017.

He draws on his experience in the military to create vast terrains and intricate systems, and his history in programming and information technology helps him bring a logical aspect to both his writing and his company while giving him a unique perspective for future challenges.

"Publishing my stories has been an incredible blessing thus far, and I hope to keep you entertained for years to come!" -Dakota

Connect with Dakota:
MountaindalePress.com
Patreon.com/DakotaKrout
Facebook.com/TheDivineDungeon
Twitter.com/DakotaKrout
Discord.gg/mdp

ABOUT MOUNTAINDALE PRESS

Dakota and Danielle Krout, a husband and wife team, strive to create as well as publish excellent fantasy and science fiction novels. Self-publishing *The Divine Dungeon: Dungeon Born* in 2016 transformed their careers from Dakota's military and programming background and Danielle's Ph.D. in pharmacology to President and CEO, respectively, of a small press. Their goal is to share their success with other authors and provide captivating fiction to readers with the purpose of solidifying Mountaindale Press as the place 'Where Fantasy Transforms Reality.'

Connect with Mountaindale Press:
MountaindalePress.com
Facebook.com/MountaindalePress
Twitter.com/_Mountaindale
Instagram.com/MountaindalePress

MOUNTAINDALE PRESS TITLES

GameLit and LitRPG

The Completionist Chronicles,
The Divine Dungeon,
Full Murderhobo, and
Year of the Sword by Dakota Krout

Arcana Unlocked by Gregory Blackburn

A Touch of Power by Jay Boyce

Red Mage and
Farming Livia by Xander Boyce

Space Seasons by Dawn Chapman

Ether Collapse and
Ether Flows by Ryan DeBruyn

Dr. Druid by Maxwell Farmer

Bloodgames by Christian J. Gilliland

Unbound by Nicoli Gonnella

Threads of Fate by Michael Head

Lion's Lineage by Rohan Hublikar and Dakota Krout

Wolfman Warlock by James Hunter and Dakota Krout

Axe Druid,
Mephisto's Magic Online, and
High Table Hijinks by Christopher Johns

Skeleton in Space by Andries Louws

Dragon Core Chronicles by Lars Machmüller

Chronicles of Ethan by John L. Monk

Pixel Dust and
Necrotic Apocalypse by David Petrie

Viceroy's Pride by Cale Plamann

Henchman by Carl Stubblefield

Artorian's Archives by Dennis Vanderkerken and Dakota Krout